PAMELA EVANS

In The Dark Streets Shining

headline

First published in 2006
by HEADLINE PUBLISHING GROUP

First published in paperback in 2006
by HEADLINE PUBLISHING GROUP

3

Cataloguing in Publication Data is
available from the British Library

0 7553 2149 9 (ISBN-10)
978 0 7553 2149 0 (ISBN-13)

Typeset in Bembo by Palimpsest Book Production Limited,
Grangemouth, Stirlingshire

Printed and bound in Great Britain by
Mackays of Chatham plc, Chatham, Kent

Headline's policy is to use papers that are natural, renewable and
recyclable products and made from wood grown in sustainable
forests. The logging and manufacturing processes are expected
to conform to the environmental regulations of the country of origin.

HEADLINE PUBLISHING GROUP
A division of Hodder Headline
338 Euston Road
London NW1 3BH

www.headline.co.uk
www.hodderheadline.com

Pamela Evans was born and brought up in Ealing, London. She lives in Wales but goes to England regularly to see her family and five beautiful grand-children.

Also by Pamela Evans

A Barrow in the Broadway
Lamplight on the Thames
Maggie of Moss Street
Star Quality
Diamonds in Danby Walk
A Fashionable Address
Tea-Blender's Daughter
The Willow Girls
Part of the Family
Town Belles
Yesterday's Friends
Near and Dear
A Song in your Heart
The Carousel Keeps Turning
A Smile for all Seasons
Where We Belong
Close to Home
Always There
The Pride of Park Street
Second Chance of Sunshine
The Sparrows of Sycamore Road

To Fred; much missed, never forgotten

Chapter One

The acrid smoke in the air was harsh to the throat, the streets still dark as Rose Brown and her cousin Joyce left the Royal Mail sorting office at Ealing to start their deliveries, each with a lamp tied to the front of her bag to be used in accordance with blackout regulations.

'Cor, it's a bit brass monkeys this morning,' shivered Joyce as they trudged past the railway station.

'You're telling me,' agreed Rose with a shudder. 'We'll have to start doubling up on our underwear soon, now that winter's on the way.' A petite brunette, Rose was small featured and pretty, with round dark eyes, a ready smile and a cheery manner. 'Still, at least it'll be getting light soon and we'll be able to see where we're going.'

Every morning before five o'clock – air raids and bad weather notwithstanding – the two cousins cycled to the sorting office in the dark to prepare their rounds for delivery.

'Trust you to look on the bright side,' Joyce chided affectionately. 'You'd find something optimistic to say if the Germans were to come marching up our street led by Herr Hitler himself.'

'You don't half exaggerate,' Rose responded amiably. 'But what's wrong with a spot of positive thinking anyway? If we let the weather get us down in this job – on top of everything else we have to put up with because of the war – we'll be going about with our chins on the ground till next spring.'

'I suppose so, especially as this is just a taste of what's to come when the winter really gets underway,' Joyce pointed out with an air of gloom. 'Not only will it be pitch dark the whole time we're out delivering, but there'll be frost and fog to battle with, as well as rain and snow.'

'Cheer me up, why don't you?' laughed Rose.

'I'm doing my best,' Joyce chortled.

'We're both young and healthy,' Rose reminded her. 'We can take whatever comes.'

'Ease up on the heartiness,' chuckled Joyce, who was tall and busty; not a great beauty but pleasantly wholesome to look at, with soft hazel eyes and hair a tad lighter than mouse-brown. 'It's too early in the morning.'

'It might be early to most people, but it's halfway through the day for us slaves of the Royal Mail.'

'You're not kidding. In fact I feel as though I've already done a full day's work.'

'You've a while to go yet,' was Rose's timely reminder. 'We've got the second delivery to do after this.'

2

'Cheer me up, why don't you?' returned Joyce in jovial mimicry.

Their rapport was the result of a lifelong friendship. Their mothers were sisters, and the cousins had been raised in adjacent houses. They were the same age too; both twenty-three.

Now they reached the point where they were to go their separate ways. Neatly dressed in dark navy coats with red Royal Mail piping and brass buttons, wide-brimmed hats worn at a jaunty angle adding a smart finishing touch to the uniform, they each had a mail bag attached to a wide strap that was slung over their shoulder so that the opening was easily accessible at the front. Inside the sacks the letters were carefully sorted and tied with string into bundles.

'See you later then,' said Rose.

'Yeah. Just as long as we don't both die of cold and exhaustion.'

'Don't be so soft,' grinned Rose. 'What's happened to your wartime spirit?'

'It's been battered to death by all the sleepless nights, I reckon,' Joyce replied.

'The raids have been bad lately, I must admit,' said Rose, frowning, 'but we're still here to tell the tale, which is more than a lot of people.'

'There you go again, making me feel guilty for complaining,' said her down-to-earth cousin in a tone of jovial admonition. 'Why can't you be like everybody else and have a good old moan now and again?'

'I do.'

'I haven't often heard you.'

'That doesn't mean it doesn't happen,' Rose said. 'I feel just as fed up as everyone else sometimes. But looking on the bright side is in my nature, outwardly anyway. I suppose it's my way of coping.'

'Yeah, yeah. I know.'

As they parted company, Joyce thought that the strain Rose was putting herself under by maintaining a brave front with such dogged persistence must be punishing for her. It was true that she had an upbeat personality, and Joyce admired her for it. But she was still grieving for her husband so she shouldn't be afraid to show her feelings.

Restraining them so rigidly couldn't be healthy, and Joyce had told her so. Rose had claimed that the less that was said about it, the easier it was for her to bear, but Joyce guessed it was more a question of her not wanting to burden other people. Still, as it was the way she wanted it, Joyce would respect her wishes, and do her part by being there if she was needed.

Rose walked as briskly as her load would allow, keeping her circulation going and trying to get warm. But the cold was the penetrating sort that made its way right through to the bone. Tiredness didn't help matters either. Having spent yet another night in the Anderson shelter while bombs rained down all around, she, like everyone else, was bone weary.

It was October 1940 and a full night's sleep had been a rare thing for most Londoners since September and the start of the Blitz. The resilience of the population in general was quite astonishing, Rose had observed. Deprived of rest and comfort, they still got up and went to work, and wouldn't think of doing otherwise.

Now, trekking along the wide streets, up and down the paths in the incipient daybreak, she noticed how grey and shabby everything now was in this elegant town known as the Queen of the Suburbs. Some of the houses were reduced to rubble; many of those surviving had their windows boarded up; others were in need of a lick of paint, which they wouldn't get until after the war because of the shortage of materials. Even some of the beautiful old lime trees were dusty and scorched.

Away from the large impressive properties in the area immediately surrounding the Broadway, and into the narrower back streets with small houses in serried ranks, she took out another bundle of letters. Reading the envelopes with the help of her lamp, her heart twisted as she realised that one of her deliveries couldn't be made because the address was now just a smoking ruin; a victim of last night's raid.

'Terrible, innit?' said a neighbour, coming over to Rose. She looked towards the bombed house. 'Gawd knows what they'd done to deserve it, the poor devils. It's criminal what's happening these days.'

'Did they cop it . . . ?' began Rose nervously. 'Or were they in the shelter?'

'The children were in the shelter, but their mum popped up to the house to get something during a lull, apparently,' the neighbour explained. 'The let-up was shorter than she expected and she was inside when the house took a direct hit. The four kiddies survived. But what sort of life are they gonna have now, with their mum dead and their dad away in the army? Poor little souls.'

Rose was imbued with sadness as she looked towards the detritus. Not usually lost for words, even she was stumped for something helpful to say.

'It's scared the living daylights out o' me, I can tell you,' the woman went on, puffing out her lips and slowly shaking her head. 'A few yards nearer and it would have been me who copped it.'

'The bomb obviously didn't have your number on it,' suggested Rose.

'That one didn't, but it's made me wonder when my luck will run out.'

'I should try not to think about it too much,' advised Rose sympathetically, wishing she could think of something more comforting to say. 'We're all in the same boat, and I think most of us feel that way each time we're spared. All we can do is try not to dwell on it and take it as it comes.'

The woman nodded, looking sad.

Rose handed her her mail, and stayed for a spot more friendly conversation because she sensed that the other woman needed company after the horrors of the night. Rose didn't live in this part of the town so knew its inhabitants only from being sociable while out on her round. With so many people away from home, most households were hoping for a letter, which meant that a visit from her could make or break their day.

Almost at the end of her deliveries – having collected mail for the latter part of the round from the official boxes along the route, where it was taken ahead of her by van – she had a package to deliver that was too bulky to go through the letterbox, so she knocked at the front door.

No reply. Further attempts were equally negative. She was about to go next door to divest herself of the package when the door opened and a frail, elderly woman in a thick maroon dressing gown stood in the doorway, thin white hair in curlers, a large proportion of scalp shining pinkly between them.

'Sorry to keep you waiting, luv,' she said hoarsely, wheezing and not looking at all well.

'Did I wake you?'

'You did as it happens, and very glad I am too,' she told her. 'What with the ruddy bombs and my cough keeping me awake half the night, I overslept. It puts me out for the whole day, that does. I'm a stickler for routine; always 'ave bin.'

'You're looking a bit poorly if you don't mind my saying,' mentioned Rose with concern. 'Maybe you should go back to bed for a while.'

'I don't feel too good as it happens, dear.' She patted her lower throat. 'It's this dreadful cough o' mine. It's gone on to my chest and made it sore; it's a perishin' nuisance.'

'Would you like me to get the doctor to call on

you?' offered Rose. 'I can easily pop into his surgery on my way back to the sorting office.'

'No. Thanks for offering, but I'm not dipping into my purse for doctor's fees just because of a cough that I get every year,' she declared. 'All I need is a bottle o' stuff from the chemist in the Broadway to put me right. He makes it up for me special, and he doesn't charge much neither.' She erupted into a fit of coughing, so violent it made her retch and splutter. 'I'll go down there later on to get some.'

Rose was cold to the marrow, eyes stinging from tiredness and lingering bomb smoke, her feet sore and leg muscles aching. When she'd finished this round she had to go back to base to do the setting-in for the second delivery, and then back out on to the streets. All she'd want to do after that was go home.

But she said kindly, 'If you give me the details, I'll get it for you when I've finished work, to save you going out.'

'It's very nice of you to offer, dear, but I don't want to put you to any trouble.'

'It's no trouble at all,' Rose made absolutely clear. 'It's the very least I can do.'

The woman wasn't in any state of health to make more than a token protest. 'Well, if you're sure you don't mind. It's ever so good of you,' she said. 'You're a proper little diamond, and we're lucky to have you on the round.' She paused, looking at Rose. 'Got time for a cuppa?'

'I'd better not stop, even though I'd love one,' Rose

replied. 'It isn't fair to keep people waiting for their post.'

'You're doing a good job; a credit to the Royal Mail; always so friendly and polite,' the old woman praised.

'Thank you.'

'I must admit, though, it did seem a bit queer to me at first to see women out on the streets with the post instead of the men. But I've got used to it now.'

'Us girls are popping up in all sorts of unexpected places these days.' Rose grinned at her.

'You certainly are,' she agreed. 'Working on the railways and the buses, even in the shipyards. The plumber who came to fix my kitchen tap the other day was a woman. A good job she made of it too.'

'You'd better watch out or they'll have you out there collecting the fares on the buses or something,' Rose teased gently.

'I wouldn't mind, but I think they'd draw the line at an old girl pushing eighty-six,' she said. 'I wouldn't be too nifty getting up and down those stairs. So I'll have to leave it to you young 'uns and do my bit by knitting for the troops; they need warm socks, the poor things.'

'Indeed.'

The old lady peered at Rose. 'Have you got a young man away at the war?' she enquired, taking a friendly interest.

'No . . .'

'Never mind, dear, you'll find the right one when you're least expecting it,' she said, failing to notice the

9

colour drain from Rose's face. 'I'll just go and get some money for the medicine and write down the details for you to give the chemist. Shan't be a tick.'

'Okey-doke,' said Rose, biting back the tears.

Going on her way, Rose felt almost incapacitated by the woman's chance remark, hardly able to put one foot in front of the other. The knot that had taken up permanent residence in the pit of her stomach ever since she'd heard that Ray had been killed in action at Dunkirk back in June had been inflamed by the unexpected reminder.

Rose had learned to contain her emotions. The tears had been copious and uncontrollable at first – many of them shed on her cousin's shoulder. It had been impossible not to indulge her grief then. But now, four months on, she thought it was time to show some real mettle, so she painted a smile on her face and went about her daily business as though nothing had changed. After all, she wasn't the only person suffering because of the war, and she certainly wasn't the only woman coping with bereavement or a parting from a loved one. Joyce was missing her fiancé Bob, who was overseas in the army, but she didn't bother other people with it.

Rose had known Ray since she was fifteen, and he seemed to have been a part of her life for ever. Their married life together had been exceptionally brief, the wedding inspired by Ray's imminent departure. Until then, they'd been content to stay as a courting couple, saving up to make a home together. But Ray's posting to the front had introduced a note of urgency and they'd got married by special licence a day or two before the end of his embarkation leave. They'd had to stay at her family home as they hadn't had a place of their own.

It hadn't been a glamorous wedding but it had been the happiest day of her life and she'd been so proud to change her name from Barton to Brown, looking forward to their future together after the war. A few weeks later he was dead. So much for those plans now . . . and yes, she did sometimes feel angry and sorry for herself, but she tried not to wallow in it; firstly because she knew it would soon tire people, and secondly because she knew she had a lot to be thankful for: a loving family, and a job she enjoyed.

The job had come about as a result of a Royal Mail advertisement urging people to join; delivery staff, in particular, were urgently required. Unlike in pre-war times, women were being welcomed into the service because so many of the postmen had gone into the forces. Rose had wanted to do something more relevant to the war effort anyway, so had left her job as a filing clerk in an office and joined the Post Office. Of a similar mind, Joyce had resigned from her job in a shop and followed soon after.

Getting out of bed around four in the morning to start work at five wasn't exactly a picnic, but once she was up and out, Rose enjoyed the feel of the morning as the first light of dawn crept over the sky. For her there was a special freshness then and a sense of hope in the day ahead.

The work was a lot more physically demanding than she'd expected but it gave her a sense of pride; made her feel as though she was involved in something worthwhile. Carrying the nation's mail was, after all, a big responsibility and a much-needed service. With this in mind she gave the job her all.

'Is there any more rice pudding, Mum?' Alan Barton asked his mother that evening when the Barton family were gathered around the table in the living room for their evening meal. It wasn't a big room but somehow they found space for dining furniture as well as easy chairs around the fire. The best front sitting room was only used on special occasions.

'Afraid not, son,' replied his quietly spoken mother May Barton, a small fair-haired woman with soft blue eyes that often exuded a worried expression. The epitome of homeliness, she was wearing a crossover apron over her clothes and a fine hairnet keeping her hair in place. 'You're still hungry, then?'

'Starving.'

'How can you be when you've just eaten a big plate of stew?' asked Alan's sister Rose.

'He's got hollow legs,' put in their father Bill Barton, a strapping dark-haired man who worked as a welder at London Docks. 'You're a bottomless pit, boy.'

'I'm not a boy any more, Dad. I'm a man with a man's appetite.' Alan was seventeen going on eighteen and making his newly acquired manhood known at every opportunity. He was well built, and had the same dark colouring as his father and sister. Alan had been blessed with good looks and more than his share of confidence. 'Besides, I have my physique to think of. Girls like a man with a good strong body and plenty of muscle, and I don't disappoint them in that respect. I don't want to lose my sex appeal.'

'We'll have less of that sort of talk at the table, thank you very much,' admonished May, who tended to be rather strait-laced. 'That's no way to speak about the opposite sex. That sort of attitude will get you a bad name.'

'All I said was—'

'I heard what you said and I don't want to hear it again,' she cut in brusquely.

'It's just high spirits, May,' put in her husband. 'He's young and full of himself. He doesn't mean any harm.'

'It's true what I said, though, Dad,' laughed Alan, his dark eyes sparkling with mischief. 'I never lack for opportunity.'

'You big-headed young sod,' rebuked his father.

'Language, Bill.' May gave her husband a stern look.

'Sorry, dear.'

'I thought fathers were supposed to be pleased if their sons did well with the girls,' joshed Alan. 'A chip off the old block and all that.'

Almost unnoticed, his parents exchanged glances. Rose had seen that look pass between them before, and recognised it as some private thing.

'Your father has always had the utmost respect for women, Alan,' said May primly, 'and I'd appreciate it if you would do the same.'

'I was only having a bit of fun, Ma. There's no need to take it so seriously.' He paused, then turned to his brother Joe, who was a year younger. 'Joe knows what a magnet I am to the women. Tell 'em, mate.'

'It is true. They do seem to like him.' Joe hero-worshipped Alan, who was everything he wished he could be: tough, assertive, witty, good-looking and popular. Joe on the other hand had a more reserved nature and was therefore a natural target for bullies, though nobody dared to push him around when Alan was near.

'Just make sure you treat them right then, Alan,' said May in a tone of quiet authority. 'You've been brought up proper, so don't let us down.'

'Don't worry, Mum, I'll behave,' he said, but he was full of devilment and didn't sound sincere.

'You don't bring any of these adoring girls home, I notice,' said Rose.

'I don't want to send out the wrong message, that's why,' he chuckled. 'Home to meet the folks is for later on, when there's somebody I'm serious about. I'm too young for all that. Meanwhile, I'm still hungry, Mum.'

'Here, have the rest of my rice pudding,' offered Rose. 'I've had enough anyway.'

'I can't do that,' said Alan, who, for all his big talk, did actually have scruples. 'I wouldn't take the food out of the mouth of one of my own.'

'I should hope not.' His mother turned to her daughter, frowning. 'You don't eat enough to keep a fly alive as it is, Rose, and you need to keep your strength up in the job you do. So finish your rice pudding and I'll get some bread and marg for Alan to fill up on.'

Rather than worry her mother, Rose forced the spoon to her mouth. While everyone else was in a state of almost permanent hunger because of the introduction of food rationing, Rose's appetite had been all but annihilated by grief.

The Barton family and their much-loved and ironically named dog Bruiser – a fudge-coloured spaniel so timid that just a raised voice was enough to send him into hiding behind the sofa – lived in Bramble Road, West Ealing; the end house in a terraced row. Rose and her brothers had been born here, but their parents were originally from the East End of London.

The slavish dedication to propriety so often found in working-class people was inherent in Rose's parents, and she and her brothers had been brought up against a backdrop of respectability.

Mentally moving around the table, Rose concentrated her mind on Alan, who worked in a factory. Gregarious and funny, there was never a dull moment when he was around. He could be a bit too full of himself at times, but there was a warm and caring side to his nature which allowed her to forgive his tendency towards conceit. He was also very good to Joe.

Dear Joe, who always seemed to struggle in his brother's shadow, had inherited their mother's gentle nature. He was the brightest of the bunch; he'd made it to the grammar school and was now employed in the drawing office of an aircraft factory at Hayes, working on designs for war planes. Much less robust and good-looking than his brother, Joe was thin, with a pale complexion, sharp features and blue eyes like his mother's, his straight brown hair usually flopping into his eyes.

Being such a spirited family, there was never any shortage of heated debate among them, but they had their share of laughter too. Despite living under the shadow of the air raids, there was enormous strength in this house that embraced Rose every time she stepped over the threshold. There was always a sense that united, the Bartons were somehow indestructible.

'Anyway,' her mother was saying, 'I'll just get that bread and marg for you, Alan, then I want to get the clearing-up done before the siren goes.'

'It's late tonight, isn't it?' observed Rose. 'Perhaps Jerry is going to give us a night off.'

'Wouldn't that be lovely?' said May wistfully. 'But I wouldn't bank on it.'

Joe went to the back door and came back with the news that the sky was heavily clouded and therefore not good flying weather for the bomber planes. 'So we might get some sleep tonight,' he said hopefully.

'We could all do with it,' said May, getting up and crossing the room, the dog at her heels.

As soon as her mother was out of sight, Rose swiftly and wordlessly swapped dishes with Alan, who made short work of her leftover rice pudding, just to save it going to waste.

★　★　★

'Evening, all,' greeted Rose's Auntie Sybil, coming in through the back door followed by her husband Flip and daughter Joyce, who perched on the arm of Rose's chair. 'Isn't it smashing not having to go down the shelter?'

'Lovely,' agreed May. 'I hope we're not speaking too soon, though.'

The family were now settled by the fire in the sitting part of the living room, though Alan had gone to see some mates, and Joe was out fire-watching. There was a kind of accidental elegance about the room, Rose always thought, mostly due to her mother's tendency to cover scratched wooden furniture with pretty pre-war embroidered cloths.

Sybil and Flip made themselves comfortable on the sofa. No one asked why they were here because the two families were so close it wasn't necessary.

'As it's all quiet outside, do you fancy going down the local for a quick one, Bill?' Uncle Flip suggested to Rose's father. A tall, broad-shouldered man with a thatch of greying brown hair and warm, laughing eyes, Flip was a London bus driver.

'Oh no you don't,' put in Sybil quickly, her blue eyes shrewd and determined. She was much more flamboyant than most women of her generation, her greying hair embellished by the wonders of peroxide, and vivid colours worn whenever she could lay her hands on any bright clothes. Dowdiness was avoided by her at all costs. 'Just because the siren hasn't gone yet, it doesn't mean that it won't. I'm not having you down at the pub while I'm here with bombs falling all over the place. If we're going to be blown up we'll all go together.'

'You're a right little ray of sunshine tonight, aren't you?' chortled Bill drily.

'The pub is only down at the end of the road, Sybil luv,' wheedled Flip. 'If the siren does go we'll be back here before you've even had time to get your coat on for the shelter.'

But she was digging her heels in over this one. 'You're not going, Flip. I'm not having it.'

'Let him go if he wants to,' said May, ever the peacemaker. 'Where's the harm in it?'

'It's the principle of the thing, May. Anyway, if my husband's involved there's bound to be some sort of mischief,' pronounced Sybil.

'Why don't you all go?' suggested Rose.

'Good idea,' added Joyce. 'We'll be quite happy here, talking and playing the gramophone.'

'We are not all going because Bill and I just want a quiet half-hour on our own in the public bar,' stated Flip with a determined air. 'No fuss or bother; no dressing up or being on our best behaviour. Just two blokes having a pint of beer together and a chat about men's things. We don't want a night out in the saloon bar with the wife.'

'Bill hasn't said that that's what he wants,' Sybil pointed out. 'He's quite content to stay at home like the decent man that he is. You're a bad influence on him, Flip Marshall.'

'Stop nagging, woman.'

'I'd like the chance, but how can I when I'm married to you?'

'You're enough to drive a man to drink,' he said. 'It's a wonder I come home at all.'

Rose had listened to a variation of this conversation between her uncle and aunt all her life. Bickering with each other was their lifeblood. As far as Rose could see, Auntie Sybil ruled the roost, and that was the way Uncle Flip liked it, even though he spent his entire life trying to outwit her. Rose always found them rather entertaining, especially as she never heard her own parents arguing. She assumed that they must have rows, like any other married couple, but never in front of the children.

'If it isn't boozing, it's betting or chasing women,' Sybil went on.

'Oh, for Gawd's sake, woman. An occasional small bet on the horses, a pint down the local . . . and as for chasing women! You must be joking. One of your lot is more than enough for me to cope with, so pipe down.'

'Yeah, give it a rest, Mum,' added Joyce.

'Yes, that's quite enough, Sybil,' rebuked her sister sternly. 'You're taking it too far now. You know perfectly well that Flip doesn't do the things you accuse him of, so stop giving him a hard time.'

'I wouldn't put anything past him.'

'Shut up, the pair of you.' This was Bill. 'We've got a night off the bombing, so let's enjoy it.'

'Go down the pub then, if you must,' said Sybil, conceding to the pressure around her. 'But don't make a night of it or there'll be hell to pay.'

'We wouldn't dare, my little passion flower,' grinned Flip, kissing his wife on the cheek then heading swiftly towards the door. 'We'll be back before you've even had time to tear my character to shreds.'

'Shall we have some music on the gramophone, girls?' suggested Rose as her father hurriedly followed her uncle from the room.

'I'm all for that,' enthused Joyce.

But at that point a familiar and depressing wail from outside scuppered their plans and turned their insides to jelly. They all grabbed coats and blankets and hurried out to the Anderson shelters.

'Looks like we're in for a long wait, May,' said Sybil the next morning as the sisters stood in the queue snaking out from the butcher in West Ealing, a line of women swathed in boots, scarves and hats, talking and laughing among themselves as though they were on an outing rather than lining up in the cold for food.

'I don't mind standing in a queue as long as they don't run out before our turn comes,' said May, stamping her feet and hugging herself to keep warm.

'It wouldn't be the first time we've got all excited over a bit of offal and it's all gone before we get anywhere near the front of the queue,' added Sybil. 'Word soon gets round when there's anything off ration about, and people seem to appear from all over the place.'

'I expect the butcher will look after his regulars, though,' suggested May, who always tried to think the best of people.

'He'd better had or we'll register with someone else.' Sybil wasn't quite so trusting.

Both women were well wrapped up in thick dark winter coats and woollen headscarves. Sybil had curlers poking out of the front of hers.

'It's hard to make sure the family get enough nourishment these days,' mentioned May.

'You're telling me,' agreed Sybil. 'They do all right, though. We're the ones who get run down and worn out, spending half our lives queuing up in the cold for food for them. If Flip had to do the queuing, we'd all go without.'

'No you would not, and you know it. You're so horrible about that poor husband of yours,' admonished May, although she knew her sister didn't mean it. 'He's out earning the money; you look after things at home, including the queuing; sounds fair enough to me.'

'You and I will soon be out working as well as doing the queuing and everything else, if they do go ahead and bring in compulsory war work for women who don't have children under fourteen,' warned Sybil.

'Yeah, I heard something about that,' said May. 'Still, it'll only apply to women under forty-five, so you'll be all right.'

'By the time it comes in you'll have had your forty-fifth, too.' Sybil paused, grinning. 'It's just as well, because you'd never get Joe to look thirteen, no matter how hard you tried.'

May smiled, taking it all in good part.

'I'd like to do my bit for the war effort.' Sybil gave a wry grin. 'It'd be nice to earn some money of my own, too. If Flip wasn't so dead set against it, I'd have already got myself fixed up. But he goes up the wall at the very idea of my going out to work.'

'Since when did you take any notice of Flip's opinion?' May asked.

'That isn't fair,' she objected mildly. 'That man has a diamond wife in me. Just because I go on at him doesn't mean I don't respect his opinion over important issues.'

'I was only teasing.'

'He likes to be the breadwinner, so I let him,' Sybil said.

'And the fact that you haven't been out to work for years and are scared stiff of doing so hasn't got anything to do with it, I suppose,' said May with a wry grin.

'Well, yeah, there is that too. I admit it.'

'Don't worry, I'm just the same.' The sisters knew each other so well there wasn't much point in pretending.

'My more immediate concern is trying to stay awake until we get to the front of this damned queue. What a night we had, eh, May? I'm so tired I could sleep on the butcher's slab.'

May nodded. 'I thought we were never going to hear the all-clear last night.'

'Bloomin' Jerries.' Sybil cast her eye around at the

other hopefuls in the queue. 'Everyone's exhausted by the air raids. They might be laughing and joking, but that doesn't hide the shadows under their eyes. Neighbours, shop girls, clippies on the buses, everyone you see is feeling the strain and trying not to show it. I don't know how Joyce and Rose manage to get up at such an unearthly hour when they've barely had a wink of sleep.'

'Still, they're young,' said May. 'You can cope with anything at their age.'

'And talking of coping, Rose seems to be doing very well,' commented Sybil. 'It can't be more than four months since she heard about Ray, but she always seems cheerful and full of beans.'

'It's an act,' announced May. 'She seems to think it's some sort of a sin to be sad, so goes about with a smile fixed on her face. She's too thin for her own good too.'

'We're all thinner than we used to be when food was plentiful.'

'I know, but Rose only eats a fraction of what she's entitled to.'

'It's the grief,' said Sybil sympathetically. 'It will have upset her nervous system, I expect, the poor dear. Don't worry, May, she'll eat you out of house and home once she begins to feel better.'

'She must use up so much energy putting on this cheerful front the whole time,' said May. 'I wish she'd let herself be miserable now and again.'

'Credit to her, though,' defended Sybil. 'At least she's not moping about feeling sorry for herself and making everyone else miserable. I take my hat off to her, I really do. I'm proud of her.'

'I am as well, of course . . .'

'She's twenty-three years old, May,' Sybil reminded her. 'You can't force food down her throat. She isn't starving herself; just not eating much. So stop worrying about it.' She gave her sister a wry look. 'But who am I kidding? You couldn't stop worrying even if you wanted to, could you? It's in your nature.'

'It comes with the territory when you're a mother, as you well know. I want to do the best I can for my family.'

'And you always do,' stated Sybil. 'No kids could have had better, more caring parents than you and Bill. You've lived for them. But you have to stop overcompensating. Stop apologising for being alive.'

'We both know why I'm like that.'

'Listen to me, May; you're a far better person than I'll ever be and you don't hear me carrying on as though I don't have a right to live, do you?'

'Quite the opposite,' May laughed.

'All right, don't rub it in.'

Sybil was a year older than May and exercised her senior position whenever it suited her. The two sisters couldn't be more different. Sybil was outspoken, gregarious, at times insensitive and often outrageous, and made no apologies for the way she was. May, on the other hand, was self-deprecating and expected nothing less than perfection from herself at all times, especially as regarded her duty to her family.

But for all that, the two of them were very close. If they had a falling-out it was resolved speedily, because they relied on each other for company and support, and were genuinely fond of one another. Sybil and Flip had only left the East End and headed west because May and Bill had moved here, and that was more than twenty-five years ago.

'The difference between us, Syb, is that you don't have anything to prove.'

'Neither do you. You've proved it time and time again over the years, so now it's time you relaxed and stopped worrying about it. None of us is perfect, so stop trying to be.'

'You make me sound like some awful holier-than-thou type,' said May.

'I don't mean to. It's just me coming out with the wrong thing as usual,' said Sybil, affection shining through her bossy persona. 'You're the least self-righteous person I know. Self-criticism; you've got that in barrelloads. I just want to see that worried look go out of your eyes.'

'I don't suppose it ever will,' May said, 'because I'm a fraud, Syb.'

'Rubbish!'

'It's true, and we both know it. I'm not who my kids think I am.'

'You're a human being as well as their mother, you know,' Sybil pointed out. 'Anyway, you're as near perfect a mother as any woman can be. So stop feeling guilty. It isn't necessary.'

'I'll try.'

'I shall hold you to that.' Sybil looked ahead. 'Ooh good, the queue is moving at last.'

As they moved up with the others towards that most precious of wartime commodities, liver, May drifted off into thought. Her sister made her sound like some sort of a saint. How very far from the truth that was.

'Here they come, the Royal Mail's answer to the Andrews Sisters,' said postman Stan Willis, grinning towards Rose and Joyce. It was later that same morning and they were walking through the sorting office on their way off duty, singing a rousing rendition of 'It's a Hap-Hap-Happy Day'.

'Hey, don't be so saucy,' joshed Rose. 'There's no need to take the mick.'

'I wasn't. I was being complimentary, as it happens.' Stan had also finished his shift and was on his way out. 'You really do sound like the Andrews Sisters.'

They were in a very large room with big tables on to which the mail bags were emptied for segregation of letters and packets prior to stamp cancellation. One whole wall was made up of sorting frames with pigeon holes, each labelled with a town or district, for the general sorting. The sorters were hard at work here. The delivery staff had their own section at one end in which to sort their rounds into the order they would deliver them, a process known as 'setting in'.

'You're having us on,' said Joyce.

'No I'm not,' he assured her. 'Maybe you're not as

polished as the Andrews Sisters, but you both have smashing voices. I love to hear you singing about the place. It cheers us all up.'

'We've always loved singing,' said Rose. 'We're never happier than when we're belting out a song.'

'I'm like that about the piano,' he told them chattily. 'I don't have much of a singing voice but I'm never happier than when I'm tinkling the ivories.'

Stan was twenty-six, tall and slim with blond hair, laughing grey eyes and a fragile look about him. Rose had heard through the sorting office grapevine that before the war he'd been a full-time music teacher in a college, and now taught the piano in his spare time at home. He was one of the few young male postmen working at this sorting office, and was only here because he had some sort of a chest complaint which gave him breathing problems and made him exempt from military service.

Rose and Joyce had both taken an instant liking to him on their first day in the job when he'd shown them the ropes. He was a terrific workmate with his easy-going ways and dry sense of humour.

'I'd like to hear you play,' said Joyce casually.

'Me too,' added Rose.

'That's easily solved.' He looked from one to the other with a thoughtful smile. 'You'd have to work for it, though.'

'Oh yeah,' said Joyce with a wry look. 'In what way?'

'In a musical way,' he replied. 'You two singing; me on the piano – in front of an audience.'

'Now you really are taking the mick,' chided Rose.

'No I'm not, honestly. I play the piano at hospitals and convalescent homes and so on as part of the war effort; to try to bring a bit of cheer into the patients' lives. I play in pubs too, sometimes, to raise money for various wartime charities.'

'That's very public-spirited of you,' said Joyce with visible admiration.

'Not really, because I enjoy it. But it does seem to cheer people up, so it's worth doing. If the two of you came along to sing, it would be even better.'

'We're not good enough to sing in public.' Rose was astonished at the suggestion.

'You're as good as some professionals I've heard.'

'We've never done any entertaining, except to our long-suffering family,' she explained. 'Besides, you're classically trained; we only sing popular songs.'

'I usually play a few well-known classics, then a range of popular songs, which is where you'd come in.' His voice rose with enthusiasm. 'You could get the audience to join in with some of the numbers. That really gives people a lift.'

'We're just a couple of amateurs,' reminded Rose.

'You won't get paid for it,' he pointed out. 'So you won't have to feel under pressure as far as that's concerned.'

'That's all right then,' said Rose.

'All entertainment, whether professional or amateur, is so important for public morale in these terrible times,' he said, becoming serious. 'I can't go and fight for my country, but I can get out there and do my best to cheer people up on the home front. Anyway, I'm not talking about the Albert Hall or even the Chiswick Empire. Just a few venues where a bit of cheerful entertainment will be welcome. Whatever contribution we are able make in this war, no matter how small, it's up to us all to make it.'

'All right, Stan; there's no need to give us a flamin' lecture,' said Joyce light-heartedly. 'And don't blame us if our warbling gets you booed off the stage.'

'You'll do it then?'

'We don't have much choice, do we, as you've gone to such pains to remind us of our public duty,' chuckled Joyce.

'I'll let you know when I've got something definite arranged, then.'

'Yessir,' said Joyce with a mock salute.

The conversation was interrupted by the appearance of the sorting office manager, Ron Partridge, who had worked for the Royal Mail for many years and was due to retire in a few years' time. A stockily built man with silver hair, he took enormous pride in his job and was an ardent patriot.

'As you lot seem so reluctant to leave the place, can I take this opportunity to have a word in your ear please, folks,' he asked.

There was a general nod of agreement, and they all waited for him to go on.

'I know that you're all exhausted because of the Germans' nocturnal antics, so make sure you get some kip this afternoon, because I need you here bright and early in the morning as usual.'

'We'll be here, Mr Partridge,' said Rose.

'We won't let you down, mate,' added Stan, while Joyce just nodded.

'I appreciate that. It isn't easy to keep the service going in these dreadful times, but by pulling together we seem to be managing it.' His voice rose as he warmed to his theme; he was almost emotional. 'The Royal Mail is an old tradition and it's our duty to get the letters delivered to the public no matter what the Germans throw at us. We've had railway stations bombed, London's main sorting office set ablaze and letterboxes reduced to rubble so that we've had to dig the mail out, to name just a few of the disasters that have made our work so difficult lately. But through it all the mail is delivered. No matter how tired you are, you still get out on the streets and keep up the service that was started long ago. I'm proud to be a part of the great institution, and I'm also proud of my staff. Now get off home and take some rest. You need it.'

'He's a smashing bloke, isn't he?' said Rose as they left the building. 'He keeps us on our toes but he's a real old softie at heart.'

'He knows how to get the best out of people,' opined Stan. 'He knows that if we don't get much sleep we'll eventually stop functioning and his sorting office will grind to a halt.'

'I think he cares about us for ourselves, too, though,' said Rose.

'Oh yeah, I'm sure he does. He's a good man.' Stan looked from one cousin to the other. 'So, you're definitely on for making your debut then?'

'Try stopping us,' trilled Joyce.

Chapter Two

When they finally left the sorting office, Joyce wanted to check on a friend after the raid last night so Rose headed for home on her own, cycling through the back streets mulling over Stan's invitation to sing for the war effort. She was quite excited about it in a nervous sort of way. Performing in front of an audience might be fun.

The pleasurable buzz of anticipation died an instant death when she found herself working out the letter she would write to Ray telling him about it. This was a trick of the mind that happened to her occasionally. For a few seconds her subconscious blotted out the awful truth and let her imagine that he was still alive and the world was rosy, the reality seeming even harsher for the lapse.

Her surroundings seemed particularly bleak because of low grey skies and a steady drizzle. A rain mist, lingering bomb smoke and brick dust merged into a grimy vapour that floated eerily over everything. The residential streets were practically deserted in this weather. The few people who were about were mostly women laden with shopping bags.

The landscape changed almost daily as more buildings disappeared, she observed, noticing fresh cavities in the rows of houses. Still, from what she'd heard, the people in east London were having it much worse. Whole streets were disappearing overnight there.

In this particular avenue, that had obviously been hit by the raid last night, the houses were big and old. Once the family homes of Ealing's elite, many of them were now divided up into rooms and rented out. So busy was she looking at what was left of a newly bombed property that she hit some stray brickwork in the road, came off her bike and hit the ground with a thud.

Cursing her own carelessness as she scrambled to her feet, rubbing her grazed knees, she got back on to the saddle and was about to move off when she heard a noise; a human sound. She stood perfectly still, listening. All was silent, so she put it down to her imagination, pushed her foot down hard on the pedal and moved off, coming to a sudden halt when she heard it again. It was the sound of someone in distress, a thin, childish cry that seemed to be coming from somewhere outside rather than inside any of the houses. But there was nobody around.

Dismounting and propping her bike in the kerb with the pedal, she scanned the area, realising with a sense of terrible foreboding that the crying must be coming from the bombed building, which was just a pile of rubble with part of the back wall of the house still standing.

'Anyone there?' she called out, walking cautiously towards it.

Not a sound.

She called again, and this time heard a muffled sob which she now judged to be coming from behind the back wall. Access from here wasn't possible because it was too high to climb, and if she tried to clamber up over the debris, that would almost certainly bring the whole lot crashing down.

Tearing down the street and around the corner, she found a narrow alleyway that skirted the back of the houses. It was muddy, overgrown and littered with bits of broken fence and garden walls that had been damaged in the bomb blast.

Picking her way through the rubbish, her heart beating so hard she thought it would burst, she located the bombed house and made her way into the back garden, which was strewn with rubble. Her initial calls met with no response, but after a while she could hear someone crying. Where it was coming from was a mystery, because there was no garden shed or outbuilding.

'Hello,' she called loudly. 'Hello, hello.'

A choking sound came from beneath what appeared to have once been a back lobby of the house, a part that jutted out from the rest and was now just a ruin apart from a small section of the roof.

Nobody could be under there and still alive, could they? Further investigation revealed that some of the brickwork from the outside wall, with the brown-painted wooden door still attached, was lying horizontally across the top of the debris.

'It's all right, I'm here,' she called reassuringly, though she was shaking all over. 'I'll get you out of there as quick as I can. Just hang on.'

Suddenly struck with panic at the magnitude and responsibility of the task, she wondered if she should go to find help. But the door and the brickwork looked precarious, and whoever was trapped beneath it must have been there since the raid last night, so there was no time to lose. She must get on and deal with this herself.

Desperately afraid of making things worse for whoever was below, she carefully reached down for the door, painfully aware that a small part of the roof of the outbuilding was hanging dangerously over the top of her. She tried to lift the door by the handle but it was wedged and immovable, which meant that, somehow, she had to pull the whole thing up without dislodging the wreckage. Taking hold of the door handle again with one hand, she put the other to the side of the attached brickwork and pulled. It was jammed solid and wouldn't move. She tried again, with no success.

With heart pounding and skin beaded with sweat, her hands bleeding from the broken bricks, she wrenched again with every last vestige of energy she could muster. At last there was a slight movement. But it wasn't enough. She daren't let go because the door would fall on top of the person underneath and take other debris with it, but she just didn't have the physical strength to heave it up. God almighty, she was stuck mid-way. Now what was she going to do?

She had to find a way. Somehow she must find the power to move it. Pulling and struggling, her nerves stretched to breaking point, she at last achieved a small shift which seemed to boost her power and enabled her to pull the door into a vertical position.

Dropping it to the ground well away from the rubble to avoid dislodging it, she peered into the opening and saw a boy of about seven, covered in brick dust and clutching a teddy bear. Rubble was packed tight all around him.

'Oh you poor little thing,' she said gently, tears streaming down her cheeks. 'Just hold on for a few minutes more and I'll have you out of there.'

Moving the bricks away from him one by one and with the utmost caution, she was finally able to lift him out. Instinctively holding him close to her, she could feel his lean little body trembling.

'There, there, it's all over and you're safe now.' She gently wiped his dirty, tear-stained face with her hand-kerchief, holding him again and noticing the sour smell of urine rising from his damp trousers. 'Does it hurt in particular anywhere?'

He didn't reply but moved away from her and peered around, looking bewildered. 'The 'ouse has gone,' he said, tears running down his face. 'Where's my mum?'

'Was she with you when the explosion happened?' Rose asked, dreading to think who else might lie beneath the ruins.

'Dunno.' He held his head, appearing to be trying to remember. 'I think she was upstairs in our room. Yeah, the siren went and we were going to the cellar to take shelter. She told me to go on without her because I needed to go to the lav, and she would get our coats and follow me down.' He thought for a moment. 'I remember being on the stairs, then I woke up and everything was dark. I called and called but nobody came and I couldn't move.' Looking very frightened and confused, he moved away from her and began to cry out in strangled sobs, 'Mum, Mum, where are you? Oh please, Mum, where are you?'

Rose's heart sank as she surveyed what was left of the house. She doubted if anyone could have survived. It was nothing short of a miracle that the boy was still alive.

'Come with me, luv,' she said kindly, taking his hand. 'We'll go and look for your mum together.'

'The poor little mite,' said May in a low voice because the boy, who had told them his name was Alfie Miller, was in the other room. Having been bathed and fed he'd finally fallen asleep on the sofa from sheer exhaustion.

'It was awful, Mum, telling that poor child that his mother is dead. But I had to do it,' Rose told her. 'He was frantic with worry about her so he had to know. It was one of the worst things I've ever had to do in my life, and I'll never forget it. His little face just crumpled and he sobbed his heart out.'

'Who told you she hadn't survived?'

'The police.'

'How did they get involved?'

'I went to the police station. I was going to bring him straight home but I thought I ought to let somebody official know that I'd found him. I also needed to find out about his mother. So I took him to the rest centre and left him there while I went to the local cop shop for information. They told me that there were no survivors in the incident. The rescue people missed Alfie altogether; they didn't realise that he was there.'

'They didn't hear him call out, then?'

'I think he must have lost consciousness for a while so wasn't able to call for help while the emergency services were there,' she explained. 'And there was no one left alive afterwards to tell them to look for him. It was a rooming house, apparently. Alfie and his mum were living in one room at the top of the house. She was an unmarried mother.'

'It didn't take you long to find that out.'

'A neighbour was quick to give me all the details when she saw me in the street with him. You know what people are like about that sort of thing. They can't wait to pass it on.'

'So the poor lad doesn't even have a dad to look out for him, then?'

'No one seems to know anything about his father,' said Rose. 'He probably did a bunk when she fell pregnant.'

'The old, old story,' sighed her mother.

'Seems like it. Anyway, I just couldn't bear to leave him at the rest centre on his own, looking so lost and lonely,' Rose continued. 'It was so sad, Mum, to see all those homeless people looking absolutely shattered, having lost everything.'

'Poor things,' May said with a slow shake of the head. 'It could happen to any of us with these raids coming every night.'

'It doesn't bear thinking about.' Rose shuddered at the thought. 'Anyway, I asked the people in charge there if I could bring Alfie home with me until permanent arrangements can be made for him. They were only too pleased to get him off their hands, I think, with so many people to look after. They said we can get a ration book for him and they'll give us some money for his keep. So can he stay here for a while? Sorry. I know I should have checked with you first, but I'm afraid I just anticipated your feelings and followed my heart.'

'Of course he can stay here,' said May without hesitation. 'It won't hurt us to give the poor lad a home. He'll be bundled off to an orphanage if they can't find anyone to look after him.'

'Perhaps some relatives will turn up to claim him,' suggested Rose.

'Let's hope so. But as his mother wasn't married, they'd probably all turned their backs on her.'

'Yeah, that's true,' agreed Rose. 'People can be very cruel about that sort of thing.'

'If no one comes forward to take him, he can stay with us for as long as the authorities need us to look after him,' said May. 'I've got a spare mattress. I'll make up a bed for him in the boys' room.'

'Thanks, Mum,' said Rose. 'I guessed you'd feel the same way as I do about it.'

'You're your mother's daughter all right.'

'Aren't you going to eat your food, Alfie?' asked May when they were having their evening meal that same day and the boy pushed his plate away.

'Nah,' he said.

'I'll have it,' offered Alan.

'I'll go halves with you,' put in Joe.

'Honestly, what a couple of gannets you boys are,' admonished their mother.

'If he really doesn't want it, we might as well polish it off,' said Alan. 'It's a sin to waste food these days.'

'Well you're not having it because Alfie is going to eat it, aren't you, son?' said May firmly.

'No I ain't. I don't want your rotten food and I'm not your son, so don't call me that.'

'There's no need to be rude,' intervened Bill in mild reproach. 'We know that you're upset and we're all very sorry for you, but Mrs Barton took a lot of trouble with the meal and food is very short at the moment.'

'Don't care.'

'The least you can do is eat what you're given,' said Bill patiently. 'Anyway, you need to build up your strength after what you've been through.'

The boy moved the plate back towards him, scooped up some food with his fork and gobbled it up as though to sate his appetite sufficiently to survive, then put his knife and fork down. 'Don't want the rest,' he said.

'It's your loss, kid.' Alan looked at his mother. 'Is it all right if we finish it up, as he isn't going to?'

'I suppose you'd better,' she said worriedly.

Everyone did their utmost to make Alfie feel at home by trying to engage him in conversation, but their attempts fell on stony ground. He just sat there stiffly, a small, skinny boy of seven with a mop of spiky fair hair, a sprinkling of freckles on his turned-up nose, and the bluest eyes Rose had ever seen. When he did speak, he did so in an insolent manner.

'We shall have to think about getting you into a school around here,' suggested Rose.

'Not goin'.'

'You'll have to go to school, dear,' said May tolerantly. 'All children have to. It's the law of the land.'

'You can't tell me what to do,' he stated sullenly. 'You're not my mum.'

'No, I'm not. But while you're staying here with us we're responsible for you and it's our job to see that you get your education. We'll have the school board man after us if you don't go to school.' May looked at him, her heart breaking at his wretchedness. 'But you can have a few days off to recover from your ordeal. How does that suit you?'

He shrugged, as though he couldn't care less.

Seeing him so ravaged with pain and angry with everything and everyone because his world had just fallen apart, Rose was full of compassion.

'Mum will spoil you rotten while we're all out at work,' she suggested hopefully.

He gave her a sullen stare, looked round at the rest of them defiantly, then left the table and marched towards the door.

'Oi,' Bill called after him, 'come back here and show your manners. You ask before you leave the table in this house.'

The reply was the sound of the living-room door slamming behind him.

'Well of all the . . .' began Bill.

'Take it easy on him, Dad,' urged Rose. 'The poor little thing is obviously feeling wretched.'

'He's only a kid, Dad,' supported gentle Joe.

'I know all that, but he still needs discipline,' said their plain-speaking father. He wasn't a harsh disciplinarian but he did believe in old-fashioned values. 'It's essential to children. They may not like it but it makes them feel secure. They need to know who's in charge. He won't know what he's supposed to do if we don't set out ground rules from the start.'

'Don't be too hard on him, Bill,' urged May, typically soft-hearted.

'It's no good allowing him to play up, luv, that won't do him any good in the long run.'

'I'll go and talk to him,' Rose intervened swiftly. 'I'd more or less finished eating anyway.' She grinned at her brothers. 'And yes, you can have the rest of mine.'

'It's a good day for us, eh, Joe,' joked Alan. 'We should take in stray kids more often.'

'You heartless bugger,' admonished Joe.

'I was joking.'

'It's a good job *I* know that you are just joking,' added Rose, giving Alan a stern look. 'Or you'd get a right old trouncing from me.'

'What's happened to your sense of humour?' asked the elder of her brothers.

'It doesn't run to jokes about a little boy who's lost his mum.'

'Sorry,' said Alan, looking genuinely contrite.

'We all know you well enough to know that you were just mucking about, son,' said his father. 'They've all gone soppy over the kid.' He held his head still for a moment as though listening, then looked at Rose. 'I think I just heard him go out of the back door. Make sure he's taken care of the blackout properly or we'll have the air raid warden after us.'

'Will do,' she said.

Rose found Alfie in the garden, standing in the dark just outside the back door. Bruiser was sitting beside him.

'Don't stand out here, Alfie luv,' she urged him. 'You haven't even got a coat on and you're shivering.'

He shrugged.

She put her arm around him, only to have him twist away from her.

'If it's any consolation, I know how much you must be hurting,' she said.

His response was another shrug.

'How about we go inside and talk about it?' she suggested. 'You'll catch cold out here.'

'Don't matter.'

'It matters to me.'

'Well, I don't care about being cold. I ain't no sissy, yer know.' He paused, looking down. 'I hope my mum isn't too cold where she is, though. She doesn't like the cold weather. It makes her chilblains worse.'

'I'm sure she'll be fine.'

'Me and Mum look after each other,' he announced with a rebellious edge to his tone. 'She would never leave me. That's why I know she'll come for me. I hope she isn't too long, because I miss her so much.'

Oh dear! He was obviously in denial. 'Sometimes people don't have a choice,' she told him. 'Your mum didn't leave of her own accord.'

'She'll be back,' he insisted accusingly. 'You don't know anything about me and my mum. If you knew my mum you'd know that she wouldn't ever leave me, and you'd stop telling me that she's dead.'

'As you say, I don't know your mum, but she sounds like a really nice lady,' Rose said, fudging the issue temporarily in the hope of calming him down.

'As soon as she comes for me, you won't see me for dust. I ain't staying here with you lot a minute longer than I have to. Mum'll find us somewhere else to live as our house has been bombed. We've moved lots of times.'

Rose really didn't know what to do. Should she tell him again what he already knew but was refusing to accept? Or would he take it in in his own time? He obviously wasn't ready to do so yet and it seemed such a cruel thing to do. She shivered, hugging herself against the cold. 'Look, I'm going indoors now. You can stay out here if you like, but don't go out of this garden because the siren might go in a minute.'

He stared at his feet, scuffing his shoe against the ground. She longed to hold him in her arms and protect him from all the ills of the world. But she knew that any such gesture of affection would be rejected at this stage. It was his mother he wanted and no one else would do.

'Well, I'm going inside.' The dog was also sniffing at the door. 'Bruiser wants to go in too. You come in when you're ready, Alfie. Make sure you don't let any light out when you open the door.'

He made a gesture that vaguely resembled a nod.

She and the dog went inside to the kitchen but Bruiser sat whining at the door. After a while, Rose poked her head out. 'The dog wants you to come in.'

'I don't care. I 'ate dogs.'

Bruiser slipped out and sat at the boy's feet.

'Well he obviously likes you. You must have made a real hit with him because that dog likes his comfort and he takes a dim view of the cold,' she said, and closed the door, confident that both boy and dog would be back inside shortly.

When she rejoined the family, she suggested to her mother that they make a bed up for Alfie in Rose's bedroom, instead of her brothers'. She wanted to be there for him if he needed someone during the night.

★　　★　　★

46

'Shame about the boy, isn't it?' remarked Bill to his wife as they got into bed that night, shivering against the cold of the room and the freezing starched sheets. They were very glad to be sleeping in their own bed, though, instead of the shelter, as there hadn't been a raid. 'Poor little bugger. He isn't making it easy for us to make him feel welcome here either.'

'He wants his mum, the poor love. He won't accept that she's dead.'

'That'll come in time, I suppose,' said Bill, 'and in the meantime we'll have to be patient and do what we can to make him feel at home here. I know I'm a bit firm with him but that's just my way. It doesn't mean I don't feel sorry for him.'

'I know that, Bill. I should do after all the years we've been together.' Shivering violently, May pulled the covers up as far as she could without fear of suffocation. 'There's one thing that's nagging at the back of my mind.'

'What's that?'

'I've been wondering if the authorities might check into our background as we're acting as sort of unofficial foster parents to Alfie.'

'Most unlikely,' he stated. 'There's far too much chaos for them to deal with at the moment for them to bother with a thing like that. They'll be only too pleased to have him taken off their hands, I should think. It's one less for them to find a home for. Anyway, we're only filling in on a temporary basis. It isn't as if we're adopting him or anything. They would start asking questions if we were. But we're not, so stop worrying.'

'If they were to start poking around, they might decide that we're not suitable people to look after him.'

'They won't poke around.'

'You can't be sure.'

'I'm as sure as I can be,' he reassured her. 'We're in the middle of a war and the number of homeless people is rising every day. They simply don't have the staff to check into every little thing. They're far too busy trying to get the victims of the bombing accommodated to worry about a temporary placement for one child.'

'Yeah, you're right, as usual. I'm worrying unnecessarily.' Bill always managed to put things into perspective for her, and was a tower of strength.

'It's no good your getting too attached to him, you know, May. It's only a short-term arrangement,' he warned.

'I know that.'

'Thinking about it, you'll probably be glad to get shot of him as he's such a little perisher.'

'I will not.' She was indignant. 'He's only being naughty because he's traumatised. He's probably a nice little lad when things are normal for him.'

'He certainly isn't much fun to have around at the moment,' said Bill.

'No, that's very true,' May was forced to admit. 'But there's something appealing about him even though he's giving us a whole load of trouble.' She sighed. 'Besides, it'll be nice having a nipper in the house again.'

'Don't get too used to it. He probably won't be with us for long.'

'I hope we keep him for a while, though. I'd like to feel I'm making a difference.'

'You've always had a soft heart. Still, I'm not complaining. Come and give us a cuddle, and then we'd better get some sleep in case Hitler's thugs come over during the night and we have to go down the ruddy shelter again.'

'G' night then, luv,' she said, kissing him lightly.

'G' night.'

She didn't go to sleep but lay there staring at the ceiling and mulling things over. The problem with having a guilty secret was that you never really felt safe.

As exhausted as Rose was, she couldn't sleep either. She lay there listening to Alfie's even breathing, hardly daring to move in case she woke him. He'd fought sleep like he fought everything else but nature had finally prevailed.

He'd eventually come in from the garden a few minutes after she'd closed the door, and had sat quietly in the corner of the living room until it was time for bed. He'd been heartbreakingly docile then, in complete contrast to earlier, when he'd been so stroppy. Rose had put him to bed and tucked him in. She even risked giving him a kiss on the cheek, for which she'd received a mumbled 'Get off, will yer.'

She guessed that the poor child hadn't had much of a life. His mother wouldn't have had an easy time, and he'd probably suffered because of the general attitude towards children of his circumstance. As if all of that wasn't enough, he'd been robbed of his beloved mother at the age of seven.

He'd obviously been well looked after, though, and had a strong spirit, probably inherited from his mother, who would have needed plenty of that to cope with the spite of society. Rose felt such strong empathy with him; she could almost feel his pain, and her eyes burned with tears at the thought of what he must be going through.

With a sudden sense of shock, she realised that for the first time since she'd heard about Ray's death she was having profound thoughts about something else; feeling deeply sad about someone else. On the heels of this came guilt, as though she was lapsing in her duty in not grieving for Ray every second of every day.

But the strong sympathy for Alfie remained. She would give a lot just to see him smile.

The next day when Rose got home from work, she found her mother distraught and Auntie Sybil not far off.

'Your mother's bitten off more than she can chew taking that boy in,' announced a flushed and flustered Sybil, in a whisper because Alfie was in the other room.

'What's happened now?' asked Rose.

'He's driven us nearly insane, that's what's happened,' replied Sybil. 'He's an absolute horror; completely uncontrollable. Your poor mother's nerves are in tatters and mine are hovering on the brink.'

Since Rose's aunt was inclined to exaggerate, Rose said, 'He can't have been that bad.'

'He was worse,' snorted Sybil.

'He is a trial, Rose,' confirmed May, filling the kettle to make tea. 'He's been an absolute little devil the whole morning. We've been at our wits' end.'

'What . . . what did he actually do?' Rose dreaded the answer.

'What didn't he do would be more to the point,' informed her aunt. 'He's been rude, naughty and downright disobedient.'

'He won't do anything he's told, Rose,' May put in shakily. 'He keeps saying that I'm not his mum so he doesn't have to do what I tell him.'

'What a performance we had when we took him up the Food Office to get him a ration book,' began Sybil. 'He said that his mother already had a ration book for him, and she'd have it with her when she came for him. He said he wasn't going with us. Screamed and carried on something alarming. We practically had to drag him down the street.'

'Oh dear,' said Rose, biting her lip.

'Since we've been back here, he's had us chasing up the street after the dog, who got out because my laddo left the side gate open after being told to make sure he closed it. He did it deliberately to upset us, I reckon.'

'That's going a bit far, Syb,' said May. 'I don't agree with you about that.'

'He emptied his porridge all over the table, didn't he, May?' Sybil was in full flow.

'That's true, Rose,' said May dismally.

'Then he crowned it all by playing with matches and nearly set the house alight,' Sybil went on.

'Oh no!' This was Rose, looking distraught.

May lit the gas under the kettle on the stove. 'You can tell him off until you're blue in the face and it doesn't make a blind bit of difference,' she said.

'He needs a damned good hiding in my opinion,' pronounced Sybil.

'That won't do any good,' disagreed May. 'Anyway, since when have you been in favour of hitting children?'

'Since Alfie arrived and made me realise that in some cases it's necessary.'

'We're not going to resort to that,' declared Rose.

'I've brought up three kids, and I won't say there haven't been times when I could have cheerfully strangled the lot of them, but I've never come across anything like this,' said May, brushing a tired hand across her brow. 'God only knows how he's been brought up. I know his poor mother must have been up against it, but surely she could have taught him some manners.'

'I expect she did,' opined Rose. 'I think the poor kid is choosing not to use them at the moment because he wants to hurt everyone around him because he's hurting so much himself.'

'I expect you're right, but it's bloomin' hard to cope with,' said May. 'I've never known such dreadful behaviour.'

'His mother probably did the best she could,' Rose went on, feeling the need to defend the woman. 'It

52

wouldn't have been easy for someone in her position. She must have had some bottle to keep him.'

'He certainly adored her,' mentioned May. 'He absolutely refuses to believe that she isn't coming for him.'

'Anyway, given what's happened this morning, do you want me to go to the council and tell them that we can't keep him? I can't look after him myself while I'm at work,' Rose said worriedly.

May looked at her in astonishment. '*Of course not!*' she exclaimed, offended by the suggestion. 'Surely you know me better than that.'

'What sort of people do you think we are?' added Sybil in support of her sister.

'It'll take more than a morning with a naughty seven year old to beat me,' proclaimed May. 'I was just letting off a bit of steam, that's all.'

'Of course she was; we both were,' added Sybil.

Rose felt immensely relieved. She'd brought Alfie into the house so felt responsible for him. But she couldn't look after him without family support, especially from her mother, since she was out for a large part of the day. For some reason she didn't quite understand, Alfie had already become very important to her.

'I think the sooner we get him into school the better,' suggested Sybil. 'He's probably bored stiff here all day, and that isn't helping matters. Children need other children, don't they?'

'They certainly do, and I'd be glad of a break from him,' added May. 'He's hard work.'

'I'll take over now anyway.' Rose looked out of the kitchen window into the small garden, where the one-time lawn was now sown with vegetables in the Dig for Victory campaign. 'It isn't raining at the moment, so if it stays dry I'll take him over to the park when I've had something to eat. Maybe I can have a chat to him and make him understand how bad he's being.'

'At least it'll give my nerves a chance to settle down,' approved May.

'What does your mum look like, Alfie?' asked Rose that same afternoon as they walked around the park. It was bleak and muddy from the recent rain though the sky was now streaked with light and promising sunshine. The dog was on the lead, and Alfie was walking with his head down, dragging his feet, determined to make heavy weather of the outing.

'What do you wanna know for?'

'No special reason,' she said. 'I'm just interested.'

'Mind your own business.'

'All right, I will.'

'Good.'

'I should think she'd be very upset if she knew how badly you are behaving,' persisted Rose. 'I'm sure she brought you up to be a good boy, so you're letting her down in a big way.'

'No I'm not,' he denied hotly. 'I wouldn't do that. I never give my mum any trouble. You can ask her when she comes for me if you don't believe me.'

Rose's heart twisted at his stubborn refusal to accept

the truth, but she said, 'Why are you giving us so much of it then, Alfie?'

'Dunno.'

'You shouldn't carry on like you did this morning, luv,' Rose admonished, trying to be firm without being too hard. 'It's unkind and wrong and my mother and aunt don't deserve it.' She paused, turning to his bowed head. 'But you already know that, don't you, Alfie?'

'I didn't do nothin',' he mumbled.

'Ooh, not much: pouring your porridge all over the table, nearly setting fire to the house. I wouldn't call that nothing.'

It was all a bit of a blur to Alfie, but he did remember turning his porridge dish upside down. A horrid pain lashed through him at the memory, and he could hardly believe that he'd done such a thing. He'd be in dead trouble with Mum if she got to know about it. But she wouldn't because she was dead. No, no, no, she wasn't. He wouldn't even let the word come into his mind because he couldn't bear it. She'd be back for him soon, thank goodness. He missed her so much. Her laugh, her voice, her smell and how warm he'd felt when she held him, no matter how cold it was in their room.

He remembered lighting the matches too. He knew he wasn't allowed to touch matches but he'd lit them anyway and then he'd wanted to cry because he knew his mum would be cross. But he'd just got angrier and angrier at the people shouting at him and telling him that he was bad when he already knew. And now this person called Rose was on at him again and there was such a huge lump in his throat he couldn't speak. So he just walked on with his head down.

Rose took the dog off the lead and let him have a run, wondering what to do next with the boy as she didn't seem able to make any sort of connection with him.

'All right, Alfie, you win,' she began. 'You don't want to talk to me and I'm not going to go on at you, but please don't keep being naughty because you'll hurt yourself far more than anyone else in the long run. Even though I'm a grown-up, I could be your friend if you'd only let me. I want you to stay on here with us, but the others will only take so much of your bad behaviour.'

Her words made his eyes burn and he wanted her to hold him, but he bit back the tears and said nastily, 'If they don't want me there, then send me away. It won't worry me. I don't wanna live with yer anyway.'

And with that he ran off after the dog, keeping his distance from Bruiser as always. He obviously wasn't used to having a dog around, and she suspected that he was a little afraid whilst wanting to befriend the animal very much. He certainly was one sad little boy.

Alfie's behaviour didn't improve, but when he started school, at least he was out of the house for part of the day, which made it easier for May, especially as Rose was around in the afternoons to help out.

However, a couple of weeks after his induction into the local school, May and Rose found themselves in the headmistress's office, having been summoned there by a curt letter in a sealed envelope brought home from school by Alfie. Rose had gone along to give her mother some support.

'I understand that Alfie Miller has just lost his mother and his home, Mrs Barton,' said Miss Atkins, a tall, authoritative woman in a grey jumper and skirt, her brown hair drawn back off her face into a bun, emphasising her pointed features and making her look fierce.

'That's right,' confirmed May. 'The poor little soul; it's such a shame.'

'Indeed, it is very sad and I am extremely sorry for him.' She paused ominously, peering at them through the thick lenses of her spectacles. 'But as much as I sympathise with him, I'm afraid I can't tolerate his bad behaviour in my school. It's too disruptive to the other children.'

'What's he been up to now?' asked May miserably.

'Fighting, Mrs Barton,' the headmistress explained. 'Fighting and . . .' she looked down and cleared her throat, 'unsavoury talk; calling the other children names of a most unpleasant kind. I heard him myself.'

'Oh dear,' said May, chewing her lip, while Rose groaned inwardly.

'He punched one of his classmates in the face the other day, and actually made his nose bleed,' Miss Atkins further informed them.

Oh Alfie, why do you do these things, Rose asked silently while her mother said shakily, 'That really is too bad of him. I shall have strong words with him about it.'

'I really do hope you can make him see the error of his ways,' said the headmistress, pushing her glasses up on to the bridge of her nose, 'because, obviously, that sort of thing can't be allowed to go on in this school. I am responsible for all the children here, not just one who is suffering from grief. This generation of children have more than enough disruption and trauma in their lives with this wretched war. I see it as part of my job to create a stable influence while they are at school.'

'Are you going to expel him?' asked Rose bluntly.

'No. Not at the moment. But it is my duty to point out to you that that sort of behaviour can't be tolerated in this school for any length of time. So if there isn't an improvement, I shall have to ask you to find another school for him. He might be better suited somewhere else.'

'The boy is suffering from shock, Miss Atkins,' May pointed out. 'I'm sure he isn't always as badly behaved as he is at the moment.'

'I am very sorry for him, as I've said, but I have a school to run and I can't have it disrupted indefinitely. It wouldn't be fair to the other pupils.' She looked at some notes on her desk. 'I'll keep him on for now in the hope that you may be able to instil sufficient discipline in him for him to behave in a reasonable manner during school hours.' She looked from one woman to the other. 'But I'm afraid if there is no improvement I shall be forced to get in touch with you again.' She stood up to indicate that the interview was at an end. 'Thank you for coming.'

Outside, Rose said, 'The little devil. What are we going to do with him?'

'Search me,' said May worriedly. 'He's his own worst enemy, that boy.'

'If the other kids were giving him stick about his mother, you can't blame the boy for giving 'em a smack and calling them names,' said Alan that evening when a defiant-looking Alfie was in bed and everyone was gathered in the living room discussing the meeting with the headmistress. They had managed to drag the facts out of the boy as to what had actually happened. Somehow Alfie's circumstances had got around the neighbourhood and the kids had been giving him a hard time. 'I'd have done the same when I was at school if anyone had said a word out of place about you, Mum. Oh yeah; not half!'

'He has to stand up for himself, May,' supported Bill. 'At least he's proved that he's no sissy.'

'A boy has to establish his strength at an early age,' put in Flip with a worldly-wise air. 'Otherwise the bullies will make his life a misery.'

'Trust you to approve of wrong-doing,' snorted his wife.

'I wasn't—'

'But then you would, as you've done more than your fair share of misbehaving yourself,' she interrupted. 'Still do, come to that, if you think you can get away with it. I bet you were a right little heathen at school.'

'Put a sock in it, you two,' rebuked Joyce. 'It's Alfie we're talking about, not you.'

'You men are a fat lot of help, I must say,' said May, clicking her tongue against the roof of her mouth in annoyance. 'You all seem to think that he was justified in beating the living daylights out of another boy.'

'He didn't beat the living daylights out of him, Auntie May,' corrected Joyce. 'There was a fight, that's all, and I bet the other boy stabbed out a good few punches. I'm with Alan on this one. Anyone who said anything bad about my mum would have got worse than that. Alfie couldn't just stand by and let the boy say what he liked.'

'Not you as well,' sighed May.

'They *were* being mean about his mother so he was bound to react,' Rose pointed out. 'Anyone worth their salt would. It's only natural.'

'What's the matter with you all?' demanded May, looking flushed and perplexed. 'Have you all forgotten the difference between right and wrong? Am I the only one in this family with any standards?'

'Don't be daft, May,' said her husband in a gentle manner. 'We're just saying that the boy was provoked.'

'Maybe he was, but that doesn't mean that it's right.' She was very hot and bothered because she was worried about Alfie's future. 'It'll be even worse for him if he has to start at another school. Another disruption is the last thing he needs on top of everything else.'

'We know it isn't right, Mum, and we know that Alfie is being a right little horror. But in this particular case we can understand why,' said Rose.

'Well, I'm at the end of my tether with the little monster, and shall be thoroughly glad to see the back of him,' declared May hotly. 'The day when he's taken off our hands can't come soon enough for me.'

Coincidentally, the following afternoon, while there was only Rose and her mother at home, they received a visit from a female officer from the Children's Department, a pleasant matronly type with untidy hair and a harassed look about her.

'I've just called in to see how things are going with young Alfie Miller,' she explained when they invited her into the living room.

Rose stayed silent, bracing herself for the explosion she was sure would come from her mother after her outburst last night.

But May said nothing.

'Not finding him too much, I hope,' said the woman, moving on swiftly as though to prevent May from replying in the affirmative. 'Only it's so dreadfully difficult to find places for orphaned children in stable homes like yours, so we haven't yet found another billet for him.' She shook her head. 'We're snowed under with cases similar to Alfie's.'

The other two women nodded politely.

'It's better for the children to be in a family environment if possible, rather than an orphanage,' she went on quickly. 'But if you don't feel able to continue we can probably transfer him to a children's home more or less right away.'

She paused, and Rose expected her mother to tell her to make the arrangements straight away. But she stayed silent.

'The powers-that-be might even recommend him for evacuation to the country,' the woman went on, 'but as this isn't one of London's most dangerous areas and he's emotionally fragile after his mother's death, personally I don't think it would be a good idea to move him.'

'There won't be any need to move him anywhere,' declared May. 'He's fine here with us.'

'You're quite sure now, only I don't want to burden you . . .'

'Quite sure, thank you,' May stated categorically. 'We'd love to have him for as long as you need us to.'

'Oh, I can't tell you what a relief that is, Mrs Barton,' said the woman, heading for the door as though fearing that May might have a change of heart. 'I'll come and see you again soon. I'm sure Alfie will thrive under your excellent care. Goodbye.'

As soon as they'd closed the door after her, Rose said, 'Well, you changed your tune a bit sudden, didn't you? You said last night that you couldn't wait to get rid of him.'

'And I'll probably say the same thing again and again if he riles me sufficiently,' May told her. 'Is it any wonder, the way he carries on? What sane person would want a little horror under their roof, causing chaos and trouble the whole time? But I won't stand by and see him go into a home, not while there's anything I can do to prevent it.'

'I'm so glad we're keeping him, Mum.'

'I can't think why, since he isn't exactly a joy to have around the place.'

'I enjoy a challenge, I suppose,' said Rose.

'He's more than a challenge,' her mother grinned. 'He's an uphill struggle.'

'You're right there,' Rose agreed.

But for all that Alfie was difficult, Rose had grown fond of him, and suspected that, despite what she'd said, her mother felt the same way.

Chapter Three

It was a Saturday afternoon in November, and a fog hung over the streets of west London in shifting, gritty clouds. People were cold, weary of Hitler's nightly onslaughts, and hungry from the effects of food rationing.

But inside one of Ealing's grand houses, now being used as a convalescent home for wounded soldiers, there was bonhomie in abundance as Rose and Joyce, with Stan at the piano, sang their hearts out in the hospital day room to a delighted audience of injured servicemen, the medical staff also enjoying the show between duties.

Their repertoire had included all the latest favourites and now they were coming to the end of the song that was on everybody's lips at the moment, 'A Nightingale Sang in Berkeley Square'. Rose was imbued with warmth and buoyancy. It was incredible the extent to which the physical and emotional experience of singing had uplifted her.

The trio had had a few enjoyable rehearsals before-hand at Stan's place – the Willis family home on the

Ealing–Acton borders. But when it had come to the real thing, the cousins had both been terrified; twittering and erupting into nervous giggles, convinced that they were going to get booed off the stage.

'It isn't the London Palladium, you know,' Stan had laughingly reminded them.

'The audience is just as important, though,' Rose had pointed out. 'Even more so really, considering who they are and what they've given for their country.'

'At least they're a captive audience,' he'd said waggishly. 'They can't go home.'

'They can shout us off stage, though,' Joyce had put in.

But they hadn't. They'd cheered and clapped and called for more. The applause was enormously exhilarating. It was almost a human bond; a feeling of communal well-being spreading through the room and touching everybody. It wasn't as if the soldiers here had much to feel happy about either. Some had lost limbs in the service of their country; others had serious head wounds; some were blind. But this didn't stop them from showing a hearty appreciation of the show. Those patients who were physically able to get to their feet had shown their approval in a standing ovation.

Having been initially wary about joining Stan in this worthy project, Rose was now proud be in the company of such valour; humbled by the men's courage. Joyce was obviously enjoying herself too.

What with the strain of the air raids at night and the constant battle with Alfie at home, this was a welcome respite for Rose. Alfie had been with them for nearly a month now and was still as difficult as ever. His belligerent behaviour was getting on everyone's nerves and putting the family on edge with one another. No one wanted to give up on the boy, but they were all fed up with having a sullen, aggressive child in the house casting a shadow over everything with his nasty temper and determination to rebel against everything he was asked to do.

As Rose had brought him into the family she felt responsible and was therefore in a state of permanent inner conflict. On the one hand she hated to see the family's life made a misery, but she was also very emotionally involved with Alfie and desperate to help him.

However, all of this had been pushed to the back of her mind by the wonderful atmosphere here this afternoon, which had refreshed and invigorated her. Now the song came to an end and she thought the applause must have been heard for miles around. The performers acceded to the calls for an encore before preparing to bring the show to a close as it was time for the patients' evening meal.

For the finale they did 'We'll Meet Again', which brought the entertainment to an emotional end. Staying long enough for a few cheery words with the patients and wishing them well, the three went out into the fog, laughing and talking.

'The buses won't be running in this pea-souper,' observed Joyce, peering into the gloom. It had been daylight when they'd arrived and the fog not so dense. Now that it was dark you could hardly see a hand in front of your face, the blackout exacerbating the problem. 'So it's Shanks's pony for us.'

'Will you two be all right?' enquired Stan, whose home was in the opposite direction to theirs. 'I'll walk home with you if you like. I don't mind.'

'There's no need,' Rose assured him. 'We'll have each other to cling on to.'

'Course we will,' added Joyce heartily. 'You concentrate on finding your own way home.'

'One good thing about the fog is that it's bad flying weather, so it might keep the Germans away and allow us to sleep in our own beds,' said Rose.

The others were in agreement.

'Anyway, girls, thanks for coming out and doing the show,' said Stan. 'It worked really well. I'm sure the boys enjoyed it a whole lot more because you two were there, rather than just me on the piano. You're a lot better-looking, for one thing.'

'Oh, so the singing didn't matter, then?' joked Joyce. She and Stan were always joshing with each other.

'If you hadn't been easy on the ear as well as the eye, they'd have soon let you know about it, don't worry,' he said. 'Soldiers aren't backward in coming forward, wounded or not.'

'Flatterer,' said Joyce with a girlish giggle.

'Don't pretend you don't like it.'

'I wouldn't dream of it.' She shrugged with an air of nonchalance, but her cheeks were flushed and her eyes sparkling. If Rose hadn't known them both better she might have suspected that there was some special chemistry at work between them. But it must just be banter between friends, because Joyce wouldn't look at any other man besides Bob, and Stan wasn't the sort to go after someone who was already spoken for, especially when her chosen one was away fighting for his country.

'Anyway, you were both brilliant,' he said. 'I hope you'll be teaming up with me again.'

'Try stopping us,' said Joyce.

'In the meantime we'd better start trying to find our way home,' suggested Rose, as her cousin didn't seem in any hurry to leave him. 'Come on, girl. Best foot forward.'

'Ta-ta then, Stan,' said Joyce, linking arms with Rose.

'Ta-ta, both. Mind how you go now.'

The cousins managed to get home safely, albeit that it took them twice as long because they lost their bearings a few times. But they were too flushed with success to let a spot of fog and blackout faze them, especially as there wasn't an air raid.

The next morning the fog had gone. Unfortunately, so had Alfie.

'At first I thought he must have gone downstairs when I woke up and saw he wasn't in his bed,' said Rose, who was still in her pyjamas having searched the house, assisted by the rest of the family.

'He isn't here anywhere.' May was pale and wringing her hands.

'The little sod,' cursed Bill. 'He'll wish he'd never been born when I get hold of him. Running off like that and getting us all into a state.'

'Never mind that now, Dad,' said Alan. 'Let's concentrate on finding him. We'd better go out looking for him before the little devil gets himself into some sort of trouble. Let's get some clothes on and be on our way, Joe.'

'I'll come with you,' said Bill with obvious concern. 'I'll go next door and get Flip to give us a hand too. If we split up we can cover a larger area.'

'The young terror must have slipped out before any of us were awake,' said May to Rose as the others left the house. 'Why would he do a thing like that, Rose? Why would a little kid want to be out in the cold all on his own in the early morning? Are we making him that miserable?'

Rose's thoughts were racing. 'No. I don't think this has anything to do with us, Mum,' she said with a sudden flash of inspiration. 'It goes much deeper than that.'

'Because of what he's been through, you mean?'

But Rose was already heading for the stairs to go up and get dressed.

'I'm going out, Mum,' she said, back down a few minutes later. 'It's just a hunch. I can't stop now so I'll tell you all about it when I get back.'

Leaving her mother staring after her in bewilderment, she rushed out of the back door, got her bike from the shed and pedalled down the road as fast as she could.

* * *

She found him sitting on a pile of broken bricks at the back of the bombed house, quite close to the part of the ruin she'd rescued him from; a small figure in a grey jumper and short grey trousers, his legs red and blotchy from the cold, his face pale and pinched. He hadn't even bothered to put a coat on so was shivering but barely seemed to notice. She sat down beside him without saying a word. He glanced at her briefly then continued to stare unseeingly into the ruins which had been made safe but not yet properly cleared.

'You've had a long walk,' she said eventually. 'I'm surprised you found it.'

'I'm not daft, yer know,' he said snappily. 'Of course I know where I used to live. I'm not a baby.'

'All right. There's no need to bite my head off.'

There was a pause. 'How did you know I was here?' he asked after a while.

'Just a lucky guess.'

A long silence. Then: 'I wanted to go home to my mum,' he said hoarsely.

'I know, luv,' she said, her heart breaking.

'I thought I might . . . I dunno what I thought really. I just wanted to feel her, yer know, close to me.'

'And now that you're here, do you?'

'Nah, not really,' he said hopelessly. 'It's all different. She's gone; she isn't anywhere.'

Rose took her coat off and put it around him, expecting him to shrug it off. He didn't, so she pushed her luck and put her arm around him. He was sitting very still but his bony shoulders trembled beneath her touch.

'Mum's never coming back to get me, is she?' he said in a small voice.

Rose swallowed hard. She didn't want to lie to him. She had just experienced bereavement herself and she'd tried to reach out to Ray many times but there had been nothing there. She was an adult, old enough to cope, whereas Alfie had been left frail without his mother's arms to shield him and show him the way. 'I'm afraid not, luv,' she said through dry lips.

'I miss her *so much*. I just want to . . . to be with her.'

'I know,' she said softly. 'But wherever she is, she'll be looking out for you.'

'But I can't see her, or touch her, so what good is that?'

'You can see her in your mind, though, can't you?'

'Sometimes. But it hurts when I think of her.'

Rose had never felt so helpless. She so wanted to make things right for him. 'I can't be your mum, Alfie, but I can be your friend if you'll let me,' she said. 'It might help having someone to look out for you.'

'Why did she have to die, Rose? Why?'

'I'm afraid I don't know the answer to that, Alfie.'

Suddenly all his repressed grief erupted in a great torrent, his cries loud and tortured, his thin little body shaking and convulsed. He didn't reject her when she cradled him in her arms and stroked his hair, shushing and comforting until he became quieter.

'Mum had dark hair like yours,' he sniffed, when the crying finally abated a little. 'She had a nice smiley face and she used to make me laugh. She said that you have to try to see the funny side of things because laughter is the best medicine.'

'You haven't done much laughing lately, have you?' Rose mentioned.

'S'pose not.'

'Did you ever have any relatives come to visit, Alfie?' she asked, interested in his background and hoping there was someone of his own out there for him. 'Aunties and uncles; that sort of thing.'

'I don't think so. I can't remember any. Mrs Bailey from downstairs used to come up to our room and stay with me while Mum was at work.'

'What sort of work did your mum do?'

'Cleaning shops in the mornings, and she worked as a barmaid in a pub some nights,' he replied. 'Before the bombs came, when we didn't have to go down the cellar of a night, she used to read me stories and make toast and dripping on her nights off. We sometimes used to eat it in bed to keep warm because Mum couldn't afford the gas fire. It was lovely.'

Rose felt an affinity towards his mother even though she had never known her. It must have been so hard for her to manage with a child to bring up alone and no support of any kind. But one thing Alfie hadn't gone short of was love; she'd given him that by the barrel-load.

Sitting here on this bomb site on a cold Sunday morning, Rose gently encouraged him to talk about how things had been with his mother, and as he chatted on about life in one room as though it was paradise, she realised that, although he'd had so little, he'd actually had a great deal. As he talked she could feel the tension gradually go out of his body. For the first time since he'd come into her life, she felt him relax.

Eventually she said, 'Shall we go home now, luv? The others will be worried. My dad and brothers have gone out looking for you.'

'I'll cop it then.'

'Very likely.'

'Oh well, better face the music,' he said, in a tone so different to his usual sulky, argumentative one that he might have been another child. 'That's what my mum always used to say.'

'She sounds like a very sensible lady, your mum,' said Rose, standing up. 'Come on then, let's go. Fancy a lift on my bike?' she suggested. 'It's a long walk home.'

'Cor, yes please.'

As she pedalled through the streets with Alfie sitting on the handlebars, she sensed that things might be better for him now. He would still have sad and bad times, of course, and he might never fully get over the death of his mother. But in his own childish way he'd said goodbye to her this morning. Rose believed that in going back to the bomb site he'd finally allowed himself to accept the fact that she really was dead. Now perhaps he could at least get on with his life, feeling less tortured as time went by. Rose was hoping that he might feel able to allow her and the family to help him through, instead of fighting them every step of the way.

*　　*　　*

Much to Rose's delight and the relief of the rest of the family, the incident at the bomb site did prove to be a turning point for Alfie. He stopped being so rude and awkward. With a little prompting from Rose, he even apologised to the others when they got back for going off without telling anyone.

He was no angel by any means and was often in trouble; mostly for transgressions related to childish overexuberance. Despite having been told not to, he would play with an old football that had once been Alan's inside the house and knock things over with it, slide down the banisters, and come home caked in mud because he'd been playing on an overgrown piece of waste ground. He still had a tendency to answer back, too, but he was saucy rather than insolent now.

One cold and sunny Sunday afternoon at the end of November, Rose and Joyce were walking in the park with Alfie, who had run on ahead with the dog off the lead.

'I reckon you're getting broody, you know, Rose,' decided Joyce suddenly.

'Oh yeah, and what brings you to that sudden conclusion?'

'The way you are with Alfie,' she replied. 'You're like a mother hen.'

'I think he's had a rough deal, that's all,' she explained. 'He needs all the kindness he can get.'

'I couldn't agree more. But it's more than just kindness with you and him. You seem like a mum to him. That indicates broodiness to me.'

'You're wrong this time, kid. I'm very fond of him but not because I'm broody,' Rose explained. 'I took an instant liking to him even though he was so difficult.'

'You're such a natural, I thought perhaps you were wanting a kiddie of your own,' said Joyce.

'No. Not really. I would have liked to have had children with Ray, but as that isn't possible I'll probably never have any,' she told her cousin. 'Naturally I'm disappointed, but I'm not using Alfie as a substitute for a child of my own, not consciously anyway. I see myself more as a big sister to him. There's something about him that makes him very special somehow.'

'He does have a certain appeal, I must admit,' agreed Joyce. 'Anyway, you're still a young woman with plenty of time to have a family. You might meet someone else eventually.'

'I don't want anyone but Ray.' Rose was adamant.

'It's still early days,' Joyce pointed out. 'You may well feel differently later on.'

'It could happen, I suppose, but I can't imagine it at the moment.'

'As regards Alfie,' began Joyce, 'you'll need to guard against getting too fond of him.'

'How could I or anyone ever be too fond of him?' queried Rose. 'Surely every child deserves to be loved.'

'I mean that he's only staying with you in the short term,' Joyce pointed out. 'You'll feel lost when he leaves if you're not careful.'

'*My* feelings are irrelevant,' Rose made clear. 'It's his

that matter. He's a little boy and I want him to feel loved, as he was by his mother.'

'He's lucky to have you.'

'Alfie is about the least lucky person I know.'

'Yeah. I suppose you're right,' Joyce said in an understanding manner.

Just then Rose spotted something that stopped her in her tracks. Alfie was rolling on the grass with the dog. For the first time the boy wasn't holding back from the animal. Immersed in his play, he was squealing with enthusiasm. After a while, he stood up and ran towards them in the winter sunshine, with Bruiser at his heels. He was doing something Rose hadn't heard him do before. He was laughing; giggling with the joy of being a child. The two women stood there smiling. The sound of that laughter brought tears of joy to Rose's eyes.

'He's going to be in dead trouble with your mum when she sees the mud all over his coat,' said her down-to-earth cousin. 'She'll go mad.'

'I reckon he'll think it was worth it,' smiled Rose.

Seeing Alfie playing like a normal, boisterous seven year old confirmed her trust in her own judgement that she had done the right thing in bringing him home with her that day. She wouldn't have missed hearing that laughter for anything.

'Are you expecting twins or something, Rose?' asked Alan one evening when they were coming to the end of their meal.

'I sincerely hope not,' said May, giving her son a

77

warning look. 'What a thing to say about your sister. I don't know what puts these things into your head.'

'She seems to have lost her own appetite and found that of at least three starving people, that's what,' he joked. 'Joe and I could always rely on a bit of extra because of her leavings. Now she doesn't leave anything.'

'So sorry to put you out by having my share, boys,' Rose said with good-humoured irony.

'I should think so too,' Alan came back at her. 'What with you and Alfie eating everything in sight, us two poor things are wasting away.'

'With Mum looking after you? Don't make me laugh,' she chortled.

'You can have my greens,' offered Alfie obligingly. 'I don't like 'em.'

'I've never known a child who did,' said May. 'But you eat them yourself, Alfie. They're good for you.'

He didn't argue as he once would have; just made painful inroads into his cabbage.

Although Alan was exaggerating, he was right in saying that Rose's appetite had returned in a big way. After months of having to force food down without even tasting it, she now thoroughly enjoyed her meals. In fact, her health had improved generally.

She wasn't constantly aching inside now. Ray was always on her mind but the pain had eased a little. Alfie had a great deal to do with it. She'd been too busy worrying about him to think about herself. He really had given her a new lease of life.

'What did you do at school today, Alfie?' enquired Alan with friendly interest.

'Nothin' much.' He thought about it some more. 'We had sums.'

'Ooh, poor old you,' Alan sympathised. 'I never could get the hang of those things.'

'I don't mind doing 'em,' Alfie said. 'I got ten out of ten for mental arithmetic the other day.'

'Well done,' said May, accompanied by cheery approval from the others.

'Perhaps you're gonna be the brainy type like Joe,' suggested Alan. 'You'll be able to get yourself a good job when you grow up then.'

'If you're good at arithmetic you can do a job for me, lad. You can help Mrs Barton to do her sums properly on the housekeeping money,' joked Bill, entering into the spirit. 'She never has got the hang of making it go around.' He gave his wife a quick, wary look and added, 'Just teasing, dear.'

'You'd better be.'

'What else did you do today?' asked Joe.

'PT,' said Alfie. 'The teacher said I'm good at that; one of the best in the class.'

'I'm not surprised, the way you're always climbing and running about,' said Alan.

'PT is my favourite lesson.'

Standing back from the scene, Rose was warmed by the atmosphere. It was so good to see Alfie joining in and seeming like one of the family. They all took an interest in him now that he wasn't so horrid to have around.

There had been no more letters summoning them to the school to see the headmistress. Since what had proved to be the watershed, Alfie seemed to have settled down at school, and had even made friends with some of the local children. Evacuation still wasn't compulsory for children, and many of the parents around here had decided to keep their offspring at home, wanting their family to stay together come what may.

Rose was brought out of her reverie by the moan of the siren, which produced a general exodus, everyone groaning and collecting coats and blankets on the way to the shelter.

It was cold, damp and sour-smelling in the shelter. The only one of them who didn't seem to mind was Alfie, who appeared to regard the whole thing as an adventure, which was surprising considering what he'd been through when his own home had been bombed. He seemed more concerned with adding to his shrapnel collection tomorrow than about the fact that he might not be alive to go round the streets looking for it.

Protected to an extent by his childish innocence, he never showed fear during the air raids. He seemed convinced that they would all be safe because his mum had told him he always would be and she didn't tell lies. Her death didn't seem to have shaken his faith in her at all. He seemed to think that even though his mother wasn't around, she still had some sort of influence on his life.

'Can we have a game of I-spy?' he asked, apparently

undaunted in the ensuing silence after an ear-splitting explosion as everyone else waited for their insides to settle.

'Oh no, not that again,' groaned Alan. 'It must be the world's most boring game.'

'Aw, go on,' Alfie persisted. 'It'll be something to do. And I've just thought of a really good one.'

'I'll play with you,' agreed Rose.

The others offered to join in, though not with a great deal of enthusiasm.

'Get started then, Alfie,' said Rose. 'You can go first.'

'I spy with my little eye, something beginning with . . .'

It was surprising how a simple game could calm the nerves, thought Rose, as the relentless raid seemed as though it would never end; probably because it was better to focus the mind on something else, no matter how tedious. Alfie fell asleep after a few games and the rest of them had had enough, so they had to find other ways to amuse themselves and stop their nerves giving out completely as the noise of battle roared all around them. There were bangs, crashes, the steely clatter of ambulance and fire engine bells, and all the while in the background the staccato cracking of anti-aircraft fire.

The terrifying whistle of another bomb in descent caused a breathless hush, everyone preparing to meet their maker while praying hard to be spared. Rose sang to herself quietly, almost without realising it. Then one by one they all joined in until there was a boisterous rendition of 'You Are My Sunshine' ringing against the corrugated walls.

'Do your worst, Hitler,' said Rose heartily. 'You won't break our spirit.'

Rose was working a split shift, and it was dark when she drove the post office van out of the sorting office to do the evening collections. She had to concentrate hard to see her way in the blackout, though there was a half-moon which helped a little. Because of staff short-ages and the extra Christmas mail, it had been neces-sary for her to learn to drive so that she could clear the pillar boxes and help with parcel deliveries as well as her usual duties. She'd been given a crash driving course and a speedily arranged test. Despite all the extra work, she enjoyed the driving experience enormously.

There were quite a few people about around the station area: people still coming home from work, some Christmas shoppers clutching packages.

Christmas shopping wasn't easy for this, the second Christmas of the war, because it was so hard to find anything to buy as presents. There wasn't going to be much festive food about either, though May had been putting tinned stuff away for months.

As Rose headed into the back streets, she cursed aloud when she heard the wail of the siren, earlier than usual tonight. She would have to continue with her work and clear the boxes because the raid might go on for hours, and the job had to be done. She decided that if the bombing got too close she would go to the public surface shelter until it eased off. Meanwhile she would get on with it.

But just seconds after the siren had died away, and even before she'd reached the first of the pillar boxes, there was a flash of light in front of her and an explosion that shook the ground so violently the van was lifted off the ground. At first she couldn't work out what had happened, but as the terrible scene in front of her fully registered, she realised that a bomb had landed on some nearby houses, which were now on fire. There was smoke everywhere. People were screaming and choking, and she could just make out some figures running in the light of the flames.

Fortunately she hadn't yet collected any mail so she could leave the van and go and do what she could to help, without breaking the rules of the job that banned delivery staff from leaving the mail unattended under any circumstances. She leapt out of the vehicle and ran towards the devastation, retching from the smoke and almost tripping over someone lying in the road.

'Oh my Lord,' she said, getting down on her knees, not sure if the woman was conscious. 'Hello there. Can you hear me?'

'Yeah, I can hear you,' came the agonised cry.

'Where are you hurt?'

'My leg.' She sounded young, but Rose couldn't see her clearly in the dim light. 'It hurts so much I don't know what to do.' She was writhing in agony.

Shining a torch on her thigh, Rose saw with a bolt of horror that blood was gushing from an open wound.

The woman must have been hit by shrapnel.

'Please help me, please, please,' she begged, sobbing with pain. 'I can't stand it. Oh God, I feel sick.'

'I'll look after you, don't worry.'

Looking around, all Rose could see was chaos and carnage everywhere. The emergency services hadn't arrived yet and bomber planes were still coming over, explosions shaking the ground.

'I'll try to stop the bleeding,' she said, wrapping her handkerchief around the wound and tying it tight, the blood soaking through and feeling sticky on her hands but not flowing at quite such a rate. 'We need to get you to hospital. Do you think you'll be able to make it over to the van?'

'No, but I'll give it a try.'

Somehow, and afterwards Rose never knew how, she managed to get the girl into an upright position and half carried her to the vehicle.

'What's your name?' Rose asked as she lifted her into the passenger seat.

'Mary,' she managed to utter through her pain, but she was groaning now.

'Hello, Mary. I'm Rose,' she informed her, thinking that a personal touch might help and talking might help her to stay conscious. 'I'm going to drive you to the hospital. If the roads aren't closed it shouldn't take long and they'll look after you there. Do you reckon you can manage to hang on until we get there? You can shout your head off if it'll make you feel any better. I don't mind how loud you yell.'

'Thanks,' Mary said in a voice tight with pain. 'I'm ever so grateful.'

Rose had never been as frightened in her entire life as she was then, driving through the air raid, flames everywhere, the sky glowing crimson above the rooftops, explosions thumping and crashing all around. Mary's wails of anguish, added to fear and an intense sense of urgency, almost shredded Rose's nerves completely, but she knew the girl couldn't help it.

At last they reached the hospital and Rose rushed into the building to ask for help. The place was a hive of activity: ambulances arriving, the injured being helped inside, people crying and blood everywhere. Much to her relief a couple of medics responded to her plea right away and came out with a stretcher.

'You'll be in good hands now, Mary,' said Rose gently as they lifted her out of the van and eased her on to a stretcher. 'Good luck. I'll be thinking of you.'

'Thanks, Rose,' Mary said weakly. 'You've been brilliant. I won't forget it.'

Bloodstained and trembling from the shock, almost oblivious now of her own safety, Rose hurried back to the van and continued with the job of clearing the postboxes. The air raid was still in full flow but she carried on until every last box was empty, then took the mail sacks back to the sorting office. Then she got on her bike and set off for home.

'Let's have "I'll Be With You in Apple Blossom Time",' suggested May.

'We've already had that once tonight, Mum,' Rose reminded her.

'No harm in having it again, is there?' said May. 'It's one of my favourites.'

'"Roll Out the Barrel" is livelier,' suggested Bill.

'Let's have some carols,' suggested Uncle Flip.

'Good idea,' said Stan, and immediately started playing 'Silent Night' before anyone could disagree.

It was Christmas night, and the Barton family and friends were gathered around the piano in the front sitting room, with Stan at the piano and Rose and Joyce leading the singing. This room was only used on special occasions so was often cold and fusty. But now there was a lovely fire crackling in the hearth, and a rousing party atmosphere.

There had been a lot of happy faces in London in the final days before Christmas, mainly because of heartening headlines in the newspapers reporting that British troops had scored a significant victory in the Western Desert. Something that had given people a lift at a more personal level was the sudden cessation of air raids, giving Londoners some of the quietest nights since the Blitz began.

For some reason, and no one knew why, though there was plenty of speculation, Hitler's boys had stayed away, even though flying conditions had seemed ideal. So everyone had had sleep at night, in their own beds, and it was such a treat, especially for Rose and Joyce, who had been frantically busy at work, doing extra shifts to cope with the Christmas rush.

They had also done a few more shows with Stan in the hope of bringing some seasonal cheer to those unfortunate enough to be in hospital during the festive season.

Food stocks in the shops had been reasonable, though there were strong warnings from the Minister of Food that things were going to worsen considerably in the New Year.

Christmas Day had been lovely, Rose thought now. They had all been up early to see Alfie open his presents. He was especially thrilled with the little clockwork car and the Rupert Bear annual Rose had managed to find with great difficulty as the paper shortage meant that not so many had been printed this year. The rest of the day had passed in pleasant gaiety, with party games following Christmas dinner, and finishing off with the sing-song now in progress.

Aunt Sybil and Uncle Flip had come for lunch and stayed all day in keeping with Barton tradition. It had been Joyce's idea to invite Stan for the evening.

'He's such a whizz on the piano, he'll make the party go with a swing,' she'd said.

As indeed he had. They were all having a lovely time. The adults were singing and Alfie was sitting quietly in a chair looking again at his presents.

'I think we'll take a break for refreshment,' said Rose as they came to the end of the carol. 'We'll have some more songs later. Phew, I need a drink.'

Rose's father and uncle departed to the kitchen to organise some liquid refreshment for everyone, while

Mum and Auntie Sybil went to the kitchen for mince pies and sausage rolls.

'You can't half play the piano, can't you, mate?' Alan said to Stan as the younger men stood around chatting.

'I'll say you can,' added Joe. 'It's a gift, being able to play like that. I don't know how you do it.'

'Years of practice,' explained Stan. 'I've been playing since I was about three.'

'We all had piano lessons when we were kids but none of us were any good so we gave up.' Joe paused, remembering. 'Well, Alan was all right but he wouldn't practise, so Mum and Dad stopped paying for lessons.'

'You have to practise all the time, but if you like a thing you want to do it, don't you? It always fascinated me, so practising wasn't a problem.'

'Liking it is all part of the gift, I suppose,' remarked Joe.

'You should hear him play classical music,' put in Joyce proudly. 'He's brilliant. He's a music teacher by profession, aren't you, Stan?'

'I used to be before the war.' He nodded. 'Just do a few private lessons in my spare time now.'

Something in Joyce's attitude caught Rose's attention. Surely the admiration she was exuding in such abundance was more than one would normally express for a mere workmate? Rose looked at her cousin, who was further extolling Stan's virtues, and she suddenly knew for certain what she'd suspected for some time: that Joyce was different when she was with Stan; she was vivacious and radiant to the point where she almost seemed to glow.

Rose's heart twisted as she thought of Joyce's fiancé Bob, away fighting in the war. Joyce probably didn't even realise it herself yet, but there was heartache ahead for her because she didn't treat her relationship with Bob lightly. But the underlying intimacy between her and Stan was so blatantly obvious it was tangible.

Because it was now so clear to Rose, it seemed odd that no one else seemed to have noticed anything. Maybe she was imagining it. She hoped so for both their sakes.

'You're not in the forces then, Stan?' Alan was saying.

'No. I didn't pass the medical unfortunately,' he explained. 'I've got a problem with my chest. I've had it all my life. I suffer a lot with bronchitis and get breathless if I overexert myself. So I'm no good to the army.'

'Sounds a bit grim.'

'The condition isn't as bad as the insults I get from people in the street because I'm not in army uniform,' he told them. 'I'd much rather be out there fighting than having to put up with that.'

'I suppose if they don't know the reason they might misunderstand,' remarked Joe. 'I mean, you look healthy enough, and you're a young man. They could mistake you for . . .'

'A coward,' Stan finished for him. 'That's what they think all right. There isn't much I can do about it, other than wear a placard round my neck with "Medically

Unfit" written on it. So I try to let it go over my head.'

'That's terrible.' Joyce was outraged. 'How dare people say such awful things to you? You can't help having something wrong with you. And what about all the good work you do entertaining for charity, risking your life in the air raids to bring people a bit of light relief? They'd better not say anything in my hearing. They'll regret it if they do.'

'All right, Joyce, there's no need to get upset about it,' said Stan, looking at her with a puzzled half-smile. 'I can look after myself.'

Joyce, Joyce, what are you getting yourself into? thought Rose, knowing for certain now that she hadn't imagined the special bond between them. Joyce was like a tiger protecting her mate, not a work colleague defending one of her own. Rose thought that the couple probably hadn't even acknowledged their feelings for each other themselves yet. But the feelings were there; very much so. It wasn't Rose's place to broach the subject, though. Joyce would tell her about it when she was ready, if there was anything to tell.

The respite from the raids proved to be a brief one. A few days after Christmas the German bombers returned with a cargo of incendiary bombs which devastated the City of London and nigh on burned it down. Some of London's most cherished buildings were gutted, and many of the thousands of firemen – regulars and part-time auxiliaries – who were called in especially to fight the blaze lost their lives. Some of these evil fire bombs also fell on the suburbs, so the Bartons went back to spending the nights in the shelter.

One Saturday afternoon in January a stranger knocked at the Bartons' front door. Joe just happened to answer it and found he was staring at the most gorgeous girl he had ever seen.

'Is Rose in, please?' asked the young woman, who had fair hair poking out of the front of her headscarf and the loveliest almond-shaped green eyes.

'Yeah, she's in.'

He was so mesmerised by her, he just stood there gawping, and not moving.

'Could I see her then, please?'

'Er, yeah, of course.'

Still he made no move; just stood there looking at her.

'Have I got two heads or something?' she asked worriedly.

'No.'

'Why are you staring at me like that then?'

'Sorry.'

'That's all right.' She smiled and he almost melted. 'I thought there must be something odd about me.'

'Quite the opposite,' he said. 'Please don't think me rude, but you're the prettiest girl I've ever seen.'

'I don't think you're rude,' she said, her cheeks turning pink. 'I'm very flattered.'

'But come on in.' He ushered her inside and called out, 'Rose, there's someone to see you.'

Rose looked puzzled when she saw her.

'Remember me? I'm Mary, the one with shrapnel in her leg,' she explained. 'I managed to track you down through your sorting office. I just wanted to come and thank you for what you did for me that night. I probably didn't thank you at the time, I was in such a state.'

'Mary.' Rose recognised her now and gave her a friendly hug. 'I didn't realise who you were, as I only saw you in the dark before. How are you? How's the leg wound?'

'I'm still limping a bit but it's much better, thanks to you. I might have bled to death if you hadn't got me to the hospital so fast.'

'Someone would have come along and helped you if I hadn't been around,' said the ever-modest Rose. 'I'm very glad that you're all right now, though. I have wondered how you were getting on.'

Rose introduced her to the others, who gave her a warm Barton welcome, offering her a seat and a cup of tea, asking about her ordeal. Bill was working overtime, Alan wasn't in, and Alfie was playing out the front with some local kids, so it was just Rose, Joe and their mother.

'Would you like another cup of tea?' offered Joe, exceptionally attentive, Rose noticed.

'I haven't finished this one yet, thank you, Joe,' said Mary, giving him a nice smile. Rose now judged her to be about sixteen, and she could see that Joe was more than a little impressed with her.

Just then there was a noisy interruption when Alan and Alfie came clattering in together, Alan affectionately teasing Alfie by having confiscated his beloved old ball. He was taunting him with it.

'Give it back, give it back,' pleaded Alfie, laughing almost despite himself.

'If you want it, you'll have to get it off me,' said Alan, holding the ball so high it was out of the boy's reach.

'How can I when it's up there?'

'Use your initiative, mate,' teased Alan.

'I can't reach up there. I ain't tall enough.'

'You'll have to find a way if you want your ball back,' teased Alan. 'Come on then, kid; show us what you're really made of. We're waiting.'

'Even if I stand on a chair I still won't be high enough,' said Alfie.

'You'll have to think of another way then, won't you?' chuckled Alan, still holding the ball out of reach.

'Stop tormenting him, for goodness' sake, Alan,' admonished his mother.

'He loves it; can't get enough of it.'

'No I don't,' denied Alfie, but they all knew that it wasn't true. He had grown to adore Alan, who always made a great fuss of him, albeit boisterously.

'Why are you laughing then?'

'Dunno.'

'Behave, Alan,' said May. 'Can't you see that we've got a visitor?'

'Have we?' He looked around the room, his eyes brightening when he saw Mary sitting in the armchair by the fire. 'Well, hello there. I didn't see you there.' He clearly liked what he saw and didn't try to hide it. 'It's this monster of a child taking my mind off things.' He gave the ball back to Alfie and introductions were made.

Mary looked at Alan in the same way as Joe had looked at her, Rose noticed with a heavy heart. Dear unassuming Joe. Alan always managed to outshine him. It wasn't deliberate, but it always happened, mainly because he was so much more assertive than Joe. No one ever forgot that Alan was around, but Joe was so quiet sometimes he just blended into the background.

Joe also noticed the look that passed between his brother and Mary, and accepted painfully that he himself didn't stand a chance with her. Joe admired Alan's good looks and outgoing personality. Alan wasn't afraid to stand up to anyone. He'd always been there for Joe; he'd been a friend and protector for as long as Joe could remember. No one dared to step out of line with Joe when Alan was anywhere near. They were good mates as well as brothers.

But watching him now blatantly flirting with Mary, and seeing her respond, Joe hated him with such a passion he wanted to hit him; to beat the smile off his face for good and all. The intense feelings shocked and shamed him, for he was not normally a violent person.

Chapter Four

The Green Cat public house at Shepherd's Bush was a family pub owned and run by the Beech family. Today it was closed to the public because of a private function. A very sad one as it happened: the funeral wake for the landlord's wife, Ida Beech, who'd been knocked down and killed by a trolley bus in the blackout.

Her death had been a blow to the whole community because the family were well liked and respected in the area and Ida had been well known for her contribution to local events. In addition to her gregarious nature, she had a warm heart and an endless capacity to listen to people's troubles, was an ardent supporter of charity projects and contributed to the social life of the neighbourhood in general.

Her widower, Ted Beech, was also a pillar of the community, but Ida's unique personality had been the essence of this pub and people had genuinely loved her. It was generally believed among the punters that the place wouldn't be the same without her.

His mother's sudden death had been more than just

a blow to her twenty-five-year-old son Johnny; it felt like a catastrophe because he and his mum had been so close. They were two of a kind, both outgoing and warm-hearted. An only child, Johnny had always enjoyed a good relationship with both parents but the maternal bond had been especially strong. He'd inherited her sense of humour and the two of them had sparked off each other. Life was going to be a whole lot duller without her, and how he was going to manage he didn't know. But it was his father he had to worry about now. He was the one in most need of support.

'Are you all right, Dad?' he asked, as they mingled with the sombrely dressed mourners.

'No, not really, son,' replied Ted, a tall man in his fifties, his square jaw and solid build giving him a look of toughness. 'But I'm getting through it . . . with the help of a drop or two of whisky.'

'I've had more than a couple myself.' Johnny looked handsome and impressive in army uniform, a black armband worn as a mark of respect. His short blond hair was combed into place for the occasion, his vivid blue eyes clouded by grief and lacking their usual vitality. 'I'm sure Mum wouldn't disapprove of us; not today.' He looked at his father, who was an imposing figure with a strong bearing, thick white hair and steely blue eyes. 'But when you've had enough of playing host, you go upstairs to the flat and put your feet up for a while. I can look after everything down here.'

'Thanks, son, but I'll stick it out to the end as people have been good enough to come. Anyway, your mother would never forgive me if I left the party early. She never did such a thing in her life.' His eyes filled with tears, though his son knew he would never shed them in public. 'And this is her party, after all.'

Johnny managed to grin. 'In a manner of speaking, yeah,' he said.

He was home on compassionate leave because of his mother's death. Having been shot in the arm and shoulder at Dunkirk, he had been sent back to England to recover and subsequently given a home posting at Woolwich barracks. His wounds had healed now and he would undoubtedly be sent back into action when someone from the army's hierarchy decided it was time. He thanked God they hadn't done so yet because had he been abroad he wouldn't have been able to get back for the funeral, and that would have been a blow for both him and his father.

Having been brought up in this pub and worked in it until he'd been called up for the army, Johnny knew the business inside out, and was concerned as to how his father was going to manage without his beloved wife, whom he had relied on totally. As well as the emotional wrench, he would miss her huge contribution to the business. She'd been the organiser; the one with flair and initiative, always thinking of new attractions, finding entertainers as well as giving the pub that homely touch.

Thinking it over, Johnny could see how the two of them had made such a great team. Dad was physically strong and competent, despite his advancing years. He stood no nonsense. If trouble erupted among the punters and a fight broke out, he removed the offending parties from the pub and had things running normally so fast people hardly knew anything untoward had happened. But it was Ida who had brought the fun and laughter to the place. Johnny still couldn't believe she'd gone and knew he would never stop missing her.

'Wotcha, Johnny,' said Bert, a friend of his father's and a long-standing customer at the pub. He shook Johnny vigorously by the hand. 'Sorry to hear about your mum. Very sorry indeed, mate. Cor, what a shock. I nearly passed out cold when I got the news.'

'It knocked me for six too,' admitted Johnny.

'Bloody blackout,' the man grumbled. 'There's been no end of people getting run over. Trolley buses are a ruddy menace in the dark because people can't hear 'em coming.' He sighed heavily, shaking his head. 'I dunno what things are coming to these days. I mean, we have enough trouble dodging Hitler's bombs; it would be nice to think we could cross the road in safety.'

'It can't be helped, I suppose,' said Johnny. 'They daren't allow light to be shown on vehicles.'

'No, I know. It's just that we seem to be getting it from all sides.' Bert swigged his beer with an air of contemplation. 'Your mum will be very much missed, lad. She was a popular woman around here. No one had a bad word to say about Ida.'

'I certainly never heard one.'

'Your dad's gonna miss her something terrible.' He

drew in a loud breath, shaking his head and looking morbid. 'I've rarely seen a more devoted couple.'

'It will be hard for him,' agreed Johnny. 'I wish I could be here more to give him some practical support. I can't take away his grief but at least I could help him with the business. But I'll have to report back for duty soon.'

'That's the war for you,' said Bert, raising his eyes. 'Kills people and splits families up.'

'Still, I'm lucky. I'm stationed near enough to get home some weekends when I can get a pass, so I'll be around now and again,' Johnny said, managing to stay positive even though his heart was breaking. 'And he's got some loyal staff.'

Bert nodded, looking thoughtful. 'Talking of your staff reminds me,' he began. 'You remember that barmaid who worked here a good few years ago?'

'There've been several,' said Johnny, not very interested because he had other things on his mind.

'This one was special; a good-looking girl with dark hair and a smashing personality. Everybody liked her. I think her name was Peggy.'

'Peggy Miller.' Johnny was paying full attention now, his heart racing at the sound of her name.

'That's the one.' Bert looked into the distance. 'We were all so upset when she left suddenly because she was such a nice person. One of the best barmaids you've ever had here, I reckon. Always had a smile; nothing was ever too much trouble for her.'

'Yeah, she was very well liked; but what about her,

Bert?' Johnny was hungry for news. 'Have you seen her or something?'

'I'd have a job, because she's dead,' the man informed him bluntly. 'Got killed in an air raid, the poor girl.'

Bert could have no idea the effect his casually uttered words had had on Johnny. As far as he knew, Peggy was just someone who used to work at the pub. To Johnny, though, she was a whole lot more. Physically weakened by the news, he thought for a moment that he was going to pass out.

'Dead,' he managed at last.

'That's right.'

'Are you sure? I mean, how do you know?'

'A pal o' mine – a local man who used to come in here with me now and again – moved out Ealing way, and I hadn't seen him for years until the other day, when I ran into him unexpectedly while he was over this way visiting his relatives. He just happened to tell me about young Peggy. She was working in his local pub apparently, and he remembered her from here. Anyway, the house she was living in was bombed with her in it.'

What a day this was turning out to be, thought Johnny miserably. As if burying his mother wasn't enough. Now there was this shattering news.

'That's terrible,' he uttered through dry lips.

'I can see how much it's upset you,' observed the other man. 'You've gone as white as a sheet, mate. It turned my stomach an' all. It's very upsetting to hear someone you know has had their lot, especially when they're still young. There's far too much bad news about lately.'

Johnny gulped his drink in an effort to steady himself. He had the shakes, acute nausea and an awful suspicion that he was going to burst into tears at any moment. Bert thought he had just passed on a piece of idle war gossip. He couldn't know that he had all but broken Johnny.

'It turns out,' Bert continued, moving forward and lowering his voice in a confidential manner, 'that she had a nipper.' He tapped the side of his nose and lowered his voice even further. 'Wrong side of the blanket, apparently.'

Johnny stared at him.

'Who would have thought it, eh? She seemed such a decent girl.'

'She *was* a decent girl,' defended Johnny, trying to gather his scrambled thoughts.

'There are people who wouldn't agree with you about that in light of the circumstances. But anyway, the sprog is a little boy, seven years old apparently.' Bert was in full flow now with this top-quality piece of gossip. 'She was bringing him up on her own, and working in the pub to help make ends meet. It couldn't have been easy for her.'

'Did . . . did the boy die too?' Johnny asked, needing to know but dreading the answer.

'No, apparently not,' Bert replied. 'I don't know any of the details, but somehow the poor little scrap survived.'

101

'That's something then,' said Johnny numbly.

'You could say that, but what sort of a life is he gonna have, with no one of his own to look out for him? He's probably been dumped in an orphanage.'

'Where did you say she was living when she died?' Johnny tried to sound casual.

'Out Ealing way somewhere,' Bert told him. 'I don't know the area at all myself. I've seen it on the front of buses but I've never been there. Anywhere further out than Acton is a foreign country to me.'

'I don't know it either,' said Johnny.

'Sorry to have been the bearer of more bad news.' Bert looked at him, wondering now if perhaps he'd been tactless in mentioning it at this sensitive time, as Johnny seemed so upset by it. 'I just thought you might want to know, seeing as she worked here.'

'I'm glad you told me, Bert. But I'd better move on and do some mingling,' Johnny told him, urgently needing to escape. 'Thanks for coming today. Mum would have been so pleased. Have what you want to eat from the buffet and drinks from the bar. It's all on the house.'

'Thanks very much.

Johnny hurried from the bar to the gents' toilets and was violently sick.

'Is it all getting you down, lover boy?' asked Johnny's fiancée Hazel, who was behind the bar getting drinks for the guests when he returned. 'You're looking a bit peaky.'

'I'm all right.'

'You're bound to feel a bit off colour today with all

the strain and everything.' A regular barmaid here, Hazel was a striking redhead with green eyes, long legs and a shapely figure. 'You'll probably feel better once this is over and things get back to normal.'

Normal, he thought. How could anything ever be normal again when he had just lost the two people he loved most in the world?

'I'm fine.' For some reason he didn't want to confide in Hazel.

'It'll soon be over,' she encouraged.

'It's my mother's funeral, Hazel,' he reminded her sharply. 'Not a trip to the dentist.'

'All right. No need to snap,' she came back at him. 'I was only trying to help.'

'It's a sacred occasion. A final farewell to my mother,' he pointed out, feeling irritable with her and knowing he wasn't being fair. 'Not something you rush through just to get it over with.'

'I suppose not,' she said, keeping it light. 'Sorry. I just wasn't thinking.'

'No, it's me who should be sorry, Hazel,' he said, genuinely contrite. 'Take no notice of me. I'm just being a miserable sod.'

'No you're not. You're under a lot of strain, that's all,' she said, eager to please him. 'I'll make sure that you get some proper comforting later on.'

'Meanwhile I must go and talk to the guests as they've taken the trouble to come and see Mum off,' he said, turning and walking into the crowd.

★   ★   ★

103

Watching him stride away, Hazel thought how absolutely perfect he was for her; he was strong, good-looking, had an entertaining personality and – most important of all – he wasn't short of a few quid. This pub was one of the most popular in the area and did a roaring trade so would provide him with a nice little wad every week. It would be his one day, and hers too if everything went the way she'd planned it.

She was twenty-four. It was high time she was married and settled down with a man who could support her to a decent standard. She enjoyed working in the pub trade, and would get a whole lot more pleasure from the job when she had the prestige and extra dough that came from being one of the Beech family.

The minute she'd clapped eyes on Johnny she'd set her cap at him. She'd had to take all the initiative, and still did even now. She was under no illusions and knew she wouldn't have his engagement ring on her finger if she hadn't coaxed him into it and convinced him that it was the right thing. Her powers of persuasion were second to none. There was a part of him that always held back from her. She accepted that she wasn't the love of his life, but didn't mind that as long as she got him and the lifestyle she wanted in the end. To own him body and soul wasn't essential.

Anyway, she wasn't head over heels in love with him either. It was more that he had all the ingredients that made him the perfect man for her. She did find him physically attractive, though; she couldn't have got this far if she hadn't. Being smart and pretty, she didn't lack for admirers, but Johnny was the only one of substance.

His mother's death had been a lucky break for Hazel. She and Ida had never hit it off. Ida had accused Hazel outright of being after Johnny for what she could get out of him. But Hazel had been a match for her and had soon told her where to get off.

Johnny had been a bit too close to his mother for Hazel's peace of mind. She'd not taken kindly to coming second to the old cow but she'd had to be very careful how she handled it, because Johnny wouldn't hear a word against his mother. Now that Ida was out of the way for good, a major obstacle had been removed and Hazel was confident that there would be another ring on her finger before very long. She daren't rush it too obviously, though. Johnny was very much his own man, and if he got so much as a hint that he was being manipulated, he would back off.

So she'd play it carefully for the moment, and give him sympathy by the bucketload. He was worth any amount of effort. She'd be the envy of Shepherd's Bush when she finally got him down the aisle.

'A son?' said Ted, looking at Johnny in astonishment the next day. 'You've got a son?'

Johnny nodded, looking pale. 'I can't be absolutely sure the boy is mine until I see the birth certificate, but I'm pretty certain. He's seven so would have been conceived at the time I was involved with his mother.'

'Bloody 'ell, Johnny. Are you trying to give me a heart attack or something?'

'Sorry to spring it on you the day after Mum's funeral, but I only learned of his existence myself yesterday and I thought you ought to be the first to know.'

'But how . . . I mean, who's the kid's mother?'

'You remember Peggy who used to work here about eight years ago?'

'Oh, so you were at it with her, were you?' said Ted disapprovingly. 'You were always told not to take liberties with the staff.'

'I didn't take liberties,' Johnny told him ardently. 'I was in love with her, and she with me. I adored her in fact. She was my first love . . .'

'So how come you only found out about the boy yesterday?'

Johnny told him about his conversation with Bert and how shocked he was to hear of Peggy's tragic death. 'She didn't tell me she was pregnant. She just left. Obviously didn't want to tie me down as I was only seventeen and she was four years older. I would have married her like a shot if I'd known. I was very much in love with her and would have done anything for her. She was very conscious of the fact that I was so young and she was older. That's why I'm so certain of her motive in leaving. I didn't know she was pregnant at the time. I was heartbroken when she left.'

'I remember her leaving without giving notice, and now I know why,' said his father. 'You should have gone after her.'

'I did. I went round to her house and she'd gone. Judging by the icy reception I got, the family had thrown her out. She must have told them she was pregnant. But I didn't know that then.'

'Did you look for her?'

'I'll say I did. I looked everywhere; went to see everyone who had ever known her. Not a soul knew where she was. They were all as baffled as I was. She hadn't told anyone she was leaving. She'd just literally vanished. I used to walk the streets searching for her. But how can you find someone who doesn't want to be found, especially in a place the size of London? She could have been anywhere; could have left London for all I knew. I'm certain she went away for my sake, so that she wouldn't ruin my life, as she thought. That's the sort of woman she was.'

'But as you say, you can't be sure that the boy is yours,' said his father.

'It's obvious to me that he is. Bert said he's seven. He's mine, Dad. He must be. I was the only man in her life at that time. She wasn't the sort of woman to play around. I shall check it out but I'm certain in my own mind.'

'Are you going to look for him?'

'Not half! I'm still reeling from the shock and a bit scared of the responsibility, but I want him, more than anything. I know they were living in Ealing, so that gives me a starting point. I shall go to the town hall and ask what they've done with him. That's why I've had to tell you about it now, when you've already got more than enough on your plate to cope with. I'm going to find him and bring him up, Dad. I want him to come and live here with us.'

'Of course you do. What else would you do with him? And why are you hanging about talking to me when you should be out looking for him?'

'Because I'll have to go back to camp soon, and I'm away in the army most of the time, so you'd have to look after him when I'm not here.'

'So what's the problem?'

'You don't mind, then?'

'Mind having my own flesh and blood about the place? What sort of a man do you think I am? Young blood in the house is just what I need.'

'Thanks, Dad.' Johnny's eyes lit up with enthusiasm. 'I can go ahead and make some enquiries now.'

His father looked overcome with sadness suddenly, his darkly shadowed eyes glistening with tears that Johnny knew he would sooner die than give in to, even in front of his own son. Strong men didn't cry in the world he inhabited. 'I wish your mother had lived to see her grandson,' he said. 'She'd have been tickled pink.'

'She'd have given me a right rollicking, though, wouldn't she? For getting Peggy into trouble.'

'Course she would,' Ted agreed. 'That's what good mothers do.'

'And she was the best,' said Johnny, his own eyes bright with tears. '*The very best.*'

★   ★   ★

108

It was a dry winter's day with a sharp breeze. The drab west London streets were bathed in pale sunlight, and shafts of it beamed into the Bartons' living room through the net curtains, making hazy patches on the wall.

But there was a dark cloud hanging over the house that no amount of sunshine could erase. First thing this morning Alan had left the house and gone to an army camp in Dorset to train to be a soldier.

'He'll be home for some leave when he's done his basic training, Mum,' said Rose over a cheese sandwich with her mother when she got home from work. 'They won't send him into action right away.'

'They will eventually, though,' her mother pointed out, dabbing at her eyes, which had been filling up intermittently all morning. 'He'll have to go and do what he's being trained for, like all the others.'

'I'm afraid so.' Having already lost her husband to the war, Rose was under no illusions as to what might happen to her brother. But her mother didn't need to be reminded of that at this point. 'We have to do our part and stay positive and wait to welcome him home.'

'I know. Anyway, I'm not the only mother whose boy has gone away. Women all over the country are sending their sons off to war.'

'And sisters are saying goodbye to their brothers, and they'll all be feeling like us.'

'The house seems so empty without him, which is a bit daft because he would have been out at work anyway at this time of the day.'

'It's knowing that he won't be breezing in at the end

of his shift, filling the house with his big personality, that's causing it,' suggested Rose. 'Still, the war will have to end sometime and then we'll all be back together again.'

'Oh, won't that be lovely?'

'I wonder if he's going to write to Mary,' said Rose, moving on.

'I hope so. It would be nice if they were to keep in touch,' said May. 'She seemed such a lovely girl. They didn't have much time to get to know each other before he went away, though.'

'Poor old Joe had his eye on her but she was smitten with Alan from the minute she saw him. I watched it happen,' remarked Rose. 'He always seems to lose out to Alan one way or another.'

'I thought he seemed a bit off towards Alan when he left. That must be why,' said May. 'He's going to miss his brother something wicked, though. They're such good pals normally.' She shivered. 'Ooh, it's freezing cold in here. Thank God it'll soon be time to light the fire.'

'That'll cheer us up,' said Rose. 'And when the others get home, and everyone's talking, it'll feel more normal, especially when Alfie comes home from school.'

'He fills the house on his own with his noise and his antics,' said May, smiling.

'It's lovely that he's finally settled in.'

'I wouldn't want to be without him now, would you?' said May.

'No. I'd hate it if he wasn't around. He grows on you, that boy.'

They finished their lunch and were in the kitchen washing the dishes when there was a knock at the front door. It was the woman from the Children's Department.

'I've got some good news for you about Alfie,' she told them as they ushered her into the living room.

'Really?' said May as the woman perched on the edge of an armchair.

'We'll be taking him off your hands soon,' she announced cheerfully.

Both women stared at her in horror. Rose saw her mother's neck turn scarlet, which was a sure sign that she was distressed.

'Well, you don't look any too pleased about it, and I thought you'd be delighted to see him go,' said the woman, peering at them over the top of her glasses.

'What on earth gave you that idea?' May enquired.

'You only took him in as a favour to us, didn't you?' she said. 'And I suspected that he might be getting a bit too much for you, even though you didn't say so, when I came round to ask if you could extend your kindness and have him for a bit longer.'

'You were wrong,' declared May.

'Oh well, it doesn't matter now, because he'll be moving out anyway.'

'I hope you're not gonna shove him into some orphanage,' said May miserably.

'No, no, nothing like that,' the woman assured them brightly. 'Quite the opposite in fact. His father has turned up out of the blue. He heard about Alfie's mother's death and came looking for him. He wants to bring him up with the help of the boy's grandfather. The father is a soldier but they are a family of publicans apparently. They have a big pub in Shepherd's Bush with spacious accommodation over the top, so there's plenty of room for the lad.'

'He's taken his time coming for him,' said May tartly. 'Seven years to be exact.'

The woman looked at her, as though choosing her words. 'It isn't my place to comment on that, Mrs Barton, even if I did know the details, which I don't,' she said in a professional manner. 'You usually find that there's more to these things than meets the eye.'

'Maybe.'

'Alfie will be thrilled anyway,' said Rose, stepping in to ease the tension and trying to be cheerful, though the prospect of not having Alfie around filled her with gloom. 'That's the important thing.'

'Yes, it isn't often we get a happy ending in these cases,' said the woman, who was a kindly soul and did the job to the best of her ability, despite the difficult circumstances created by the war. 'The children usually end up going from one foster home to another, or growing up in an orphanage.'

'Poor little devils,' said May.

'Anyway, Alfie's father will be coming to collect him on Saturday, provided he can get a weekend pass. I'll leave you to tell young Alfie the good news, and have him ready when Mr Beech comes if you would be so kind. It'll be sometime in the afternoon. I'm sure the lad will be delighted. If there's any change to the arrangements I'll let you know.'

When May returned from showing the woman out, she looked very downhearted.

'You'll miss him, won't you, Mum?' said Rose.

She nodded.

'Me too, but it will be lovely for Alfie, being with his own family.'

'I know, and we must be happy for him,' said May. 'That little boy deserves a break.'

When Alfie got in from school and they sat him down on the sofa between them and broke the news to him that his father had tracked him down after all this time, and wanted to have him to live with him and his grandfather, they expected whoops of delight. So they were more than a little taken aback by his reaction.

'I ain't going,' he stated categorically, the old defiance they had come to know so well glinting in his eyes.

'Why not?' asked Rose.

'Just don't wanna go, that's all.'

'But he's your dad, Alfie,' Rose reminded him kindly. 'Your very own flesh and blood; someone of your own to look out for you. It'll be wonderful for you. You'll have a great time.'

'No I won't.'

'Of course you will, luv,' put in May patiently. 'He'll be able to do much more for you than we can.'

'He won't, 'cos I ain't going.' He was adamant. 'I'm staying here with you.'

'That isn't possible I'm afraid, luv,' Rose informed him gravely.

'Why?'

'Because we only took you in as a temporary measure,' she explained. 'Now that they've found something permanent and better for you, you'll have to go.'

'So you don't want me to stay?'

'Of course we want you to stay, and we're upset that you're going,' Rose assured him ardently. 'But it isn't a question of what we want, luv. Your future is at stake here and we don't have a say in the matter.'

'You're grown-ups and grown-ups can do what they like,' he said, his freckled face suffused with pink, his eyes bright with tears despite the brave performance he was putting on. 'You could tell 'em I'm not going because I'm staying here. If they know you want me here, they'll let me stay.'

'It doesn't work that way, Alfie, not now that your father has turned up,' Rose told him gently. 'Honest to God, if there was any way we could keep you, we'd do it. But we have to do what the authorities say, especially as it's the best thing for you.'

'No it ain't.'

'I can't understand why you don't you want to go.'

'Because I like it here with you,' he replied.

'That's really sweet, and we've loved having you, but—'

'I 'ate the sight of me dad, whoever he is.'

'How can you hate someone you don't even know?' asked May.

'Because he made my mum sad, that's why. She was poor, and people said bad things to us, and all because he didn't look after us.'

Rose and her mother exchanged looks. 'You must give him a chance to make things better for you,' said May. 'I'm sure he wants to.'

'I wanna stay 'ere.'

'We'll still see you,' Rose told him. 'I'll come and visit you as often as I can, I promise. It isn't far on the bus.'

He shrugged sulkily.

'Now don't start all that again,' said Rose in a tone of mild admonition. 'I thought you'd stopped playing up. You've been such a good boy lately. Don't spoil it.'

Alfie looked from Rose to her mother, his eyes full of emotion, all pretence stripped away. 'Please let me stay here with you,' he begged in a small voice. 'I'll be so good you'll hardly know I'm here. I'll do as I'm told. I won't answer back. I'll do all the errands.'

Rose almost choked on the lump in her throat and she could see that her mother's eyes were moist.

'We don't want you to go, Alfie,' she said, managing to stay in control. 'We all love having you here. If there was any way we could keep you, we would. But the authorities won't allow us to now because your dad wants you, and he's your family. We don't have any rights as far as that's concerned.'

'It's true, luv,' added May. 'We're ever so sorry, we really are.'

Alfie looked from one to the other, and Rose could

see the pain of rejection clearly visible in his eyes. He really did think they were abandoning him, and she felt like the devil himself. The last thing Alfie needed now was another disruption to his life, having finally settled down here with them, but blood was thicker than water.

'So he's coming for me on Saturday then, is he?' he said at last.

They nodded.

'Right. So can I go and read my comic now, please?'

'Course you can,' said May.

The two women watched him go, sad but relieved that he finally seemed to have accepted the situation.

Hazel looked steadily at Johnny across a table in the empty saloon bar of the Green Cat where they were sitting just prior to opening time on Saturday morning.

'Cor, you don't half know how to make a girl sit up and take notice, Johnny,' said Hazel, reeling from the shock he'd just given her. 'I mean, I didn't expect you to be whiter than white before we met. I knew you'd been around a bit. A man of twenty-five wouldn't come without a past. But why on earth do you want to take on some kid you don't even know because of a bit of fun you had years ago?'

'It wasn't just a bit of fun,' he corrected firmly. 'It was much more than that. I was in love with her, and I want to take him on because he's my son.'

'But you've managed without him up until now; why not just leave things as they are?'

'Because I don't want to do that,' he replied with a

hard edge to his voice. 'If I'd known about him I'd have had him in my life long before this. But now that I have found him, I am not going to turn my back on him. The boy needs me, Hazel. His mother is dead so I'm all he has. My father and I are his only family.'

'How can you be so sure that he is yours anyway?' she asked with more than a hint of cynicism.

'I found his birth certificate at Somerset House. She named me as the father.' He paused, looking pleased. 'She gave him my name as his second name, too. Alfred Johnny Miller.'

'Oh, I see.' She pondered for a moment. 'So where exactly do I fit into all this?' she wanted to know.

He wasn't absolutely sure about this because his thoughts were full of his new responsibilities towards his son. 'Just be nice to him,' he suggested. 'He's going to be around so I'd like you to get on with him.'

'Oooh, I dunno about that, Johnny. I haven't got a clue how to go on with kids.'

'Me neither. I'm just going to have to pick it up as I go along,' he told her. 'It would help me a lot if I could have your support in this.'

'And after we're married, I'll be expected to look after him, I suppose?' she asked.

He hadn't thought that far ahead. He rarely did think of actually being married to Hazel. She'd wanted to get engaged so he'd gone along with it to make her happy. 'No. Not necessarily. I wouldn't expect that of you. Inasmuch as you'd be his stepmother and we'd be living as a family, you might need to do the odd thing for

117

him from time to time. But he isn't a baby. He won't be any trouble, and I'll do most of the looking after, with Dad's help. Anyway, that's a long way off; we don't even have any wedding plans yet, do we?'

'No.' That was something that needed fixing, but now wasn't the time to broach the subject.

'The war will probably be over by then and I'll be around all the time,' he continued, 'but right now, I'm more concerned with the present, and getting this fatherhood thing right. Having my son in my life means a very great deal to me, Hazel.' He shook his head slowly as though to emphasise the point. 'I just can't tell you how much.'

There was a new buoyancy and bloom about him, she observed with a great deal of annoyance. He was almost childishly excited about this new-found son of his. This development had come as a terrible blow to Hazel. No sooner had his damned mother been removed from the picture than she was faced with another rival for his affection, a blasted child.

Having a kid in her life was the last thing on earth she wanted. She wasn't ready for all that malarkey. Maybe she never would be. She certainly hadn't had so much as a flicker of a maternal urge so far. She didn't even want a child of her own, let alone someone else's. Anyway, she hadn't the faintest idea of how to go about dealing with one. Childcare was foreign territory to her and she wanted it to stay that way.

But she had a strong suspicion that if she made a stand over this, and Johnny had to choose between her and the boy, at this stage she would lose hands down. She had to box very clever and get the boy out of their lives by other, more subtle means.

'As I've said, I don't know anything about kids, but it can't be that difficult to learn, can it? So I'll do what I can to help you with him,' she said sweetly. 'We're partners, you and me. We do things together.'

'Oh Hazel, that is such a load off my mind.' He looked at her closely. 'I know it's a lot to ask of you.'

'It was a bit of a shock at first, I admit, but now that I'm used to the idea, I don't mind.'

'You're a real diamond, do you know that?' He beamed at her. 'It isn't every woman who'd be willing to accept a child from her fiancé's past.'

'Whatever you want, I want too, my darling,' she said, reaching for his hand. 'Would you like me to go with you to collect him?'

For some reason he didn't want her there when he met his son for the first time. But neither did he want to hurt her feelings, so he said, 'I'd better go on my own, I think. He might be a bit shy, you know, meeting his old man for the first time. Anyway, you'll be needed here. It's always busy on a Saturday lunchtime session. I don't want Dad overdoing things while he's still frail from Mum's death.'

'I'll stay here then.'

'Thanks for being so good about it.'

'That's all right.'

But it was very far from all right. Already he was excluding her, wanting to be by himself with the wretched infant. She'd have to nip that in the bud right away, because she wasn't going to allow some snotty-nosed little bastard to come between her and the man she'd worked so hard to get this far with.

Chapter Five

The likeness to Alfie was so stunning, Rose would have known who he was even if they had not been expecting him.

'Hello there,' she greeted, opening the front door to him. 'You must be Alfie's dad.'

'Johnny Beech,' he said in a strong, exuberant voice, thrusting forward his hand.

'Rose Brown.' She returned his firm handshake. 'Pleased to meet you.'

'Likewise.' He had certainly fared well in the looks lottery, she thought, observing the strong jawline and clean-cut features. His smile was warm; his blue eyes – so much like Alfie's – were expressing a look of apprehension, presumably about meeting his son for the first time. He looked beyond her into the hallway. 'Is he ready to go?' he asked nervously.

'Yeah, he's all ready,' she replied. 'Come inside while we say our goodbyes.'

As he crossed the threshold, he courteously removed his cap to reveal blond hair cut short, army style. This was Alfie twenty years down the line, she thought.

Unbeknown to her, Johnny was struggling with disappointment he knew was unreasonable. He'd been harbouring a picture in his mind of his son waiting for him at the door, as eager to see his father as he was to see Alfie. He admonished himself for expecting too much; that sort of thing probably only happened in sentimental films and children's storybooks.

Rose took him into the living room and introduced him to the family, who gave him a warm welcome. Predictably, May put the kettle on while the others made friendly conversation.

'Where is Alfie anyway?' asked Rose after a while.

Nobody seemed to know.

'He was here a few minutes ago,' said her father, frowning. 'He must have popped upstairs to collect some last-minute thing from the bedroom.'

A thorough search revealed that he was neither in the house nor the garden, and nowhere to be seen in the street.

'He's probably feeling a bit shy,' May said in an effort to spare their visitor's feelings. 'He'll be hiding somewhere, as a prank. Boys will be boys.'

'The little perisher,' grumbled Bill, also sensitive to Johnny's feelings, and extremely embarrassed by the situation. 'It's just childish high spirits but he doesn't half pick his moments.' He shook his head, tutting and looking at Johnny. 'It's too bad of him to keep you waiting like this. Still, that's kids for you: unpredictable and always up to something.'

'I hope you don't think we make a habit of letting him go off to roam the streets without permission,' said May, on the defensive. 'He knows he has to ask before he goes out to play. I don't know what's got into him.'

'I'm sure you've done a great job in looking after him, Mrs Barton, and I'm very grateful to you,' Johnny said.

There was an awkward silence.

'I'll go out and see if I can find him,' offered the ever-obliging Joe. 'He's probably lost track of the time. He'll have gone to say a last goodbye to one of his pals, I expect, and you know what kids are like when they get together; they're lost in a world of their own.'

'No, you stay where you are, Joe. I'll go. I think I know where to find him,' intervened Rose. Spotting the chance of a few quiet words with Johnny, she turned to him and added, 'Perhaps you might like to come with me.'

'Good idea,' he enthused. 'I am eager to meet him, I must admit.'

To speed things up, they took the bus for a couple of stops then walked the rest of the way, which gave Rose the opportunity to emphasise a few salient facts.

'Alfie's been very badly traumatised, you know, being buried alive and losing his mother, and all the upheaval of living with strangers,' she said.

'Yeah, I have been given the gist of it by the people at the Children's Department,' he told her. 'He's had a rough time, the poor kid. I'll do my best to make it up to him.'

123

'It might not be that easy. We had a lot of trouble getting him settled in when he first came to us. If I'd been through a fraction of what he has I'm sure I'd have been difficult. But he did get used to us. Now that he has to leave, it's only natural that the boy is upset.'

'Upset? Because he doesn't want to come and live with me, you mean?' Johnny burst out. 'That's why he's made himself scarce. It isn't just a prank.'

'The family were just being diplomatic.'

'I guessed as much but didn't want to admit it to myself,' he said miserably. 'I hoped he'd be pleased to have his dad come for him.'

Rose halted in her step and turned to him, fiercely protective of Alfie. 'I suppose you thought he'd be waiting at the door and would wrap his arms around you in gratitude for coming for him,' she blurted out.

'No, of course not,' he said sharply, 'but I did hope he might be a little bit pleased to see me.'

'He's seven years old and he's never seen you in his life before,' she pointed out. 'Of course he doesn't want to go with you. As far as he's concerned you're just a stranger who wants to take him away from people he's only just got accustomed to and feels comfortable with.'

'He'll have a good home,' he informed her. 'I intend to do my very best for him.'

'I don't doubt it, but it's a *new* home in a different neighbourhood,' she reminded him. 'He'll have to make friends, get used to living with new people, when he's only just got used to us and this area.'

'Why are you trying to make me feel guilty when all I want to do is care for my son?' Johnny asked, his voice rising.

'If you feel guilty, that's nothing to do with me,' she replied. 'I'm just passing on some facts I think you need to know as he's going to be your responsibility from now on.'

'I think I've enough savvy to realise that it'll take the boy a while to settle,' he said. 'Anyway, it's my job to worry about him now. Not yours.'

'Just because he's leaving us doesn't mean I shall stop worrying about him,' Rose said, miffed at the suggestion. 'I think the world of him and I can't bear the idea of him being unhappy all over again. He's had enough misery to last him a lifetime. From what I can make out, his mother had a hard time bringing him up on her own, and he's taken a lot of flak from other kids all his life. He's too young to understand exactly how the system works, but he knows that he's been taunted and made to feel like an outsider because his mother wasn't married.'

He stared at her, his eyes hardening. 'You've no right to judge me,' he objected, over-reacting because he was feeling so emotional. 'You know nothing about the circumstances, and I'm buggered if I'm going to explain myself to you.'

She knew she had overstepped the mark in her anxiety about Alfie. 'Sorry if I seem to be judging you. It isn't my place to do that,' she said, her face brightly suffused.

'I'm glad we agree about something.'

'I suppose I'm a bit overanxious because I suspect that Alfie will give you a hard time at first. He can be an absolute monster when he wants to be, which is understandable for a child who's been through so much,' she told him. 'He began to feel like one of the family with us. Now his security is threatened yet again, as it was when he lost his mother. Naturally it will have an effect on his behaviour until he settles down again.'

'I'll bear in mind what you've said,' Johnny said curtly.

'Good.'

'Where are we going exactly?'

'You'll see,' she said. 'We're very nearly there.'

Alfie was there, just as Rose had known he would be, sitting on a low piece of remaining wall with his back to them, a small, still figure in a navy school raincoat. The bomb site had been cleared so it was just a piece of waste ground now, shabby and overgrown with weeds. It seemed even sadder to Rose now because there was no sign that the house had ever been there. It must be so painful for Alfie to find the landmark erased from the landscape altogether.

'That's him, is it?' Rose and Johnny were standing on the other side of the road, keeping a distance from Alfie.

'Yes, that's him,' she whispered. 'We'd better keep quiet. If he spots us, he'll run away.'

'How did you know he'd be here?'

'He came here before when he was going through a

crisis,' she said in hushed tones. 'He used to live here. It's the site of the house where he and his mother had a room. The place where she died. I think he feels it's his only link with her. He comes here to feel close to her.'

It was the saddest thing Johnny had ever heard and he was unbearably moved. 'Shall . . . shall we go and get him? He must be so cold sitting there,' he suggested thickly.

'Would you mind if I have a few minutes on my own with him first?' Rose asked.

'If you think it'll help, please go ahead,' he told her. 'I'll wait here.'

'So, here we are again then, kiddo,' she said, perching beside him and slipping her arm gently around him.

He shrugged.

'Did you come here to be near your mum?'

'I s'pose.'

'Has it helped?'

'Dunno.'

'It wasn't a very clever thing to do, you know, going off without a word when you knew your dad was coming for you,' she reproved. 'It isn't a good idea to get off to a bad start with him.'

'I don't care. I don't wanna go with him anyway.'

'I know you don't, luv, but we all have to do things in life we don't want to do.'

'Why?'

'Because it builds our character; makes us better people, I suppose.'

'How?'

'It makes us appreciate the things we like to do if we do the others as well,' she explained. 'It creates a balance, and life is made up of that; a mixture of the good and the bad.'

'Why can't they get rid of the bad things?'

'Because it wouldn't be right.' She had to admit that Alfie's life hadn't been terribly well balanced so far. 'You just take my word for it that it's the best way in the long run and it's the way life is, so you'll have to get used to it. Anyway, I think you'll like it, being with your dad and your grandad, once you get to know them.'

'Is that him?' he asked, looking surreptitiously across the road.

'Yes, that's him. He looks just like you.'

'Ugh, I don't wanna look like him.'

'Alfie,' she said reprovingly. 'That isn't nice.'

'I dunno why he can't just leave me alone.'

'He must care about you or he wouldn't want to bring you up.'

'Well I don't care about him.'

'I don't think you're being fair to him. You haven't even given him a chance.'

'I want to stay with you and the others.' He paused. 'I'll miss Bruiser too.'

'They might have a dog at the pub to guard the premises,' she said. 'They often do at those places.'

'I don't like other dogs. Bruiser is the only dog I've ever liked.'

'Only because he's the only one you've ever got to know,' she pointed out. 'Besides, once you've settled in at your dad's, you can come over to see us all sometimes, if your dad doesn't mind. I'll come and fetch you myself. I'll be coming to visit you anyway, and that's definite.'

'Promise?'

'I promise. So, now that we've established that, are you going to stop being such a flippin' pain, and come with me to meet your dad?'

'I s'pose I'll have to.'

'Good boy. I knew you wouldn't let me down.'

Watching events from across the road in a state of heightened emotion, Johnny had to admit to being impressed with the way Rose handled the boy. She was so natural with him. There was something achingly touching about the two of them sitting on a bomb site wall in the middle of winter, huddled close together in conversation. His own nerves felt shot to pieces now that he'd actually come this close to his son. He felt sick and breathless, and when he saw them get up and walk towards him, he thought his legs would give out altogether.

'We finally made it,' said Rose. 'Come on then, Alfie, say hello to your dad.'

Johnny didn't know if he spoke or not. Everything paled into insignificance: the war, the street, the woman standing beside Alfie; everything. It was as though there were only two people on earth, himself and this small boy, whose blue eyes were studying him uncertainly. Love for him consumed Johnny totally. It was raw, instinctive and painful, and not at all conducive to an easy mind. He was humbled by the feeling and knew it would make him vulnerable for the rest of his life. This was his son, the creation of himself and the woman he'd loved, and he wanted to protect and guide him. He knew without a doubt that he would give his own life for him if it was ever necessary.

He'd had all sorts of fine speeches ready in his head for this moment but he was so choked up he couldn't speak at all. Eventually, he managed to utter, 'Wotcha, Alfie. How's it going, mate?'

'All right,' responded Alfie in a subdued manner, keeping his eyes fixed on his feet.

'Come on then, we'd better get back to the house and collect your things,' said Rose in an effort to ease the tension. 'Before we all freeze to death out here.'

Back at the house, belongings were collected and goodbyes said. Johnny gave hearty thanks to them all for looking after his son. Auntie Sybil and Uncle Flip came in to wish Alfie well. Then he left the house and walked down the street beside his father, keeping carefully at a distance. The entire family stood outside watching them until they turned the corner out of sight.

They were all very quiet when they trooped back inside. It was as though some of the vital life force had been sucked out of the house.

'I never thought I would ever say this,' said Bill eventually. 'But I'm going to miss the little perisher. He gave us plenty of headaches, especially when he first came here, but he brought fun and new life to the house as well. It'll be strange without him around.'

Even Auntie Sybil admitted to being sorry to see him go.

'He wasn't a bad little lad once you got to know him,' added her husband.

'I hope they're kind to him,' said Joyce.

Rose was having similar thoughts. Johnny Beech seemed a decent enough type, but if Alfie took it into his head to be difficult – as she suspected he would – he could try the patience of a saint, let alone a man embarking upon fatherhood for the first time.

'I'll put the kettle on,' said May thickly.

'I'll give you a hand,' said Rose, following her mother into the kitchen.

Bruiser was sitting by the back kitchen door, his dark, hopeful eyes looking at them expectantly. 'It's no good you waiting for Alfie to come back,' May said to the dog tearfully, 'because he's moved out.'

Rose cleared her throat. 'I know we're all going to miss him like mad, but it's the best thing for him, Mum,' she said, taking the cups and saucers out of the cupboard. 'It'll be nice for him to have a proper family, once he's got to know them. It's up to us to be pleased for him.'

'I know,' agreed May, heaving a sigh. 'It's just that he's had so much upheaval already, I hate the idea of his being uprooted again.'

'Let's hope this is the last of it for him.'

The conversation was interrupted by Joyce wandering into the kitchen.

'Can you lend me something to wear tonight, Rose?' she asked casually. Being the same size, she and Rose often swapped clothes, to add a little variety to their limited stocks. This evening they were doing a show at a special unit for wounded soldiers at a hospital in Acton. 'I'm fed up with everything of mine. They've all been worn too often.'

'You're welcome to have a look through my wardrobe to see if there's anything you fancy,' offered Rose. 'I'm wearing my red jumper and black skirt. You can take your pick from anything else that's there; such as it is.'

'Thanks, kid,' she said and headed for the stairs.

Witnessing the close companionship between the cousins, May experienced a feeling of warmth and gratitude. She was so glad that her sister lived next door. Life would have been a whole lot lonelier had Sybil and Flip not made that momentous decision, all those years ago, to leave their life in the East End behind and follow her and Bill here to west London.

'So, what sort of things do you enjoy doing, Alfie?' asked Johnny as the two of them waited at the bus stop.

'Nothin'.'

'There must be something you like to do.'

The boy replied with a shrug.

Johnny wasn't usually lost for words, but he was finding this heavy going. The fact that he was so desperate to build some sort of a rapport with Alfie made him even more vulnerable to the boy's indifference. 'What about school?' he asked, clutching at straws. 'What's your favourite subject?'

'Dunno.'

'I wasn't all that keen on lessons myself,' Johnny persevered, adding so as not to create a bad example, 'I always tried my very best, though.' At that moment he realised that being a parent changed everything. From now on he must have a responsible attitude and reflect this in the way he behaved. He had to choose his words more carefully and encourage his son to try hard and grow up to be a rounded and decent human being. It was a whole new world, and not easy for a beginner, especially when he was getting no response whatsoever from Alfie. 'My favourite lesson was games.'

'Was it?' said the boy without interest, turning his head away from his father towards the approaching trolley bus.

'You're not on your own any more, you know, Alfie,' Johnny burst out in an urgent bid to win him over. 'You've got me now; me and your grandad. When I'm away in the army he'll be there for you.'

'I wasn't on my own before,' Alfie replied. 'I had Rose, and the others. And before that I had Mum.'

Johnny's heart twisted at the mention of Peggy. He wanted so much to know about Alfie's life with her, but the proud tilt of his son's head warned him that now wasn't the time to broach the subject. As for trying to win the boy's favour by telling him the truth as to why

133

he'd lacked a father for all these years, it wasn't even an option, given Alfie's love for his mother. Johnny himself experienced a moment of anger towards Peggy for the large chunk of his son's childhood that he'd been excluded from. He daren't risk passing that bitterness on to Alfie when he was far too young to understand how adults' emotions often impaired their judgement.

'Rose isn't your family,' he pointed out.

'She's my friend, though,' he said. 'All the Bartons are. I liked living with them.'

Johnny ached to earn Alfie's love and respect. But he felt unworthy and inadequate for the task. He'd learned one thing already: forging a bond with his son wasn't going to be easy, and it certainly wasn't going to happen overnight.

Joyce was so hyped up and talkative after the show that night, she didn't immediately notice that Rose was quieter than usual on the way home. Because it was still fairly early they managed to get a bus, and the siren was mercifully silent for a change.

'Performing gives me such a lovely feeling,' Joyce prattled on as they got off the bus and made their way carefully towards their street, faltering every so often in the blackout.

'Me too,' said Rose.

'I get a real buzz from the applause. It makes me want to cry for joy,' Joyce went on. 'Do you know, kid, I reckon I must be getting a bit stage-struck in my old age.'

'You're struck with something,' Rose blurted out unintentionally, 'but it's a bit more than just the call of the stage.'

'Rose,' Joyce said, stopping and taking her arm. 'What's that supposed to mean?'

'Surely you must know what I mean.'

'No I don't. I've obviously upset you somehow, but what have I done?'

'Made me feel like a complete gooseberry, and not for the first time either,' Rose informed her firmly. 'You and Stan are all over each other. Apart from adding some volume to the singing, I might as well not have been there. It's so damned embarrassing, Joyce. I've tried to tell myself that I'm imagining it, but I know in my heart that I'm not. The two of you positively drool over each other.'

'Don't be so ridiculous,' Joyce denied hotly.

'Maybe you don't realise that you're doing it, but you are, both of you, all the time when we're not actually doing the act; you're obviously besotted with each other, and wanting to rip each other's clothes off.'

'That's disgusting,' protested Joyce. 'You know I would never cheat on Bob.'

'I know you wouldn't want to, which is why you're setting yourself up for a whole load of heartache.'

'I don't have to justify my actions to you.'

'No, you don't,' agreed Rose, 'and if I wasn't with the two of you together, I wouldn't be affected. But you make me feel as if I'm in the way. I don't enjoy feeling as though I'm the only obstacle between you and Stan's bed, and I certainly felt like that tonight. So if you're going to carry on like a couple of star-struck lovers, you and Stan can do the act on your own.'

'Now you're being stupid,' Joyce snapped.

'You're the one who's doing that,' retorted Rose. 'Honestly, if you could see yourself, carrying on like some dewy-eyed teenager with a crush.'

'You're just jealous,' Joyce spat at her. 'Jealous because Stan pays more attention to me than to you.'

'Oh, do me a favour . . .'

'I've been very supportive to you since Ray died,' said Joyce, extremely miffed. 'I've always been there for you – *always* – and how do you repay me? You make horrid accusations just because you're feeling frustrated.'

'Stop lying to yourself as well as to me,' said Rose. 'You know as well as I do that there's something between you and Stan which is going to become a problem if it's allowed to develop. Do what you like, but don't involve me in it. Stan's a nice bloke but so is Bob, and he's away at the war fighting for his country.'

'Oh, here we go; here comes the lecture,' Joyce objected. 'Don't you take the moral high ground with me just because Stan doesn't fancy *you*.'

'Now you really are being childish.'

'And you're being extremely petty,' Joyce came back at her, her voice high and tight. 'Just because you don't have a man of your own, you don't have the right to carry on like some Mother Superior.'

They had both said things they didn't mean, and they fell into a stony silence for the rest of the journey.

At their gateways, they each marched up the path to their front door without even saying goodnight.

Rose hated bad feeling, especially between her and her beloved cousin, and she was still smarting from the altercation as she got undressed for bed that night. Maybe she should have stifled her feelings and kept quiet. But it was becoming almost unbearable to be around Joyce and Stan lately, and the words had come out almost of their own volition because she was worried about her cousin.

Joyce's love life was her own affair, but Rose knew her better than anyone; she knew how loyal she really was and how she would torment herself if she did betray Bob, which seemed the most likely outcome of the flirtation that was currently in progress between her and Stan.

Perhaps her cousin was right and Rose was just a frustrated widow who was envious when she saw other people enjoying themselves. But she knew herself better than that and she wasn't going to be bullied into believing otherwise. It was true to say, though, that she did feel a void in her life without a man in it, and she still missed Ray.

Shivering as she got into her pyjamas, she turned the light off and made her way to the bed in the dark, kicking her slippers off at the side.

What's that? she wondered as her foot touched something soft on the floor at the side of the bed. She turned on the light again and inspected the area, her heart sinking when she saw that it was Alfie's teddy bear Rupert, the one he'd had with him when she'd found him in the ruins; the one that went to bed with him every single night. He'd be miserable without that scruffy old bear when he went to bed tonight. That ragged piece of furry material with black button eyes was his comfort and salvation.

She couldn't bear to think of him without Rupert at this unsettling time. It was Sunday tomorrow. She'd take it over to him at Shepherd's Bush in the morning.

'We're not open yet,' shouted a man from inside the Green Cat as Rose banged on the door.

'It's Rose Brown.'

'Oh.' A brief silence. 'Hang on a minute.'

The door rattled as it was unlocked then opened by Johnny, who was standing there in a khaki shirt and trousers looking at her with a puzzled expression.

'Alfie forgot this,' she said, handing over the soft toy. 'I thought I'd better bring it over to save him being without it again tonight, because he's so fond of it. His mother gave it to him and he takes it to bed with him every night.'

He gave Rupert the once-over. 'He didn't say anything about missing it when he went to bed last night,' he told Rose.

'He wouldn't, for fear you might think him a baby because he still takes a teddy to bed.' She lowered her voice. 'So can I ask you to put it in his bed so that he thinks that he just mislaid it last night, rather than making a big thing of it and embarrassing him. He does love old Rupert so.'

'It's very good of you to come all this way with it,' Johnny said with an air of finality.

'It was no trouble; the bus stops at the end of our street.'

'I'll make sure that he gets it.'

'How is he settling in?' She couldn't resist asking because she was concerned about him.

'Wonderful. No trouble at all.'

'Is he getting used to his new surroundings?'

'I think so. Fortunately we have plenty of accommodation here,' he informed her coolly.

'It's quite a place,' she said, glancing towards the wide pub frontage which was situated on the corner of a side street in a prime position overlooking Shepherd's Bush Green.

'We like to think so, and I'm sure Alfie will be happy here with us.' He was overly defensive and edgy. 'Now if you'll excuse me, I have to start getting the pub ready for opening now. Thanks again for bringing his bear over.'

'A pleasure,' she said, turning to go. 'Give him my love, won't you.'

'Will do.'

'Cheerio.'

'Ta-ta.'

Rose walked away feeling well and truly snubbed. Johnny had made it obvious that he didn't welcome her interest in his son. The least he could have done was to invite her in for a few minutes. They never kept anyone waiting out in the cold at the Barton house. She did hope he wasn't going to be difficult about her visiting Alfie. She'd promised the boy that she would and she couldn't bear to let him down. She was feeling churned up and worried as she joined the bus queue.

Johnny was feeling terrible as he locked the door behind Rose. Why had he treated her so badly when she'd gone out of her way to bring something of value to his son? How could he have kept her standing out in the cold like that? His mother would turn in her grave.

Did he feel threatened by Rose because she had Alfie's love and he didn't? Was he jealous of the special bond she appeared to have with the boy that seemed out of reach for him? Whatever the reason, his behaviour was reprehensible.

Making a sudden decision, he ran out of the bar to the pub's private entrance and left the premises, tearing across the green towards the bus stop. A bus had just come and Rose was moving towards it with the rest of the queue.

He tapped her on the shoulder. 'I think I owe you an apology,' he said. 'I was very rude to you back there.'

'I have had warmer welcomes, I must admit,' she said, seeing no point in denying it. But her spirits were surprisingly uplifted by this unexpected turn of events.

'You must feel free to visit Alfie as often as you like,' he said, keen to appease her.

'I'm relieved that you've said that. I promised him I would, and I'd hate to let him down.'

'If you're not in too much of a hurry now, would you like to come back to the pub to say hello to him, meet my dad and have a drink with us?'

'Thank you. I'd like that.'

'The truth is,' he found himself confiding as they walked back to the pub together, 'it isn't going at all well with Alfie, and I haven't got a clue how to turn things around. He's really uncommunicative. He doesn't seem to want to get to know me at all.'

'He was like that with us at first,' Rose told him. 'You'll have to be patient, and remind yourself what he's been through. You didn't expect it to happen overnight, did you?'

'No. But I didn't expect it to be as difficult as this,' he confessed. 'The truth is, I'm completely out of my depth. I don't know what to talk to him about. No matter what subject I bring up, he shows no interest whatsoever. I'm as nervous as a kitten when I'm with him. I mean, what do I know about kids?'

'You were one yourself.'

He turned and smiled at her. 'You're a great help, you are,' he said jokingly.

'I do my best,' she joshed back, feeling extraordinarily light-hearted suddenly.

'Rose!' whooped Alfie, rushing up to her and wrapping his arms around her.

'What's all this?' she said, smiling down at him. 'I

didn't used to get big hugs like this when I saw you every day.'

He clung on to her as though he never wanted to let her go, and when she looked into his face she saw tears in his eyes.

'Why don't you show Rose your bedroom, Alfie?' suggested his father.

'Come on, Rose,' Alfie said, happy now that she was here.

The flat was on two floors and extremely spacious, Rose noticed, as Alfie led the way upstairs. More than twice the size of the Barton residence, it was an old-style property with big rooms, sash windows and high ceilings. Alfie's room was large and comfortably furnished; there was a train set, a punchball on a stand and a well-used old football.

'They were all mine when I was little,' Johnny explained. 'I'm glad I hung on to them now.'

'You're a lucky boy to have such things, and such a lovely room,' Rose said, looking round. 'Better than having a corner of my room, eh?'

Alfie nodded vaguely.

'I'll leave you two alone to chat in private,' said Johnny diplomatically and left the room.

As soon as he'd gone, Alfie said, 'Did you bring him, Rose? Did you bring Rupert?'

Rose gave him a look. 'You little horror,' she admonished. 'You left that teddy behind on purpose because you knew I would bring him over, didn't you?'

'I had to make sure you'd come.' At least he had the grace to look sheepish.

'I told you I would visit you. Surely you know me well enough to realise that I wouldn't let you down.'

'But I might have had to wait ages,' he said, 'and I couldn't bear that.'

So much for her worrying about his sensitivity, she thought. 'I've given the bear to your dad.'

'I bet he thinks I'm a sissy.'

'Course he doesn't. Anyway, it's your own fault for leaving the bear behind on purpose.'

'I wanna come home, Rose,' he whispered. 'Can you get me out of here?'

'Alfie, luv,' she said, sitting on the edge of his bed, 'this is your home now.'

'It's horrible.'

'Now that just isn't true,' she said, waving her hand around. 'You've got a smashing room of your own and much more space than you had at our place.'

'I don't care about those things,' he said bleakly. 'I wanna be with you. I miss everyone.'

She swallowed hard and bit the tears back. 'And we all miss you, but this is where you live now with your family. You know that.'

Alfie looked very downcast.

'Your dad seems nice,' Rose said hopefully.

'I don't like him.'

'You're not even trying.'

'Why should I, when he didn't care about my mum? He was there all the time but he never came to see us.'

'Oh Alfie, Alfie,' she said despairingly. 'There could have been any number of reasons for that. Your dad has come for you now, when you really need him, so you must try to stop being horrid to him.'

'I don't need him.'

'You'll make things a whole lot worse for yourself with that sort of attitude,' she advised. 'You can have a nice life here, so make the most of it.'

'I don't want to be here.'

'Look, luv, if you carry on like this when I come to visit, your dad won't let me come.'

'Please take me back with you.'

'No, Alfie,' she said firmly, standing up. 'Now you're not being fair to me. You know I can't take you back. I've explained to you how these things work.'

'I thought you were my friend.'

'And I thought *you* were *my* friend,' she came back at him. 'But if you were you wouldn't be giving me all this trouble. All of this is hard for me too. Now will you stop going on about coming back with me and make an effort here, or I'll begin to think that you're behaving like a spoiled little brat. Please, Alfie, I mean it.'

'All right, s'pose I'll have to.'

'That's better. No more whingeing. Promise?'

'I'll try not to.'

Back downstairs in the sitting room – large but homely with an old-fashioned fireplace and tall windows overlooking the green – Johnny introduced her to his father, Ted Beech, to whom Rose took an instant liking. The older man was wearing a black armband, and seeing Rose notice it, he explained that his wife had died recently.

'I'm sorry to hear that,' she said with an understanding look. 'I know how that feels. I lost my husband last year. He was killed at Dunkirk.'

'Sorry to hear that, love,' said Ted, turning to his son. 'Johnny was at Dunkirk too. He got wounded, didn't you?'

'Just a bit.'

'It wasn't just a bit,' disagreed Ted. 'He had bullets in him all over the place.'

'All right, Dad,' interrupted Johnny. 'I'm sure Rose doesn't want to hear about that, and I'm damned sure I don't want to be reminded.'

'Don't worry on my account,' Rose assured them. 'I'm happy to listen.'

'Don't encourage him, because he won't know when to stop once he gets going.' Johnny grinned. 'Anyway, I'm going to open up downstairs now, ready for the punters. Would you like to join me for a drink before you go, Rose?'

'Yes, I'd like that,' she said graciously.

'Good.' He looked at Alfie. 'You know where I am if you need me, son. Your grandad will be up here anyway.'

Rose gave Alfie a warm enveloping hug, promised him she'd come to see him again soon and followed Johnny downstairs to the bar.

★   ★   ★

Hazel recognised trouble when she saw it, and she spotted a whole load of it when she saw a small, attractive brunette sitting at a table in the saloon bar with Johnny. The brass neck of the woman; sitting there like Lady Muck, having a drink and chatting and laughing with Hazel's fiancé while muggins here served behind the bar.

She was the only woman in the place besides Hazel because the Sunday lunchtime session was predominantly male. It wasn't as if this Rose woman didn't know that Johnny was spoken for, because Johnny had introduced Hazel as his fiancée. Rose was a war widow, Ted had told Hazel when he'd popped down to the bar for a bottle of beer; as though that made her special somehow. She probably had Johnny in mind as a replacement for husband number one.

It was just one damned thing after another since Johnny's mother had slipped conveniently out of the picture, Hazel thought miserably. First some awful illegitimate child had dropped into their lives, and now some woman from the boy's foster home had come to visit and was flashing her big brown eyes at Johnny and showing all the signs of becoming a regular visitor.

Well, neither she nor the boy would be staying around here for long. Hazel was determined about that. She knew exactly how to deal with the woman; she was an expert at beating off the opposition. But removing the boy from his father's life was going to take a bit more planning and could take a little time. He'd have to go, though. Oh yes! Once Hazel set her mind to something, she always succeeded.

This Rose person shouldn't be too difficult to shift, once Hazel got to work on her. She'd never want to come back here again after Hazel had finished with her.

'So I expect you're up even earlier in the morning than I am when I'm at camp then,' remarked Johnny on hearing that Rose was a postwoman.

'I get up about four o'clock, ready for duty at five,' she told him.

'Blimey, even the army doesn't drag us out of bed that early,' he said lightly. 'Not when we're not in action anyway.'

'The Royal Mail has a reputation to maintain, especially difficult in wartime, with railway stations and sorting offices being bombed. People need their letters more than ever these days, with loved ones being away.'

'I bet it's a bit parky out at that time of the morning; we nearly freeze to death at camp, trooping to the shower block, and we're not up quite as early as that.'

'You get used to it.'

'There's snow on the way, I reckon,' he said with a wicked gleam in his eye. 'So I hope it holds off until you've done your round tomorrow.'

'Me too. One thing is for sure: I can't turn over and go back to sleep no matter how thick the snow is. The mail has to be delivered whatever the weather. Thank goodness it does too. Heaven knows how much longer Alfie would have survived trapped in the wreckage if I hadn't come along after my round and found him.'

147

'You actually got him out yourself?'

'That's right.'

'I didn't realise that. I just assumed the rescue people did it.'

'There was no time to call them.'

'Oh Rose, how can I ever thank you?' Johnny said emotionally.

'You don't have to. Alfie's alive, that's reward enough for me.'

'I'm very grateful to you, just the same,' he said with enormous warmth. 'I dread to think what might have happened to him if you hadn't come along when you did.'

'Well I did, so there's no need to torment yourself.' She cleared her throat and changed the subject because his gratitude was beginning to embarrass her. 'Anyway, are you home on a weekend pass?'

He nodded. 'I have to be back at camp by this evening, which means I haven't had much time to get to know my son,' he told her. 'My father will know him better than I do.'

'That sort of thing can't be helped in wartime,' Rose said. 'At least he's with his family now. It's better for him.'

'For all the good it seems to be doing him.'

'He gave us a hard time at first, as I've said,' she informed him. 'Basically there's only one person he wanted to be with and that was his mother. It still is, come to that. He got used to us eventually, but it took quite a while and a whole lot of patience.'

'You're wonderful with him,' Johnny said with overt admiration. 'I've seen the way he is with you.'

'I love the bones of him.'

'He obviously feels the same about you.'

'Yes, I think he does. But it wasn't always that way,' she reminded him. 'That son of yours has a mind of his own, and a stubborn streak. He's very strong-willed.'

'I've gathered that.'

'He can be quite a handful if he's in the mood. It's tempting to give in to him, because of what he's been through, but he needs a firm hand. He'll run rings around you otherwise.'

'I think he's doing that already.'

'Anything I can do to help, you know where I am.'

'Thanks, Rose. I'll bear that in mind, and thanks again for looking after him,' he said.

'We loved having him and were sorry to see him go,' she said, finishing her shandy. 'And talking of going, it's time I was on my way.'

Johnny stood up. 'Thanks for coming,' he said. 'Sorry I was rude earlier.'

'Forget it.'

'And don't you forget to come and see Alfie whenever you want to. If I'm not here, Dad will be.'

'There's no chance I would ever forget.'

He walked to the door with her and opened it, watching her as she swung off down the street, a trim figure with a red muffler worn over a dark coat, enhancing the colour of her lustrous near-black hair.

'Can you come and give me a hand over here, please,

Johnny?' Hazel's strident tones came from behind the bar. 'I need some help.'

No reply. Johnny was still standing at the door watching Rose crossing the green.

'Put the wood in the hole, will yer, mate?' said a customer who was sitting with a group of old men. 'You're letting in a hell of a draught over here.'

'Sorry, boys,' he said, shutting the door. 'Can't have you catching your death in your local, can we?'

'Johnny,' called Hazel again. 'You're wanted over here . . . now!'

'Sorry, luv,' he said, coming to his senses and hurrying across to her. 'I thought I ought to be polite as she'd taken the trouble to come over.'

The preoccupied look in his eyes put Hazel on full alert. But she had to be a bit crafty.

'The rush is over now, but we were busy and I could have done with another pair of hands,' she admonished.

'I was keeping an eye on things while I was talking, and you seemed to be coping,' he told her. 'But I'm sorry if I stayed away too long.'

Just then there was a rush of customers, so they were busy working for a while.

'Do you think it's a good idea for Rose to stay in touch with Alfie?' Hazel said as soon as there was a lull.

'I certainly do. He needs all the support he can get. Why? Don't you?'

'No. I think she might unsettle him.'

'Why on earth should she?' he asked. 'She thinks the world of him, and vice versa.'

'Exactly! While she keeps turning up here, it'll make it harder for you to get close to him.'

'I don't agree with you, Hazel. Rose will do everything she can to encourage Alfie to settle in here,' he told her. 'She really cares about him and wants him to get along with me.'

'She's a rival to you for Alfie's affections.'

'Oh no, you're wrong there,' he disagreed heatedly. 'She's very fond of him but not in a selfish or competitive way. She really does want the best for him and is keen for him to get closer to me so that we can have a father-and-son relationship. The last thing she intends is to come between us.'

'You hardly know her,' Hazel reminded him. 'You don't know what she's like.'

'You know me, Hazel; I take people at face value.'

'It doesn't do to be too trusting. I reckon she's allowed herself to get too fond of Alfie,' she kept on, determined to poison Johnny's mind against Rose. 'Why else would she bother to come and visit him so soon if she isn't clinging on to him?'

'She brought something that he'd left behind at her place, as it happens,' he explained.

'Any excuse.'

'No. It was quite genuine,' he said. 'Anyway, I've told her to feel free to visit whenever she wants to. Alfie is very keen to keep in contact with her and her family, and I'm not going to interfere with that. They are obviously genuinely fond of him. And he of them.'

'I'm only thinking of you,' she lied. 'It's going to be

hard enough for you getting used to having a child in your life. You don't need someone making it even harder. In my opinion the boy needs to cut his ties with the past and concentrate on his life here.'

'I appreciate your concern, but I'm sure you're worrying unnecessarily.' Johnny turned towards the bar and a waiting customer. 'The usual, is it, mate?'

Hazel was fuming as she stood beside Johnny while he pulled a pint for another customer. She didn't allow anyone or anything to deter her in the pursuit of her own personal ambitions. As the problems arose she knocked them down, and she would do so in this case. That big-eyed brunette would be dealt with at the earliest possible opportunity.

Chapter Six

The snow that Johnny had jokingly predicted on Sunday was thick on the ground on Monday morning when Rose struggled through the dark streets on her early round. Fingers numb inside her gloves and toes aching from the cold, she found it very hard going, especially as it was so slippery underfoot. She'd had to walk to the sorting office this morning instead of going by bike because the roads were treacherous.

However, she had far too much on her mind to dwell unduly on her own physical discomfort. First there was Alfie, who had to adjust to living with different people, and suffer the agonies of finding friends, yet again. The lad would be starting at his local school today, and her stomach churned at the thought of him having to face the initial loneliness of being the new boy.

Someone else was very much on her mind too: her cousin Joyce, who obviously hadn't forgiven her for her speaking out on Saturday night. She'd gone to work on her own before Rose this morning, instead of waiting for her in the normal way.

Rose herself had been miffed by what had been said so had stayed away from her cousin over the weekend. But now she was beginning to realise that if things weren't put right quickly, a serious rift could develop. So she would swallow her pride and apologise at the earliest possible opportunity because her friendship with Joyce was too important to lose over a few impulsively uttered words. In future she would try to hold her tongue about her cousin's private life.

She paused on a street corner to get a fresh bundle of letters from her bag, her normally nimble fingers clumsy and fumbling in the bitter cold. Using the light from her lamp, she carefully untied the string, holding the wad of letters in her hand. Because she was shivering so violently, her grip lacked control, and the string and one of the letters slipped from her grasp. About to bend down to retrieve it, her feet went from under her, and all the letters shot out of her hand and floated down to the snow, while she landed with a thump on the side of her buttocks on the ice, a sharp pain searing across her shoulder.

Initially stunned, she eventually managed to struggle up on to her hands and knees and began picking up the letters out of the snow, concerned that some of the addresses written on the economy labels – commonly stuck on re-used envelopes these days because of the paper shortage – were blurred with the wet and difficult to read.

Her shoulder was throbbing, her knees smarting and she was frozen to the bone as she struggled to retrieve all the letters in the dark, her uniform trousers now wet through and clinging icily to her legs.

'You having a bit of trouble, Postie?' asked a woman in a turban with curlers poking out of the front.

'I slipped over.'

'Well, I didn't think you were down there out of choice, luv,' chortled the woman.

'I've dropped a whole load of letters in the snow,' explained Rose, ashamed to feel her eyes burning with tears from the sheer bodily misery of her circumstances. 'It's so hard to find them in the dark, and I must get every single one. It's my responsibility to make sure they're delivered.'

''Ere, let me give you a hand,' offered the woman cheerfully. 'I've just come off the night shift at the munitions factory and I'll be home in a minute and in bed soon after when I've had a nice cup o' tea. You've obviously got a while to go before you finish your shift, so let's help you on your way. This is no weather to be out on the streets.'

'Thanks ever so much,' said Rose, as the woman got down beside her and began plucking letters out of the snow. 'It's very kind of you.'

'We're all on the same side, aren't we, luv?' she said chirpily, brushing the snow off the envelopes as she collected them. 'Whether we're working in a factory, in the forces or out delivering the mail, we're all doing our bit to win the war. Pulling together is what it's all about these days.'

This small kindness from a stranger in the street

warmed Rose's heart. After that, the long, arduous trek through the frozen streets to finish her round – with a bruised shoulder and grazed knees – was easier to take, especially as the woman had further illustrated her generous spirit by taking Rose into her house and giving her a cup of hot tea to help her on her way.

'What do you think about this invasion that everyone's on about?' asked one of a group of postwomen in the staff canteen at the sorting office later that same morning. 'Do you reckon the Germans are coming?'

'Let 'em come; our boys will soon give them what for,' said Rose, remaining positive even though she was as nervous as everybody else as the newspaper headlines created a general mood of feverish apprehension about an imminent German invasion of the British Isles. 'No one is going to take over our country.'

'I bloomin' well hope you're right,' said one of the women.

'The military will have made special plans to deal with them if they do come, so we'll just have to have faith in that,' said Rose, who was taking a short break in between finishing her first delivery and starting the second. 'Anyway, a lot of it is just newspaper talk and rumours.'

'There's no smoke without fire, Rose,' opined one of her colleagues. 'The government wouldn't have warned us to stock up our invasion larders and reminded us to make sure we always carry our gas masks if they're not expecting something big.'

'There is that,' she agreed. 'But I suppose they have to make sure we take precautions just to be on the safe side; it doesn't mean it's certain to happen.'

'We've been expecting to be invaded since war broke out and it still hasn't happened,' someone pointed out.

'Get it over with, I say,' said a sanguine member of the gathering. 'Let the Germans try and land here and see what they get. They won't know what's hit 'em.'

'That's the spirit,' said Rose.

The subject moved on to the other popular talking point: the current lull in the Blitz.

'Some people say the Jerry bomber pilots are just resting to get ready for a massive attack during a full moon,' said one cheerful soul.

'Let's just enjoy the quiet nights while we can,' was the way Rose saw it.

The gathering began to disperse as people went back to work. Rose finished her tea and was about to leave when Joyce came into the canteen.

Eager to make her peace with her cousin, Rose hurried towards her, realising as she did that Joyce was heading her way.

'Joyce, I'm—' she began, meeting her halfway.

'Rose, I have to talk to you,' Joyce interrupted, looking grave, and glancing around the canteen where postmen and women were coming and going. *'In private.'*

'I can't stop now. I've my round to do.'

'I'll wait for you after work and we can walk home together.'

'See you later then.'

Judging by her cousin's tone, Rose guessed that she was in for a real roasting after work. The annoying thing was, she hadn't even had a chance to say sorry.

As it happened, it was Joyce who made the apology.

'Sorry, kid, I shouldn't have gone off the deep end at you like I did,' she said as they walked gingerly through the snow, which had mostly turned to slush on the main road, though the back streets still hadn't thawed.

'It was my fault. I had no right to interfere,' said Rose. 'But it really got to me on Saturday. I suppose I was worried about what you were getting yourself into.'

'You had every right to speak up if I was making you feel uncomfortable,' Joyce told her. 'I didn't realise I was making my feelings so obvious. It must have been my guilty conscience that caused me to blast off at you like that. Sorry I went off to work without you this morning. I was still angry. But walking through the streets on my own, I finally calmed down and admitted to myself that you had a point.'

'There is something between you and Stan then?'

'I'll say there is. I'm nuts about him,' she confessed. 'And there's no point in telling me to get over it, because I've already tried and there's not a damned thing I can do about it.'

'Oh, Joyce . . .'

'Don't panic. Nothing's happened,' Joyce assured her quickly. 'But I want it to.'

'What about him?'

'He feels the same but he's too decent to let it go any further, knowing that I'm engaged to Bob. If a move is made, it'll have to come from me.' She sighed. 'I know this sounds corny, but I just light up when I'm with him.'

'I know. I've seen you.'

'I've never experienced anything like it before.'

'Not even with Bob? At first, when it was all new and exciting?' suggested Rose.

'No, not like this,' Joyce confirmed. 'I'm not proud of myself, believe me, with poor Bob away fighting, but I want to be with Stan; to share my life with him.'

'Blimey, Joyce, you have got it bad,' exclaimed Rose worriedly. 'Are you sure you don't just fancy him?'

'I do, of course, but there's much more to it than just that. It's everything, the whole works: love, lust, caring, and wanting to be with him for the rest of my life. There's an urgency burning inside me. It's as though he's my only chance to touch real love, and I have to grab it with both hands.'

'That's all very well, but what about Bob?' asked Rose.

'I know this makes me the worst kind of selfish cow, but Bob has become just a distant threat at the back of my mind, keeping me on the straight and narrow.'

'Perhaps you'll feel differently when you see him again,' Rose suggested.

'Who knows? I heard from him last week and there's no chance of him getting leave. But the way I feel at the moment, my engagement to him is just a burden,' Joyce told her. 'It was never the love affair that dreams are made of; more something we just drifted into. We'd been going out for a while, so got engaged because it's what people do. Bob's a lovely man and I'll always think a lot of him, but it wasn't ever the same kind of thing that I feel for Stan.'

'Are you sure it isn't the idea of Stan being a talented musician that you've fallen for?' Rose wanted to find a solution to the problem so was looking at it from every possible angle. 'Those sorts of people do have a certain glamour about them.'

'I admire his talent enormously, but that isn't what I'm in love with. You know as well as I do, Rose, that Stan is no oil painting, and he's certainly no beefcake. If I was looking for some hunk to fancy there's no shortage of choice among the servicemen around in London at the moment. I didn't go looking for love. I was quite happy to settle for Bob until Stan came into my life. I don't know why I feel this way about him or why I've changed towards Bob. It just happened. How can anyone know what makes them feel one way or another?'

'They can't, but I think the war has a lot to do with it,' Rose suggested. 'It splits couples up, and causes them to meet people they wouldn't in normal times.'

'That's true.'

As they walked on, Rose noticed — in a preoccupied sort of way — as the snow melted, that some of the mess left by the bomb damage at the height of the

Blitz had been removed from the streets. The piles of rubble in the road had disappeared, and damaged shop fronts had been made tidy. The respite from the air raids had given the authorities the chance to get on with the job of clearing debris and boarding up blown-out windows. The area looked better for a bit of a spruce-up. But how long before it was battered down again was anybody's guess. Still, hope springs eternal in the human breast, as was clearly demonstrated by the local shopkeepers, who had worked hard to reopen their bombed shops.

'I suppose you think I'm being really stupid,' Joyce said. 'I bet you think I should grow up and get over it.'

'If only it was that simple,' Rose sighed. 'I know how sensible and down-to-earth you usually are. So I know how serious this must be to you. That's why I've been so worried.'

'I don't know what to do.' Joyce's voice broke into a sob. 'The last thing I want to do is betray Bob. I've always intended to stay true to him. But I love Stan and I don't want to hurt him either. He wants me and he needs me, I know that without a word having been spoken.'

'Bob will need you when he comes home too.'

'I know,' she wept. 'You are the only person in the world who I would admit this to, and you'll probably hate me for saying it, but I don't want to be with him any more. I've changed, Rose, and I wish I hadn't. I hate feeling like this. I loathe myself for the hunger eating away at me for what I shouldn't have. But the joy of being with Stan is so special I can't get enough of it.'

'Oh dear,' said Rose. 'You really are in a state.'

'I can't force feelings for Bob that aren't there any more. I know that compared to all the terrible things that are happening in the world, all the bombing and our boys dying overseas, my personal life is utterly unimportant. But I can't turn my feelings off. What should I do, Rose?'

She didn't answer right away. 'Over the years, you and I have turned to each other for advice about everything. But this is one of those rare occasions when I can't advise you,' she said as they walked on, Joyce struggling to stop crying. 'No one else can make your mind up for you about this. It's too important and too personal.'

'I suppose you're right.'

Rose linked arms with her cousin in a companionable way. 'It'll work out one way or the other, though,' she said. 'Things always do in the end.'

She didn't feel as optimistic as she sounded, though. Love triangles always ended in tears for someone, and she had the horrible suspicion that most of those resulting from this one were going to be shed by her cousin.

It wasn't really the weather for a walk, but Joe Barton felt the need for some fresh air and exercise in his dinner break so took to the streets near the factory. Hands sunk deep into his pockets, head down against the cold, he walked as briskly as he could in the melting snow to get his circulation going. The temperature was so low in the office they all had to work in their outdoor clothes.

He was feeling oddly frustrated and unfulfilled; as though he was lacking in his contribution to the war effort. He helped at the ARP control centre, running messages, and took his turn with fire watching, but he never felt as though he was making much of a difference. Alan was the heroic soldier in the family, while feeble Joe just sat at a desk all day, he thought resentfully.

Knowing that his day job was vital didn't seem to help, even though everyone who worked in an aircraft factory played an essential part in the war. Maybe if he were to apply for a transfer to the shop floor he might feel more involved in things, though he knew it wasn't really the answer. It was something with more action that he needed.

He was about to turn round and go back to work when a placard on a brick wall caught his eye. It was a picture of some firemen working with hoses on a burning building. Across the top, in large striking letters, were the words *AUXILIARY FIRE SERVICE: LONDON needs Auxiliary Firemen NOW*. The compelling message at the bottom was: *Enrol at Any Fire Station*.

It struck an immediate chord with Joe. He'd show Alan that he wasn't afraid of danger. Full of enthusiasm, he decided to call in at the fire station on his way home from work tonight.

'Alfie seems to be settling in all right, Ted,' observed Rose the following Saturday afternoon as she looked out of the window of the Beeches' living room to see Alfie playing on the green with some other boys, the well-worn triangular open space suffused with winter sunshine. The pale light seemed to emphasise the sadness of the bomb-damaged buildings around the green, one of which was a cinema, now closed as the result of a hit last year. 'He's found some friends by the look of it, anyway.'

'Yeah, he soon latched on to some local kids at school,' said Ted, his brow furrowed under a thatch of white hair. He had the look of a rough diamond about him but he struck Rose as a man with a kind heart.

'It was probably easier for him starting school this time as he's with his own family and the people around here don't know about his background,' she remarked. 'At least he won't have to put up with name-calling now.'

'Mm, there is that.'

'Is something wrong, Ted?' she enquired.

'Not with me,' he replied. 'But Alfie seems such a sad little boy, and that upsets me.'

'He's still grieving for his mum, I expect.'

'I wish I could make it better for him. I feel so help-less.'

'I know the feeling well,' Rose said with a wry grin.

164

'But I thought he seemed happy enough when I arrived.'

'That's because he was so pleased to see you, I expect. He thinks the world of you.' She had come over to see how Alfie was and was delighted when some lads had called for him to go out to play. She'd told him not to stay in on her account because it made her happy to see him with boys of his own age. At this time of day the pub was closed, so Ted had time for a companionable chat over a cup of tea. 'Sadly, he doesn't feel the same way about us, especially his father.'

'Johnny's away at camp this weekend, is he?'

'He hasn't turned up, so I suppose he couldn't get a pass.' Ted nodded. 'It's a pity, because he needs to spend as much time as possible with the boy to get to know him during these early days with us. Not that Alfie wants anything to do with him. But Johnny has to persevere.'

'I'm sure Alfie will come round,' she encouraged, 'but he can be a stubborn little so-and-so.'

'You're telling me. I had a right old battle with him the other day and I was determined to win. I knew I had to or he'd walk all over me for ever more.'

'What was it about?'

'I asked him to lay the table for tea and he wouldn't. He did it in the end, though.'

'It wasn't really about laying the table, though, was it?' she speculated.

'Oh no, not for either of us,' he explained. 'It was a battle of wills and could have been about anything. I

165

could easily have done the job myself as usual. But I wanted him to do that small thing because it's good for him to muck in, especially as he's living in a working household. I also thought it would make him feel like a permanent part of the family rather than just someone who's staying here.'

'Very sensible.'

'Anyway, he took it as a chance to test me; to find out just how far he can push me. He probably didn't even realise that was what he was doing, but I knew,' Ted continued.

'Did you have to get tough with him to resolve it?'

'I had to stand my ground, but I didn't shout or lift a finger to him. I just stood firm and he did what he was told in the end.' Ted drew on his cigarette. 'I've had to lay down some ground rules with Johnny being away most of the time or I'll have no control over the boy at all. It's a long time since I had a little 'un to deal with. But I do remember a bit about it. Johnny could be stubborn at times. Must be where his son gets it from.'

'I think a lot of it with Alfie is caused by all the disruption,' Rose said. 'And he really did love his mum. If there's anything I can do to help, you only have to ask.'

'Thanks, dear, but I'm managing. Anyway, trying to get to grips with my new-found grandson helps to take my mind off my own troubles and how much I miss my wife,' he continued. 'I've got staff downstairs in the pub, so I'm covered if I have to spend more time up here with Alfie.' He grinned. 'Though I shouldn't tempt fate as far as that's concerned, because there are times when people don't turn up for work and I'm running around like a blue-arsed fly trying to cope.'

They chatted for a while longer, and Rose was getting her coat on to leave when there was the thunder of footsteps up the stairs and Alfie came in, cheeks flushed and smudged with dirt.

'I was just coming over the green to see you, to say cheerio,' she told him.

'Oh. Are you going already, Rose?' He sounded disappointed.

'Yes, it's time I went. I've been here ages.'

'I wanted to show you my collection of cigarette cards,' he burst out. 'I've nearly got the whole set in the Air Raid Precautions series now. The boys at school have got loads of 'em, and I've done lots of swaps.'

'I think I can spare the time for you to show me those,' she said, and turning to Ted added, 'As long as your grandad doesn't mind.'

'Stay as long as you like, ducks,' he said.

So she stayed for a while longer while Alfie showed her his collection of cigarette cards, the pre-war array of film stars and sportsmen now replaced by more serious images relevant to the war. Little boys these days collected cards illustrated with air raid precautions and various aspects of civil defence, including fire-fighting and how to cope in a gas attack.

When she finally left, having assured Alfie that everyone at home, including his beloved Bruiser, was fine, and promised that she would come again soon, she felt easier in her mind. Maybe some time still had to pass before the sad look went out of his eyes, but he'd get there in the end, she hoped. He was with people who cared about him; that was the important thing.

Crossing the green on her way to the bus stop, engrossed in her own thoughts, Rose was recalled to the present by someone greeting her.

'Hello there,' said Johnny's fiancée Hazel with a friendly smile. 'What are you doing in these parts? Have you come to visit our famous market?'

'No. I've been to see Alfie, as it happens,' Rose replied. 'I'm just on my way to catch the bus home.'

'How did you find the lad today?' Hazel enquired.

'He seems to be getting along all right,' replied Rose, thinking how attractive the other woman looked in an emerald-green coat that complemented her bright auburn hair. 'I was pleased to see that he's made some friends.'

Hazel nodded but looked worried suddenly. 'Yeah, I suppose that's an encouraging sign,' she said, implying that all was not well otherwise.

'It's bound to take him time to settle in,' Rose said.

Hazel nodded. 'It's a difficult situation for them all,' she said. 'I don't think Johnny realised quite what he was taking on when he decided to face up to fatherhood.'

'There will have to be a period of adjustment for them all,' said Rose, prickling slightly at the implied criticism of Alfie.

'Johnny so much wants it to work,' Hazel went on, her voice full of caring. 'He wants to be a good dad to Alfie, but the boy isn't making it easy for him.'

'Alfie's had a rough time.' Rose was fully on the defensive now. 'He needs to get used to being with different people. I know Johnny and Ted are his own flesh and blood, but they are strangers to him, after all. Once he gets to know them I'm sure they'll all get along famously, and he'll settle down and become part of his new-found family.'

The other woman appeared to be mulling something over; she looked at Rose, seeming embarrassed suddenly. 'Look . . . er, there is something I was wondering about as regards his settling in with Johnny and his dad.'

'Oh?'

'It's a bit awkward really,' began Hazel, biting her lip. 'I don't want to cause offence.'

'Well, I might as well hear about it, as you've obviously got something on your mind.'

'It's just that . . . well, I know you mean well and everything, but I was wondering if you might be doing more harm than good by continuing to visit Alfie.'

Rose was too taken aback to reply at first. 'I very much hope not,' she said at last. 'That's the last thing I would ever want to do.' She gave Hazel a look. 'What exactly do you mean anyway?'

'Well, while you're still in his life, I don't think he can properly settle down with them.'

'Why?'

'Because he'll continue to hanker for you and your family,' she said with astounding authority for someone who knew nothing about children. 'He enjoyed living with you and he's hanging on to it. But he needs to shut the door on the past now and move on to a new life. God knows he's had it rough in the short time he's been around. Johnny has told me all about it. But it's time to put all that behind him now and make a new start.'

'But he sees me as a friend; a sort of big sister,' Rose explained. 'I can't just stop going to see him. He'll think I've abandoned him, and be so hurt. He doesn't need that kind of a blow, especially at this time.'

'There are times when we have to be cruel to be kind,' Hazel said, her green eyes resting on Rose as though in concern. 'It's up to us adults to work out what's best for him. When a child is adopted, I believe they stop all contact with the past so that the child can move on to a new life.'

'But this is completely different, because I'm his friend and he trusts me. It would be so awful for him if I stopped seeing him, especially coming on top of everything else,' said Rose, feeling utterly distraught. 'He'd think I'd let him down. He'd never trust anyone again.'

'I think it might be best not to tell him that you won't be coming again, because that'll upset him and he'll beg you not to do it.' Hazel looked grave. 'It will be best for you to just disappear from his life altogether.'

'It seems so cruel.'

'Yeah, it does, but it will be for his own good in the

long run,' she said. 'Look, I know it might hurt him initially, and God knows that's the last thing I want for him, but he'll soon get over it. He'll forget all about you in no time at all, once you stop appearing. A child of that age wouldn't hang on to memories for long.'

'He'll think I've stopped caring about him.'

'It doesn't matter what he thinks *now*; it's his future we have to worry about, isn't it?' Hazel said chummily. 'I haven't known him for long, but I think the world of my future stepson. So I feel obliged to speak my mind on his behalf.'

'I love him to bits too.'

'In that case you'll want to do right by him, won't you? Though you must do what you think is best, of course.' She leaned forward and put her hand on Rose's arm. 'You've done a wonderful job so far. Johnny was saying how well you and your family have looked after him. But now it's time for someone else to take over. He's our responsibility from now on.'

'Yes, I realise that,' Rose said miserably.

Hazel shivered and hugged herself against the cold. 'Anyway, I have to be going now. I've a bit of shopping to do before my evening shift at the pub. It's up to you what you do about Alfie. I've said my piece; the rest is up to you. I hope you didn't mind my speaking out. I felt I had to for the boy's sake.'

'Of course not.'

'Ta-ta then.'

'Cheerio.'

*　　*　　*

Going on her way, hips swinging, a triumphant look in her eyes, Hazel was full of self-congratulation. Oh yes, she was wasted behind a bar counter. With her acting talent, she ought to be playing to packed houses on the West End stage. Judging by the worried look on the daft cow's face, she'd fallen for it hook, line and sinker, and Hazel hadn't even had to raise her voice. How clever she was to think of it on the spur of the moment when she'd just happened to run into Rose unexpectedly.

Rose was the type to have a conscience. She was obviously one of those irritating do-gooders who gave Hazel the right hump. Still, with a bit of luck she'd got rid of her for good and all. If Hazel was any judge, Rose wouldn't come sniffing around the Green Cat again, putting temptation in Johnny's way.

So that was one problem solved. The boy was the next item on the agenda. That was going to be much more difficult and called for cunning of the highest order.

Rose sat on the bus, staring out of the window at the Saturday afternoon crowds thronging the Uxbridge Road, and mulling over her meeting with Johnny's fiancée.

Hazel seemed genuinely to have Alfie's interests at heart, and she was right in what she said about Rose's continuing friendship with the boy. Rose couldn't imagine why she hadn't thought of it herself when it was so blindingly obvious. She must have been so emotionally involved in the situation she hadn't seen the wider view: that Alfie wouldn't move on properly if she kept going to see him, reminding him of the past.

Nevertheless, the thought of doing what Hazel suggested hurt Rose so much, it was a physical, grinding ache that seemed to drag the heart right out of her. But her feelings didn't matter. Alfie's future was the important thing. No matter how painful it was for her, she had to do right by him.

Despite all the rumours about an imminent German invasion, the weeks went by and British troops didn't have to fight off enemy troops from the beaches, so people stopped being so jittery. There weren't many air raids either, which also helped to boost morale. The Barton family had a special uplift to their spirits when Alan came home one Friday night at the end of February for the weekend.

His mother wept with pride at the sight of him in uniform; his dad slapped him on the back and Rose gave him a hug and smacked a kiss on his cheek.

'Hey, steady on, sis,' he said with mock embarrassment. 'I haven't been away that long.'

'We've got a fireman in the family now,' Rose informed him when things had calmed down, keen to give Joe some of the limelight. 'Joe has joined the Auxiliary Fire Service.'

'Well done, mate,' Alan said to his brother, genuinely pleased for him. 'Have you seen any action yet?'

'Not yet.'

'Good job too,' pronounced May. 'Fighting fires is a dangerous business.' She paused, looking at Alan. 'I hope you're not going to see any action just yet either.'

'Who knows,' he said, full of masculine aplomb. 'I could get posted abroad at any time. I'm a proper soldier now, you know, Mum. All trained up and ready to go.'

'Change the subject and stop depressing me, for goodness' sake,' admonished May lightly. 'I don't want to think about that part of it until I absolutely have to.'

Rose thought that Alan looked even more handsome in uniform, and seemed taller somehow. Never lacking in confidence, he was even fuller of himself now that he had successfully completed his army training.

'This calls for a celebration,' suggested Bill. 'Let's see if we can get a few bottles in and have a bit of a knees-up. We can have it tomorrow night; that'll give us a chance to get it organised.'

This was greeted with a roar of approval. Nobody noticed that Joe wasn't saying much . . .

Joe was watching his brother, who was nothing short of magnificent. So tall and broad-shouldered, so sociable and confident, he simply filled the room with his powerful presence. Joe felt hopelessly inadequate and incapable of ever matching up to him. The hero-worship of earlier years was turning to hate.

'Fancy doing a thing like that to a little child,' said Hazel stridently. 'That's plain evil, that is.'

'It isn't very nice,' agreed Ted. 'I'm surprised at her.'

'I never trusted her,' said Hazel.

'I did. I really trusted Rose,' Ted said with emphasis. 'I thought she had a heart of gold. And what does she do? She lets young Alfie down good and proper.'

'The nasty cow,' said Hazel, relishing the situation.

As well as concern for his grandson, Ted's attitude was also influenced by disappointment in Rose, who he'd taken a real liking to. 'Fancy staying away without as much as a word of warning,' he said. 'I didn't think she was capable of such a thing.'

'I must say, I was very impressed with her. She seemed to be genuinely fond of Alfie,' Johnny put in. It was a Saturday evening and this conversation was taking place behind the bar of the pub during a lull between customers. Johnny hadn't long got back from camp as he only had a thirty-six-hour pass this weekend, and his father was getting him up to date with all the news as he hadn't been home for the last few weekends. 'I think there must be a good reason why she hasn't been to see him.'

'Yeah, there is,' Hazel piped up. 'She can't be bothered to come over. It's as simple as that.'

'She didn't seem the type not to bother,' said Johnny. 'Quite the opposite, in fact.'

'She didn't seem like the sort to let anyone down,' added Ted. 'It just goes to show how wrong you can be about people.'

'Alfie's upset about it, I suppose,' said Johnny.

'Not half. He's too proud to make much of it, but she's really hurt him,' replied Ted.

'The poor thing,' said Hazel.

'He's been at the window looking out for her all afternoon the last two Saturdays.'

'Shame.' Hazel again.

'It isn't as though she expects him to stay in the whole time she's here or anything,' Ted went on. 'He goes out to play while she's here, but I think just the fact that she's come to see him gives him a feeling of stability.'

'Perhaps she's ill,' suggested Johnny. 'I can't believe she would do that to him for no good reason.'

'I wondered about that too,' mentioned Ted thoughtfully. He wanted to think well of Rose despite the evidence against her. 'But if she wasn't well, surely she'd have got someone to give us a bell. She knows how much Alfie thinks of her and looks forward to her visits. It isn't as if we're not in the phone book.'

'I doubt they're on the phone,' Johnny pointed out. 'Not many people are unless they're rich or in business.'

'They have phone boxes in Ealing,' Ted reminded him sharply. 'She could have got someone to call us if she wasn't well enough to go out herself.'

'Course she could.' Hazel was revelling in the successful outcome of what she'd set up.

'Perhaps something happened to her in an air raid,' suggested Johnny.

'We haven't had any since she was last here.'

'They might have over her way.'

'Might have done, but I get the impression it's been pretty quiet all over.'

'It's obvious that she's just dumped him,' put in the scheming Hazel. 'The best thing to do is to just forget all about her and encourage young Alfie to do the same.'

'Don't you think you're being a bit harsh?' said the fair-minded Johnny.

'No, not at all,' she replied. 'The woman is obviously not to be trusted, so why waste a single scrap of mental energy thinking about her?'

'Because you might be wrong about her. I think the two of you should stop judging her until you know the facts,' said Johnny in a firm tone. 'Anything could have happened to her for all we know. There's a war on, remember. We don't get to know about every raid that happens outside our own neighbourhood.'

'Why are you so keen to defend her?' asked Hazel, annoyed by his attitude because her plan had worked so well apart from that. 'She means nothing to us.'

'I'm not keen to defend her especially,' he replied evenly. 'I don't like to think of anyone being found guilty without a trial, that's all. It just isn't fair.'

'Actions speak louder than words,' she came back at him. 'Or in her case, no action.'

'She does have a point, son,' put in Ted.

'I think we'd better drop the subject before we fall out over it,' suggested Johnny wisely. 'There are customers waiting to be served now anyway.'

'He's right, though, Hazel,' added Ted. 'We shouldn't be so quick to judge her. She could have a valid reason for not turning up.'

'Why can't you both face up to the fact that you

were wrong about her?' she said huffily. 'You've been fooled by her sweet-talking ways. But you're my employers, so I won't say another word about it.'

'Thank God for that.' Johnny looked towards one of the regulars, an elderly man who was standing waiting at the bar. 'Evening, Syd. How are you keeping?'

'Mustn't grumble.'

'What can I get for you?'

'A pint of brown ale, please, Johnny.'

'A pint coming up, mate. Right away.'

He took the man's glass and held it under the pump, pulling the handle slowly and making conversation with the customer at the same time. His mind wasn't on the job, though. It was a few miles down the road in another part of west London.

Chapter Seven

There was a party in progress at the Barton house and the evidence of it could be heard right down the street and beyond. But the family didn't expect any complaints. It was very much a live-and-let-live sort of a neighbourhood. Everybody was used to noise after dark anyway, and the sound of people enjoying themselves was far preferable to the horrendous din of the air raids. Just in case any offence was caused, however, the neighbours at close proximity had been invited to join in the fun.

There was quite a crowd packed into the small terraced house. As well as family friends and neighbours, Alan had invited Mary, to whom he'd been writing while he'd been away at camp. Although it was generally expected to be just a passing thing as the couple weren't of an age to settle down, the family were delighted that they were together because Mary was so unassuming and always a pleasure to have around. Joe was on duty at the AFS. Rose wondered if he'd engineered it to avoid seeing Alan and Mary together.

Stan was here because of his talents at the piano; at

least that was Joyce's excuse to the family for inviting him. Now that Rose was in the picture about Joyce's feelings for him, she was able to be more tolerant, though since her cousin had bared her soul, the subject had been wisely avoided by them both. It was far too emotionally charged for regular exposure to discussion. Rose guessed that things had progressed, though, because Joyce wasn't at home much outside of working hours lately and no explanation was given. But she maintained a diplomatic silence. If Joyce wanted to confide in her she would do so, but the initiative must be hers. Rose was especially cautious about that now.

At the moment they were taking a break from the sing-song for refreshments.

'Sandwich, anyone?' said Auntie Sybil, sailing into the room with a plateful. 'There's only a scraping of margarine and barely a taste of cheese, so you'll have to use your imagination about the filling; it's just something to keep you going.'

'Same thing with the cheese straws,' said May, following her sister into the room with a plate in her hands. 'They are definitely more straw than cheese.'

'It's very good of you to provide anything for us,' remarked Mary, 'rationing being as it is.'

There was a roar of hearty agreement.

'It's only a few bits and pieces,' May said. 'It isn't every day your son comes home on his first leave, is it? We couldn't let it pass without a party.'

'Letting our hair down is just what we need to help us forget about that weasel Hitler,' said Sybil.

They all agreed about that.

May walked over to the piano, where Stan was talking to Joyce and Rose. 'Take some of these before the gannets eat the lot,' she advised him. 'You deserve first pick as a thank you for providing us with the music.'

'Oh yeah, and what about our singing?' asked Joyce in a bantering tone. 'Doesn't that deserve a mention?'

'We can hear that any day of the week – and we do,' laughed her mother. 'But nobody can play the piano in this family, so Stan is the hero of the hour.'

'The piano is too complicated for me,' said Joyce. 'My voice is my instrument.'

'Ooh, hark at Miss Modesty,' teased Alan.

'And a lovely voice it is too,' said Stan, adding quickly to hide his adoration for Joyce, 'And that goes for you too, Rose. You're my two special songbirds.'

'Flattery will get you everywhere,' Rose joshed.

'What's this? Empty glasses at a Barton party,' said Sybil in a tone of mock horror. 'That will never do, wartime or not. Somebody is lacking in their duty and half of that somebody is my old man. He and Bill are supposed to be looking after the bar. They'll have found a quiet corner somewhere and are yapping, I expect.'

'It doesn't matter, Mum,' said Joyce, hoping to ward off one of her mother's tirades. 'One of us will do it.'

But Sybil wasn't that easily deterred when it came to her husband's shortcomings. 'Trust your father to leave everything to other people,' she went on. 'That's him all over. But I'll soon put a stop to his little game.' She handed the plate to her daughter. 'Pass the sandwiches round, please, luv, while I go and sort your father out. Flip . . . Flip,' she shouted in an authoritative tone and marched from the room.

'Give it about five seconds and he'll be in here reporting for duty,' said Joyce, and when Flip and Bill both came into the room asking if anyone wanted their glass filling, everybody burst out laughing.

Rose went to the kitchen to give the men a helping hand to serve the drinks from the meagre selection on offer: just a few bottles of beer they'd managed to obtain by paying over the odds, and some sherry they'd had left over from Christmas. When all the guests were taken care of, Rose poured herself a small glass of sherry before going to rejoin the party, which was back in full swing with a riotous version of the hokey-cokey.

She was in the hall, on her way from the kitchen to the sitting room, singing along with the others, when there was a knock at the front door. Smiling in anticipation of greeting a latecomer, she opened it.

'Johnny,' she said in astonishment, her hand flying to her throat. 'What are you doing here? Oh my God, is it Alfie? What on earth has happened?'

'As if you care,' he blurted out.

She stared at him. 'Of course I care. What on earth are you talking about? For goodness' sake, tell me what's happened to bring you here.' The door was only open a fraction because of the blackout. 'Come inside quickly before we have the air raid warden after us.'

'No thanks. I wouldn't want to gatecrash the party,' he said, obviously miffed about something.

'It's only a bit of a do because my brother's home for the weekend,' she explained, because his attitude made her feel compelled to do so. 'Please come inside and tell me what the matter is.'

'You're clearly having a good time so I'll leave you to have your fun,' he said with implied criticism.

'Johnny . . .'

But she was speaking to his back as he marched up the path in the dim light.

Grabbing her coat from the hall stand, she went after him, glad of the light from the half-moon to help her see her way. She caught him up at the end of the street.

'Hey,' she said, grabbing him forcefully by the arm. 'What's this all about?'

He shrugged away from her.

'I'm not having it, Johnny,' she stated categorically. 'You turn up at my door with a face like thunder and make snide comments for some reason best known to yourself. The least you can do is to tell me what I've done to upset you.'

'If you must know, I came to find out if you're all right, and as you are obviously very much more than all right, I'll be on my way,' he said coolly. 'I shouldn't have wasted a minute of my time worrying about you.'

'You've been worrying about me? Why on earth would you do that?'

'Because I mistook you for someone who cares,' he ground out. 'But I got you all wrong apparently. I thought you really cared about Alfie.'

'I do, of course I do.'

'That's why you've broken his heart, is it?'

'Oh . . . oh, I see.' The reason he was angry now hit her with a bolt of compunction. She'd felt terrible about not going to see Alfie and had had to force herself to stay away, telling herself repeatedly that it was for the boy's own good. 'He's taken it badly then, has he?'

'Of course he's taken it badly. What do you expect when you let him down like that; just don't turn up after you promised faithfully you'd continue coming to see him.' He looked at her and she could just make out his fury in the dim light, his countenance set in a grim expression. 'I know I'm late coming into my son's life, but now that I am in it, I'll defend him to the ends of the earth, and I won't have people hurting him. If you were a bloke I'd knock your block off. As I can't do that, just get out of my way.'

'Oi,' she came back at him stormily. 'As you've come here throwing your weight about, the very least you can do is listen to my side of the story.'

'The facts speak for themselves,' he snapped. 'You didn't bother to come and see him as you promised. End of story. You're obviously not ill or anything, and to think that I was worried about you.'

'I didn't come to see him because I thought I was unsettling him by continuing to visit.' She was shouting now. 'I did it for him. I didn't stay away because I just didn't bother. That isn't my way. I did it because I thought it would be best in the long run, for all of you. I believed it would be easier for him to bond with you and his grandfather if I was out of the picture, reminding him of the past and renewing his hankering to come back here to live with us. I've been as upset about it as he has, believe me. Keeping away has been one of the hardest things I've ever had to do. I forced myself to do it with his best interests at heart.'

Johnny didn't respond immediately. When he finally spoke, his manner was much more subdued. 'Oh, I see. But what on earth put an idea like that into your head?'

She could have told him the truth; that it had been Hazel. But Hazel had only made the suggestion. Rose had given the matter thought and made up her own mind about it. She wasn't so pathetic she couldn't make her own decisions.

'Just common sense, I suppose,' she replied. 'I knew he'd be hurt at first but I thought it would be the best thing for him in the long run.'

'And it never occurred to you to mention your theory to any of us at the pub; to get our opinion on the matter?'

'It seemed best to just disappear,' she explained. 'I knew that if I told Alfie he would beg me to change my mind and I would give in to him because I love him so much. I've been through hell knowing how hurt he would be, but I had to do what I thought was the right thing for him.' She paused. 'I adore that kid and I've missed him terribly. It's been awful.'

Johnny was silent for a moment. 'I don't agree with this new theory of yours,' he said. 'I don't think it is the best thing for him. In fact, it couldn't be more wrong.'

'Oh, come on,' she said. 'He hasn't exactly warmed to you, has he? Your father told me how cold he is towards you. So I'd have thought you'd be glad to see the back of me as a rival for his affections.'

'You? A rival?' He seemed astonished at the suggestion. 'That's the last thing I would ever think about you.'

'Really?'

'Yes, really,' he confirmed in a definite tone. 'I see you as valuable support; some extra stability in the boy's life; a friend and comforter for him.'

'Oh . . . oh, that's nice. If I tried to define it, I think that would be the role I had in mind for myself.' Rose pondered on the matter. 'But surely you can see that there is another way of looking at it. I really did think it would make it easier for all of you.'

He thought about it for a moment. 'Yeah, I can see why you might think that,' he admitted. 'But in this case, I don't think you're right. We all want you to continue to visit.'

'In that case I'm sorry to have caused you any trouble. And I'm even sorrier for hurting Alfie,' she said with sincerity. 'I genuinely believed I was doing the right thing. But you're his father and you make the rules. If you believe it would be right for my friendship with him to continue, then it will.'

'Who knows what is right or wrong in a situation like this? Certainly not me; I'm a complete novice as regards this sort of thing and have only my instincts to go on. I suppose it varies with each individual case anyway. But yes, I would like you to start coming to see him again. I really will feel so much easier in my mind, going back to camp, if I know that you're around as a bit of back-up for Dad.'

'In that case I'll be there.'

Johnny cleared his throat. 'Look . . . I'm sorry I had a go at you,' he apologised. 'I was bang out of order. I should have given you a chance to explain.'

'Yes, you should, so I won't argue with you about that.'

'I'm probably a bit overprotective towards Alfie, having come into his life at such a late stage,' he suggested.

She nodded.

'I was concerned about you too, though,' he added. 'I don't know you well but you didn't strike me as the sort of person to break a promise without good reason, so I thought you must have been ill, or worse. You never know what awful things are happening to people these days with all the bombs about, so I came tearing over here.' He shrugged. 'Then, when you opened the door laughing all over your face, I just saw red after being so worried.'

'Yeah, I can understand how it must have seemed to you,' she assured him. 'It really is just a bit of a knees-up for my brother. Why not come back and say hello to everyone?'

'Thanks, but I have to get back to the pub. I promised Dad and Hazel that I wouldn't be long.' He shook his head in a gesture of self-deprecation. 'I just walked out and left them to it without even saying where I was going, which wasn't at all fair. But they'd told me how you'd stopped coming and how upset Alfie was. I couldn't get it out of my mind. I just had to find out what had happened.'

'You'd better get back then.'

'Can I tell Alfie you'll be coming to see him?'

'I'll be over tomorrow afternoon,' she replied.

'I'll look forward to seeing you,' he said. 'I'm not going back to camp until late afternoon this week, so I should still be there.'

'See you then. G'night.'

'G'night, Rose.'

Johnny headed off down the street, leaving Rose with a plethora of emotions. She still wasn't absolutely certain if it was the right thing to visit Alfie, but as his father had made the decision it was good enough for her. The altercation had left her feeling churned up but oddly excited too. She was still inwardly quivering from the incident when she got back to the party, where they were all belting out 'Knees Up Mother Brown'.

Winter was beginning to draw to a close, thought Rose the following afternoon as she sat on a bench on Shepherd's Bush Green watching Alfie kicking a ball about with his pals. There was a scattering of crocuses around a nearby tree, and the lush green shoots of daffodils and tulips were pushing up at random through the patchy grass. There was still quite a nip in the air, though, despite the pale sunlight that spread over the green and the bomb-damaged buildings around it.

Alfie's rapturous welcome had moved her to tears. She couldn't remember anyone being quite *that* pleased to see her before. When his pals had come to call, he'd so much wanted her to come to watch his football game, she couldn't refuse. So she'd pulled her muffler up closer around her throat, braced herself against the elements and come over here. Johnny had wandered over later and was sitting beside her.

'He was very pleased to see you, wasn't he?' he remarked now.

'I'll say. I thought he was going to squeeze the life out of me with his hug.'

'It was a treat to watch the two of you,' he told her. 'I never get greeted in that way.'

'You will, given time. It's still early days.'

'To tell you the truth, Rose, I don't know how to play it with him,' he confided. 'He isn't actually rude to me, not in so many words anyway. It might be easier if he was because I could give him a good trouncing and that would be that. But he's just cold and unresponsive. Never calls me Dad. Doesn't call me anything.'

'He's obviously feeling awkward.'

Johnny sighed. 'You can't make a child like you, can you?'

'You can have a damned good try.'

'Short of doing somersaults around the green to impress him, I don't know what to do.'

She laughed. 'All somersaults would do is have him cringing with embarrassment. I should think the best thing to do is carry on as you are, making an effort

189

without seeming too desperate about it, and let nature take its course. I'm sure you'll win him over in the end.'

'I do hope so.'

'Thank goodness spring is on the way,' she said with a swift change of subject to lift the mood. 'I can't wait for the light mornings. It will be heaven not having to fumble about in the dark when I'm out on my round.'

'How many more springs will we be at war, I wonder?' he said in pensive mood.

'That's the question on everyone's lips, I should think. Let's hope this will be the last,' she said, in her usual buoyant manner. 'Meanwhile, when do you have to go back to camp?'

'Fairly soon,' he told her. 'I'm waiting for Hazel to come back. She's gone home to Hammersmith for her dinner. She likes to walk down to the station with me to see me off. I've told her there's no need, but she seems to want to do it.'

'That's sweet.'

'I suppose it is really,' he said casually, though 'sweet' wasn't an adjective he normally associated with Hazel. Attractive and amusing, but not really sweet. 'Anyway, that's why I've come over to watch his nibs, because I won't be seeing him for a while.' He gave a wry grin. 'Not that he's in the least bit bothered, of course.'

'Just be happy that he's found some pals.'

'I am, really I am.'

'If he worshipped the ground you walked on, he'd still rather be with his friends than his dad for a lot of the time,' she pointed out. 'It's only natural for a boy of that age.'

'I know.' He turned and smiled at her, his blue eyes seeming to warm her right through. 'And I'm so glad he's got you. I know that you'll look out for him.'

'I'll do what I can.'

'It's a bit of a drag for you, coming over here, though, isn't it?' he said.

'No, not at all. It doesn't take long on the bus.'

'It's very much appreciated, you know; not only by him but by me too.'

The game seemed to be breaking up, and Alfie's friends were dispersing. When he came over, Rose praised his soccer skills and said it was time for her to go. Taking a good look around to make sure that his friends had gone and the coast was clear, he reached up and gave her a peck on the cheek, then walked off towards the pub, catching up with the other boys who lived in the nearby back streets.

'Thanks for everything, Rose,' said Johnny, looking down and smiling at her. 'I'm glad we got the misunderstanding sorted out last night.'

'Me too,' she said, looking up at him and meeting his gaze. 'I'll see you again soon, I hope.'

'I hope so too.'

Then they went their separate ways; he to the pub, she to the bus stop. Unfortunately, Hazel had been watching their innocent farewell from the window of an incoming bus and completely misinterpreted it.

★   ★   ★

Rose hadn't even got to the other side of the green when someone slapped a hand on her shoulder, causing her to turn.

'Hello, Hazel, how are you?' she said innocently, smiling at her.

'Don't ask me how I am,' roared the other woman. 'I'm not your friend, and the way you're carrying on, you and I are likely to become arch-enemies.'

'What on earth are you talking about?' Rose was completely nonplussed.

'We agreed that you would stay away from Alfie,' Hazel ranted, far too angry to choose her words. 'So why are you here?'

'It wasn't set in concrete, as I remember it,' said Rose, bewildered by Hazel's obvious fury. 'You merely suggested that it might not be a good idea for me to continue to visit Alfie, and I thought you might be right, so I stayed away.'

'So why are you here now?'

'Because Johnny has ideas of his own on the subject,' Rose explained. 'He thinks it will be good for Alfie for me to carry on seeing him. And as Johnny is the boy's father, what he says goes as far as I'm concerned. So you don't have to worry about Alfie any more.'

'I'm not worried about *him*,' Hazel declared, all pretence swept away by anger and the need to protect her plans for the future. 'I never was. As far as I'm concerned, all that kid is is a bloody nuisance.'

'So what was it all about then?' asked Rose, still a

little puzzled but beginning to be fearful for Alfie. 'Why did you suggest I keep away from him?'

'It's Johnny I want you to keep away from, you silly cow,' Hazel replied.

'But why would you want me to do that?' Rose enquired. 'Johnny is nothing to me. My only connection with him is Alfie.'

'Exactly! That's why I asked you to stop visiting the boy,' Hazel explained. 'You and Johnny are getting a little bit too matey for my liking.' She reached out her hand, placed it on Rose's chest and pushed her to emphasise her point. 'So keep away from us; stay right away.'

'I certainly will not,' asserted Rose, beginning to get the measure of the woman. 'Not from Alfie, anyway, and if my seeing him also involves seeing his father, that's just too bad.'

'You scheming bitch,' rasped Hazel. 'You don't have a man of your own so you go after someone else's.'

'I'm not after Johnny.'

'Ooh, not much. Women like you are after anything you can get hold of, regardless of who they belong to. You're just a frustrated widow looking for something you're not getting any more and a meal ticket for after the war.'

'How dare you . . .'

'Oh come on, don't tell me you've been so busy playing the do-gooding big sister to Alfie that you haven't noticed how gorgeous his father is.'

'Of course I've noticed, since there is nothing wrong with my eyesight.'

'I knew it, you bitch.'

Rose looked at her studiously. 'Why are you so insecure when you have the man's ring on your finger?' she enquired. 'Isn't that enough for you?'

'It doesn't pay to be too trusting,' Hazel announced. 'So keep away from here. Stay on your own manor.'

'I couldn't do that now even if I wanted to, because you've shown me what you're really like and how you feel about Alfie, so I'll have to keep a close eye on him to make sure you're not mistreating him.' She put her hand on Hazel's upper chest and pushed her in a reciprocal gesture. 'You harm a hair on that boy's head and you'll have me to deal with, and I can be every bit as tough as you if necessary.' She gave another little shove to prove it. 'Now get out of my way, I have a bus to catch.'

She turned and continued across the green, leaving Hazel gawping. If she'd expected a pushover in Rose she'd been sadly mistaken. Rose had surprised herself with her own forcefulness. She was uneasy, though, knowing how Hazel felt about Alfie. Johnny and Ted obviously had no idea. To tell them could be risky, because Hazel was Johnny's intended and well established in that family. She was also an extremely good actress, as she'd proved to Rose at their last meeting. The scheming way Hazel operated, they would believe her if she chose to tell them a pack of lies about Rose, and that could result in her being asked not to visit Alfie any more, despite Johnny's feelings on the subject now. She just couldn't take the chance.

*   *   *

Hazel was seething as she marched across the green towards the pub. Why was she beset with obstacles standing in the way of her future happiness with Johnny? First it was his mother; now she was threatened not only by a wretched child taking all his attention but by some cow of a woman who looked as though butter wouldn't melt but who was actually as hard as nails.

She needed to be rid of them both, and soon. It suddenly occurred to her that this could be done in one operation. If she got rid of Alfie, the woman would disappear too, because there would be no reason for her to come to the pub. All supposing she hadn't got her claws into Johnny by the time Hazel managed to bring her plan to fruition. Don't panic, she told herself. All that was needed was a definite strategy.

It came to her like a gift. Evacuation! That was the answer. All she had to do was convince Johnny that it would be in Alfie's best interests to send him away to the country on the government scheme, and all her problems would be over. It wasn't a permanent solution, of course, but it would do for now. By the time the kid came back, she might be Johnny's wife and, as such, would have a say in what happened to her stepson, and whether or not he lived with them.

But now she had arrived at the pub.

'There you are, Hazel. I wondered where you'd got to,' said Johnny, opening the residential door of the pub to her and leading her upstairs to the living room. 'What kept you?'

'Mum was a bit late with dinner because Dad overstayed his lunchtime session at the pub,' she lied. 'Sorry about that. I got here as soon as I could.'

'It doesn't matter,' he said amiably. 'It's just that I don't have much time before I have to go back to camp, and I wouldn't want to go without seeing you to say goodbye.'

'That's nice. You don't have to go just yet, surely?' she said, her manner becoming suggestive. 'You've got a little time before we need to go to the station, haven't you?'

'Well, not really,' he said.

'Oh come on, Johnny. Your dad always has a kip at this time and Alfie's outside in the back yard playing with his ball. So we've got this room to ourselves,' she said, leading him towards the sofa.

'I've been doing some thinking, Johnny,' she said later, as they walked to the station together.

'Ooh, that sounds as if it's going to cost me a few quid,' he joked.

'No, nothing like that,' she assured him. 'It's about young Alfie, actually.'

'Oh, that's good! I'm glad you're taking an interest.'

'You know me, Johnny. I always rise to the occasion, whatever it is.'

'So what's on your mind?'

'I'm a bit worried about him being here in London,' she explained, sounding deadly serious. 'I think it's far too dangerous for him here at the moment.'

'The raids have eased up a bit lately,' he reminded her.

'We haven't had so many, it's true. But we do still get them, and they are lethal when they come. I just don't think it's right to put his young life at risk.'

'So you think I should send him away?'

'Yes, I do,' she said, her voice full of feigned concern. 'I think it's up to us, as responsible adults, to do everything we possibly can to protect the children from the war.'

'I quite agree.'

'Oh.' This was proving to be a breeze, and she could hardly contain her joy. 'I mean, it isn't as if you're around to look after him, is it?'

'No. But Dad is.'

'Your dad's getting on a bit in years now, Johnny,' she reminded him.

'Give over. He isn't in his dotage yet; nowhere near.'

'Maybe not, but he isn't a young man, and he does have the pub to run,' she persisted. 'It's a lot for him to have to look after Alfie as well as that, without your mum by his side. It would be different if she was still around.'

'I've discussed it with Dad thoroughly and he's assured me that he thrives on it; in fact looking after Alfie is helping him though his grief,' Johnny told her. 'And it isn't as if the boy is a baby or a toddler needing constant attention.'

This was beginning to look less good for Hazel, but she daren't let her true feelings show. 'Mm, there is that. I was more concerned with Alfie's safety than whether or not your dad can cope. That was only a secondary thought. The government are urging people to send their children away.'

'I have given a lot of consideration to the idea of evacuation for him, as it happens,' he informed her.

Ah, that sounded more promising. 'Good, I'm glad, Johnny.' She tried not to sound too delighted. 'I know how hard it will be for you to send him away when you've only just found him. But it'll be in his best interests, believe me.'

'I'm not sending him away, Hazel,' he told her in an even tone. 'After what he's been through, he needs to be with his family. Emotionally, I don't think he can take any more upheaval. It just wouldn't be fair.'

'Children are very resilient, so they say,' she pointed out. 'And as a parent you have to do what is right for him even if it isn't what either of you want.'

'He isn't going, Hazel.' Johnny was adamant.

'Oh, I see,' she said sharply. 'And do you think that's fair to him?'

'I don't know, to be perfectly honest,' he told her. 'I'm not a child psychologist. I have only my gut instinct to go on, and that is telling me that it would be wrong to send him away.' He paused, looking at her shrewdly. 'So, as much as you want him out of the way, he's staying put.'

She hadn't been expecting that, and was ruffled for a moment. 'That isn't fair, Johnny. I don't want him out of the way,' she said, managing to sound suitably outraged. 'I've done what I can to help with the boy.'

He thought about this. From what he'd heard, she

didn't have much to do with his son when he himself was away at camp, but she always seemed kind to Alfie when he was around. There was something lacking in her attitude towards him though. She seemed stilted and ill at ease. Or was he comparing her with Rose, and the way she was with the boy? Just the thought of Rose and Alfie together gave him a warm feeling. But it wasn't fair to Hazel to make the comparison. Anyway, he wasn't in any position to criticise when he couldn't even strike up a rapport with Alfie himself.

'I'm sure you have, and I wasn't having a go at you,' he told her, and meant it. 'But on your own admission, you're not the maternal sort. So I understand how you might not feel comfortable with a child around. I'm not blaming you.'

'Thanks very much,' she said with withering sarcasm. 'I suggest something I genuinely believe would be right for the wellbeing of your son and I get accused of wanting him out of the way. All right, so I've never been particularly maternal. That's probably because I've never had a child.'

Rose didn't have any children of her own, but she was a natural with Alfie, thought Johnny. Maybe it wasn't anything to do with motherhood and everything to do with having a natural warmth and sensitivity towards people in general. But there he went again, comparing Hazel with Rose, which wasn't fair. Rose was taking up far too much space in his thoughts lately.

'Sorry if I've upset you, luv,' he said in a warmer tone, putting his arm around her.

'You'd better be.'

'I am. I know you do your best. It'll probably get easier with time, the same as it will for me,' he suggested, his conscience troubling him over his preoccupation with Rose. 'Let's face it; we're both raw beginners at bringing up kids. It's definitely a case of the blind leading the blind. But we'll learn.'

'Yeah, course we will,' she said.

In fact Hazel had no intention whatsoever of learning anything about looking after that wretched boy. She wasn't beaten just because the evacuation idea had failed. It was simply a question of finding another way to remove him from their lives.

Although diligent in her pursuit of Johnny, Hazel was rather less dedicated to her work when he wasn't around, as Rose discovered one Saturday afternoon when she was visiting Alfie.

'That's torn it,' muttered Ted, looking worried when he came into the living room after receiving a phone call. 'Now I'm really in the soup.'

'What's happened?' she asked.

'Hazel's just phoned in sick,' he grumbled, scratching his head and frowning. 'I'm already short-staffed because I've had a couple of my part-timers leave to go on to war work, and my potman's gone down with flu. So I'll be on my own down there on the busiest night of the week, dammit.'

'Perhaps Johnny will turn up and give you a hand,' she suggested.

'No. He definitely won't be home this weekend because he's on guard duty. He told us that last weekend.' He gave a wry grin. 'Hazel wouldn't stay away if there was the slightest chance of his being here, don't worry. I've got nothing against the girl personally, but she isn't one of the workers of this world.'

'She can't help being ill, Ted—'

'She no more ill than I am,' he cut in. 'She just fancies a night off. I know her tricks of old.' He shrugged. 'I'd have got rid of her long ago if it wasn't for the fact that she's engaged to Johnny and therefore almost family. Unfortunately she knows that and pushes her luck something awful. Anyway, you can't get the staff these days, with so many women being on war work, so I need her behind the bar.'

'Perhaps Rose will help you tonight,' Alfie piped up.

'Don't be daft, luv,' she said, grinning at him. 'I don't know one end of a beer pump from the other. I've never pulled a pint in my life.'

'You'd be able to do it,' said Alfie confidently. 'You can do anything.'

'Ooh, it's very flattering of you to say so, Alfie, but it isn't true, I'm afraid. I have my limitations.'

'Rose is probably busy this evening anyway,' said Ted.

'I'm not doing anything special, as it happens.'

Ted gave her an appealing look. 'Any chance of you doing a shift for me? Just this once to help me out of a jam?' he asked. 'I'll pay you more than the going rate. I'd be ever so grateful.'

She was extremely doubtful. 'I know nothing about bar work,' she said.

'Once I've shown you what to do, you'll pick it up in no time,' he encouraged. 'I'm not expecting you to be brilliant; just do the best you can and keep the customers happy.'

'Don't blame me if you get complaints from your customers because they've got more froth than beer, then.'

'I'll take you by the hand. You'll soon get the hang of it,' he assured her.

'May I use your phone to leave a message with a neighbour of ours down the street who is on the phone, to say that I'll be late home? Mum will worry if I don't.'

'Help yourself,' he said, looking relieved as he waved his hand towards the hall.

As Rose had predicted, there was no shortage of froth in the glasses at the beginning of her shift.

'Slowly does it,' instructed Ted, standing behind her while she pulled nervously on the pump. 'Hold the glass at an angle so that the beer goes in from the side, not the bottom. That's it.' He inspected the filled glass. 'Look at that; a definite improvement, not bad at all.'

The customers were very patient, and she did begin to improve after a while. What's more, she started to enjoy herself. Even the saucy banter from some of the male punters was quite fun, as long as it wasn't taken seriously.

'I told you you'd be good at it,' said Alfie, peering round the door from the hallway behind the bar. He'd come downstairs in his pyjamas to see how she was getting on.

'What are you doing out of bed, young man?' said Ted in a tone of light admonition. 'I'll cop it from your dad if he finds out you've been down here at this time.'

'It is Saturday, Grandad,' Alfie reminded him in a persuasive tone. 'There's no school tomorrow. Can I stay down here for a little while? Please?'

Ted didn't reply. He head was slightly bowed. 'All right. Five minutes then, and no longer,' he said gruffly. 'But don't make yourself too obvious or I could get into trouble with the law for having a child in the bar. And go back to bed when the time is up. Don't let me have to remind you, there's a good lad.'

'I won't,' he said, going back behind the doorway to watch from there.

Giving Ted a close look, Rose observed that he was on the verge of tears.

'What is it, Ted?' she asked worriedly. 'What's the matter?'

'Take no notice of me,' he said, wiping his eyes with the back of his hand. 'I'm just a daft old fool.' He dragged a handkerchief from his trouser pocket and blew his nose. 'It's just that, well, that's the first time Alfie's ever called me Grandad. He doesn't usually call me anything.'

'Aah, that's lovely. It just shows that you're getting somewhere with him.' Rose was delighted.

203

'Yeah, I think perhaps I might be.' He leaned back and squinted along the bar, where there was a view of the counter in the public bar. 'Will you be all right here for a minute? There are people waiting to be served in the public bar. I won't be long.'

'I'll be fine.'

He went off and Rose looked after things in the saloon bar. Ted had told her earlier that he thought it would be too rowdy for her to serve in the public bar as she was new to the trade. The crowd in there was almost entirely male, and they didn't watch their language as there weren't any women around, whereas the saloon bar attracted more of a family crowd, and they were a friendly bunch. When her hands finally stopped trembling, and she managed to pull a half-decent pint, she felt very much at home here.

Later on, having noticed a piano closed and silent in the corner, she said to Ted, 'A spot of music wouldn't go amiss in here, even if no one can hear it above the noise. A piano playing in the background would make the atmosphere complete on a Saturday night.'

'I agree with you,' he said. 'But I can't get anyone to play it. Our regular pianist got called up, and I haven't found anyone to replace him yet. There just aren't the people about these days; so many of them are away.'

'Well, I can't promise to get you a regular pianist, but I can offer you a musical evening on a one-off basis for charity,' she said, and went on to explain to him about the musical act she was part of. 'I'd have to check with the others, of course, but I'm sure they'd be more than happy to do it one night. Any money that you pay us will go to charity. How do you feel about that?'

'That sounds smashing, luv,' he enthused. 'Get it organised as soon as you like.'

'Will do.' Seeing a movement out of the corner of her eye, Rose said, 'In the meantime, shall I go and settle your grandson into bed? He's come downstairs again.'

'That would be a great help,' said Ted. 'The little monkey. Tell him I'll be up there to read the riot act to him myself if he comes down again.'

'I'll tell him.'

'You're going to be in real trouble with your grandad if you don't settle down and go to sleep now, Alfie,' she told him. 'You don't want to upset him, do you?'

'I only wanted to see how you were getting on.'

'You've seen now, so you don't need to come down again,' she lectured. 'I won't be able to help out down there if I'm a bad influence on you.'

'I wish you were here all the time, Rose,' he said wistfully. 'I wouldn't keep coming downstairs then because I could see you the next day.'

'I can't work here all the time, luv,' she said.

'Why not? You're very good at it,' he said hopefully.

'It would be too far for me to travel every day,' she said. 'Anyway, I already have a job, remember, and you know how early I have to get up.'

'I wish you lived here.'

She smiled as she covered him up, his impish face

so small and sweet against the pillow. 'I think you're doing a bit too much wishing, young man.'

'It's only that one thing.'

'Well, it isn't going to happen, so forget it and go to sleep,' she said.

'Don't you like it here?'

'Yes, I like it. But I can't move in,' she said. 'I live with my family.'

'Yeah, yeah, I know,' he said with a sigh of resignation. 'But it feels so lovely when you're here. It feels like home.'

'That's very sweet of you to say so, Alfie,' said Rose, emotions aroused unbearably. 'But now settle down and no more going downstairs tonight.'

He yawned. 'All right, Rose,' he said sleepily.

'Good boy.'

She kissed him lightly on the brow. Saturday was bath night, and the clean smell of carbolic soap emanated from him in a sweet, homely cloud.

Making her way downstairs, she found herself mulling over what Alfie had just said. It was the strangest thing, but her feelings were in tune with his. She was very much at home here at the pub and felt inextricably linked with the Beech family. Yet her only connection was Alfie. It was odd.

Chapter Eight

The saloon bar of the Green Cat was packed to the doors and brimming with conviviality as the musical trio brought their show to a close by inviting everyone to join in with them for 'The White Cliffs of Dover'.

Observing the scene from behind the bar, Johnny thought he had rarely seen the place more vibrant. It was such a joy to see his punters – people for whom bombing, shortages and hardship had become a way of life – brought together in song, and all because three people had taken the time and the trouble, for no personal gain, to provide them with an evening of heart-warming entertainment.

He was impressed by all three performers but particularly taken with Rose. One of a growing number of young war widows, she hid her grief almost completely. To a discerning and interested eye like his own, sadness could be seen lurking beneath the surface in those big dark eyes. But it wasn't easy to spot because of her outwardly cheerful persona.

While most people were still sleeping, she was out

delivering the mail; she handled Alfie as though born to it; and she still found time to go out singing for charity, looking lovely in a white blouse and black skirt, her hair worn in a loose pageboy. She exuded heart and vitality. There was an inner strength about her somehow, and he knew instinctively that he could trust her completely.

'Getting a good eyeful, are you?' asked Hazel accusingly, breaking into his thoughts. 'Perhaps you'd like some binoculars to get a closer look.'

'They're very good entertainers, aren't they?' he said innocently, ignoring her insinuation. 'They've certainly put new life into this place tonight. It's positively buzzing.'

'If you're getting ideas about that Rose woman, you can forget it,' she blurted out, unable to restrain herself. 'Because you're engaged to me, remember.'

'I don't need reminding, thank you, Hazel,' he said edgily.

'You haven't taken your eyes off her all night.'

'Honestly, you don't half exaggerate.'

'I've seen you doing it, Johnny, so there's no point in denying it.'

'Oh come on, luv, you know how it works,' he said, trying to be patient. 'Men look at women; women look at men. It's a fact of life and what nature intended. It doesn't mean anything is going to come of it. Anyway, I'm not ogling her or anything. I've been watching the show, which just happens to entail looking in her direction.'

'I suppose I'll have to take your word for it,' Hazel

muttered disagreeably, 'but you do seem to be getting rather friendly with her.'

'She's very good to my son, so of course I treat her in a friendly manner,' he informed her. 'But we don't have an actual friendship as such. In fact I hardly know the woman. I only see her when she comes to see Alfie and I'm not here very often.'

'She's trying to worm her way in here,' Hazel stated. 'She even worked a shift here when I was off sick.'

'Only to help Dad out because you let him down at the last minute,' Johnny reminded her. 'He told me about it.'

'I couldn't help being too ill to come to work.'

'No, of course you couldn't. But it did leave Dad in urgent need of help. I think it was very good of her to step in without any prior notice,' he said, irritated by Hazel's increasing possessiveness towards him. 'I expect there were other things she'd rather have been doing than serving behind a bar. Anyway, why would she want to worm her way in, as you put it?'

His impatience didn't escape Hazel's notice, and she knew she must control her tongue or she might begin to seem too clingy. Men hated that in a woman.

'She seems a bit pushy, that's all,' she said, wisely changing her attitude. 'But I'm probably just imagining things. I suppose I ought to be grateful to her for replacing me when I was off sick.'

'You don't have to go that far,' said Johnny, turning and grinning at her. 'Just stop accusing me of being after her.'

'I'm sorry, Johnny,' she said, taking his hand and squeezing it. 'I trust you. Course I do.'

'That's my girl.' He hoped that he never betrayed her trust. Johnny was no angel, but he was fiercely loyal, and definitely a one-woman man.

But now there was a roar of applause as the song came to an end. He clapped and cheered along with the others.

'I'm going over to thank them now, and to pay the bill,' he told Hazel, going to the till and taking out some money.

'I thought they gave their services for nothing.'

'They do; their fee will be given to a charity of their choice,' he explained. 'The pianist deals with that side of it, apparently. I won't be a minute.'

'I hope you won't be long, because there'll be a rush for the bar before last orders.'

'I'm sure that you and Dad can cope,' he said evenly, and made his way across the crowded bar to the piano.

Rose always felt elated after a performance and was positively glowing when Johnny came over.

'You were marvellous,' he said, addressing all three of them. 'Absolutely wonderful! You've given this place a real boost, I can tell you.' He handed Stan some money. 'You'd be worth it at three times the price.'

'We don't want to rob you, even if it is all in a good cause,' smiled Stan.

'We'd love you to come again, if you can fit us in sometime in your busy schedule,' Johnny told him.

'We'll fix something up some time soon, eh, girls?' said Stan, looking pleased with himself.

The cousins responded with enthusiasm, then Joyce and Stan drifted into conversation, as they so often did. It was almost as though they'd forgotten that anyone else was there.

'Has Alfie gone to bed now?' Rose asked Johnny, finding herself alone with him, in a manner of speaking.

'Yeah.'

'I know you let him stay up past his usual bedtime because I saw him tucked away in a corner watching us earlier on. He's got you organised, has he?'

'Not completely,' he smiled, taking it in good part. 'I only let him watch the first part of the show.'

'He told me he was hoping to stay up to see us, so I guessed that he'd get to work on you. He can be very persuasive when he wants something.'

'You're telling me. But I only gave in because you were part of the entertainment and I know how much he would have hated to miss it,' he explained. 'I think I would have been stricter otherwise. I'm not very keen on his being down here in the bar too often of an evening. It isn't the healthiest sort of environment for a kid of his age.'

'I bet you used to sneak down here when you were a boy, didn't you?' Rose suggested to make conversation, as he showed no sign of moving away.

'Oh, all the time,' Johnny confessed with a grin. 'But that doesn't mean that I want the same for my son.'

'It doesn't seem to have done you any harm.'

'No, I suppose not,' he agreed amiably, 'except make me into a publican.'

'You're not looking too bad on it.'

'I enjoy pub life. It's the only job I've ever wanted to do and I grew up knowing that I would go into it eventually.' He pointed towards his uniform. 'I can't wait to get out of this lot for good, and back to where I belong.'

'You won't be the only one wanting that.'

'I know,' he said, becoming more serious. 'There are plenty worse off than I am. I saw mates blown to bits in action and I survived. That makes me feel guilty sometimes.'

'From what I've heard, you've no need to feel guilty. Far from it,' she said. 'Who lives and dies in this war is completely out of our hands.'

'It's hard to see your mates die, though,' he said sadly. 'It shakes you up. Young men with their lives ahead of them, gone just like that.'

'It must be awful, being in the thick of it.'

During this conversation something had been happening to Rose. It was as though all the grief and heartache was being lifted away, and she felt something she hadn't experienced in a very long time. Instinctively she was ashamed. It wasn't yet a year since she'd lost Ray. It didn't seem decent to feel the unmentionable for another man so soon, especially one who was already seriously involved.

She was recalled to the present by Joyce telling her that they ought to be going or they would miss the last bus.

'I'll leave you to it then,' said Johnny. 'And thanks again for cheering us all up. It was a belter of a show.'

As he made his way back to the bar, Rose found herself staring after him approvingly.

'Come on then, Rose,' urged Joyce. 'Get your coat on, girl, and let's get going. I don't fancy walking home.'

'I must just pop to the ladies' before we go, Joyce,' she said. 'Shan't be a minute.'

She had washed her hands and was trying, somewhat unsuccessfully, to dry them on the damp, threadbare towel when she heard someone come in. Immersed in thought, she paid little attention. That is until she was grabbed roughly from behind, dragged across the room and pushed against the wall. She was then pulled back and the process repeated with such force, her head throbbed.

'Hazel, what on earth's got into you?' she gasped, reeling from the shock.

'How many more times must I tell you to keep your hands off my bloke?' the other woman said through gritted teeth.

'Get off me,' Rose objected, trying to pull away and failing because she'd been taken unawares so was at a disadvantage. 'You're hurting me.'

'That's the general idea,' she was told. 'Perhaps a bit of pain will make you realise that I mean what I say when I tell you to stay away from this place.'

'Oh, stop getting your knickers in a twist, for goodness' sake, you silly woman,' snapped Rose. 'I have no intention of stealing your man.'

'Don't lie,' Hazel growled. 'I saw you making up to him just now; and don't you dare call me a silly woman.'

'What else do you expect when you act like one? And don't threaten me.' Rose was back in control and furious at this assault. 'How dare you attack me?'

'I'll do whatever it takes to keep you away from here.'

With a sudden burst of strength, Rose thrust herself forward and pushed the other woman away. Before Hazel had a chance to fight back, Rose turned the tables by grabbing her by the arms and pinning her against the wall.

'Let's get this straight once and for all, shall we, lady? I am *not* trying to steal your man,' she informed Hazel, putting her face close to hers. 'But I will not stop visiting this pub so long as Alfie is here. I've told you that before, and nothing has changed. So grow up and get used to it.'

'You bitch . . .'

'If you're so unsure of your man, maybe you shouldn't be with him,' Rose suggested.

'I *am* sure of him.'

'Then stop acting like a jealous schoolgirl with a crush. And don't give me any more trouble.' Rose tightened her grip. 'Now for the last time, I will be coming here again to visit Alfie whenever it suits me. If you don't like it, that's your problem. But if you lay a finger on me again, I shall make a formal complaint to the police.'

'You wouldn't dare.'

'Try me,' Rose challenged.

'I will.'

'You'll be sorry if you do,' she said. 'Now I have a bus to catch.' She released her grip on Hazel's arms, confident that the other woman wouldn't come at her again as she was still gawping at her in astonishment, having obviously mistaken a dainty build for a lack of strength and courage. 'Now, if you'll excuse me, I'll be on my way.'

With that she picked up the towel that had fallen to the floor in the rumpus, put it back on the hook and walked out.

'You seem a bit quiet, Rose,' remarked Joyce, on the bus on the way home. 'Is something wrong?'

For some reason Rose didn't want to talk about the scrap with Hazel, not even to Joyce. Fighting wasn't natural to her and she wasn't proud of it. She was also overly sensitive about the half-acknowledged sensations Johnny evoked in her which made Hazel's accusations seem less outlandish somehow, even though Rose had every intention of casting such notions out of her mind. There was the fact too that if no one else knew about the altercation, Johnny wouldn't get to hear about it. Hazel wasn't likely to tell him, and Rose certainly wasn't going to.

Hazel was Johnny's fiancée, and if he thought Rose was causing her problems he might tell her to keep away, despite what he had said previously. After all, she was nothing to him, and he was hardly likely to blame the woman he was engaged to. Rose just couldn't take the risk. Alfie seemed to be settling in at the pub now, but he still needed her, and she couldn't let him down.

'No, nothing's wrong,' she replied now. 'I'm probably a bit tired.'

'She's exhausted from the performance, aren't you, Rose?' said Stan, leaning round from the seat in front and winking at her. He had a talent for sensing when someone had something on their mind they'd rather not talk about.

'That must be what it is,' agreed Rose, giving him a grateful look.

'That's all right then,' said Joyce, satisfied with the explanation.

When they got off the bus, Joyce said she wasn't going straight home and was going to Stan's place for a while. Rose surmised that his people either didn't know that Joyce was engaged to someone else or were more broad-minded about such things than Joyce's parents, who were very fond of Bob and would be upset to know that she was seeing someone else.

But Rose didn't ask questions, criticise or judge. She merely walked the rest of the way home on her own.

Apart from the performance she put on for Johnny's benefit, Hazel hadn't had much to do with Alfie on a one-to-one basis since he'd been at the pub. Children gave her the screaming abdabs; she never knew what she was supposed to do with them or talk to them about. She usually managed to avoid being with Alfie on her own, which wasn't difficult, because when Johnny wasn't around she hardly ever went upstairs to the flat.

But since all her attempts to remove the boy and his hanger-on Rose had failed, she was now seeking an opportunity to get him on his own to set her latest plan in motion. Her chance came one spring Sunday morning on her way to work when she came across him on the green kicking a ball about on his own.

'Hello there, Alfie,' she said with feigned friendliness. 'You're all on your own today then?'

'My mates can't come out yet,' he explained. 'They'll be out later.'

'I've been meaning to have a little chat with you, as it happens,' she said, sitting down on a nearby bench and patting the space beside her for him to do the same. 'It'll help pass the time until your pals come.'

He was wary because she wasn't usually nice to him when his father wasn't around. But he sat down, staring at the ground and swinging his legs.

'So how are things going at the pub with your dad and grandad?' she asked.

He shrugged. 'All right,' he said.

'You're a very lucky boy.'

'Am I?'

'I'll say you are,' she said with emphasis. 'There aren't many men of your grandfather's age who would be willing to look after a child as well as run a busy pub.'

'Aren't there?' he said dully.

'No, there aren't,' she told him. 'To be perfectly honest, Alfie, it's too much for him.'

'Why does he do it then?' he asked simply.

'Because he's a good man,' she said with the air of one who cared. 'But he isn't a young man, and he gets very tired having to look after you.'

'I keep my room tidy like he's told me to, and make my own bed,' Alfie defended. 'I make the toast by the gas fire, and lay the table; things like that.'

'I'm sure you do everything you can to help,' she said in a syrupy tone. 'But you're just a little boy who still needs looking after. Having you around is too much for him. The truth is, Alfie, you're just a bloomin' nuisance around here.'

'Why did they make me come then?' he asked, his cheeks burning. 'I didn't ask to come here. I didn't even want to come. I liked it where I was with Rose and the others.'

'Your dad felt responsible for you so felt obliged to take you off their hands,' Hazel said cruelly. 'But he finds it difficult having you at the pub because he's away in the army and worried about his father having too much to do.'

Alfie just sat there watching his feet swing to and fro, saying nothing.

'There's no point in beating about the bush. You might as well know the whole truth. Your father didn't want to take you on but he felt he ought to show willing,' she went on, becoming more brutal with every word because it was imperative that Alfie be receptive to what she was leading up to. 'In actual fact, you're just a burden to him.'

'Oh.' He still didn't look up.

'So how do you feel about going away to school?' she asked.

He didn't reply at once. 'They're going to put me in a home, are they?' he asked at last, looking up at her, his face pale, lips trembling.

'No, not exactly,' she replied. 'But there are schools where you can live in. Boarding schools, they're called.'

'They're only for posh kids.'

'Not necessarily,' she said. 'Successful publicans sometimes send their children away to school to get them away from the pub environment as well as give them a good start in life. Your dad and grandad have a thriving business so they can afford to pay the fees.'

'Is that where they want to send me, boarding school?' Alfie asked, staring at his feet again.

'They are seriously considering it,' Hazel lied. 'They want you off their hands, and it would be better for you too. They have lovely sports fields and things like that at those places. The kids have terrific fun, all sleeping together in the dormitory. Pillow fights and midnight feasts. It'll be lovely for you.'

'I don't wanna go.'

'You ungrateful little sod. It's about time you stopped thinking so much about yourself,' she snapped, all pretence at friendliness eradicated by her need for his co-operation in this plan. 'Now listen to me. You mustn't tell them that you don't want to go. You must tell them that you think it would be good fun to go away to school. Make it seem like your idea so that they don't feel guilty about sending you. Tell them before they tell you. Make it easy for them.'

When he didn't reply, she took hold of his hand and bent his fingers back so hard, he cried out. She kept her body turned towards him to hide her actions from passers-by.

'Stop that noise or you'll get worse,' she said out of the side of her mouth.

Somehow he managed to stifle his cries, but his eyes were watering with the pain.

'Let me spell it out for you,' she went on. 'You're not wanted around here by any of us. They don't want you and neither do I, and the sooner you get used to it the better.' She was speaking to him with her mouth close to his ear. 'So stop being so selfish, and help your father and grandfather by telling them that you want to go away to school. Tell them that you've read about it in one of your storybooks and think it seems a good idea.' She paused, bending his fingers back again even harder. 'You *do not* tell them that I put you up to it. You don't tell them that we had this conversation.' She clutched his face with her free hand and turned it towards her, her eyes fixed on him. 'If you breathe a single word about any of it, something terrible will happen to your friend Rose, something really bad; worse than you can possibly imagine. I can promise you that. This conversation didn't happen. Do you understand?' Back went his fingers some more. 'Well now . . . what do you have to say about that?'

'All right, all right. I'll do what you want,' he agreed

in a tortured tone; it felt as though the bones in his fingers were going to snap.

'I should think so too.' Hazel released his hand. 'I'm going to work now. Just do as I say and everything will be all right. Boarding school will be fun. So just make sure you're grateful that you have folks who can afford it.'

She got up and swung off towards the pub, leaving Alfie sitting on the seat. His fingers were painful and he didn't feel very well; sort of sick and wobbly inside, as though he was having what his mum used to call a bilious attack. But he was hurting inside somewhere too, with the sort of pain that made him feel choked up and tearful. He mustn't cry; not here. If his pals got to hear about it, they'd take the mickey something awful.

It was just that he'd thought his dad and grandad really did want him, and to know that they didn't made him feel sick and achy inside. It wasn't as if they were a patch on his mum, or Rose. But he'd just begun to think that they weren't too bad, especially Grandad, when all the time they'd wanted rid of him.

Swallowing hard, he walked back to the pub with his head down and his ball under his arm. He went in through the back door and hurried upstairs to his room, his eyes burning with tears.

'I'm going downstairs to help your grandad open up,' said his father, poking his head around the door a few seconds later.

Alfie nodded, keeping his head down.

'I try to give a hand in the bar as much as I can when I'm home for the weekend,' he went on, as though his son needed an explanation, 'but you know where I am if you need me. All right, Alfie?'

'Yeah, fine,' he said, sitting on the edge of his bed.

Listening to his father's footsteps receding down the stairs, he suddenly knew what he must do. Wiping his eyes with the back of his hand, he went downstairs to the kitchen, pulled a chair up to the cupboard and reached for the jar in which his grandfather put money for something called odds-and-sods. He took out a sixpenny piece and put the jar back on the shelf. Then he crept down the stairs and slipped out of the back door. Tears were streaming down his cheeks as he walked across the green. He just couldn't stop them and was past caring if anyone saw him.

When Johnny went upstairs to the flat to check on Alfie and found that he wasn't there, or playing in the back yard, he assumed he must be over on the green and was annoyed with him for not telling them. It was one of the house rules that he asked them before he went out to play.

'The little devil,' said Ted when Johnny put him in the picture on his way out to look for Alfie. 'Still, boys will be boys. We all did that sort of thing.'

'Your dad's right,' put in Hazel, who was behind the bar serving a customer. 'You know what kids are like for mischief. Don't be too hard on him when you find him.'

Johnny's anger turned to fear when there was no

sign of Alfie on the green or in the street behind the pub where the local children often congregated.

'He won't have gone far,' his father tried to reassure him when Johnny came back to let them know. 'He'll be playing a bit further afield, I expect. Try some of the other streets.'

'Calm down, Johnny,' said Hazel, carefully concealing her fury with Alfie for causing this hoo-ha and making himself the centre of attention. 'He'll just be with some pals somewhere.'

Johnny was back half an hour later having scoured the streets. 'There's no sign of him anywhere,' he announced, ashen-faced and grim. 'Someone's gone off with him. One of those perverts has taken him.'

'Now you're just being overdramatic,' said Hazel, managing not to show that she was seething. 'He's a sensible boy. He won't go off with any stranger.'

'Don't go jumping to conclusions, son,' urged Ted, but he too was pale with worry.

'I'm going to call the police.'

'Perhaps that wouldn't be a bad idea,' said his dad, trying not to panic, 'just to be on the safe side.'

'Meanwhile we'll go out looking for him,' said one of the regulars. 'Come on, lads.'

Within minutes, the bar had emptied of its Sunday lunchtime male clientele as the search party headed out into the streets of Shepherd's Bush.

Johnny was no stranger to fear; he'd had it in spades when he was in action. But that was as nothing

223

compared to what he was feeling as he went to the telephone. It was much worse than being afraid for his own life. It wasn't just fear either; his guts were twisted with worry and anguish at the thought of some stranger's hands on his son. He could have murdered the boy by now. Such things did happen. You read about them in the papers. Consumed with a primal instinct to protect, he was frustrated because he was helpless.

He blamed himself entirely. He should have kept a closer eye on Alfie. But going out to play was part of a child's life. Johnny himself had spent his days as a boy playing in the streets around here and on the green.

His palms were sweaty and his hands were trembling as he dialled the number.

'Police, please,' he said to the voice at the other end. 'My boy's gone missing. I need them to find him — fast.'

It was Sunday afternoon and there was tension in the air in the Barton household as they waited to say their goodbyes to Alan, who was going back off embarkation leave prior to going overseas. May was trying not to cry, Sybil was sniffing into her handkerchief, Rose and Joyce were moist-eyed and struggling to stay composed, and Dad, Joe and Uncle Flip were staying true to their gender and keeping their emotions under wraps.

'Cor blimey, I'm not going to the gallows, you know,' Alan reminded them, coming into the room ready to go to the station, battledress buttoned and boots

224

polished. 'You'd think I was about to have my head chopped off to look at you lot.'

'You wouldn't like it if we were all jumping for joy, would you?' challenged Rose.

'No. But you don't have to turn the house into a flaming funeral parlour.'

'Sorry, son,' said May, managing to smile. 'It's only because we care about you.'

'Come here,' he said, taking his mother in his arms and hugging her. 'I'll be back before you know it, driving you mad with my wisecracks and piles of dirty washing.'

'Course he will,' said his father, in an awkward attempt at humour. 'We won't be left in peace and quiet for long.'

'Is Mary going to Paddington with you, to see you off?' enquired May.

'No fear,' he replied, full of bravado. 'I don't want all of that malarkey in public: women crying on the platform and waving handkerchiefs as the train pulls out of the station. We said our goodbyes in private last night. We don't need to go through it all again.'

'Is your big sister allowed to walk to the end of the road with you?' asked Rose, keeping her tone light. 'I was thinking of taking the dog out for a walk anyway.'

'All right then. As long as you don't start blubbing all over me,' he joshed, though it was clear to Rose that he wasn't quite as immune to emotion as he pretended.

'Carry on like this and we'll all be glad to see the back of you,' she said, laughing it off.

'Come on then, if you're coming.'

'I'll just get the dog's lead.' She looked down at Bruiser, who had heard the 'w' word and was quivering and woofing in anticipation. 'Come on then, you dozy hound.'

Rose waited at the gate while all the others gave her brother a heartfelt send-off, then he came swaggering out, kit bag on his back.

'Are you scared, Al?' asked Rose, the dog pulling at the lead as he sniffed around every little weed, wall and crevice. 'You wouldn't be human if you weren't.'

'Yeah, a bit, I suppose,' he admitted. 'But the job has to be done, so I'll get on and do it since I don't have a choice. There's no point in moaning about it. You know me, sis, I take things as they come. I'm lucky in that I've got a good bunch of mates. We're all in the same boat, so we cheer each other up and have a laugh and do our best to stay positive. My army mates are the best pals I've ever had.'

'That must help.'

'It does. It's a bit of an adventure in a way; going overseas,' he said thoughtfully. 'I probably wouldn't have got the chance to see anything of the world if it wasn't for the war. Though God knows which foreign bit of the world we're going to be seeing. They don't tell you anything.'

'I suppose in the interests of security they daren't,' she commented. 'Careless talk costs lives and all that.'

'Exactly. Anyway, not knowing makes it all the more exciting somehow.'

It was typical of her brother to find a positive angle to even the most daunting of tasks. When they reached the corner, she decided that it was time for a parting of the ways.

'Before you go, sis,' he began, a worried look coming into his eyes, 'Joe's been a bit offhand with me lately. Any idea why?'

'Probably just a touch of sibling rivalry,' she said, not wanting to worry him by enlarging on such a sensitive subject when he was about to go away to war. 'He'll get over it.'

'I hope so.'

'Anyway, I won't embarrass you by going right to the bus stop with you,' she said, moving on quickly. 'I'm heading for the park anyway. So I'll say goodbye here.'

'If you like.' He looked at her with affection and said hoarsely, 'Well, take care of yourself, sis, and look after the others for me, especially Mum.'

'I will, don't worry.'

He cleared his throat. 'Just when you've got used to having a bit more space around the place,' he said, 'I'll be back to get in your way.'

Emotions welled up and Rose could feel hot tears rushing into her eyes. 'Oh, bugger embarrassment and come here,' she said, wrapping her arms around him and smacking a kiss on his cheek. 'Ta-ta, Alan. Take care and come back soon. We'll all miss you and be thinking of you.'

He gave her a warm hug, bent down and patted the

dog's head, then went on his way, the metal tips on his army boots clicking against the paving stones and echoing into the quiet of a Sunday afternoon in a London suburb. Rose walked on with the dog, seeing everything through a blur of tears.

She had just managed to recover and was about to go into the park when she saw him: a small figure in short trousers and a dark jumper. It must be a trick of her imagination. It couldn't possibly be him; not around here. But he saw her and ran towards her.

'Alfie,' she cried, running to meet him. 'What in God's name are you doing here?'

If ever a family needed a diversion that afternoon, it was the Bartons. Alfie's arrival was the perfect antidote to the aftermath of Alan's departure.

'Poor little mite,' said May, back at the house, having been told that the bus conductor hadn't let Alfie on the bus because he was too young to travel alone, and he had walked all the way here. He had run away from home, he said, because his folks were going to send him away to boarding school. 'Fancy walking all that way on your own. It's a wonder your little legs got you here.'

'Your father and grandad will be worried sick about you,' said Rose. 'I'd better go to the phone box and let them know where you are.'

'Please don't do that.' The runaway was sitting on the floor, cuddling the dog. 'They'll come and get me and make me go away to school with all the posh kids. I came here because I thought I'd be safe.'

'As much as we'd like you to stay here, we can't keep you because we'd be breaking the law,' Rose reminded him.

'Please . . .'

'We've been through all this before, luv,' she said, feeling terrible. 'Anyway, are you absolutely certain that boarding school is what they have in mind for you? It doesn't seem like their kind of thing at all.'

'It's all planned,' he informed her. 'They want me out of the way.'

'Have they actually told you?'

'Well, no . . . but they are gonna do it.'

'How do you know?'

He didn't reply; just sat there looking shifty before burying his face in the dog's coat.

'Alfie . . .' Rose prompted him.

'I, er . . . overheard them talking about it,' he lied, because the consequences of telling the truth were too awful for him even to consider.

'You're sure you heard them right?'

'Yeah.'

'I'm sure there must be some mistake. It seems most unlikely to me,' said Rose.

'It's true,' said Alfie.

'Well, you stay there with the dog for a minute while Mum and I go and get you something to eat.'

He nodded.

In the kitchen, May said to Rose in a low voice, 'It seems a bit cruel, to send him away after all he's been through.'

'I can hardly believe they would do such a thing,' said Rose. 'They must have decided that it will be safer for him to go away.'

'A boarding school, though,' expressed May worriedly. 'They're very strict, those places, from what I've heard. Surely if they want him to go away it would have been better for him to go to a family in the country.'

'I suppose they think it'll give him a good start in life,' suggested Rose. 'And it probably will in that he'll learn nice manners and get a decent education. It's just the timing that's all wrong.'

'We need to let Johnny know where he is. The poor man's probably beside himself,' said May.

'I'll do it now.' Rose found some coppers and left the house en route for the telephone box.

'Boarding school!' exclaimed Johnny when Rose met him off the bus from Shepherd's Bush and they walked back to the house together. She'd only had time to give him the basic facts on the phone before the money had run out so had come to meet him with the idea of calming him down before he saw Alfie. 'What on earth has given him that daft idea?'

'You mean you're not sending him away?' she said, almost weak with relief.

'Of course I'm not sending him away,' he stated categorically. 'I wouldn't do a thing like that to him after all he's been through. Surely you must know that.'

'I was surprised when he said it, I must admit,' she told him. 'But he sounded so sure about it. He said he overheard you and your dad talking about it.'

'Whatever he heard, it wasn't that,' he assured her. 'That's the last thing we'd be discussing since it's never even entered our heads. The only reason I would send him away is if it got impossibly dangerous for him here. Then I would make sure he went to a good and caring family. I certainly wouldn't pack him off to boarding school at this young age.'

'It's a case of taking pot luck with evacuation, I think,' Rose said, 'unless you know someone who lives in the country and can send him privately. I've heard a few unsavoury tales about the people who take the evacuees in.'

'Me too. And that puts me off, as well as the fact that I don't want him disrupted again.'

'All's well that ends well. He's safe, that's the important thing,' she said chattily.

'I'll say,' Johnny said. 'Phew, what a day it's been. I've been tearing all over the Bush looking for him; me and the pub clientele, not to mention a substantial portion of the Metropolitan Police. That boy's going to get a real roasting, I can tell you.'

'I don't think he'll care how much you go on at him as long as he doesn't have to go away to school.'

He halted in his step and turned to her. 'He's still got you wrapped around his little finger then?' he said.

She nodded, smiling. 'I'm afraid so,' she confirmed.

'It's odd that he was so upset at the idea of being sent away,' he remarked. 'I mean, he doesn't seem exactly overjoyed to be living at the pub with us.'

'Perhaps he likes it more than he's showing,' Rose suggested. 'The idea of going to boarding school obviously frightened the life out of him.'

'That's no excuse for running off and giving us all such a scare,' Johnny said.

'Don't be too hard on him. It was a genuine misunderstanding. It was a long walk for little legs like his. He wouldn't have done it unless he was desperate.'

'He'd walk to the ends of the earth to get to you, I think,' he said.

'Yeah, I believe he would too, if he was in trouble,' she replied, affection for Alfie noticeable in her voice.

'Thanks for being so good to him, Rose. All this bother he puts you to.'

'No trouble,' she assured him. 'Seeing Alfie is always a pleasure, whatever the circumstances.'

She was so wonderfully warm, Johnny thought, seeing her eyes soften as she thought of his son. How grateful he was that Alfie had someone like her looking out for him after the loss of his mother. Johnny would like to know her better too. Through Alfie she'd become a part of his life, but he hardly knew her at all at a personal level.

But he knew he shouldn't harbour such thoughts so he just said, 'I'd better get a move on. I've got to go back to camp when I've taken his nibs home. I'll be on a charge if I'm late back.'

'Let's get our skates on then,' Rose suggested, quickening her step.

★   ★   ★

'Have you any idea the amount of worry and trouble you've caused?' said Johnny to Alfie on the way to the bus stop. Johnny hadn't wanted to upset the Bartons by reading the riot act to his son in front of them. But the boy had to learn that he couldn't just go running off every time he felt threatened. 'Not only have you shattered mine and your grandfather's nerves with the worry of wondering where you were, but you've disrupted the Bartons' afternoon too.'

'Sorry.'

'You will be if you ever do anything like that again, and that's a promise,' he made clear. 'You're lucky I haven't given you a good hiding.'

'I really did think you were going to send me away,' explained Alfie.

'And you got it all wrong, didn't you?' rebuked his father.

'Yeah.'

'So the next time you're earwigging and you hear something that worries you, you ask me or your grandad about it. Right? You do not – ever again – do what you did today.'

Alfie's past life had given him a strong survival instinct, and he sensed that he could get himself out of trouble if he were to tell the truth about how he had come by the idea that he was going to be sent away to boarding school. But the memory of Hazel's vicious warning about something happening to Rose if he breathed a word removed all temptation.

'I took this money from the jar for the bus fare,' he

said, digging into his pocket for the sixpence and handing it to his father.

'Oh Alfie,' said Johnny in a tone of strong admonition, 'you've been stealing, on top of everything else. What am I going to do with you?'

'I only borrowed it. I didn't know they wouldn't let me go on the bus.' He was very subdued. 'I was going to pay it back as soon as I could. And I've given it back now.'

'I should damn well hope so too. This is getting worse by the minute. As soon as we get home you're grounded until further notice,' said Johnny, astonishing himself with his authority. It was amazing how instinct guided you through this fatherhood thing. 'And I shall tell your grandfather not to let you go out except to school, until I say different.'

'Sorry,' the boy said again.

'You won't get round me by saying sorry; not like you get round Rose.'

'I wasn't trying to . . .'

'Well, don't even try because it won't work. You've met your match in me, boy.' They reached the bus stop and stood in the queue. 'What puzzles me,' said Johnny on impulse, 'is how you managed to walk that distance.'

'I didn't.'

His father looked down at him in a questioning manner. 'No?' he said, eyeing him shrewdly.

'No, I ran for quite a bit of the way.'

It was as much as Johnny could do to keep a straight face. He wouldn't dream of setting a bad example by telling Alfie, but he admired his spirit enormously. 'Same thing, son,' he said. 'Same thing.'

'You've managed to calm down at last, have you?' said Hazel to Johnny later as she walked to the tube station with him.

'Just about,' he told her. 'I wouldn't want to go through that too often.'

'I don't think any of us would.'

'It just never occurred to me that he would go all the way to Ealing.'

'It is quite a distance for a child of that age.'

'What I still can't understand is what put this boarding school idea into his head.'

She tensed. 'I thought you said he overheard you and your dad talking.'

'That was what he said, but he couldn't have done because such a thing has never even occurred to either of us,' he said. 'Boarding school just isn't a subject that ever comes up in our household.'

'So you think the boy is lying then, do you?' she enquired artfully.

'No, not really. I don't see any reason for him to make up a story like that.'

'Devilment,' she suggested. 'He fancied an adventure so went off just for the hell of it, and when he got caught he needed an excuse so came up with the boarding school idea.'

'I think it's more likely that he misheard something that was said.'

'In that case I should just accept that as the reason and put it behind you.' She didn't want too many questions asked on the subject for fear that the boy would give in under pressure and blurt out the truth. 'He's back home safe and sound, that's the important thing.'

'You're right,' Johnny agreed. 'No point in going over and over it again in my mind, especially as I'm not going to be around all the time. I'll just have to leave it to Dad.'

'I'll keep an eye on things while you're away, too,' Hazel assured him.

'Thanks, luv, I'd appreciate that.'

'No problem.'

'He's got some spunk, though, I'll say that much for him,' he said with unconcealed pride in his voice. 'He's no sissy; that's for sure.'

'It's just typical of a man to take that attitude.'

'You must admit, he was pretty impressive.'

'Maybe, but I hope you've made sure he realises that he can't go waltzing off like that whenever he feels like it,' she said. 'It wasn't so bad as you were around but it wouldn't be very nice for your dad to have to cope with something like that without you. He isn't a young man.'

'Alfie knows he mustn't do it again, don't worry,' he assured her.

'I hope you're right for all our sakes.'

So much for all her plans now, thought Hazel. She could cheerfully throttle the kid for going off like that instead of following her instructions. At one point she'd thought that his running away might work in her favour, in that Johnny could have taken the view that it would be better for them all if Alfie went away to school if he was going to cause so much trouble. Instead of that he saw the flaming kid as a hero. The whole thing had made him love the boy even more.

Putting the child at a safe distance from her life with Johnny was certainly proving to be a whole lot more difficult than Hazel had anticipated. She'd have to think of another plan now, because she couldn't give up.

Maybe she should change tack and make a friend of Alfie; or at least seem to, and work something out from there. It wouldn't be easy, seeing as she couldn't stand the sight of him, but it might be worth some more thought.

Chapter Nine

As a few hardy daffodils added a welcome splash of colour to the public parks, and pale spring sunshine illuminated the shabbiness of the bomb-damaged streets, Londoners were treated to some wonderfully silent, bomb-free nights which lifted their spirits, even though there were no illusions about it being a permanent situation.

Realising that she hadn't been to the West End for ages, Sybil suggested that the women of the family make the most of the respite from the air raids and have a Saturday afternoon outing. So the four of them – Sybil, May, Joyce and Rose – decided to go up to town to see a film; whichever one they could get in for, since the cinemas were always packed, especially at week-ends. Their first choice was *Gone With the Wind*, but the queue for that looked to be the longest in London, so they settled for an American musical called *Down Argentine Way*, starring Betty Grable and Carmen Miranda.

It didn't matter to Rose that the plot was somewhat

shallow, and the Technicolor exaggerated the colours so that all the pinks were the shade of strawberry blanc-mange, and all the reds like ripe tomatoes. This was a lavish extravaganza, and a welcome escape for the war-weary inhabitants of this island. There was quite enough reality on the streets outside; she could do without it when she went to the pictures.

She thought how daft Ray would have found the film, and smiled to herself. A Western or a murder mystery was more to his taste. On the heels of this thought came the sudden realisation that she could now think of him without wanting to cry. She could look back on the happy times and treasure the memories. Not so long ago she'd thought there could only ever be sadness ahead for her. Now she could take some pleasure in her own existence.

Alfie popped into her mind because she usually went to see him on a Saturday afternoon. She would go tomorrow instead, and had called the pub from the call box to let them know. It was probably about the time the ban was lifted on his going out, as a month had passed since the running-away incident. The whole thing had distressed Rose terribly, because she'd known how desperate he must have been to go off like that. What had given him the idea that he was going to be sent away to boarding school still hadn't been explained satisfactorily. But Rose had her suspicions . . .

For now, though, she was going to sit back and allow herself to be transported away by all the larger-than-life characters to a place where there was colour, music and romance.

Joe Barton and his AFS mates were having a game of football with an old tennis ball on the tarmac playground of a requisitioned school which was being used as an Auxiliary Fire Service sub-station. Joe had become quite nifty at footie since he'd been in the service because a kickabout passed the time when they weren't out on a shout.

'Take a shot at goal, Joe,' shouted one of the men of the watch as Joe dribbled the ball towards the two woolly jumpers that were serving as goalposts. 'Shoot, mate, shoot.'

Raucous cheers rang out as he kicked the ball through the middle.

At that point, the game was interrupted by a couple of soldiers in the street who were looking over the railings and let rip with a verbal attack.

'You gutless load of gits,' one of them taunted. 'Nice work if you can get it; being on three quid a week for doing bugger-all except playing about in the school yard.'

'We do our bit,' one of the firemen shouted back. 'When the bells go down we're out there. We can't fight a bleedin' fire if there ain't one there to fight.'

'You ought to be in the forces, like the rest of us,' shouted the soldier, 'not biding your time waiting for something to go up in flames.'

'You're a bit behind the times, aren't you, mate?'

yelled one of the older firemen. 'We auxiliaries have been in the thick of it since the beginning of the Blitz. We've saved lives and lost a lot of men, and our contribution has been recognised for fire-fighting and other dangerous rescue work. So clear off and leave us alone.'

But the soldier was undeterred. 'You're yella, the lot of yer,' he sniped. 'You only joined the AFS to get out of going in the army.'

'We're volunteers, mate. We do this in our spare time when we're not at work in our ordinary jobs,' the fireman reminded him. 'Anyway, if and when the army wants us, they'll let us know and we won't hang back. We don't need the likes of you mouthing off.'

The soldier replied to that by clucking and making chicken movements with his arms.

This was too much for one of the men, who rushed over to the railings in a fury and started to climb over. He was restrained by two of the senior officers, who told him not to rise to the bait, pointing out that the members of the AFS had proved their worth and no longer needed to defend themselves against people who were too ignorant to get their facts right before opening their mouths.

Joe agreed wholeheartedly. He'd seen courage of the highest order since he'd been in the service; men risking their lives to save others in the battle against fire, with ludicrously makeshift equipment. He had no idea if anyone did actually join this service to avoid the army, but doubted it, since the job carried plenty of danger.

Anyway, the government weren't fools. If they wanted you in the army, that's where you went.

Some of the auxiliary firemen were too old for military service. At the other end of the scale, Joe still had a few months to go until he was eligible but was planning on joining up rather than waiting to be called up. He'd fibbed about his age to get into the AFS, and they were so desperate for volunteers, they'd conveniently taken his word for it.

Being a part-time fireman kept him busy. When he wasn't at work at the aircraft factory, he was on duty here; nights and weekends. It left no time for anything else, which suited him, because he'd never had much of a social life, even less without Alan for moral support.

The AFS had taught him a great deal; he found the technical side of fire-fighting fascinating. There was so much more to it than just aiming a hosepipe at the flames. He'd found companionship in the service, too, and experienced the true meaning of team spirit.

Now the soldiers were moving away at last, muttering and mumbling aggressively. The football game petered out because dusk was falling, and the men went inside the heavily sandbagged school building where they lived while on duty. Joe wondered if this would be another quiet night or whether they would be called out.

'Well, I reckon that film did us all the world of good,' commented Sybil as they came out of the cinema and walked through Piccadilly Circus to the tube station in the dusk of early evening. There were plenty of people about, despite the blackout. They refused to be kept at home by the limitations of the war, and were queuing in large numbers outside the cinemas; others were just milling about. 'There's nothing like a spot of glamour to cheer you up.'

'It was well worth queuing for,' agreed May. 'All that lovely Technicolor is a real tonic.'

'I loved the sheer gaiety of it, and the bright lights and colour,' said Rose.

'Me too,' agreed Joyce, linking arms with Rose in a companionable manner. 'It doesn't half seem dark and dismal out here in comparison.'

'It wasn't so long ago that we could rely on the West End for bright lights and elegance,' Sybil mentioned as they paused by the ugly sandbagging covering the Eros pedestal and fountain, the statue having been evacuated to the safety of the country. 'Now look at the place. Even our lovely London statues have gone.'

'They'll be back,' said the ever-optimistic Rose as they carried on towards the station. 'One day soon, the lights will come on again and all the statues will be back where they belong and everything will be back to normal. Meanwhile let's enjoy the quiet nights while they last.'

'She's right,' said her mother.

'Ooh, I've been meaning to tell you,' began Sybil, remembering something, 'I'm going to the Labour Exchange on Monday to get a part-time job. No more talking about it. I'm doing it, I've decided.'

'Good for you,' said her sister. 'What's brought this on all of a sudden?'

'Well, Flip can't make a fuss about my going out to work now that the government are definitely making it compulsory for women to do a job outside the home,' she explained. 'So I think it's time I made myself useful.'

'The new law doesn't apply to women of your age, Mum,' Joyce pointed out. 'Not yet anyway. But I suppose they'll raise the age limit if the war goes on and on and they need more people.'

'Thanks very much,' Sybil said with feigned umbrage. 'I know I'm getting on a bit, but there's life in the old girl yet. I'm sure they'll find something worthwhile for me to do.'

'I didn't mean it that way,' Joyce said, laughing with the others. 'I meant that younger women will be the first to be called up.'

'I know what you meant, luv, and I was only pulling your leg,' her mother said. 'But seriously, this new employment act will mean that married women can get a job without their husbands making a great to-do about it because they feel threatened by their wives going out earning. We're all needed out there to help with the war effort.'

'You'll be the next one to register, Mum,' Rose suggested to May lightly.

'I have been seriously thinking about it, as it happens,' May informed her. 'I've no young children dependent on me now, so I think I ought to make some sort of an effort.'

At that moment, the quiet night they had been going

to make the most of was brought to a sudden end by the wail of the siren.

There was a general groan.

'We're heading for the right place, anyway,' said Rose in an effort to cheer things up.

'Us and the rest of the population by the look of it,' added Joyce as the West End crowds surged towards the underground station.

'I hope those men of ours will be all right at home,' said May worriedly.

'They'll be all right. There might not even be an air raid out our way,' suggested Rose, as they elbowed their way through the jostling masses to join the queue that was surging towards the escalator. It felt as though the entire London populace was in this station, trying to get down on to the platforms. Anxiety was palpable in the air, but there was no actual chaos, despite the general desperation to get below ground level.

'The bombing does vary from mile to mile,' added Sybil hopefully.

'I'll be glad to get home just the same, though,' fretted May. 'I hate it when the family is split up during an air raid, though it's difficult not to be these days with Alan abroad and Joe spending all his spare time on duty down at the sub-station. I hope to God the trains are running.'

'It's all my fault,' said Sybil. 'I shouldn't have suggested that we come up the West End. We always knew the air raids would start again at some time. Now we're caught out in one because of me.'

'Don't be daft, Auntie,' chided Rose gently. 'If we thought that way we'd never go anywhere and Hitler will have beaten us. Anyway, we all wanted to come.'

'She's right, Mum,' agreed Joyce. 'We've had a smashing time. It was a good idea.'

'Oh, that's all right then.' Sybil paused. 'I hope your father has the sense to go down the shelter without me there to see that he does.'

'I think he can manage to do that for himself,' laughed Joyce. 'He doesn't need you to hold his hand.'

'I'm not so sure about that,' she said, making a joke of it to hide her fear. 'He doesn't know his right foot from his left without me there to show him.'

'He and Bill will have each other for company, so that's one good thing,' put in May.

'Good thing, my eye,' grinned her sister. 'They've probably gone down the pub.'

'Not this early,' defended May.

'With us out of the way, who knows what mischief they'll get up to?' she said with the attitude many people adopted during a raid, which was to behave as though nothing untoward was happening around them.

The platform was heaving with people; many sheltering for the night, others waiting for a train, the air a pungent mixture of sweat, cigarette smoke, disinfectant and urine. Fortunately the tubes were still running, and when one finally rumbled in, Rose and the others were pushed through the doors by the crowd surging forward.

'Thank God we're on our way at last,' said Sybil as

they stood together, strap-hanging and wedged in by a solid block of people. 'We'll soon be home now.'

'There'll probably be nothing much happening over our way,' said Rose.

'I do hope you're right,' said her mother.

Rose was right, as it happened. They heard explosions and saw the sky lit up when the train first emerged from underground on to the overland section. But they left all that behind and all was quiet when they came out of Ealing Broadway station and walked down to the main road to catch the bus. Not for long, though. The miserable drone of the siren soon made itself heard.

There was a chorus of complaint.

'I don't think we'd better try to make it home,' suggested Rose.

'Nor do I. Let's make a run for it to the nearest public shelter, girls,' said Sybil. 'There must be one around here somewhere.'

Rose and Joyce were more familiar with this part of the town than their mothers because they worked around here, and they assured the older women that there was a shelter close by.

'It's so bloomin' hard to see where we're going, though,' said Rose, leading the way down one of the streets off the main road with the others following, hanging on to each other so they didn't get lost in the dark.

There were nine men besides Joe on the watch, and three women manning the telephones in the watch room. The men were playing cards when the air raid siren sounded, and it wasn't long before the fire alarm went. One of the telephone girls came out and gave them the details.

Since this was the Auxiliary Fire Service and not its superior big brother the London Fire Brigade, there was no shiny pole to slide down and no red fire engine to ride on with its bells clanging. For these men there were just commandeered taxis with ancient fire pumps tied to the back.

But amateurs or not, there was no lack of speed or enthusiasm in their response. Kitted out in rubber boots, tin hats and overalls with AFS printed in red on them, they trooped out to the taxis and sped through the dark streets towards the address they'd been given.

'Judging by the colour of the sky, they're dropping incendiary bombs by the hundred,' said the sub-officer. 'It looks as though the whole of London is in flames.'

'Let's hope they don't drop parachute mines as well,' said one of the men, referring to the latest enemy weapon: landmines the size of pillar boxes that were dropped from enemy planes by parachute and drifted down on the wind, exploding on impact on the surface with maximum blast effect. 'Two of those buggers can obliterate a whole street, so they say.'

Several houses were ablaze when they arrived at their destination. The pumps were quickly attached to the water hydrant in the road, and as soon as the water came through, the men started work, playing their hoses on the conflagration.

When the fire was under control and the order to go inside was given, Joe – armed with a hose, an axe and a spanner attached to his belt – walked into the smouldering building with his mate beside him; two dark figures disappearing into the smoke.

Rose and the others were still searching for the shelter, greatly hampered by the blackout, the air sharp with smoke under the fiery, orange-tinted sky. Then they heard the terrifying whistle of a descending bomb, its close proximity making death seem inevitable. Throwing herself on to her stomach on the ground, along with the others, every nerve in Rose's body was stretched to breaking point and her heart seemed to stop as she waited for her dreadful fate to be sealed. When the explosion came, it shook the ground beneath them but, astonishingly, she was still alive.

'Blimey. I thought my end had come that time,' muttered her mother next to her as they began to scramble to their feet. 'The sooner we get inside that shelter the better. Is it much further, Rose?'

'It's hard to say in the dark, but it's along here some-where, so it can't be far.'

'Come on, Mum,' urged Joyce, as her mother showed no sign of getting up. 'It's no good staying down there with bombs falling so close. We need some proper protection . . . Mum . . . Mum . . .'

'Auntie Sybil,' added Rose as flames could be seen rising behind a nearby building in great yellow tongues, 'Auntie, are you all right?'

When the lack of response indicated that she certainly was not all right, Rose and Joyce went down on their knees. In the light of her torch, Rose could see that her aunt wasn't lying on her front as she should have been. She had obviously been knocked over by the blast and was on her back with her eyes closed, face wet with blood.

'God almighty,' said Joyce with a sob in her voice. 'Mum, oh Mum.'

Managing to stay in control even though she was shaking all over, Rose felt for a pulse and, much to her relief, found one. It was weak, but at least her aunt was still alive.

'It's all right, Joyce. We haven't lost her. But we need help right away. You lot stay with her. I'll go and find someone or ring for an ambulance.'

Inside the burning house, the smoke was so dense Joe and his mate could hardly see a hand in front of them. The heat was intense too. There didn't seem to be anyone downstairs so they made their way up the stairs.

Coughing and wanting to be sick, his eyes streaming and throat feeling as though it had had a thorough going-over with a cheese grater, Joe peered through the fog and could just make out a woman slumped in the corner of one of the rooms with a baby in her arms.

His instinct was to open the window and let some of the smoke out, but he knew from his training that it was too risky. In a burning building in which the windows are closed, the temperature could reach a point where a sudden burst of oxygen would make the whole thing burst into flames.

Overwhelmed by the blistering heat, his chest as raw as razor blades, Joe continued onwards with his mate until they reached the two trapped people. The other man took the child from the mother, who was coughing and retching, and carried it swiftly out of the room. Forcing back the urge to vomit, Joe picked up the woman in the fireman's lift he'd been taught in training and carefully carried her out of the room, down the stairs and out into the welcome fresh air.

Gently handing her over to the medics, and knowing that both she and the baby were alive, gave him a great sense of satisfaction. He knew at that moment that he was right for this job. But there was a lot more work to be done before the night was out, he thought as he followed orders and started up a ladder on the outside of the building.

The look of complete devastation on her uncle's face when she told him that his wife had been injured and was in hospital was something Rose knew she would never forget. Auntie Sybil and Uncle Flip had always been like sparring partners rather than a happily married couple; a bit of a family joke because of their warlike behaviour. But looking into his eyes now, Rose saw utter devotion.

'It's all right, Unc,' she said reassuringly, taking his arm. 'She's regained consciousness now and we think she's going to be all right.'

Flip looked frozen with shock, his face ashen and his mouth set in a grim line.

'She's got some nasty cuts on her face from splintered glass when the explosion blew the windows out, and she banged her head when she was knocked down by the blast,' Rose went on. 'I didn't realise until afterwards, but she didn't get down as quickly as the rest of us when we heard the bomb and she was blown off her feet. But she'll be OK. Auntie's a survivor.'

They were at the Barton house, where her uncle and her father were. Rose had left the others at the hospital and had run all the way home through the air raid to her uncle.

'I'll go on my bike,' said Uncle Flip.

'I'll come with you,' said Rose.

'Me too,' said her father, taking his cycle clips off the mantelpiece.

As her uncle went next door to get his bike, and Rose and her father went outside to the garden to fetch theirs, the all-clear sounded.

'Thank you, God,' said Rose, raising her eyes towards the heavens.

Sybil was discharged from hospital a few days later. Medically speaking she was in good shape. Some splinters of glass had been removed from her face, and the cuts were healing up nicely; the bump on her head from where she'd hit the ground had proved to be only superficial, and the bruises were expected to take their natural course and disappear in time.

But the woman sitting in the armchair when Rose went next door to visit bore little resemblance to the Auntie Sybil she had always known. Physically she was the same, though a little thinner. But she was shaky and meek; seemed frail and a lot older than before the accident. It was difficult to get a word out of her, and that wasn't at all like her.

'Lovely to have her home, isn't it, Rose?' said Uncle Flip. 'She gave us all quite a scare.'

'I'll say.'

Rose expected some sort of rude retort from her aunt, but Sybil just gave a twitchy smile and nodded.

'Obviously not your time to go, Auntie,' said Rose cheerily. 'You're a survivor, and long may it remain.'

'That's right, dear,' Sybil said absently, almost as though she hadn't even been listening.

'I'll put the kettle on for a pot of tea,' said Joyce and departed to the kitchen.

'We'll soon have you back on your feet, love,' said Flip, sitting on the arm of his wife's chair with his arm around her shoulders. 'You'll be back to normal, bossing me around, in no time, so I'd better make the most of your being in a quiet mood while I can.'

That sort of comment was guaranteed to produce a scathing response from his wife.

But not this time.

'If you say so, dear,' she said with a weary sigh, sitting with her shoulders bent and her hands clasped together in her lap.

Even her voice sounded different, observed Rose; it

was weak and hesitant. Where was Sybil's raucous sense of humour and indomitable spirit? This was a woman who'd always spoken her mind without the slightest hesitation and had sailed through life like some great ocean liner, oozing with confidence and making her presence felt wherever she went. Normally she would never say one word when four dozen would do. Now it was as much as they could do to get one out of her.

'She's bound to be shaken up,' Rose said to Joyce later in the kitchen. 'Anyone would be. I mean, one minute she was walking home from the flicks; the next thing she knows she's in hospital with bandages all over her face.'

'On the other hand, having lived to tell the tale, it could have had the opposite effect and made her feel invincible,' suggested Joyce.

'There is that. Everyone reacts differently to these things, I suppose,' said Rose.

'She seems so timid and frightened,' Joyce went on with a sad shake of the head. 'Not like my mum at all.'

'She'll be back to her old self in a few days, I'm sure,' said Rose reassuringly.

'Yeah, course she will,' agreed Joyce, forcing a cheery tone. 'You can't keep my mother down for long.'

Sybil didn't snap out of it in the next few days. If anything, she sank even deeper into a world of her own.

'She doesn't want to go out of the house,' Joyce told Rose one morning over a cup of tea in the staff canteen after their first delivery. 'It isn't like her at all.'

'Mmm. Mum was saying that she has a hell of a job

persuading Sybil to go down the shops of a morning. She really doesn't want to go,' Rose told her cousin.

'I can do the shopping for her, but it isn't good for her to stay indoors all the time.'

'Exactly,' agreed Rose.

'She's always enjoyed their trips to the shops together of a morning,' Joyce went on. 'Off they go with their shopping bags, like a couple of soldiers going into battle, to get a good place in the queue.'

'They used to have a chat and a bit of a laugh with the people in the shops,' Rose mentioned. 'Now, apparently, they go straight there and back because Auntie Sybil is desperate to get home. She doesn't speak to a soul except Mum.'

'I can't understand it, because she knows the bombers aren't likely to come over at that time of the morning. So what is she so frightened of?'

'Everything, I think. Her nervous system has taken a battering,' suggested Rose.

'She was full of herself and determined to get a job before this happened.'

'Has she said any more about that?' asked Rose.

'Oh no, I reckon that's all gone by the board now,' replied Joyce. 'It's as much as she can do to get to the front gate, let alone to a place of work. She won't go out anywhere else apart from that quick trip to the shops in the morning. I suggested the pictures the other day and she nearly had a fit. She just sits about at home doing as little as she can get away with. All she wants to do is sit in the chair or go to bed.'

'She's usually such an energetic person,' said Rose. 'The accident must have really unnerved her.'

'Seems to have wrecked her nerves altogether. She's lifeless; it's as though all the energy's been knocked out of her,' said Joyce. 'She gives the house a lick and a promise these days, and you know how house-proud she usually is.'

'She and her sister both.'

'Do you know what the weirdest thing of all is?' asked Joyce. 'She doesn't seem to care what Dad does. I think if he told her he was carrying on with another woman she wouldn't turn a hair.'

'Blimey, she must be ill.'

Rose wasn't being serious, but Joyce picked up on it.

'I've been wondering if she should see a doctor, to tell you the truth,' she said. 'But I don't want to risk upsetting her by mentioning it. You know, seeing as there's nothing physically wrong with her. I was thinking perhaps he could give her a tonic to perk her up.'

'Good idea. But I should have a chat with your dad about it first,' suggested Rose. 'See what he thinks.'

Joyce nodded in agreement. 'He's wonderful with her, and has the patience of a saint.' She paused. 'I've never seen this side of his character before. He's so gentle with her. Never tells her to get off her arse and pull herself together.'

'I've noticed how sweet he is to her.'

'It's weird seeing him like this. I'm so used to their constant banter – Mum bossing him about, and him trying to outwit her – it seems funny the way they are now. Dad's become quite the pipe-and-slippers man when he's not on duty. And the oddest thing about it is that Mum couldn't care less if he's late home or goes to the pub or not. I much prefer the fiery couple they were before.'

'Me too. Auntie Sybil being so quiet doesn't seem natural. The two of them were always good for a spot of entertainment,' said Rose. 'Poor Auntie. Something awful must have happened to her when she got caught in that blast.'

'I'll see what Dad thinks about trying to persuade her to see the doctor,' said Joyce.

'I would.'

'Meanwhile, we've got the second post to get out,' said Joyce, finishing her tea. 'Come on, kid.'

Sybil listened to what her husband and daughter were saying to her as they finished their evening meal. 'Why on earth would I want to see the doctor when there's nothing wrong with me?' she wanted to know. 'That's just a waste of time and money.'

'We thought the doc might be able to give you a pick-me-up,' said Flip kindly.

Sybil shook her head. 'I don't need picking up,' she said curtly. 'I'm quite all right as I am, thank you very much.'

'But you don't seem to be enjoying life much, Mum,' suggested Joyce.

'Who is, these days?'

'You were until you had your accident.'

'Oh, I dunno about that,' she mumbled. 'Anyway, that was then and this is now. How can any of us enjoy so much as a second of our lives with the threat of bombs all around us day after day?'

Joyce and her father exchanged looks. It was like listening to a stranger.

'We have to get on and do the best we can, Mum, bombs or no bombs,' Joyce pointed out.

'I cook and clean for you,' said her mother defensively. 'What more do you want?'

'We want you to be like you used to be,' replied Joyce. 'We want you to be happy again.'

'I'm perfectly all right,' insisted Sybil. 'Now will you please finish your food so that I can wash the dishes; and for goodness' sake just leave me alone.'

'We're only trying to help, luv,' said Flip.

'If you want to help me, stop telling me to be cheerful,' she said, and she picked up the plate with her half-eaten meal on it and marched out to the kitchen.

Joyce and her father did as she asked and finished their food, since it was the last they'd get for a while. But neither of them had much of an appetite now.

In the kitchen, Sybil took her plate outside and scraped the food that was left into the pig bin. Then she sprinkled some soda crystals in the washing-up bowl and ran some water, which was heated by a temperamental geyser which obliged her today by doing its job. Her eyes were hot with tears as she rubbed the plates with the dishcloth. She had never felt so miserable in her life, hating herself for shutting her husband, daughter and sister out but not seeming able to do anything about it.

She felt isolated from them; alone and frightened of the new dark world she'd found herself plunged into when she'd woken up in that hospital bed. It was as though she had lost control of her moods. She could remember being happy, but it didn't seem possible to feel like that again.

The shame of not being able to pull herself together was awful. She was the luckiest woman alive; she'd been a hair's-breadth away from death and she'd come through it with nothing more than a few cuts and bruises. She had a family who cared about her. So she ought to be down on her knees thanking God for sparing her, and making the most of being alive. But there was grey mist over everything. It was as though she was living in a dark, empty space.

Tears began to flow. She dried her hands on a tea towel and wiped her eyes with a hanky, struggling to compose herself. If Flip or Joyce found her crying, they'd worry and fuss even more, and try to help her when they couldn't. Sybil didn't know what had happened to her to make her feel like this, but some sixth sense told her that the cure lay within herself. The problem was, she hardly had the strength to put the milk bottles out, let alone wrestle with something she didn't understand.

Joyce appeared with the plates, picked up the tea towel and began the drying-up.

'I'll do that, Joyce,' said Sybil, because she wanted to be on her own. 'I remember you saying that you're going out.'

Joyce could tell that her mother had been crying. She went up behind her and put her arms around her.

'Don't cry, Mum,' she said.

'I'm not,' Sybil said thickly.

'Whatever it is that's troubling you, you've got Dad and me to turn to.'

Sybil stiffened, not wanting to distress her daughter any further.

'How many more times must I tell you that I'm perfectly all right?' she assured her. 'Honestly, dear, I really am. I'd rather potter about out here on my own if you don't mind. You go and get your glad rags on.'

'Well, if you'd really rather do it yourself,' Joyce said, accepting that her mother wanted solitude.

'Yes, yes, you get off,' said Sybil, and, forcing an interest, added, 'Did you say that you're going to the pictures?'

'No. I'm just going to see a friend.'

The old Sybil would have wanted to know all the details. But now she just said, 'Have a nice time then.'

'Thanks, Mum.'

As soon as her daughter had gone, tears welled up again, and Sybil forced them back, because it was only a matter of time before Flip would appear in the kitchen wanting to know if she was all right. He'd become a

261

bit of a fusspot since the accident; it wasn't like him at all.

She wanted to sink into his arms and beg him to help her, but how could he when she didn't know herself what the matter was? The only thing she did know was that, somehow, she had to drag herself out of this trough for the sake of the people who loved her.

As Joyce left the house, she thought how shocked her mother would be if she were to learn the identity of the friend her daughter was going to see, and the nature of their relationship. It might jolt her out of the doldrums. On the other hand, it might just send her over the edge. Joyce wouldn't dare take the risk. Her mother was far too precious to her.

Chapter Ten

One evening a week or so later, Joyce went next door on the pretext of a clothes swap with her cousin for the show the trio had been invited to take part in on Saturday. It was being organised by an amateur group of performers to raise money for the growing number of bombed-out homeless in London, and was to take place in a church hall in the back streets near Ealing Broadway.

As soon as they were in Rose's bedroom with the door safely closed, Joyce said, 'I don't really want anything of yours to wear on Saturday. It was just code in front of your folks to get you on your own, because I need to talk to you.'

Rose perceived a kind of inner radiance about her cousin, despite her worried frown. 'No prizes for guessing the subject matter. It's bound to be about you and Stan,' she said with a wry grin.

'Naturally,' Joyce replied, sitting on the edge of Rose's bed while Rose sat on a wicker chair nearby. 'But it's primarily about Bob's part in it.'

'He doesn't have a part in it, does he?'

'Of course he does. He's always on my mind, making me feel guilty,' Joyce said. 'I've had a letter from him, and I really think I shall have to tell him the truth when I answer it.'

'Oh, Joyce!' Rose couldn't hide her concern. 'Wouldn't that be too cruel, with him being so far away from home and living under God knows what conditions?'

'It isn't the best way to break it off, I admit,' Joyce said, looking extremely sheepish, 'but is it worse than continuing to deceive him?'

'Inasmuch as what he doesn't know can't hurt him, yes, it is worse.' Rose paused, giving Joyce a look. 'There is, of course, another way around all this.'

'That isn't even an option,' Joyce declared. 'I'm not giving Stan up.'

'It would save a lot of pain, not only for Bob but for you and Stan too. Neither of you is the type to be able to ignore your conscience. I know what you're like, Joyce. You'll torment yourself in the years to come.'

'I am *not* giving him up, Rose.' Joyce was adamant. 'I've tried. We both have. It wouldn't be right for us to part, because we're meant for each other. We can't fight it. We don't want to fight it. We just want to be together. If it's selfish, then let it stand. We only get one life and I want to spend mine with Stan.' She studied her finger-nails and muttered almost to herself, 'The question is, do I write and tell Bob about it or not?'

'It might ease your conscience, but it won't do Bob any favours,' opined Rose. 'As far as I know, the general

264

advice is not to ditch a bloke by letter while he's away on active service; that's what the magazine agony aunts seem to think anyway. It's common sense, because news like that could upset a soldier's concentration as well as break his spirit and cost him his life. Surely it would be best to wait until he comes home?'

'How long is that going to be, though?' queried Joyce. 'It could be years the way the war is dragging on. There doesn't seem to be any sign of it ending.'

'It will eventually, of course. But I don't think even Mr Churchill knows when.'

'Exactly.'

'It's your life; it must be your decision,' said Rose. 'All I can do is offer you my opinion.'

'I know,' sighed Joyce. 'In my heart I know that you're right, but − even apart from the guilt of deceiving him − I don't want Bob hearing about it from someone else. One of his mates might think it's a good idea to drop him a line to let him know what's going on.'

'How can they? No one knows about it apart from me, and I'm not going to write and tell him.'

Joyce gave her an odd look. 'They will know soon, Rose, because Stan and I are getting married.' It came out all of a rush and she couldn't keep the excitement out of her voice. 'He's asked me and I've said yes.'

'Oh Joyce,' Rose blurted out, clamping her hand to her brow.

'It can't be that much of a shock, surely?' Joyce said, looking disappointed. 'Marriage is what people in love usually want to do, after all.'

'Not when they're engaged to someone else.'

'All right, don't rub it in. I feel bad enough about Bob as it is.' She threw Rose a dark look and heaved a sigh of irritation. 'There's no need to look at me as though I've just told you that I'm planning on murdering my parents or something. All I want to do is end a relationship. These things happen. It isn't a crime, you know.'

'Sorry, kid. I just feel so sorry for Bob, that's all,' Rose explained, recovering. 'I know you and Stan are smitten. I just didn't realise you would get married so soon.'

'What's the point of waiting when none of us know if we'll still be around from one day to the next? This is the biggest thing that's ever happened to me,' she said. 'That's why I feel I must tell Bob, even though the last thing I want to do is hurt him. I'm not in love with him any more, but I still care about him. But I care about Stan too, and I don't want our love to be hidden away like some sordid guilty secret. I want it out in the open. You've been married; you must know what it feels like. You want to tell the world.'

'Yeah, that's true.'

'Try and be a little bit pleased for me, Rose,' Joyce urged. 'It's what Stan and I want more than anything else in the world. I know Bob wouldn't want me stay engaged to him out of duty. He's far too nice for that.'

'Yes, he is.' Rose looked at her. 'So when are you planning on getting married, then?'

'As soon as we possibly can. We'll just have a register office wedding. No fuss or big preparations,' Joyce replied. 'Trouble is, I want it to be all open and above board. I don't want to get married without the family being there, but with Mum being so peculiar at the moment, I don't feel I can land this on her. She'll be upset, because she's very fond of Bob.' She made a face. 'If she can feel anything outside of her own miserable world, that is. So I'll have to wait until she shows some sign of improvement.'

'It'll probably be best.'

'I don't want to wait too long, though.' She looked at Rose accusingly. 'Oh, come on. Can't you try to look as though you're just the tiniest bit pleased for me?'

'I am pleased for you,' Rose said, getting up and giving her cousin a hug. 'I really hope it works out for you.'

'Thanks, Rose,' she said. 'It would spoil it for me if you turned against me.'

'I would never do that. It isn't my place to tell you how to live your life.'

Emotion drew tight in the air.

Joyce cleared her throat. 'I think I will see if I can find anything half decent in your wardrobe for Saturday after all,' she said to smooth over an awkward moment.

'Help yourself, kid.'

Together they went through the sparse selection of garments hanging up on the rail, the atmosphere between them reverting to normal.

*　　*　　*

It was Saturday evening and May and Bill were sitting in their living room with the dog at their feet and the wireless playing at low volume in the background. Bill was reading the newspaper; May was busy with her knitting, listening to a play on the wireless with half an ear.

'Quiet without the kids, isn't it?' she remarked.

'Very.'

'I don't know where the time goes,' she said wistfully. 'One minute they're under your feet and you're longing for some peace and quiet; the next they're grown up and gone and the silence isn't nearly as nice as you thought it would be.'

'They haven't left home, luv,' he pointed out, lowering his newspaper to look at her. 'Rose is out singing with Joyce, Joe's on duty down at the substation and Alan's away in the army. They'll all be back.'

'They'll all be flying the nest soon, though. It's only natural now that they're grown up,' she said, sighing heavily. 'So this is what it will always be like; just you and me – a proper old Darby and Joan.'

'They'll still be back and forth from here even when they're married with kiddies of their own,' he told her. 'They won't leave us in peace for long, you can bet your sweet life on it. They'll always look on this as their family home; somewhere they can come and go as they please knowing they'll be welcome, no matter how old they are. You've done a really good job, luv. You've built a strong family base for them.'

'We have; the two of us,' she corrected. 'I haven't done it on my own.'

'I've just provided the back-up,' he said. 'You've always been at the centre of things.'

'The mother of the family usually is. But you and I have made a good team.' She looked at him fondly. 'Any regrets?'

'Not likely.'

'Me neither,' she was quick to assure. 'Apart from the one sadness we've both had to live with all these years, I wouldn't change a thing.'

'I'm glad.'

May rested her knitting on her lap, her brow furrowing. 'I'm blowed if I know what to do about that sister of mine, though,' she confessed. 'It's awful the way she is. It's tearing me apart to see her like it.'

Bill frowned. 'Is there no sign of improvement at all?'

'Not a flicker. She's in a world of her own and there's no shifting her. I miss her, Bill, I really do. We've always been friends as well as sisters, and it's as though she isn't there any more. I feel as though I've lost my best mate. Even when we're together, she isn't really with me; she's just going through the motions. We never used to stop talking; now we hardly say a word,' she added sadly. 'She's lost interest in everything. And that isn't Sybil. She always wanted to know every last detail about what was going on; some might even have said she was nosy. I'd give anything to have her back to her old self.'

'I must admit, I miss her coming in and out of here, larking around and bossing her old man around.'

'She could be a bit overpowering at times, but she has a good heart. I much prefer her being too full of herself to the way she is now, a strange, frightened little woman.'

'Perhaps she'll come out of it in her own good time,' Bill suggested reassuringly. 'She's probably still suffering from shock. It affects people in different ways.'

'I've tried everything I know to perk her up,' May went on. 'I've been kind, I've been firm. I've tried to appeal to her sense of humour and begged her to cheer up. But she either bursts into tears or says nothing. I tell you, Bill, although I feel sorry for her because I know she can't help it, it's really beginning to get me down. I don't know what to do to help her.'

'It's wearing Flip down too, I think,' mentioned Bill. 'The poor bloke is worried sick about her. It's so depressing for him with her mooning about the house all the time, hardly saying a word. He must get fed up with it.'

'I don't suppose it's any picnic for Joyce either, having her mother creeping about the place like a zombie.'

'Still, at least Joyce has Rose to turn to for company while Bob is away,' Bill pointed out.

'That's something I'm always thankful for; the fact that those two are so close. I'll forever be grateful to Sybil and Flip for coming to west London. They didn't judge or make a fuss. They just arrived. The girls have been able to grow up together and I've had my sister's friendship for all these years. I so want her to get better.'

The conversation came to a halt as the dog became

restless suddenly, a low rumble in the back of his throat turning into a full-voiced bark that heralded the wail of the siren.

'His sixth sense has been at work again,' said May, because Bruiser often seemed able to anticipate an air raid before the official warning came.

'Come on, boy, let's go down the shelter,' said Bill, picking him up and carrying him while May got the coats and blankets.

As they felt their way across the garden in the dark, May said, 'I hope to God that Rose and Joe will be all right. I hate it when they're out during a raid.'

'I was just thinking the same thing myself,' said Bill affectionately.

May wasn't surprised, because she and Bill were usually of one mind, especially when it came to their family.

The trio were in the middle of 'Over the Rainbow' when the siren went. Panic swept through the audience. There were screams and a frantic rush for the exits while the songsters warbled on until there was no one listening at all.

They had just left the stage when there was an ear-splitting crash and the building seemed to crumble at one end. In all the noise and confusion, initially Rose couldn't make out exactly what had happened.

'It's a bomb,' gasped Joyce. 'Flipping heck, Rose, a bomb's come through the roof down there.'

Even as she spoke, flames and smoke filled what was

271

left of the hall. Rose held a handkerchief to her face, but the choking vapour still seeped into her throat, making her retch, her skin wet with perspiration. Those people who hadn't managed to get out were cowering back as the great tongues of flame leapt higher and closer. Rose went to grab Joyce's arm only to find that she wasn't there.

'Joyce, Joyce. Oh no . . .'

Her cousin was on her knees beside Stan, who was lying on the floor. As Rose stared in horror, Joyce lifted his head and cradled him in her arms, stroking his face.

'He's out cold. Must have been overcome by the smoke,' she muttered as Rose crouched down beside her. 'We've got to get him out of here.'

'We'll carry him between us,' said Rose, the violent fumes feeling like a knife in her chest. 'You take his top half, I'll take the bottom.'

But the searing heat was suddenly too much for her. She came over dizzy and sick and had to lean forward on to her hands with her head bent forward.

'You go, Rose, get out of here,' shouted her cousin, coughing and spluttering. 'I'll see to Stan.'

'I'm not leaving here without you.'

'I'm not going without him,' her cousin panted, eyes and nose streaming, her strength waning from the effects of the conflagration. 'Go and get help, Rose, please . . . quick, before it's too late.'

Rose knew she must do as she was asked, so struggled to her feet. As ill as she felt, the sight of her cousin on her knees cradling Stan in her arms with flames creeping ever closer moved her unbearably. It spoke volumes about Joyce's love for Stan that she would rather lose her life than leave him. That was about the last thought she had before she was overpowered by the noxious vapours and blacked out.

There were fires all over the borough when the men of Joe's watch headed off in their taxis.

'God almighty, that's one hell of a blaze,' said the sub-officer as they drew up outside the community hall that was on fire at one end. 'We need to get it under control sharpish, before it engulfs the whole ruddy building.'

'Let's hope they didn't have anything on in there tonight,' said one of the men.

'Oh my God, they did,' said Joe, frozen with horror as he remembered. 'There was a show on there and my sister and cousin were in it. I've got to get in there to find them.'

'You'll follow the proper procedure and go in when I tell you to,' ordered the sub-officer firmly, 'which is after the hoses and not before.'

'This is my sister and cousin we're talking about. They could be burning to death in there.'

'A dead hero is no use to your relatives or to me, so calm down and do what you're told,' said the sub-officer. 'You know you can't go in until we've done some hosing. Anyway, we don't know that anyone is in there. They might all have had time to get out.'

'I bloomin' well hope so,' said Joe.

The men scrambled out of the taxis and set up the pump, but had to wait until the water came through, which seemed to Joe to take for ever. His instinct was urging him to make a run for it into the fire to find Rose and Joyce, but he knew the sub was right: it wouldn't help them because he probably wouldn't live to be of any use unless the time was right. As soon as the water came through, the men played their hoses on the flames on the outside of the building, moving forward gradually.

Inside it was like the world's worst pea-souper. At first sight there didn't seem to be anyone in there, but as they advanced, hoses hissing and turning the flames to steamy smoke, Joe could see people lying on the floor, either dead or unconscious. His mates were already lifting them out.

Then he saw a woman holding a man in her arms with another woman on the floor beside her. As the smoke cleared a little he saw with a racing heart that it was his sister and cousin. Joyce was gagging; Rose was lying on her back on the floor. He couldn't quite make out who the man was.

Feeling as though his legs would buckle at any moment, he shouted for help to the men at the back. As soon as someone replaced him on the hose, he got down on his knees to his sister. A couple of his colleagues came to his assistance, and between them the three men lifted the trio and carried them out into the fresh air.

★　★　★

When Rose came round, she was lying on the ground outside the hall with her brother leaning over her, holding her hand.

'Thank God for that,' he mumbled thickly. 'You scared the living daylights out of me.'

'Oh, my head,' she groaned.

'You'll be all right; it'll go off after a while,' he comforted. 'The medics will get to you as soon as they can. There are so many people injured, it's taking them a while to see to everyone. It's one of the worst nights we've had. There are fires everywhere.'

She felt very muzzy; couldn't think straight.

'Sorry, Rose, but I'm going to have to leave you,' said Joe apologetically. 'Only I'm on duty and there's still more work to be done because the fire isn't quite out. I know you'll be in good hands.'

Rose's head was beginning to clear. 'I'll be fine; you go and do what you have to.' She thought for a moment. 'What about Joyce and Stan? Are they all right?' she muttered, but Joe was already heading back towards the smoking ruin.

A man nearby said, 'We'll be with you in a minute, luv. Try to stay calm.'

Was he kidding? she thought, as ambulances drew away ringing their bells and enemy planes roared overhead, bangs and crashes reverberating all around her. But she said, 'I'll be all right. Don't worry about me.'

Sitting up and putting a hand to her throbbing head, she could just about make out people moving like shadows through the mist of the smoking building.

Gingerly she got to her feet. Her head was splitting, she had chronic nausea and a rasping throat, but she was reasonably steady on her feet.

Near to her, the medics were dealing with someone on a stretcher. Moving closer, she watched in the dim light as they pulled the blanket over the person's face with silent finality. But not before Rose had recognised the owner of it.

'Oh no, please God no,' she gasped, legs weak and voice breaking. 'Poor, poor Joyce.'

'You did well tonight, Joe,' said the sub-officer, taking him aside as the men gathered the equipment together and prepared to stand down, having fully satisfied themselves that their job here was done.

'Thanks, Sub.'

'You've got the makings of a damned fine fireman,' he went on as they rolled the hoses up. 'I know that some people still look on us auxiliaries as a bunch of amateurs, but you behaved like a real professional tonight. It isn't easy to stay in control when there are people you know involved.'

He was right about that, thought Joe. He'd fallen apart inside when he'd seen Rose lying there, and been consumed by panic. But somehow, and he'd never know how, he'd managed to muster the mettle to do what was required of him. It had given him confidence to know that he could cope under stress, and was able to curb his natural impulses sufficiently to do the right thing in the circumstances.

'This might sound strange, given the danger and discomfort involved, but I really enjoy the work,' he said.

'It doesn't sound strange at all, lad. I'm glad to hear it. We'll be sorry to lose you when the army come calling,' the man added. 'You'll be missed.'

'I shall miss being here, but we have to go where the government sends us, don't we?'

The sub nodded in agreement. 'Our lives aren't our own in wartime,' he said.

There were shouts from the other men for them to stop skiving and come and give a hand. They had to be on their way pronto because a message had come through on the walkie-talkie telling them they were needed at another fire.

'Jerry is really keeping us on the hop tonight,' said the sub-officer, as the raid showed no sign of easing up. 'Let's go and put some more fires out, boys.'

As they hurried over to the taxis and attached the equipment to the back, Joe knew that he had passed through some sort of a watershed tonight. He wasn't sure exactly how or when it had happened, but at some point in the proceedings he'd left his boyhood behind and become a man.

It was the policy at the Green Cat to keep business going as usual during an air raid for as long as there were people in the pub who wanted to stay. But on that particular night in May, the raid was so long and intense Ted was forced to abandon the bar and take shelter in the cellar, inviting the few indomitable punters left in the pub to join him.

Alfie was already there with Hazel. He was lying under a blanket on one of the bunks Johnny had rigged up down here; she was sitting on another. Ted always took Alfie to the cellar at the first wail of the siren and made sure that there was someone with him, a member of staff usually; sometimes a customer would sit with him until Ted could get there himself. Johnny hadn't made it home this weekend, so it was just the two of them when Ted and his regulars came down the steep cellar steps.

Down here among the barrels and pipes, the stone walls creating an earthy chill, the mingled stench of dampness, beer-soaked wood and cigarette smoke filling the air, the noise of the raid was reduced but the explosions and gunfire could still be heard.

For some reason Ted felt more jittery than usual tonight. He'd been generally more nervous of the raids since Alfie had been with them, which was only natural, he supposed. There was a young life to protect now; the boy was his own flesh and blood and his responsibility when Johnny wasn't around.

There were only a few punters and they sat down on upturned beer crates, finishing their drinks and smoking. They were all well acquainted but nobody was saying much. The sheer viciousness of the attack had them all wondering if they were about to breathe their last.

Sitting facing his grandson, Ted felt impotent because

there was nothing more he could do to make him safe. None of them could do anything about the German bombs except sit the raids out in the bowels of the earth, hoping and praying to be spared.

Alfie didn't mind the air raids. There was something quite exciting about being down here in the cellar in the candlelight. It wasn't as boring as going to bed in the normal way, and was quite cosy under a blanket on the bunk. Grandad told him that he should try to go to sleep, but he wasn't nearly so strict about it as he would be if they were upstairs. The usual bedtime rules didn't seem to apply down here.

Glancing across at his grandfather, the candle flame flickering across his wrinkled face, his eyes sad, his mouth tight with worry, Alfie felt something piercing inside of him; something he hadn't felt in a long time, and used to feel for his mother. It made him feel weird inside; sort of happy but sad at the same time. A salty lump rose in his throat and his eyes filled with tears. He brushed them aside and swallowed hard.

'We'll be all right, Grandad,' he said, reaching across and taking Ted's hand. 'There's no need for you to worry. Those rotten Jerries won't get you because I'm here with you and they won't get me. My mum told me that, and she was always right about everything.'

Ted couldn't speak for the overpowering emotions the boy evoked in him. How could he tell him that it was for Alfie, not himself, that Ted was afraid? He must appear calm and make the child feel safe. No point in frightening him with the truth when there was nothing they could do except stay in the cellar and hope to God that the pub didn't take a direct hit and kill the lot of them. Time enough for reality when the lad was older. He'd had more than enough of it in his short life already. He was entitled to be protected from it as much as possible during what was left of his childhood.

How Alfie had loved his mother, and trusted her so completely, Ted thought. She must have been quite a woman.

'I'm all right, boy,' he said. 'Don't worry about me.'

'You can sit next to me if you like,' said Alfie in the matter-of-fact manner he used when he wanted to hide his feelings. 'I can budge up to make room.'

Ted did as he suggested without a word, and when the boy curled his hand into his, Ted felt invulnerable.

'If Rose was here she'd get you all singing,' said Alfie brightly. 'What about "She'll be Coming Round the Mountain"? That's a good one.'

'Good idea, son, good idea,' approved Ted, and launched into an out-of-tune version supported by an equally tuneless effort from Alfie. The others joined in, shakily at first, but soon gaining spirit and momentum. Not only did it help to blot out the noise from above, it also calmed the nerves.

Sitting on another bunk watching the touching scene between Ted and his grandson, Hazel noticed with annoyance that they were getting closer every day, which from her point of view was just another obstruction in the battle to remove Alfie from all of their lives. The reference to that dreadful Rose woman hadn't gone unnoticed either; anyone would think she was flaming Vera Lynn, to hear them talk.

But Hazel had a far more urgent matter on her mind at the moment which pushed everything else into the background . . . even that dratted child.

The all-clear had gone by the time Rose and Joyce finally made their way home from the hospital through the smoky streets, some of the bombed buildings still smouldering, the smell of cordite potent in the air.

The cousins had been checked over by a doctor and told that neither of them had sustained any serious damage from the smoke, and that the uncomfortable symptoms would clear up quite soon.

Neither of them cared about their own sore throats and headaches. A bit of discomfort was nothing in comparison to Stan's terrible fate.

'He would probably have survived if he hadn't already had a chest complaint,' said Joyce tearfully. She'd been weeping on and off ever since they'd put that final blanket over poor Stan's lifeless body. At one point she'd been so hysterical Rose had had to slap her face. 'He'd be here now, walking home with us, making us laugh.'

'I know,' said Rose gently. 'It's a tragedy. Stan was such a smashing bloke.'

'People don't realise just how brave he was,' sobbed the heartbroken Joyce. 'They see a young man in civvies and label him a coward without knowing the facts.

People had no idea how hard he had to fight for breath sometimes. I've seen him when he was bad, Rose. It was awful.'

'I'm sure it was,' she responded kindly.

'But his condition didn't stop him getting up early and going out on to the streets to deliver the mail, or going out of an evening entertaining people, at terrible risk to himself with all the fire bombs about. He knew smoke inhalation could kill him but he still went out playing the piano despite the air raids . . .' Her voice tailed off. 'Oh Rose, what am I going to do without him? He was my strength, my comfort . . . everything.'

'I know now how very much he meant to you,' said Rose, turning and holding her cousin in her arms while she sobbed. 'I saw you with him. I know you would have lost your own life rather than leave him in that burning hall.'

'I don't want to live if he isn't with me. Without him there's nothing for me.'

'Please don't say that, Joyce,' urged Rose, not far off tears herself. 'What would I do if you weren't here?'

'I'm sorry, I shouldn't have said that. It's just that it hurts so much.'

'I know. I feel gutted too,' said Rose. 'I was very fond of him. He was a good friend.'

'Everyone at the sorting office will miss him,' said Joyce. 'He was very popular.'

'He certainly was.'

'One thing I will never do again is wear Bob's ring,' stated Joyce determinedly. 'It really would be a travesty now. I never wore it when I was with Stan on my own anyway. I just kept it on in public to stop people asking questions. From now on I shall never wear it again. It's going back in the box ready to give back to Bob when he gets home.'

'Will you write and tell him now?'

'Probably not; not now,' she responded. 'I know I said I was thinking about it, and as far as I'm concerned our engagement is over. But I'll wait until he comes home and tell him to his face. It'll be kinder that way. It isn't as though I'm going to marry Stan now, is it? So there's no rush.' She paused. 'There's no way I could ever make a go of it with Bob, though. Stan's death doesn't change that.'

'I guessed it wouldn't.' Rose paused. 'Will you tell your folks why you're not wearing your engagement ring?'

'Eventually they'll have to know, but not right away,' she replied. 'There's no hurry now, and I don't want to be put into a position where I have to defend my love for Stan just because they think a lot of Bob and could never understand how it was for Stan and me.'

'I can see your point.'

'Anyway, they probably won't even notice that my ring is missing. Dad won't because men never do notice things like that, and Mum doesn't notice anything any more.'

Rose wanted to weep at the cruelty of it all; people's lives ruined by the war. Her own had been torn apart because Ray was buried in a foreign field somewhere,

Auntie Sybil had had the heart and spirit knocked out of her by a bomb blast, and now Joyce had lost the love of her life.

As they approached their front gates, Rose realised that they had a welcoming party. Mum, Dad and Uncle Flip were all outside waiting for them. It was a relief to Rose, who'd been worrying about them.

'Oh thank God,' said May, rushing up to them and throwing her arms around one and then the other. 'We've been going out of our minds worrying about you; the bombing's been that bad. It must be the worst night ever, I reckon.'

As Joyce hugged her father, fresh tears flowed. But everyone assumed she was crying because she was pleased to see him after the ordeal of the night. No one commented on the fact that Sybil hadn't come out to greet her daughter. They had all become accustomed to her being a shadowy figure on the periphery of the family. It made Rose feel so sad.

Hazel stayed in the spare room at the pub for what was left of the night after the all-clear. Although she was exhausted, she couldn't sleep because of the serious worry that nagged at her incessantly. She hadn't had a moment's peace since she'd heard that women in her age group were now being required by the government to register for war work. She was expecting a letter about it any day. A woman of her age she knew had already had hers.

As a young single woman with no dependent children she could get called up into the services or into some dreadful munitions factory. They could send her anywhere and there wasn't a damned thing she could do about it. Even if she managed to escape the horrors of a barrack room somewhere miles away, or a factory, they could force her to go into the public services like the railways or the Royal Mail. A barmaid she knew had gone on the buses as a clippie recently.

Every one of these options was anathema to her, being far too much like hard work for someone with her delicate constitution. She was all in favour of everyone doing their bit for the war effort as long it didn't involve her in work she wasn't suited for.

In her opinion, bar work was absolutely essential to the war effort in that it helped to keep up public morale. But the employment people might not see it that way. She didn't know for sure, but she suspected that the officials at the Labour Exchange might take the view that her work could be done by an older person, someone too old for the forces or a factory. They were ruthless from what she'd heard, and didn't brook argument. You simply did as you were told.

Her job here at the Green Cat was a cushy little number. As the only woman on the staff, she never had to heave crates about or do anything much beyond light duties. Apart from pulling a decent pint and washing glasses, her main purpose was to look good and be nice to the customers.

Being engaged to Johnny helped enormously, even though he wasn't around much, because as she and Ted were practically related, he didn't like to come down too hard on her if she took time off or didn't pull her weight.

So the idea of actually having to work hard for a living filled her with dread. Anything too physically demanding was abhorrent to her. In fact it terrified her. She had to think of a way out of it, and quickly. It was all very well for these married women who were getting themselves pregnant to get out of it, since no woman with a child under fourteen was going to be forced to go out to work. There was such a glut of unexpected pregnancies, people were calling it 'the prevailing disease'. In fact, even some unmarried women were getting themselves in the club too, for the same reason.

Perhaps that was the answer for her. Johnny had principles. He was the sort of man to feel duty bound to stand by her and marry her if she were to fall pregnant, so she wouldn't have to endure the disgrace and castigation that unmarried mothers had to put up with. Pregnancy would get Johnny up the aisle as well. He was certainly dragging his feet as far as that was concerned at the moment.

But pregnancy was too high a price to pay even in dire circumstances like this. Going about like a hippo, with swollen ankles, varicose veins and boobs like water melons for nine months didn't appeal to Hazel in the slightest.

From what she'd heard on the subject, even after you'd survived nine month of physical torture and were left with stretch marks and sagging breasts, the misery didn't end, because you then had a screaming baby keeping you awake all night, demanding your attention during the day and puking all over you the whole of the time. That wasn't for her. Anyway, Johnny was away a lot, so she might not get pregnant in time to be safe from the government's new rules. So what on earth could she do to avoid them?

It came to her in a sudden burst of inspiration, and she couldn't imagine why she hadn't thought of it before. A ready-made house-trained child was the answer, and Johnny already had one of those.

As Hazel's stepson, Alfie would be her dependant, as far as the law was concerned anyway. She had no intention of actually carrying out the role in any physical sense. Not likely! Ted seemed happy enough to look after the boy, so he could continue and she needn't get involved. Alfie need interfere with her life hardly at all.

Anyway, as soon as the war was over and people were free to choose their line of work, she'd see about getting him sent away to school. The position of wife and stepmother must carry a certain amount of clout. Once she was Mrs Beech, Johnny would have to take her opinions seriously.

But first she had, somehow, to persuade Johnny to get married with all possible speed. That wouldn't be easy, as he wasn't in any hurry. He never had been exactly eager, and had been even less so since Alfie had come on to the scene. But now, instead of being a hindrance, that boy could become the key to her success.

If she made a point of getting friendly with Alfie,

Johnny would be more receptive to the idea of a speedy marriage. He wanted the best for his son, so if she could persuade him that the boy really did need a mother, her problem would be solved. And the sooner the better! Once the Ministry of Labour got their hands on you, you were in uniform before you had time to say 'hang on a minute, mate'.

A serious flaw in her plan was the fact that she didn't actually like children, and she disliked Alfie in particular. But now that she could see him in a different light, it might be easier. It wasn't as though she'd have to keep it up indefinitely. Once she'd got that ring on her finger and was his legal stepmother, out of harm's way from the government, she need only feign friendliness when Johnny or his dad were around.

Meanwhile, she would have to put on the performance of her life to win Alfie over. He would be no pushover, and he didn't like her any more than she liked him. Still, no little kid was a match for Hazel when she was on form. Alfie might be bright like his father, but she was brighter. As long as she acted to perfection and hung on to her temper, all would be well.

If she got started right away, by the time Johnny came home again she and Alfie would be the best of pals. She would have to make all the running and push hard for it, of course, because Johnny would let things stay as they were indefinitely if she didn't take a firm stand.

That was the way men were. They had to be led by the hand to the altar by their women. They would never do it of their own accord because they were selfish and liked to have their cake and eat it. They were all the same; every damned one of them.

Still, there was no point in dwelling on that, especially now that she had a definite plan. Hazel congratulated herself on her presence of mind in thinking of it. If she said so herself, she was no fool when it came to handling men.

Chapter Eleven

While out on her round one morning the following week, Rose found herself mulling over Joyce's situation. It hardly seemed possible that her cousin's life could have fallen apart so completely and no one except she and Rose was aware of it.

To Rose, the love between Joyce and Stan had shone so bright as to be obvious to anyone who saw them together. But if any of the staff at the sorting office suspected what had been going on, or how much Joyce was suffering now, they hadn't indicated it. Unless, of course, they were just being tactful.

The saddest part was the absence of family support, except, of course, from Rose. She remembered how much she'd valued her parents when Ray had died. Their support and sympathy had never been suffocating; they had just been there, quietly, in the background if she'd needed them.

As much as Rose wanted to offer Joyce some words of comfort, she wasn't going to lie to her and tell her that the pain would go away in a few weeks or even months. All she could do was assure her that it did lessen with time. Poor Joyce still had to make that agonising journey, and Rose intended to be there for her every step of the way.

Meanwhile, she had the early post to deliver, and she already had some letters to take back to the sorting office because the addresses no longer existed. The borough had taken a real battering, as had the rest of London, last Saturday night. No one would forget 10 May in a hurry.

'Got anything for me this morning, Postie?' enquired a woman of advanced years. She was waiting in the street for Rose in her dressing gown and slippers, a thick hairnet over her curlers.

Rose looked carefully through her bundle. 'Not today, luv,' she replied.

'Oh. Oh dear.' The woman's disappointment was obvious. 'I'm hoping for some news of my son. He's overseas and I haven't heard for a while.'

'Maybe there'll be something in the second post, or the first post tomorrow,' Rose suggested hopefully.

The woman tutted. 'I hope I hear something soon; just a line to let me know that he's all right is all I need,' she said. 'It's a worry when you don't hear and they're out there somewhere fighting.'

'We're the same about my brother, so I know what it feels like,' Rose said in an understanding manner. 'Let's hope I'll bring you some good news soon.'

The woman nodded, seeming reluctant to go back inside her house. 'The bombing was terrible on Saturday night, wasn't it?' she remarked, sucking in her breath and shaking her head slowly. 'I thought the end had come for us all.'

'I think we all did,' Rose responded. 'They say it was the worst night since the start of the Blitz.'

'It's been quiet since, though.'

'Thank goodness.'

'It's a breathing space for us anyway; gives our poor shredded nerves a chance to heal a bit before the bombers come back.' She gave Rose a questioning look and paused for a moment before saying, 'Got time for a cuppa?'

Rose hesitated. She still had the rest of her round to do and hated to keep people waiting for their letters any longer than was necessary. But she sensed, somehow, a kind of desperation about the woman which a spot of company might lessen, so she said, 'That's very kind of you. But I'll have to make it a quick one.'

'Come on in then, luv, and I'll put the kettle on right away,' said the woman, looking hugely cheered.

Following her up her front path, Rose thought it was worth being a little inventive with her job description if it helped someone to get through the day.

When Rose arrived at the pub on Saturday afternoon to see Alfie, she got the shock of her life to hear that he'd gone to the cinema with Hazel.

'There's a Western on at the Palladium,' explained Johnny, who'd managed to get home for the weekend.

'Ooh, Alfie will love that,' she enthused. 'He's very

partial to a nice big helping of cowboys and Indians. I think all little boys are.'

'And some big boys,' laughed Johnny. 'I'd have gone with them myself, but I was still busy in the bar when they left. We let Hazel go off a bit early as she was doing us a favour.' He paused, remembering. 'Ooh, by the way, I've strict instructions from Alfie to ask you to wait until he gets back if you have the time. He was worried you might think he didn't want to see you because he isn't here when you've taken the trouble to come over.'

'I'm only too delighted that he's doing something he enjoys,' she said.

'He didn't seem all that keen to go, funnily enough,' he told her, frowning. 'Hazel really had to coax him into it.'

I bet she did, thought Rose, guessing that the other woman had her own personal reasons for giving Alfie this treat. It certainly wouldn't be for Alfie's happiness, and the boy would sense that. But in the interests of diplomacy she said, 'He'll enjoy himself once he gets there, I expect.'

'I hope so as she's making an effort with him. I did suggest to her that she take one of his pals along as well for company for him, but I think one eight-year-old boy at a time is more than enough for her.'

Rose nodded politely.

'Anyway, seeing that you'll have a while to wait, and the pub's closed, which leaves me free, I'll make some tea and keep you company until they get back,' Johnny suggested. 'Dad's having his afternoon nap so there's only us.'

After the trauma of the past week – the pain of seeing Joyce suffer as well as having to endure her own personal grief for the loss of Stan's friendship, the carnage in the streets everywhere you looked, and the continuing worry of her depressed Auntie Sybil – Rose felt her spirits lift slightly. A distraction was just what she needed, however brief.

Hazel's foray into friendship with the younger generation wasn't going well. In fact she was hating every second, and her nerves were in tatters from all the noise and nonsense on the screen: endless gunfights, bow-legged cowboys who looked as though they could do with a damned good wash, swaggering down a dusty street that was supposed to be a town when it only had one dismal store and a pub they called a saloon with swing doors that everybody seemed to burst through instead of entering the place normally. Awful! The cinema was crawling with children too, all shouting and calling out to the screen at the slightest bit of action.

Hazel's idea of a good film was a nice sentimental romance; something she could lose herself in. All this cowboy rubbish was giving her a thumping headache. Even more depressing than the discomfort in the cinema was Alfie's lack of response towards her, which made her feel as though the whole thing was a waste of time.

She'd sacrificed her Saturday afternoon to take him out and it was as much as he could do to talk to her.

She'd tried to strike up a conversation on the way to the cinema but he'd hardly said a word. And if all of that wasn't enough, he hadn't even wanted to come out with her in the first place, the ungrateful little toerag.

Perhaps he was still wary of her because of that boarding school business. He'd ruined her scheme completely by running off to Ealing, and she'd given him the trouncing he deserved afterwards, also reminding him of the serious consequences if he didn't keep schtum about her part in it.

So he was probably a little confused by the change in her attitude towards him, which she'd been forced into because of her latest plan. It had been rather sudden, she had to admit. But she didn't have the time to be subtle; not with the Ministry of Labour likely to track her down at any time.

Oh, thank God for that; at last the film had finished. As they left the cinema and emerged into the sunshine, she wondered which was worse: trying to make friends with a boy who had no wish to become better acquainted with her, or sitting in a cinema surrounded by the loud and unruly infant population of the area. She decided on the former. At least she hadn't had to make any effort at conversation while the film was in progress. Heaven knows what you were supposed to talk to a young boy about. Their interests didn't go beyond tin soldiers, catapults and cigarette cards as far as she could make out.

'So what would you like to do now?' she asked, as they stood outside the cinema, the streets thronged with Saturday shopping crowds, the town bathed in sunlight.

'I'd like to go home, please,' he said politely.

'Home already?'

He nodded.

'What about half an hour in the park first?' she suggested, desperate to make progress with him. She had so little time to win him over.

'I'd rather go home, please.'

'How about a wander down the market?' she persisted. 'There might be some bargains about.'

'I'd rather go home, if you don't mind,' he said, his voice quivering slightly. 'Rose will be there waiting for me.'

Oh, so it all came down to her again, did it? It was as much as Hazel could do to keep her hands off him. She'd gone to a great deal of trouble to give him a nice time and all he wanted to do was go home to see that interfering cow. Her temper was so fierce she had to clench her hands to keep them by her sides and not around his throat.

Clutching at every last vestige of self-control, she said, 'All right then, Alfie. If that's what you really want, let's head for home.'

'Thank you for taking me to the pictures,' he said courteously.

I should damned well think so too, she thought, but said through gritted teeth, 'It was a pleasure. We'll have to do it again some time soon.'

Alfie did hope not. But his mother had liked him

to be well mannered, and he didn't want to let her down, so he said, 'Thank you; that will be nice.'

Back at the pub, Rose was having a lovely time. Johnny was such entertaining company, she found herself relaxing for the first time in ages. Cosily ensconced in armchairs opposite one another, they talked about serious things: the terrible bombing of last Saturday night and the general state of the war. But he also amused her with anecdotes about the lighter side of life in the army, leaving out his time in action when he'd received his injuries. He had a comical way with him, and had her crying with laughter at one point.

Inevitably the subject got around to Alfie, since he was their mutual interest.

'He can be quite a comic, that boy,' Johnny told her. 'Some of the things he comes out with make me roar. Usually when he doesn't know that I'm listening.'

'He's a chip off the old block, then.'

Johnny smiled at her, one of those huge uplifting grins. 'You don't know how much it pleases me to hear you say that,' he said. 'I love it when people say he's like me. Is that vain of me, do you think?'

'Not at all,' she replied heartily. 'It's only natural to want to see yourself in the next generation. I'd be the same if I had a child of my own.'

He studied her, looking pensive. 'I always forget that you don't have any kids,' he mentioned. 'You're so comfortable with Alfie, and get on with him so well . . .'

'You'd expect me to have a brood of six, I suppose,' she finished for him.

'I don't think you'd have had the time to gather that many,' he grinned, 'but maybe one or two.'

'I would have liked to have children if Ray had lived,' she told him. 'We planned to have a family after the war.'

'You might yet, you're still a young woman.'

'No, not for me,' she said. 'I'll just borrow Alfie from time to time if that's all right with you.'

'You won't get any argument from me about that, I promise you.'

The conversation petered out but the ensuing silence was a comfortable one.

'I still feel as though I hardly know him,' Johnny continued at last, 'which isn't surprising as I'm away most of the time. I'm not around for long enough to build any sort of a relationship with him, and it doesn't help that he hasn't wanted to know about me from the start.'

'It's awkward.'

'He's quite matey with Dad now, though, so that's something,' he went on, sounding pleased. 'Dad says he's a proper little treasure. He does the errands without argument and even washes the dishes to help out. He can't wait to be old enough to serve in the bar, apparently.'

'I can just imagine him in a few years' time, chatting up the customers, just like his father,' Rose said lightly. 'I should think he'd be a natural.'

'Growing up in the trade, he'll have a head-start, that's for sure.' Johnny paused as though recalling something. 'It was really sweet earlier today. He put Dad's slippers out ready for him when he came up to the flat from the bar. It's a bit of a ritual apparently. He does it all the time.'

'Aah, how lovely.' Rose smiled. 'I can just imagine Alfie doing that. He's a very kind little boy and a great one for routine, because of his background, I suppose. I get the idea that he and his mum moved around quite a bit, probably because of the nature of their circumstances.'

'It's a shame they had such a hard time,' he said, but made no attempt to enlighten her further about the past. 'I shall know I've made the grade when he puts slippers out for me; except that I don't wear them.'

'He'll find another way of showing you.'

'As long as he doesn't put stinging nettles in my bed, I suppose I'm still in with a chance.'

She burst out laughing. 'Honestly, Johnny, what a thing to say.'

Her laughter was infectious and they were both chuckling when Alfie and Hazel came into the room. Rose leapt up and went towards Alfie with her arms outstretched; he ran over to her and threw his arms around her waist.

'Wotcha, big boy,' she said, lifting him up and swinging him around, the two of them laughing together. 'How smashing it is to see you!'

Watching this happy scene, Johnny was filled with

admiration for Rose and her natural gift of making his son happy. The boy simply lit up when she was around. It saddened Johnny that he wasn't able to create such a rapport; maybe it was because he was always so eager to do the right thing that all spontaneity was lost. But Rose seemed to get it right instinctively. He didn't feel so much as a hint of jealousy; only respect. He knew she had something that money couldn't buy.

Observing the same events, Hazel was also affected, but in a totally different way. She was beside herself with rage and envy. How did that wretched woman do it? How did she achieve such a close and easy relationship with the boy without so much as a smidgen of effort?

It was so damned unfair. She had spent the best part of the afternoon in purgatory at the cinema with the child, while that bitch was here having a good time with Johnny, and now the kid was all over her, making Hazel feel completely excluded. It was a mystery to her how the woman knew what to say to a boy of that age when he quite clearly inhabited another world. It must be her infantile mentality, she thought bitchily.

Rose wasn't lost for words when it came to bigger boys either, judging by the way she and Johnny were enjoying a good laugh together when Hazel and Alfie had come in. She'd soon put a stop to that. But how many more times did the awful woman have to be told?

★　　★　　★

'And how many more times must I tell you that I am not trying to steal your man?' said Rose, pushing Hazel away when she accosted her halfway across the green and immediately launched into a tirade of verbal abuse.

'I don't believe you.'

'If you're that scared of losing him, why don't you work harder at trying to keep him happy instead of suspecting every other woman on the planet of being after him?'

'It isn't every other woman.'

'Just me?'

'That's right.'

'You're off your flamin' head.'

'Don't wriggle out of it by trying to make me look silly.'

'You're managing to do that very well on your own,' Rose retorted.

'Stay away from—'

'No I will *not* stay away from here. I've already told you that,' Rose finished for her, 'and neither will I listen to any more of your paranoid accusations. So get out of my way.'

'You're not going anywhere until I've finished saying what I have to say . . .'

'Oh for goodness' sake.' As the other woman grabbed her arm roughly in an attempt to restrain her, Rose decided it was high time she asserted herself more positively, so gave her a shove firm enough to force her back. 'Keep away from me when I come to see Alfie in future, or I really will do what I threatened before and have you done for assault and harassment. I mean it, Hazel.'

Leaving the other woman staring after her, she marched towards the bus stop. For all that she seemed calm and composed, she was actually extremely worried. Because every time Hazel showed her true colours by physically assaulting Rose, she illustrated just how spiteful and malicious she really was. And this was the woman who was going to be Alfie's stepmother!

Hazel wasn't of a nervous disposition. Her heart raced a bit during the air raids, but life in general didn't frighten her. But as she watched Rose walk away, apparently undaunted, she was very afraid; terrified of losing Johnny. He admired Rose; she'd seen it in his eyes. And that could be the first step towards other, more dangerous feelings.

Her insecurity lay in the fact that she knew she wasn't the love of Johnny's life. It wouldn't be the end of the world for him if she wasn't around, whereas for her it was vital that she become his wife.

She daren't let him slip through her fingers; there was far too much at stake. He would be her meal ticket for the future and her saviour now, in the present, if things went to plan. With him being away so much there was no time to lose. Somehow she simply had to persuade him to name the day.

'We're happy enough as we are for the moment, aren't we, Hazel?' was his response to her efforts to get their wedding plans underway. It was later that same night. The pub had closed, everyone else was in bed and the two of them were sitting on the sofa together. 'I don't know why you're in such a tearing hurry to get married.'

'The reason you don't know is probably because you're a man,' she said, keeping her tone jovial and trying not to sound too desperate. 'Women see these things differently. Anyway, we are engaged, and marriage is the next step, so why don't we just get on and do it? When you got engaged to me you were making a promise, remember.'

'Yeah, I know, and it isn't that I don't want to get married, it's just that there's such a lot going on at the moment,' he pointed out. 'What with trying to get to know Alfie and learning to be a good father, which isn't easy as I'm away so much. Then there's all the disruption because of the war. I'd rather wait until everything is back to normal and we can do things properly.'

'I can see your point and I know you mean well,' she said, clinging to her temper with the utmost tenacity. 'But honestly, Johnny, I really believe that the sooner we do it the better. I can see no point in waiting . . .' She paused for a moment in sweet anticipation of the bargaining tool she'd been saving up and believed would swing things her way. 'Especially as Alfie needs a mother.'

He looked at her in surprise. 'Oh . . . he does, does he? Since when have you been interested in that sort of thing?'

'I'm not,' she responded, guessing that if she lied about that he would find it too hard to swallow, and begin to question her motive in suggesting it, 'but Alfie is the son of the man I love, and that makes all the difference.'

'That's nice.' Johnny thought for a moment. 'Oh, so that's why you're being especially friendly towards him, is it? You're getting some practice in.'

'That's right. I thought it was about time I made a real effort with him,' she lied. 'If I'm going to be his mum, I need to get to know him better.' She paused, realising her mistake and adding quickly, 'Not that anyone can ever replace his mother, of course. I wouldn't even try.'

'Very wise.'

'But I can be the next best thing,' she continued eagerly. 'At least if we were married there would be a woman in the house, and that's what he really needs, especially if you're sent overseas again. A female influence will be the best thing for him. Every child needs that. It would take some of the burden off your dad, too.'

'Mmm, there is that.' He could see her point and hated himself for wanting to escape. He was engaged to the girl so it was his duty to do the decent thing and follow through to the next stage, especially as she was making such an effort with Alfie. Johnny's sense of responsibility had been sharpened by what had happened to Alfie's mother. True, her fate had been out of his hands after she'd disappeared, but he still felt responsible for the hardship she and Alfie had had to endure because he'd got her pregnant.

Anyway, what was so bad about the prospect of marrying Hazel? She was easy on the eye and good fun to be with – most of the time anyway – so why not? He didn't love her enough, that was why. It was his own fault that he was being forced into marriage. He should never have let himself be persuaded into the engagement when it wasn't what he'd wanted. He should have been stronger against Hazel's seductive charm and persistence. However, since he had made the commitment, there was no going back.

'Well?' she said.

'I tell you what, as soon as I get some leave that's longer than just a weekend, we'll arrange something,' he said, feeling doomed. 'Unless, of course, you want the works, a long white dress with a veil and church bells and bridesmaids. Then we really will have to wait until after the war, when things will be plentiful again and we can do it in style.'

'I'd like all of that, of course,' she told him. 'But I can see that it just isn't possible at the moment. Anyway, you mean more to me than all the trappings of a white wedding. So a register office wedding will do for me.'

'In that case we'll apply for a special licence once I get some decent leave.'

It wasn't exactly what she'd been after, but Hazel supposed it was the best she could hope for under the circumstances, so she snuggled up to him and said, 'That's wonderful, Johnny. I just can't wait.'

Johnny wondered if wanting to run a mile from this situation was a normal male reaction to deciding to get married. But knowing it would please her, and feeling very guilty, he said, 'Neither can I.'

Alfie was nervous of Hazel since she'd started being nice to him because he knew that she was only pretending to like him. She hated him; he could tell from the way she looked at him, her horrid green eyes hard and angry, even when she was smiling.

He disliked being with her and lived in dread that she would ask him if he'd like to go to the park or down by the river at Hammersmith. He enjoyed going to both places but not with her. She was too scary. Quite often when she was being friendly towards him, she would suddenly fly into a temper and tell him he was a wicked, ungrateful little heathen. Then, even before he had a chance to get used to that, she would change again, telling him that she didn't mean it and he wasn't to tell anyone she'd got cross with him.

It was all very peculiar. Maybe his father had told her to be nice to him for some reason. You could never tell what grown-ups had in their minds. They were a weird lot; except Rose and Grandad, of course. They were both smashing.

Much to everyone's relief, the bombless nights continued, spirits dampened only slightly by yet more rumours of an imminent enemy invasion, mostly fuelled by the view that silence must mean that something big and nasty was brewing.

News of the organisation of mobile teams of ARP

officials being prepared to go instantly to the assistance of any heavily attacked towns gave credence to the current stories that were circulating.

Being an occasional driver of a post office van, Rose was given a memorandum from the Ministry of Transport, outlining instructions for the immobilisation of a motor vehicle in the event of an invasion. It set her thinking that there must be something serious in the offing for the government to issue such reading material.

But despite all the tales of impending doom, nothing untoward happened, so everyone got on with their lives, confidence boosted by the lack of enemy activity. The anniversary of Ray's death in June passed quietly for Rose. She shed a good few tears and thought about Ray for most of the day, and as she didn't have a grave to visit, she spent a few moments in quiet contemplation in the local church. When it was over, she felt as though she'd stepped over some sort of milestone.

Joe's hero status in the family continued as a result of his courage in the fire service, and Rose was delighted. Having so often watched him being overshadowed by Alan, it was lovely to see him shine.

Rose's mother took the momentous step of volunteering for war work and was given a part-time job in a munitions factory canteen in Acton. After years of total domesticity, she seemed to enjoy being part of the workforce outside the home. They heard from Alan, who was somewhere in the Middle East; just a note to say that he was alive and well.

Auntie Sybil remained depressed and utterly oblivious of her daughter's grief, which Joyce was coping with admirably, in Rose's opinion. Because of the secrecy of her love affair, she had only one shoulder to cry on, and Rose made sure it was available to her whenever she needed it.

A month or so after Stan's death, however, Joyce seemed to perk up to rather an astonishing degree. She seemed cheerful and buoyant, an even happier version of her old self, in fact. Rose assumed she must just be making a special effort to put up a front, because surely she couldn't be feeling this good so soon.

But she was, and there was a reason for her new radiance. When she told her cousin what it was, Rose was the one suffering from shock . . .

'Pregnant?' she gasped. 'You're having Stan's baby?'

'That's right,' her cousin beamed, eyes sparkling joyfully. 'Isn't it wonderful?'

Rose wasn't at all sure if wonderful was the way she would describe it. Calamitous or disastrous sprang more readily to mind in this particular instance. Pregnant by her dead lover while officially engaged to a man who was away in the service of his country. It wasn't exactly the stuff that happy families were made of.

'You're . . . you're pleased, then?' she muttered.

'Very.'

'That's all right then.'

They were in Rose's bedroom, where the walls were ingrained with more than twenty years of the cousins' shared secrets. Joyce was sitting in the wicker chair near the bed where Rose had just collapsed in a state of shock.

'I always used to think that getting in the club if you weren't married would be the worst thing that could ever happen to any woman,' Joyce confided. 'But it's the best thing that's ever happened to me. Stan's gone but he's left me a part of him and I'll cherish it for the rest of my life. I feel honoured to be carrying his baby.'

Rose clutched her head. She didn't want to be a damp squib, but there were harsh realities to be faced. 'Have you . . . have you thought of the practicalities, though?'

'Of course I have. I'm not a fool.' Joyce was overly defensive and the emotional temperature rose. 'If you're implying by your attitude that I should find some woman who'll see to it for me in her back room, if I can scrape together enough cash, you're out of luck, because I'm not getting rid of it.'

'I wasn't implying anything of the sort; you know me better than that,' corrected Rose edgily.

'Yeah, I know. Sorry.'

'It's all right,' said Rose. 'But it won't be easy for you or the baby if you keep it.'

'Well I'm not going to give it away, so I'll take what-ever comes,' she stated categorically.

'Good for you.'

'I know there's going to be shock and horror all round and people are going to be hurt, Bob in particular when he comes home,' she went on. 'Mum and Dad will go up the wall because of the shame it will bring on them. They'll probably throw me out on the street. But if I end up living in a room the size of a broom cupboard, on my own with the baby, I shall bring it up and do my very best for it.'

'In that case, I'll be beside you all the way. I'll do everything I possibly can to help,' Rose said, standing up and opening her arms to her cousin.

'Thanks, Rose,' Joyce said, hugging her tearfully.

'No one else knows, I take it,' said Rose as they drew back and sat down.

'You're dead right about that,' she said, 'and it's going to stay that way for as long as possible.'

'You can't be very far gone.'

'I've just missed a second period,' she told her. 'I was late at the time Stan died but I was too grief-stricken to even think about it. Now I've missed another, and I've been feeling a bit queasy, so I've been forced to put my mind to it, and am thrilled to bits to accept that I'm pregnant. I've been dying to tell you but wanted to wait until I was sure.'

'You've kept the queasiness well hidden, even from me,' said Rose.

'I've had to be on my guard the whole time in case Mum suspected anything, so I suppose it got to be a habit when I was out of the house too,' she explained. 'Mind you, I don't suppose Mum would notice if I gave birth in the middle of the living room. She's far too wrapped up in herself.'

'You'd be wise to tell your mum and dad before other people notice anything, though,' suggested Rose. 'It'll make it worse for you all if they find out from someone else. And other people will notice your change in shape, even if your mum doesn't. It'll soon get around.'

'Yeah, I know, and I will tell them,' she agreed, 'but not for a good while yet. I need some time to get used to it myself, and to work out what I'm going to do if they do want me to leave home. It's time I was out from under their feet anyway.'

'I'd be very surprised if it came to that,' opined Rose. 'They're not the sort of people to throw their daughter out, whatever the circumstances.'

Joyce shrugged. 'I'm not so sure. Mum and Dad are good people, but it is every parent's worst nightmare, isn't it, their daughter bringing this sort of trouble home. It's the biggest shame a daughter can bring on her family, and a damned sight worse when the father of the baby isn't the man she's engaged to.'

'I'm glad you're under no illusions,' said Rose. 'But I think you might be making it sound worse than it is.'

'There's no point in kidding myself. The way I've said it is the way Mum and Dad will see it.'

'I agree that you'll probably have a hard time with them when they first get to know, but I think they'll come through for you in the end. I can't imagine them abandoning you. They just wouldn't do something like that, no matter how angry and upset they are.'

'If they do, they do. I'll get by somehow.' Joyce fell

silent for a few moments, thinking. 'The thing is, Rose, I hate the idea of hurting and shaming them, and it's going to break my heart to cause Bob to suffer, but I just can't feel ashamed of what's happened. I loved Stan so much, you see, and I shall love his child. I'm never going to apologise about my baby. I shall hold my head high and be proud no matter how tough it gets.'

'I know, kid. I know.'

'Anyway,' Joyce began wiping the sudden rush of tears from her eyes with a handkerchief, 'for the time being it's just you and me and our little secret.'

'I won't say a word.'

'Thanks, kid.'

'A baby in the family, eh?' said Rose, thinking about it and smiling. 'It'll be fun.'

'I think so too,' Joyce said with a wry grin, 'even though I'll probably be evicted from the family.'

'You'll always have me,' said Rose. 'Whatever happens, I'll be there.'

Chapter Twelve

Hazel woke up one summer Saturday morning and decided not to go to work at the pub today because she fancied a day off. She would have a long lie-in, then maybe go out and have a leisurely wander around the dress shops; she might even use some of her clothing coupons if she saw something she couldn't resist. But with only sixty-six coupons to last a year and a frock using eleven of them, it would have to be something really special.

The word on the street was that a few shrewd market traders could be persuaded to sell clothes without coupons if the customer was willing to pay a higher price for them. Maybe she could find one of those in Shepherd's Bush market. But on second thoughts, she couldn't really afford to pay over the top. Anyway, it wouldn't be wise to risk going to the Bush today in case she was seen, since Ted was going to be told that she was ill in bed.

She wasn't worried about getting the sack if the worst happened and she was found out, because her status as Ted's future daughter-in-law protected her from anything as drastic as that. But he was sure to get more than a little narked and she didn't want any hassle if it could be avoided. Feigning friendship with that dreadful child was stressful enough; she didn't want to have to cope with Ted's wrath as well when she went back to work tomorrow.

Johnny wouldn't be home this weekend so there wouldn't even be any light relief to make it more palatable. It would just be the same old monotonous routine: pulling pints, washing glasses, being nice to boring old windbags and making sure that the flirting she did with servicemen home on leave didn't get out of hand. No, she couldn't face it today. She'd get her mother to go to the phone box later on and tell Ted that she had an upset tummy or some other minor ailment.

Meanwhile she'd grab some extra beauty sleep. She might as well make the most of it while she could. If things didn't go according to plan and she was sent on to war work, it wouldn't be so easy to take the odd day off without supplying a doctor's certificate. Ooh, what bliss, she thought, as she pulled the covers up and snuggled down.

The shafts of sunlight streaming through the windows of the bus that was taking Rose to Shepherd's Bush to see Alfie later that same day gave her a sudden idea.

'Do you fancy going somewhere for the afternoon, Alfie, as it's so lovely out?' she asked after she'd greeted him. 'If it's all right with your grandad, of course.'

'Cor, yeah.' He looked at Ted, who had just come up to the flat after the lunchtime session in the bar. 'Can I go, Grandad, please?'

'Course you can, son. It'll be nice for you to get away from here for a while.'

'Where do you fancy going then?' Rose asked brightly. 'The park, or the river, maybe? Don't suggest the pictures because the weather's too nice to be inside.' She gave the matter some more thought. 'We could go to the West End if you like; maybe take a rowing boat out on the lake in Hyde Park.'

'Cor, I'd love to go out on a boat,' he enthused. 'Can I do the rowing?'

'You might have to if I can't make the boat move,' she chuckled, adding more seriously, 'We'll sort it out between us when we get there.'

'Go and wash your hands and face then,' said his grandfather. 'Put a clean shirt on and comb your hair.'

'We'll have to make sure you don't get wet, if you're going to get yourself all done up,' Rose said laughingly.

'I'm not letting him go out with you looking like a scruff,' explained Ted responsibly.

'Go on then, Alfie, do as your grandad says,' added Rose supportively.

She and Ted were chatting in the living room while they waited for Alfie when they heard someone coming up the stairs.

'Blimey, son, where have you sprung from?' said his father when Johnny appeared with a beaming smile. 'I thought you couldn't get home this weekend.'

'So did I. But I got an unexpected chance of a twenty-four-hour pass, so hopped on the train,' he explained. 'It's only a flying visit. I have to be back midday tomorrow.'

'I'm especially pleased to see you, as it happens,' said his father, 'because I'll be in need of some help in the bar tonight as Hazel isn't coming in.'

'Not coming in?' Johnny frowned. 'Why is that?'

'She's got lazyitis,' replied Ted. 'According to her mother she's got a stomach upset but I don't believe that for a moment. You know how she likes a day off every now and again.'

'Come on, Dad. You don't know that for sure,' admonished Johnny in defence of Hazel. 'It isn't fair to judge someone without knowing the facts.'

'I'm as certain as I can be,' said Ted. 'Surely being engaged to her hasn't blinded you to the fact that she doesn't exactly embrace the work ethic.'

'She could be really sick,' Johnny pointed out. 'I'll go round to her place in a minute to find out how she is.'

'You'll be lucky if you find her in.'

'We'll see.' He turned to Rose. 'Has Alfie gone out to play and deserted you?'

'No. I'm taking him out for the afternoon, and he's gone to get ready.'

'How lovely. Where are you going?'

'Hyde Park. We're planning on taking a boat out on the Serpentine.' She made a face. 'I don't know if I've bitten off more than I can chew, though. My rowing experience is limited to a small lake in a local park with my cousin when we were kids, and our fathers were in charge. But don't worry, I'll take good care of him and make sure he doesn't fall in.'

'I trust you. I'm sure you'll have some fun,' he said. 'I wish I was coming with you.'

'Why don't you then?' suggested Ted cheerfully. 'An afternoon out will do you good.'

'No, I'd better go round to see Hazel,' he said, giving his fiancée the benefit of the doubt. 'I'll never live it down if I don't visit her when she's under the weather.'

Ted shrugged. 'Oh well, that's up to you,' he said with obvious disapproval. 'I'm going to tell that boy to hurry up.'

'Thanks, Ted. We need to be on our way,' said Rose. 'The queue for boats will probably be miles long on a nice day like this.'

As Johnny sat on the bus en route to Hazel's, he was ashamed of himself for wanting to be with Alfie and Rose instead of his girlfriend. He felt constrained by duty; angry that he couldn't spend what little time he had at home with his son. Poor Hazel, he seemed to spend all his time lately wanting to distance himself from her. It was a sad state of affairs when you didn't even want to visit your intended when she wasn't feeling well.

Off the bus and striding along the main road towards her turning, he stopped and stared in astonishment as he saw her come round the corner and swing off up the main road, unaware that he had seen her. Done up to the nines in a summer frock and high-heeled shoes, she was obviously in the best of health. So Dad was right. She was idle; a liar with no thought for her employer.

His first instinct was to run after her and give her a piece of his mind. But he was so angry he didn't even want to look at her, let alone talk to her. Anyway, there was something else he'd much rather be doing than arguing with Hazel, who would doubtless have some excuse. He'd deal with her tomorrow before he went back to camp. She couldn't be allowed to get away with treating his father so shabbily.

When she was safely out of sight, he crossed the road and got the next bus to Marble Arch.

'How much longer do you think we'll have to wait, Rose?' asked Alfie with childish impatience, peering towards the front of the queue.

'Not long now,' she said hopefully. 'We're gradually moving towards the front.'

'There are lots of people here, aren't there?'

Indeed there were. The sunshine had attracted the crowds, and servicemen and women were out in force, as well as hordes of civilians. There were families, groups of young boys and girls, courting couples; everyone wanting to make the most of the fine weather. The sun was reflecting on the gently undulating water in ever-changing splinters of light, the green and luxuriant trees on the other side of the lake topped by the London skyline etched against the clear blue sky.

'Wotcha, you two,' said Johnny, unexpectedly appearing beside them. 'I hoped you might still be waiting to get on. Mind if I join you?'

'Of course not,' said Rose. 'But how come you're here? How is Hazel?'

'She'll live,' he replied with an edge to his voice that deterred Rose from enquiring further. 'So I thought I'd have an afternoon out with you two.'

'Does this mean that I can sit back and enjoy the sunshine while you do the rowing?' she enquired.

'If I can have a little help from Alfie, yeah, you can relax,' he grinned.

'This is getting better by the moment,' she said, smiling at him.

It continued to improve. There were some hilarious moments until Johnny got into his stride with the oars. The boat went round in circles just yards from the starting point, giving those waiting in the queue some splendid entertainment. But he eventually got to grips with it and they moved out into the shimmering lake, Alfie, who was sitting beside him, being given a turn with one of the oars from time to time, under his father's strict supervision.

At one point when Johnny was working both oars, they wobbled so violently Rose thought that the boat was going to turn over.

'Whoops,' she said, keeping a firm hold on Alfie.

'Sorry about that,' Johnny apologised. 'There has never been much call for rowing in my life before.'

'I'd never have guessed,' said Rose with irony.

'Cheeky,' he said, but he was smiling.

Alfie wanted another chance to show what he could do, and his father conceded.

'Hey, careful does it,' warned Johnny when Alfie was a little too boisterous with the oar and they all got a soaking.

'Talk about the blind leading the blind,' teased Rose. 'I must have been mad to let myself in for this. I'm rapidly reaching the point where dry land is beginning to seem very desirable, but I have a terrible feeling that I'm not going to get back there without a ducking.'

'Oh come on, Rose, you've got to give us a chance to get used to it, isn't that right, Alfie?'

'Yeah, we're doing our best,' said Alfie with the sort of father-and-son chumminess that warmed Rose's heart.

'We'll make you do the rowing if we have much more cheek,' said Johnny.

'I don't mind taking my turn,' she said. 'I was going to be in charge of this boat if you hadn't turned up.'

'Just as well I did turn up then, isn't it?' he said jokingly. 'This rowing lark is hard work. I doubt if you'd have got the boat away from the starting point.'

'You didn't exactly have a smooth take-off yourself,' she came back at him.

'I got away eventually, that's the important thing,' he pointed out. 'I doubt if you've got the muscle power for it.'

'Are you offering me a challenge?'

'I'm far too much of a gentleman,' he said with a

wry grin. 'Anyway, if we change places now, the chances are we'll all end up in the water.'

'In that case, I'll just relax while you sweat it out,' she said, leaning back and raising her face to the sun. 'Oh yes, this is the life for me.'

And so it went on: joshing, jokes and laughter. By the time, the boat was due back in, Johnny was becoming quite a proficient oarsman and guided the vessel into the hands of the lake staff a lot more skilfully than when he'd started off.

They spent some more time in the park, then walked down to Marble Arch for tea in Maison Lyons. It was very busy and they had to wait a while to get a table. But it didn't seem to matter because there was such a happy atmosphere between the three of them, even though Alfie and his dad were still a little awkward with each other. Rose guessed that her presence was acting as a sort of buffer, and was happy for it to be so.

'Well, I hate to break up the party, but we'd better be making tracks,' Johnny said eventually when they'd finished their tea. 'I want to get back to the pub in time to give Dad a hand with opening up.'

When they got back to the Green Cat, they found Ted sitting in an armchair looking extremely poorly.

'It came on suddenly,' he told them. 'One minute I was perfectly all right, the next I was in the lavatory heaving my guts up.'

'You need to be in bed,' suggested Rose, noticing how pale and ill he looked.

'How can I go to bed when we're short-staffed downstairs without Hazel?' he pointed out.

'You get off to bed, Dad, and let me worry about that,' said Johnny.

'I think I shall have to, son,' said Ted weakly, looking more ashen-faced by the second. 'I really do feel rotten.'

'I'll go with him,' said Alfie as Ted got up and walked very unsteadily across the room towards the stairs. 'Wait for me, Grandad. I'll help you up the stairs.'

'That's kind of you, son.'

After they'd gone, Rose said to Johnny, 'That leaves you in a bit of a fix, doesn't it?'

'Right in the cart,' he affirmed. 'But I'll manage. I'm just glad that I'm here to take the responsibility off his shoulders for tonight.'

Being so worried about his father exacerbated his fury towards Hazel. He was about to go storming around to her place to tell her to get her lazy arse over here and do some work when Rose made an unexpected suggestion.

'I can stay and give you a hand if you like,' she offered. 'As long as you don't mind me using your phone to leave a message at a neighbour's for my folks.'

'That's very nice of you, but don't you have other plans for the evening?'

'No other plans,' she assured him. 'I'm all yours. And I did help your dad once before, so I'm not a complete beginner.'

'In that case, thanks very much. It will be an enormous help to me,' he said, all thoughts of Hazel fading.

* * *

Having dipped her toe into these particular waters before, Rose found the bar work less difficult this time. Admittedly, there was no shortage of excess froth about until she got back into her stride, but before long she was pulling pints like a veteran and getting on like a house on fire with the customers. Johnny was easy to work with, which made the shift an enjoyable experience.

'It's been a smashing day,' said Alfie when she went upstairs to tuck him in.

'Yeah, I've had a good time too.'

'It's lovely when you're here.'

'That's nice.'

'I wish you could live here.'

'Don't start that again,' she said in a tone of gentle admonition. 'You know what I've told you about too much wishing. Anyway, you've got your grandad, and your dad is here sometimes. Then there's Hazel.'

Alfie didn't reply, and Rose tensed when she saw fear in his eyes at the mention of the other woman's name.

'Hazel is nice to you, isn't she, Alfie?' she enquired.

Alfie became more frightened of Hazel every time he saw her because she was so changeable. One minute she was being nice, the next she was shouting at him and telling him he was a horrible little nuisance who nobody wanted. She changed back so fast he was bewildered but knew he hadn't imagined it because he could feel her hatred of him even when she was being friendly.

But he daren't tell anyone, because of what would happen to Rose if he did.

'Yeah, she's all right,' he said now.

Rose wasn't convinced, but sensed she wouldn't get any more out of him so she just said, 'You'll let me know if there's anything wrong, won't you?'

'Course I will,' he said.

'Make sure you do.'

She was worried, though. Something definitely wasn't right with him.

Although they were affected by the national beer shortage at the Green Cat, by staying open for fewer hours during weekdays and rationing what the customers had then, they could usually make sure that the punters had a good time on a Saturday.

That particular Saturday night the bar was busy right through until closing time, by which point Rose was beginning to feel like a proper barmaid.

'You've been a real diamond tonight, Rose. I don't know what I'have done without you,' said Johnny when the last punter had gone and the door was finally locked. He took some money from the till and handed it to her. 'You've earned that, so don't get any daft ideas about refusing it.'

Rather than complicate matters, she did as he asked. 'I've enjoyed myself as it happens,' she told him, 'but I'd better be getting off home now or I'll miss the last bus, if I haven't already. The service is a law unto itself these days, and they stop running ever so early some nights.'

He looked concerned. 'You should have said something earlier,' he told her. 'Come to that, I should have had it in mind that you have to get home.'

'I was so involved in what I was doing, I forgot the time,' she said lightly.

'I wish all bar staff felt that way.'

'It's because it's a novelty, I expect,' she suggested. 'Anyway, I can always try for a train if there are no buses. But either way, I must fly.'

He pondered the matter. 'Why not stay here instead of being at the mercy of public transport?' he suggested. 'The least I can do is offer you a bed for the night when you've done me such a big favour. There's a spare room upstairs in the flat. Hazel sometimes uses it when I'm home.' He gave her a knowing look. 'Is it too late to phone that neighbour to let your people know you won't be home?'

'It is a bit cheeky but I'll chance it.'

'Would it help if I did it, and explain what's happened?'

She chuckled. 'A strange man calling a neighbour to say that I'm staying the night at his place? I don't think so. They're not that broad-minded in our street. So thanks, but I think I'd better do it myself.'

'As you wish,' he said. 'I'll go on upstairs to see if Dad's all right.'

Rose was smiling as she went to the phone in the hallway behind the door to the bar.

'It's been a really good day, Rose,' he said when they were settled in armchairs in the Beeches' living room.

Johnny had a glass of beer and was smoking a cigarette; Rose had a shandy. 'I can't remember when I've enjoyed myself more. It was a good idea of yours to take a boat out on the lake.'

'Alfie had a good time, which was the object of the exercise,' she said. 'He enjoyed it all the more because you were there.'

He beamed. 'Do you really think so?'

'Of course,' she confirmed. 'There's no need to sound so surprised.'

'I still don't feel altogether comfortable with him,' he confessed, his brow furrowing. 'There's a barrier between us. He won't let me into his heart.'

'I'm sure he will do, in time,' she encouraged.

'It made all the difference your being there this afternoon,' he told her. 'You're so natural with him; I just relaxed and enjoyed myself.'

'Maybe when you're on your own with him you're overanxious because you want him to like you so much,' she commented. 'It could be that you're trying too hard.'

'You've hit the nail on the head there,' he said. 'It might sound odd, but I'm quite nervous when I'm by myself with him. I know I'm too eager to get everything right but can't seem to stop myself.' He looked at her. 'I so admire the way you handle him. How do you do it?'

'I don't do anything special. I'm just myself. Remember, Alfie wasn't always as easy with me as he is now,' she said. 'He was a right little horror when we first took him in. The poor kid was in a hell of a state.'

'When I think of how frightened he must have been trapped in that rubble; then to have to face up to his mother's death, it makes me go cold,' Johnny confided. 'I want to make it up to him for everything he's been through. But he won't let me.'

'Being away so much doesn't help, I suppose,' she remarked. 'But nothing can be done about that.'

'I'm not sure if it would be any better if I was at home more,' he responded. 'There's something inside him that won't let him love me. Probably because he adored his mother and he thinks I let her down.'

'And didn't you?'

'Only because I had no choice,' he tried to explain.

'Oh, I see.'

He looked across at her, the immeasurable depth of her lovely dark eyes seeming to draw him towards her. Without any prior intention, he blurted out the whole story.

'Peggy meant everything to me,' he said in conclusion. 'Sometimes I think *she* let *me* down by not allowing me to be a part of my son's life. She did what she thought was best for me but she made the wrong decision; it wasn't the best thing at all. I lost all those years of Alfie's life, and I can never get them back. I may never get him back. It may be too late to gain his respect. I know it isn't fashionable for a man to think this way. We're all painted as villains by you women if we get a girl into trouble, especially if we don't do the decent thing and marry her. But what I felt for Peggy was true love. I would have gone to the ends of the earth for her at that time.' He looked into space, his blue eyes shining with tears. 'But she went away and made sure that I couldn't find her and the child I didn't know she was carrying. I find that hard to forgive.'

Rose wasn't surprised by the truth. She didn't know Johnny well but he'd struck her as the sort of man who wouldn't let anyone down.

'Don't you think it might be a good idea to tell Alfie how much you and his mother loved each other?' she suggested. 'It might please him to know that he was born of love.'

'Definitely not!' He was emphatic. 'He's far too young to understand the ways of adults. It would just be another burden for him to carry.'

'Don't you think it might help your relationship with him if he were to know that you didn't let his mother down?' she wondered thoughtfully.

'It very well might, but I'm not going to do it at this stage,' he wisely decided. 'One day, when he's old enough to cope with it, I'll tell him the truth, but not now. I want him to love me for myself as a person, and I have to earn his respect as I am now, not for what happened all those years ago. Anyway, if I tell him what really happened, he might start to blame his mother for stopping us all from being together.'

'I suppose there might be a faint chance of that.'

'There's every chance. Think about it, Rose. He would have had a much better life if I'd been there to look after them. I would have given them a good home, security and a proper place in society. He might start

330

to think badly of his mother for depriving them both of that if I tell him at this stage, and I don't want that. I don't want to gain popularity with him at her expense.'

'Maybe if you explain that she made the sacrifice for you because she was a truly good and caring person, he won't react that way.'

'But Alfie came off badly because of it, didn't he?' he reminded her. 'From what I can make out, they never had any decent accommodation, and he was made to live with the stigma of illegitimacy, probably bullied at school and shunned by everyone else. He could have been spared all that if Peggy had told me about the pregnancy and let me marry her. He isn't old enough yet to understand about adult love and the sacrifices people make for it. He'll look at it from his own point of view. It's only natural at that young age. I don't want the memory of his mother tarnished in any way for him. If he had to hate either of us, I'd much rather it was me. I'm here to win him back; poor Peggy isn't.'

'I don't think he would ever think badly of his mother for long, no matter what she'd done. He absolutely adored her, and would forgive her anything,' Rose pointed out. 'But yes, I can see that you do have a valid point, and I admire you for sticking to your principles.'

'Thank you,' he said warmly. 'Anyway, I'm not the only father who's lost years of his child's life. Very few young married men are at home to see their kids grow up these days.'

'I know,' she said. 'But maybe the war will soon be

over. At least we've got Russia on our side now, after Germany invaded their country.'

Johnny nodded. 'We all have the same dream,' he said. He was more circumspect than Rose about the progress of the war, but saw no point in being pessimistic. 'The end of the war is everyone's fantasy.'

'It isn't a fantasy, because it will happen and we will win it,' said Rose.

'We certainly will,' he said heartily. 'That's another thing that we're all agreed on.'

He sipped his drink and inhaled deeply on his cigarette. 'Anyway, we've talked about me and my misspent youth,' he said. 'What about you, Rose? Do you have any skeletons in your cupboard?'

'Heavens, no,' she grinned. 'I'm the dullest person you could ever wish to meet. I married my long-standing steady boyfriend. Got widowed soon after and now work as a postwoman. No illicit affairs; no pregnancies and no glamorous job. Ordinary is my middle name.'

'The last thing you are is ordinary,' Johnny said. 'You are the most extraordinary person I've ever met.'

'Oh . . . am I, really?' Rose said, her cheeks burning. 'Are you sure we're talking about the same person?'

'We certainly are,' he stated. 'You don't have to have a glamorous life to be a very special person.'

This was getting embarrassing, so she said, 'I think you'd better tone it down a bit. Too many compliments might go to my head.'

'You're far too modest,' he grinned. 'But tell me, how long have you been widowed?'

'It's over a year now, incredibly,' she said. 'I didn't think I could get through one day knowing that I'd never see him again. But here we are, in the second year, and I'm surviving.'

'I'm glad you're coping.'

'It's amazing how we find the resilience to carry on, isn't it? I suppose it's because we have no choice but to put one foot in front of the other every day. I still miss him, though, I suppose I always will.'

'I'm the same about my mother,' Johnny confessed. 'I still miss her a hell of a lot; knowing that she's not there any more, for a chat and a joke, makes me sad. I just hate the fact that she'll never be around again. Sometimes I can't believe that she's gone. She was so full of life. She and I shared the same sense of humour. No one could make me laugh like she did.'

His love for his mother was a palpable presence in the room, and Rose was touched by it.

'It's a shame you lost her so early. I don't know what I'd do without my mother.'

'I'm still wondering how I'm managing,' he said.

Rose could have stayed there, basking in his warm and entertaining company for ever. But she felt she ought to make a move because she sensed a hint of intimacy creeping into the atmosphere,

'Well, I suppose we'd better get some sleep or we'll be like death warmed up tomorrow,' she said, finishing her shandy and rising. 'Thanks for the drink.'

'Thank you for helping me out in the bar tonight.'

'A pleasure,' she said, walking towards the door.

'I'll stay here a few minutes and finish my drink.'

'Goodnight, then,' she said.

'Goodnight, Rose,' he said softly. 'Thanks for making the day so special.'

She smiled, then left hurriedly because she was feeling oddly emotional.

Sitting in the chair reflecting on the day, Johnny's thoughts were all of Rose. He admired her more each time he saw her. How could anyone so beautiful, brave and full of heart think of herself as ordinary? And yes, he was attracted to her, very much so. What normal man wouldn't be?

But he daren't allow himself to be ruled by his feelings. Having had his sense of responsibility heightened by Alfie's arrival in his life, Johnny would hate to betray Hazel. She had her faults; she was often shallow and self-centred. But she was good fun, loving and loyal to him. The last thing he wanted to do was let her down.

She was, however, going to hear a few strong words from him tomorrow about another matter . . .

Rose lay in bed staring into the dark. Because she'd been up so early for work that morning, she was exhausted. But sleep eluded her. She felt warm and excited; how she'd felt when she'd first begun to fall in love with Ray.

This had to be nipped in the bud right away, because there was no future in it and she didn't want to find herself wishing for something she couldn't have. She'd suffered enough pain grieving for Ray.

It was a surprise to find that she was functioning as a complete woman again. She'd thought that that part of her had died along with Ray, but obviously not. Still, it was probably just a passing thing, brought about by the congenial mood of the day. She really must try and get to sleep, she thought, sighing and turning over on to her side, but the face she kept seeing in her mind was Johnny's.

Hazel was surprised to see Johnny at the pub when she arrived for her lunchtime shift the next day. He was on his own in the bar, bottling up ready to open.

'Johnny! I didn't expect to see you here,' she said. 'When did you get back?'

'Yesterday.'

She threw him a look. 'Which part of yesterday?' she asked, her eyes narrowed suspiciously.

'Early in the afternoon.'

Her eyes flashed angrily. 'You mean to tell me that you've been home for almost a full day and you haven't been round to see me?' she rebuked.

'Oh but I have, Hazel,' he informed her, his eyes flint hard. 'I came to visit you in your sick bed, and saw you walking up the street in the best of health.'

Her eyes widened. 'Oh . . . so you were spying on me, were you?' she accused, using attack as a form of defence.

'Don't be so ridiculous; of course I wasn't. I was on my way to see you to let you know that I was home, and to find out how you were, as you'd phoned in sick,' he explained. 'But before I got to your house, I saw you strutting along the road all dressed up and feeling fine.'

'Why didn't you come up to me, when you saw me out?' she asked accusingly.

'Because I was angry with you and disappointed to find out that you'd lied. I just didn't want to talk to you,' he replied. 'I don't like to see my father being taken for a ride.'

'I wasn't well,' she claimed feebly. 'I only went out to get some fresh air because I thought it might make me feel better. I had to go home and go back to bed.'

'Don't insult my intelligence by continuing to lie,' he said gruffly. 'You've been caught out. The least you can do is come clean and admit it.'

'Well, I didn't feel too good when I first woke up,' she said untruthfully. 'I felt better as the day wore on but not well enough for work. I didn't stay out long.'

He looked at her overly made-up face, her gorgeous green eyes and her peachy skin. 'I'm not a fool, so for goodness' sake stop treating me like one.'

'Well all right, maybe I did just want a day off,' she finally admitted. 'I get tired the same as everyone else. I wanted to have a look round the shops.'

'If you want time off, ask in advance so that Dad can get cover,' he admonished. 'As it happens, I was at home, which is just as well because Dad took sick last night so he couldn't work down in the bar.'

'Oh dear,' she said, biting her lip and having the grace to look sheepish. 'Is he all right now?'

'Yeah, he's feeling much better this morning,' he replied. 'Whatever it was went as suddenly as it came. It was some sort of a stomach upset. Probably something he'd eaten.'

'You must have been rushed off your feet in here then,' she said.

'It was very hectic, yes. But luckily for me, Rose stepped in to help out so it turned out all right in the end.'

Hazel's expression became thunderous. 'Rose,' she burst out. 'You let that woman stand in for me?'

'I certainly did,' he replied in an even tone. 'And you have no right to object since you didn't bother to turn up and left us with a problem. She was a real godsend too. It was fortunate for me she happened to be here at that time. She's usually gone before opening time.'

'Why was she still here?' Hazel demanded.

'Because we'd been out for the afternoon with Alfie,' he explained. 'We took him out on a boat on the Serpentine, and then to Lyons for tea.'

Her eyes were slits now, her mouth tight with fury. 'You . . . you went out with her?'

'Yeah, that's right. She was taking Alfie out so I tagged along,' he informed her with a casual air. 'It was nice to spend some time with him.' He paused before adding meaningfully, 'I could see that you had plans of your own.'

Incandescent with rage, she could hardly get her words out. 'You are supposed to be engaged to me, you know. You ought to remember that.'

337

'It's a pity you don't remember it when you lie to my father and let him down.'

'You went out with another woman,' she accused.

'Don't be so melodramatic,' he snapped. 'I didn't "go out" with her as such. I went out with her and Alfie, the purpose of which was to give Alfie a nice time. It's entirely your own fault that I was with her and not you. If you're going to tell lies, you must take the consequences.'

'All I did was take a bloomin' day off,' she mumbled.

'No, what you did was lie to my father and let him down for your own ends; and this is the man who is going to be your father-in-law,' he spelled out for her. 'That cuts deep with me because it means that you don't respect him enough to treat him decently. You could at least be straight with him. He's a good man and a fair and generous employer; he doesn't deserve the treatment you give him.'

Seeing how angry he was, she was terrified he might break off their engagement there and then. A large helping of humble pie was definitely needed.

'Sorry, Johnny,' she said, sounding very repentant. 'I was well out of order.'

'I'll say you were, and if you let him down again for no good reason, you're fired,' he warned her.

'Oh Johnny . . .'

'I've told Dad to go ahead and give you your cards the next time you leave him in the lurch,' he cut in determinedly. 'In future he's to treat you the same as any other employee. There'll be no more perks just because you're engaged to me.'

The situation was deadly serious and called for her special brand of persuasion. She raised her left hand, spreading the fingers so that her ring sparkled, and looked at him from under her thick, curling lashes. 'Can the ring stay where it is?' she asked in a girlishly seductive tone. 'Or do I have to give it back to you for being a naughty girl?'

Usually her sexy playfulness amused him, but this time he was irritated by it. But he gritted his teeth and said, 'Of course you don't. This isn't about you and me; it's about you and the job and my father.'

'Sorry, Johnny, it won't happen again.'

'Well, you know the consequences if it does, so let's just leave it at that, shall we?' he suggested coolly. 'Now I have to go back to camp. I only have a twenty-four-hour pass so I can't stay to do the lunchtime shift. I'll pop upstairs to get my things, then I'll be on my way.'

'I'll walk to the station with you.'

'No, not this time, if you don't mind,' he told her in a tone that defied argument. 'I want you to stay here and help Dad. I don't want him to have to cope on his own, not after being under the weather last night. He's probably still a bit weak.'

'Oh, all right then, if that's what you want,' she said meekly.

'Can you manage here now?' he asked. 'I've done the bottling-up. The float is in the till.'

'Yeah, I'll be all right.'

'I'll pop upstairs to get my stuff then. I'll be down in a minute, and so will Dad,' he said, and hurried through the door at the back of the bar to the stairs.

Hazel hardly knew how to control the fury that was eating away inside her. She wasn't so much angry with Johnny as with Rose. That woman really was beginning to push her too far. It was just as well she wasn't around now, because Hazel knew that if she could get her hands on her this minute, she would kill her. Yes, she would go that far to keep her away from Johnny . . .

Chapter Thirteen

The tendency of British people to talk about the weather had been superseded by the bombing. Now that there was a respite from that, food became a favourite topic, especially as the shortages worsened. Everybody talked about it. Women endlessly exchanged views on how to make the rations go further, how to make wartime recipes tastier, and constantly strived to come up with new substitutes for unobtainable items. Men mourned the passing of big meaty dinners and the fact that fish and chips from the shop had become a rarity.

Most people found themselves yearning for some item of food that was no longer readily available. Rose fantasised about real fried eggs instead of the powdered stuff, and bacon with bread spread with lashings of butter instead of a scrape of margarine. She also brooded from time to time on milk chocolate.

One person who wasn't bothered by her meagre wartime diet was Joyce, who was having an extremely nauseous pregnancy. Just the sound of her cousin's detailed eulogy to a fried breakfast was enough to send her scuttling to the bathroom. It was a mystery to Rose how she managed to keep her condition secret, especially from her parents.

But with the shrewd use of roomy clothes to hide her thickening middle, and timely employment of the lavatory chain to drown out the noise of her morning vomiting, Rose remained the sole sharer of her secret. They both knew that Auntie Sybil would have spotted the signs ages ago had she been her usual self, but she remained in her distracted state. Joyce's parents would have to be told some time soon, of course. But as well as dreading the fall-out from her bombshell, Joyce also hated the idea of her much-cherished pregnancy becoming the subject of shame and disgust, as it undoubtedly would once it was out in the open. So she was staying silent for as long as possible.

Through it all, she remained happy and serene. Although she felt like death, she looked well. Her sheer joy in the child she was carrying by far outweighed any physical discomfort and she was radiant.

Until, that is, one day in the autumn when she came looking for Rose in the staff canteen after her early round, tearful, whey-faced and trembling.

'I think I'm going to lose the baby, Rose,' she whispered shakily, sitting down at the table opposite her cousin. 'There's blood . . . down there. Oh Rose, I can't bear to lose it. I'm so scared.'

'Is it much?'

'Enough to frighten the life out of me.'

342

'Have you got any pain?'

'Not much; just a slight ache.'

Although Rose was unnerved by the news, she knew she must take control since Joyce was clearly in no condition to do so. She went with her cousin to Mr Partridge's office, where she was forced by the circumstances to be extremely economical with the truth. She told him that Joyce wasn't feeling well and she needed to take her home as she wasn't in a fit state to go by herself. She was actually intending to take her to the doctor's surgery, but the fewer details Mr Partridge knew the better.

'I'll get back here as soon as I can to do the second delivery,' she told him. 'I'll do Joyce's round as well.'

'Don't worry about that. I'll get someone else to do them both,' said the understanding man, taking a worried glance at Joyce, who looked about to pass out cold. 'You get off home.' He glanced at Rose. 'As she's feeling so groggy, you'd better take her in one of the vans.'

'Ta very much, Mr Partridge,' she said gratefully. 'But is that allowed?'

'Who's running this sorting office, you or me?' he said in a kindly manner. 'There are times when I have to be the judge of what is right, and this is definitely one of them.' He looked at Joyce again, his concern obvious. 'Now get off home with your cousin before we have to pick you up off the floor.'

Because Joyce had always had such a strong character, it was a new experience for Rose to see her in such a

343

nervous state. It wasn't so much for herself she was frightened, but the baby she wanted so much.

'You don't know for sure that you're going to miscarry,' Rose tried to reassure her, as Joyce sobbed uncontrollably all the way to the doctor's surgery. 'It might be nothing to worry about; just a passing thing. Women do sometimes see a bit of blood during a pregnancy, so I've heard, and then go on to produce a perfectly healthy baby. Maybe the fact that you don't have much pain is a good sign.'

'There must be something wrong or I wouldn't be bleeding, would I?'

Rose couldn't argue with that so she just said, 'Let's wait and see what the doctor says, shall we, before we jump to any conclusions?'

'Step on it, Rose,' urged Joyce in a panic.

'I don't want to make things worse by bumping you about too much,' she told her. 'The roads are full of holes and craters left by the bombs.'

'Just get there as fast as you can, please.'

'That's exactly what I am doing,' she said. 'A few more minutes and we'll be there.'

'Complete bed rest is absolutely essential if you are to stand any chance of keeping your baby,' the doctor advised Joyce, after hearing all the facts and giving her an examination. 'It's the only thing that will do it. You may lose it anyway, but bed rest will at least give the baby a chance.'

'I can't take to my bed.' As much as she wanted the

baby, Joyce had to be realistic. 'It just isn't possible.'

'I'm afraid you'll have to,' said the kindly man, who was their family doctor and had known Joyce all her life, though not very well because he wasn't consulted unless someone was seriously ill, on account of the expense. 'And I mean complete rest. You don't even get up for meals.'

'It's rather awkward for her, Doctor,' intervened Rose, who had gone into the consulting room with Joyce at her cousin's request.

'My parents don't know I'm pregnant, that's why,' sobbed Joyce, far too distressed to care what he thought of her. 'I'm not married.'

'Oh . . . oh, I see.' He doodled with a pen on his blotter, then looked up at her with a grave expression. 'Your private life is none of my concern, of course, but your health is, and the health of your baby. I understand that it might be difficult, but you really will have to go home to bed, my dear. You'll need to be looked after for a while.'

'But I have to go to work.'

'That's out of the question, I'm afraid.' His tone was uncompromising. 'At least until this crisis is over, maybe not until after the baby is born, if you go the full term. You'll have to face that possibility.'

'Oh God,' said Joyce, the grim reality of her situation registering fully after months of joy and optimism. How could she go home to bed and expect her parents to look after her, given the nature of her condition? What was she going to do for money if she couldn't go out and earn it? She couldn't sponge off her parents. It wouldn't be fair. Anyway, they probably wouldn't even want her in the house when they knew the truth.

'I can't force you to take my advice, but neither can I be held responsible for the consequences if you don't,' the doctor made clear. 'How you organise things is up to you, but if you don't go straight home to bed you will be putting your baby's life at risk, as well as your own.'

'Leave it to me, Doctor,' said Rose as Joyce was in such a state of distress. 'I'll see to it that she does.'

They thanked him and paid him two shillings, and he said he would call to see Joyce in a few days for no extra charge but that they were to contact him at once if there were any further developments.

'Gawd knows what I'm gonna do now,' said Joyce once they were outside.

'You're going to do exactly what the doctor told you,' announced Rose with an air of authority. 'Just leave it all to me and concentrate on looking after yourself and your baby. I'll sort out everything else.'

Joyce was far too worried, and grateful for Rose's support, to argue.

When they got to Joyce's house, she went straight up to bed while Rose stayed downstairs and confronted her aunt in their living room, a homely chamber with a superabundance of ornaments that gave the room the look of a seaside gift shop.

'There are a lot of coughs and colds about this time

of the year as we head towards winter,' said Sybil, having been told that her daughter had gone to bed because she wasn't feeling well. 'We're all run down through lack of nourishment and prone to pick things up easier, that's what it is.'

'She doesn't have a cold, Auntie,' said Rose.

'Oh? What is the matter with her then?'

Rose braced herself to say what couldn't be avoided. 'She's pregnant,' she blurted out.

Sybil's eyes widened momentarily and she looked at Rose, puzzled. 'Pregnant?' she uttered.

'That's right. She would have told you herself but she asked me to do it for her because there's a problem with her pregnancy and it's important that she doesn't get upset or excited at the moment,' she explained.

'Rose, dear,' began Sybil in a tone only narrowly escaping condescension, 'you've made a mistake. Joyce can't possibly be pregnant. Bob hasn't been home.'

There was an awkward silence and Rose's skin was burning as she summoned up the courage to keep the rest of her promise to Joyce. 'She was seeing someone else, Auntie, one of the postmen from the sorting office, and, er, well . . . it's his baby. He was killed in the fire at the community hall.'

Sybil's eyes were full of accusation. 'You should know better than to say such a wicked thing,' she rasped, refusing to accept the truth. 'Joyce wouldn't do that. She's been far too well brought up for that sort of carry-on.'

'Upbringing has nothing to do with it,' said Rose,

clinging doggedly to her patience and resisting the urge to shake her aunt for her narrow attitude, which wasn't worthy of her. 'She fell in love with someone else. It happens to people from all backgrounds.'

'Not to my daughter it doesn't. Oh no, Rose, you've got it all wrong.' Her voice wobbled on the verge of tears. 'And I'd rather you didn't come in here telling me lies about my daughter. You know I haven't been well.'

Rose was very fond of her aunt and didn't want to hurt her. But certain things needed saying.

'I know you haven't been well, Auntie, but you're better now and Joyce is the one who is poorly and needs looking after. There's a chance that she might lose the baby. She has to have complete bed rest and no upset or excitement; on doctor's orders!'

'The doctor . . .' Now Sybil was forced to take Rose seriously. 'She's spoken to the doctor about it?'

'Yes, we've just come from there,' Rose explained. 'She was taken ill at work so I took her straight to the surgery.'

'Oh my God! My daughter is pregnant outside of marriage,' Sybil wailed, clutching her head. 'The doctor knows about it too. What must he think?'

'It doesn't matter what he thinks. It isn't his place to make moral judgements,' Rose pointed out. 'His only concern is Joyce's health and that of her baby.'

'What is her father going to say?' Sybil muttered, almost to herself.

'He'll be shocked at first, naturally. But knowing Uncle Flip, he'll be pleased to know that he's going to be a grandfather once he gets used to the idea,' suggested Rose.

Sybil tutted, clamping her hand to her brow dramatically. 'An illegitimate baby in the family,' she muttered, apparently with no thought for her daughter. 'Oh dear, oh dear. What are we going to do?'

'There won't be a baby at all if Joyce isn't properly looked after.'

'Oh dear,' she said again feebly, her face and neck suffused with strawberry-coloured anxiety blotches. 'I can't cope with something like this in my state of health.'

'Yes you can, Auntie.' Rose forced herself to be firm. 'The Auntie Sybil I used to know would have been right there by her daughter's side, and I wouldn't have fancied the chances of anyone who said a word out of place about her or her baby. You had plenty of spirit back then. You'd have taken anyone on in defence of your family.'

'I don't know about that,' she grunted.

'I know you've had a bad time, but that strong woman we all loved and admired is still in there somewhere. Auntie Syb, Joyce needs you very much at the moment. Please give her your support.'

'Who was the lowlife who did this to her?' Sybil asked miserably.

'He wasn't a lowlife, and don't let Joyce hear you call him that, for goodness' sake,' warned Rose. 'He was a good man and a talented musician. Before the war he was a full-time music teacher and played at classical concerts.'

'He should have been away fighting for his country, not getting my daughter pregnant.'

'He was medically unfit for the services, which is why he joined the post office,' she explained. 'He was a brave man. He lost his life while out entertaining for charity.'

'No decent man would do that to a woman who's engaged to someone else.'

'They don't come more decent than Stan,' Rose informed her. 'He was a lovely bloke, and he and Joyce adored each other. There was nothing they could do about it, no matter how hard they tried. Joyce felt terrible about betraying Bob, and she still does, but she couldn't help loving Stan. It was meant to be between them, and now, God willing, there will be a baby for her to love and to remind her of him.'

'Some stranger's child,' Sybil mumbled disapprovingly.

'He isn't a complete stranger to you, Auntie,' Rose told her. 'You met him once or twice at our place. You remember Stan, who used to play the piano for us?'

'Oh, it was him, was it?' she snorted. 'He seemed like such a genuine type too.'

'He was; completely genuine.'

Sybil sighed. 'I suppose everybody is talking about her,' she said gloomily.

'Nobody knows about it except me . . . and the doctor now, of course,' she told her aunt.

'They will be yapping about it before long,' Sybil said. 'Anyway, the doctor knowing is bad enough. It makes me feel sick to my stomach to think of it.'

'Joyce was devastated when Stan was killed, Auntie, she really was,' Rose told her, hoping to make her see the problem from a perspective other than her own. 'She's had such a horrible time, grieving for him in secret. This baby has really perked her up. She'll be heartbroken if she loses it.'

'Why didn't she tell me if she was feeling so bad?' Sybil asked. 'I am her mother, after all.'

Rose hesitated for only a moment. 'With respect, you haven't been behaving much like her mother lately, have you?' she blurted out. 'Anyway, she knew you would disapprove of Stan so thought it best not to tell you.'

'Of course I would have disapproved. She was engaged to someone else.'

'If you'd been your old self you would have noticed the signs of pregnancy for yourself.'

Sybil didn't reply; just stared at the floor.

'Look, she knew you would be upset because you're so fond of Bob,' Rose went on. 'You know your daughter; she always has other people's feelings in mind, and that didn't change when she fell in love with Stan. She always knew she would have to hurt Bob and it made her miserable. The important thing now is that we do what we can to help her to avoid a miscarriage. It might happen anyway, of course, but if there's a chance of saving this baby we have to try. She has to have complete bed rest, and someone has to look after her so that she doesn't have to get up. Willingly would I do it, but I have to go to work.'

Sybil just stared worriedly into the distance.

'I have to go now, Auntie, because I have to take the post van back to the sorting office,' she said. 'I won't be long, though. Mr Partridge will have got someone else to do my second delivery. I'll be back as soon as I can.'

Her aunt was still staring miserably into space when Rose saw herself out.

Sybil found herself trembling from head to toe after Rose had gone. She stood there in the middle of the room wringing her hands, feeling sick and wanting to cry. Why did these awful things keep happening to her? Why couldn't life be simple like it was before the war?

If it wasn't one damned thing it was another. No sooner was she back on her feet after almost being killed by that foul rat Adolf's bombs than she was knocked down again; this time by a shocking family scandal. Her daughter was having a baby out of wedlock by a different man to the one she was engaged to. Joyce was going to bring a baby into the world with no father. Oh, it was too awful for words. She couldn't even bear to think about it.

There was an ache deep inside her, and she realised suddenly that it wasn't just pity for herself but concern for her daughter. In some far corner of her mind she felt ashamed, because it was a feeling she hadn't had in a long time.

A baby; the words resonated in her mind, taking on a new meaning. It wasn't just an inconvenient pregnancy that was going to set tongues wagging. It was going to be a child, her grandchild, hers and Flip's. But it might not come to that, because Joyce might lose the baby. If it wasn't meant to be, there was nothing anyone could do, but if there was a chance of saving it . . .

So what was she doing standing here feeling sorry for herself when her daughter was upstairs unwell and worried out of her mind? She scaled the stairs with the speed and agility she'd thought she'd lost for ever.

'Joyce, love,' she said, going over and sitting on the edge of the bed, looking at her daughter's pale, tear-stained face against the pillow. 'Now dry your eyes and stop worrying. Everything is going to be all right. If this pregnancy can be saved, we're going to do it. You do the resting, I'll do everything else.'

Joyce sat up and put her arms around her mother, sobbing even more but with relief and joy now. 'You've been away too long, Mum,' she said thickly.

'I know, luv, I know,' said Sybil. 'But now that I'm back, I'm here to stay.'

'Has Joyce gone out?' asked Flip that evening as he and Sybil sat down for their meal of savoury mince with vegetables.

'No, she's in but she's upstairs in bed. I've taken a tray up to her,' she explained.

'Is she poorly?'

'In a manner of speaking, yes,' she replied.

'What do you mean by that? She's either poorly or

she isn't.' He paused. 'Oh, I see . . . it's the time of the month, is it?'

'No, it isn't that.'

'What is the matter with her then?'

'I have something to tell you, Flip,' Sybil said in a forceful tone of voice he hadn't heard from her in a long time. 'But I want no shouting and hollering. No flying off the handle. You've got to promise to stay calm.'

He put his knife and fork down and looked at her. 'Well, spit it out then, for Gawd's sake.'

She told him the whole story.

'Bloody 'ell,' he exploded, his face turning red then becoming bloodless. 'My daughter's up the duff by some bloke we hardly know, and you expect me to stay calm?'

'That's right,' she said evenly, her gaze resting on his face. 'You can blow your top at me all you like, but not at Joyce, because she's in danger of losing the baby. We must both give her our full support. The baby's father is dead and can't help, so it's up to us.'

Flip got up and paced the room.

'What about Bob, how's he gonna feel when he comes home and finds out what's happened?'

'We'll have to cross that bridge when we come to it,' she said. 'Meanwhile we have to do what we can to help our daughter to hang on to our first grandchild.'

'Grandchild,' he echoed.

'Of course,' she said. 'It might be a boy, Flip. You always wanted a son.'

Flip stroked his chin, mulling it over. 'Well, I can't pretend to be pleased about it. No father would be,' he grunted. 'But as it's happened, I suppose we'll just have to put up with it. I'll go up and see her.'

'Oh no you don't. You're not going anywhere near her until you've properly simmered down,' she said bossily. 'I'm not having you upsetting her.'

'Can't a man do what he wants in his own house?'

'Not if I don't think it's the best thing, no, he certainly can't,' she confirmed. 'So sit back down at the table and eat your meal. It's a sin to waste food in these hard times, and we have to keep our strength up now that we have Joyce to look after.'

Flip did as she asked without argument and they ate in silence, each lost in their own thoughts.

'A grandfather, eh?' he said after a while. 'It doesn't half make me feel old.'

'Your grandchild will soon change that when it arrives,' Sybil said. 'Kids keep you young, so they say.'

'Yeah, there is that. I remember our Joyce when she was little,' he said. 'She was a proper livewire.'

Flip finished his meal, making short work of the plain suet pudding which would have been spotted dick if currants weren't in such short supply. 'I'm going next door to tell Bill,' he said excitedly, rising. 'I can't wait to see his face. We've beaten them to it for a grandchild.'

'You'll do no such thing,' ordered Sybil. 'You are not to breathe a word to Bill or anyone else until I've told May, and I'm not doing that until I've had Joyce's permission. So show your manners and sit down and wait until I've finished eating before you leave the table.'

'Yes, dear.'

Flip knew he would always remember this day. Not only because it was the day he learned that he was to become a grandparent for the first time, if all went well. But because it was the day he got his wife back.

'And don't you go blabbing your mouth off to those pals of yours down the pub neither,' Sybil continued in full voice. 'We don't want the tongues to start wagging before they have to. So keep schtum.'

'I won't say a word, dear.'

Oh what a relief! Sybil was back to normal, nagging away like a good 'un. He could put up with anything, including an unmarried pregnant daughter, when Sybil was on form. He'd been like a lost soul without his sparring partner.

'Thanks for breaking the news to Mum, Rose,' said Joyce the next day when Rose called in to see her after work. 'I don't know how you put it to her but she's being fantastic. So is Dad.'

'That's none of my doing,' Rose told her. 'They are just running true to form. They're good people. I knew they'd come through for you once they got used to the idea.'

'Dad is like a dog with two tails because the whole thing seems to have shocked Mum back to normal. She's back in charge, bossing him about like mad, and it's the way they both like it.' Propped up against the pillows, Joyce smiled. 'Apparently Mum wouldn't let him come up to see me last night until she was sure he wouldn't upset me. He said it's just like old times with her ruling the roost.'

'It's the way we all like it,' said Rose. 'It gave me the creeps to see Aunt Sybil going about like a little mouse.'

'They've said they'll support me financially while I can't work, which has taken a load off my mind.'

'That's good.'

'I hate to sponge off them but I don't have a choice, and I'll make it up to them later on when I'm earning again. Mum's offered to look after the baby when I go out to work, which I shall obviously have to do to feed and clothe it.'

'I told you they'd turn up trumps, didn't I?'

'I suppose I knew that too in my heart. But it was such a huge thing I was hitting them with. About the worst thing a girl can land her parents with,' she said. 'I think they're dreading the scandal and worried about Bob, but they seem pleased about the baby.'

'They'll have a wonderful time spoiling it.'

Joyce frowned. 'I'm still scared stiff I might lose it, but I'm trying to stay calm,' she confessed.

'Are you still bleeding?'

'It seems to have stopped, for the moment anyway, so I'm feeling a bit more optimistic, but I'm not taking anything for granted,' she told her. 'I'll see what the doctor says when he comes, but if I have to stay here in bed for the next three months to keep it, I'll do it, though I don't know how I'll stand Mum fussing over me for that long.'

'You didn't like it when she went all withdrawn, remember,' said Rose.

'I know I didn't, but she can get a bit much at times when she's on form,' Joyce said. 'I love her to bits, though, and am very grateful to her.'

'Would you like me to come and sit with you later on?' Rose offered. 'It might help to pass the time if you have a bit of company of your own age. It isn't much fun being in bed on a Saturday.'

'I'd love that, Rose, if you don't have anything else to do,' she said.

'Nothing that I can't do at another time,' Rose replied thoughtfully.

The next day was Sunday, and Sunday mornings were very special to Rose because she didn't have to get up at four o'clock.

It was always a homely sort of time, and she usually gave her mother a hand by tidying up and preparing the vegetables for Sunday lunch. Then they would have a companionable cup of Camp coffee together in the kitchen while her father read the paper in the living room. This Sunday, Joe was still in bed as he'd been on night duty at the sub-station.

Joyce had given her mother permission to tell her sister about her pregnancy, so the news was out and naturally May was full of it when they sat down for coffee. Rather to Rose's surprise, however, she was not judgemental. Given the scandalous nature of Joyce's circumstances, Rose had automatically expected any member of the older generation to be beside themselves with disgust.

'I nearly passed out cold when Sybil told me,' May confessed, looking at Rose over the rim of her cup. 'But it's happened and it's up to us, as her family, to do all we can to help. She'll need all the support she can get. She'll get plenty of trouble from the world outside.'

'She knows it's going to be hard.'

'But with the help of her mum and dad, and us lot in the background, she'll get by,' said May. 'We'll make bloomin' sure that she does.'

'You're not full of moral outrage, then?'

'I'm not happy about it, naturally; she's been a silly girl and I wish it hadn't happened this way, for her sake. I feel very sorry for Bob, too,' she made clear. 'But these things happen; we're all only human.' She cradled her cup in her hands. 'One thing is for sure, Joyce isn't going to be the only woman in the same position by the time this war is over. When couples are split up for long periods, it's bound to happen.'

Rose nodded.

The conversation was brought to a halt by the dog, who was staring at Rose beseechingly to remind her that it was time for his Sunday morning walk.

'All right, Bruiser, I can take a hint,' she said to him, stroking his head. 'I'll just finish my coffee, then I'll get my coat.'

She'd just gone out of the front gate with the dog on the lead when she stopped dead in her tracks as she saw a man and a boy walking towards her. She ran up to Alfie and hugged him while the dog barked and jumped up at him, woofing rapturously and wagging his tail.

'What a lovely surprise,' said Rose, beaming at both Alfie and his father. 'To what do I owe the honour?'

'As you didn't get to see Alfie yesterday, I thought I'd bring him to see you,' Johnny explained.

'I rang the pub and told your dad I couldn't make it because my cousin isn't well. I told him I'd be over today. I was going to come this afternoon,' she said. 'Did he forget to give you the message?'

'No. We got the message, but I thought Alfie could come to see you instead of the other way around. It's about time we made some effort.'

'That's nice,' she beamed. 'The others will be delighted to see you, Alfie. Let's go indoors.'

Indeed, the family were thrilled to have unexpected visitors, and gave them a real Barton welcome.

'Well you're a sight for sore eyes, young man,' said May, hugging Alfie. 'We've missed you around here.' She grinned. 'It's been very quiet without you and all your cheek.'

'It's good to see you, boy,' added Bill. 'How have you been getting on?'

'All right thanks, Mr Barton,' he replied chirpily.

'I'll put the kettle on,' said May. 'And I might be able to find a few biscuits.'

Joe came downstairs to see what all the excitement was about and everyone began talking at once. Except Johnny, who was standing back watching with a smile on his face.

The dog wasn't prepared to be done out of his walk, visitors or no visitors, and was woofing at the door.

'I'll have to take him out or we'll get no peace,' said Rose. 'You stay and talk to everyone, Alfie. Bruiser and I will see you when we get back; shan't be long.'

She put the dog back on the lead and hurried out of the house.

'Mind if I join you, Rose?' asked Johnny, catching her up at the gate.

'Course not,' she said. 'I'm only taking him to the park to let him have a bit of a run. It isn't far.'

'It's just the weather for a walk,' he said.

It was a cold, clear autumn day, a hazy sun shining from a misty blue sky. Not a sign of a cloud anywhere. 'It feels so good not to have the air thick with bomb smoke, doesn't it?' she remarked.

'Not half.'

'They reckon the raids will start again in the winter, though,' she added.

'That seems to be the general opinion,' he said. 'I think the Germans are still being kept busy giving Russia a hard time at the moment.'

'It's ever so nice of you to bring Alfie over,' she said, changing the subject. 'I really did intend to come to your place later on today.'

'I thought it would make a nice change for you both if he came here,' he told her. 'It'll give him a chance to see the others too.'

'It's a good idea. In fact maybe he could come to ours for the whole weekend some time, when you're not at home, to give him a chance to spend some time with the family and the friends he made when he lived here,' Rose suggested. 'I'll come and get him and bring him back.'

'I think he'd like that,' Johnny said. 'I'll talk to him about it later on.'

'It's a while since you've been home, isn't it?' she remarked in a casual manner to suggest, erroneously, that she'd barely been aware of his absence.

'It's been much too long,' he said. 'Still, I mustn't grumble. I'm lucky to be posted near to home so I can get back more than most of the other blokes. I'm making the most of it. I'll miss it when I go back overseas.'

They entered the park and she let the dog off the lead. They stood together watching him tear across the sunlit grass.

'All that energy,' she said with a casual air, though she was acutely aware of Johnny's disturbing proximity. 'I could do with some of that when I get up for work at four o'clock in the morning.'

'I'll bet.' He paused. 'How have you been this long time, Rose?' he asked, the interest and tenderness in his voice creating a sense of intimacy.

'Fine.' There was a vibrancy in the air that filled her with joy and a sense of anticipation.

'You look well,' he said hoarsely, observing her lovely bright eyes, cheeks rosy from the cold, the red muffler around her neck so perfect with her dark hair.

Trying to still her thudding heart she said, 'Yes, I'm one of those people who are always disgustingly healthy.'

He wanted to hold her in his arms and tell her much he'd missed her; tell her how often he thought about her. But he reminded himself of his commitment to Hazel and just said softly, 'I'm glad.'

As she nervously fiddled with the dog's lead, it slipped from Rose's grasp and dropped to the ground. Before she could bend down to retrieve it, Johnny picked it up for her. As he passed it to her, his hand brushed against hers. It felt so agonisingly sweet, all her instincts were crying out for her to ignore the fact that he was engaged to someone else and show him how she felt.

But common sense finally prevailed and she just said, 'Ooh, it's a bit chilly when you stand around, isn't it? I think we'd better get moving.'

'Yeah,' he said sadly.

She called the dog and they walked on, saying little, the atmosphere between them charged with emotion.

Chapter Fourteen

Hazel was seething when she got home from her lunchtime shift at the pub that day, and in no mood to listen to her younger sister pestering her for a favour.

'Can I borrow this frock?' asked eighteen-year-old Sheila. She had removed the item from the wardrobe she and Hazel shared in their joint bedroom, and was holding it up against herself in front of the mirror. 'I think it'll look nice on me.'

'No, you can't,' snapped Hazel, who was lying on her bed staring miserably at the ceiling. 'Put it back in the wardrobe and get out of here. I want to be on my own.'

'It's my bedroom as well as yours.' Sheila was pretty like Hazel but not quite so cosmetically enhanced. 'I've as much right to be here as you.'

'Just shut up and go away.'

'Let me borrow this red dress then,' she persisted. 'Then I'll go away and leave you alone. I promise.'

But Hazel was in no mood to do anyone a good turn. 'No, I am not lending it to you, so stop going on about it,' she said.

'Oh please,' wheedled Sheila. 'You've got loads more clothes than I have.'

'Some of them I've had for years; since before clothes went on ration,' Hazel pointed out irritably. 'Anyway, I need more things than you do. I'm not some scruffy factory girl who wears overalls all day. I have to look glamorous when I go to work.'

''Ere, you watch who you're calling scruffy,' her sister retaliated. 'You've got a bloomin' cheek.'

'I'm only saying what's true; factory gear isn't exactly smart, is it?'

'At least I'm doing my bit for the war effort, which is more than can be said for you. I help to make munitions. All you do is stand behind a bar counter flirting with blokes.'

'I do not flirt,' Hazel denied hotly. 'I've no need to since I'm engaged to be married.'

'That doesn't stop you flashing your eyes at the men and sticking your chest out, does it?' Sheila challenged. 'Don't deny it, because I've seen you do it.'

'They flirt with me and I have to be careful not to upset them because they are punters,' said Hazel. 'It's all part of the job.' She put a hand to her brow as though in pain. 'Anyway, I don't have to explain myself to you. Just go away, will you, you silly kid? You're getting on my nerves and giving me a headache.'

'You've no right to call me scruffy when I'm doing an honest job of work and helping my country.'

'Oh for God's sake, just go away and let me have some peace,' snarled Hazel.

'You hardly ever wear this frock anyway,' said the indomitable Sheila, who had a good teacher in her older sister on how to get her own way. 'Just one night, that's all I want it for. It isn't much to ask.'

'No. How many more times must I tell you?'

'Oh please, sis,' she kept on. 'I've got a date . . . with a gorgeous Yank, as it happens, so I want to look my best. Go on, just this once. I'll take your turn with the washing-up for a week in return.'

The fury within Hazel that was being exacerbated by Sheila's dogged persistence actually had nothing to do with her sister, or the red frock. It had everything to do with Johnny going over to Rose's house this morning. He'd told her about it when he got back as though he had no shame; claimed that he just went over there to take Alfie.

Unfortunately Hazel had been unable to contain her vociferous disapproval. How she'd managed to stop herself from lashing out at him physically, she'd never know. All her instincts told her not to overdo the remonstrations; it wasn't wise to antagonise him at this stage. Once they were married her security would be assured so she could do as she pleased as regards to making sure he didn't step out of line.

He definitely fancied Rose; there was no doubt in her mind about that. There was something in his voice when he mentioned her name. He tried to sound casual but it just didn't ring true. Hazel's anger grew ever more ferocious the more she thought about it. He'd had the audacity to go and visit another woman when he was engaged to be married to her. Just friends, my Aunt Fanny! Since when could a man and a woman have a platonic relationship, apart from relatives and people who were past it?

'Two weeks washing-up in exchange for the loan of your red frock for one night only,' her sister was bargaining. 'I'm being more than generous; so how about it, sis?'

The irksome drone of Sheila's attempts to coax her finally sent Hazel's temper soaring to uncontrollable levels. She shot to her feet, grabbed Sheila by the arms and banged her against the wall very hard. 'Just do as I say and get out of this room,' she rasped through clenched teeth. 'I don't want to hear any more of your whining.'

'Hey, stop that; you're hurting me,' objected Sheila, her face screwed up with pain. 'You bashed my head so hard against that wall it's throbbing. I'm telling Mum.'

Hazel's strength was magnified by the rage that was driving her, and she pulled Sheila away from the wall and pushed her down on to her bed. Before the younger woman had a chance to escape, Hazel had pinned her down with her knees and one hand gripping her arm, then pulled her hair so hard her sister cried out, her eyes filling with tears of agony.

'You're telling Mum nothing,' Hazel said, slapping her sister's face. 'Is that clear?'

'You're bleedin' barmy.' Sheila was frightened. Hazel had always had a vile temper and had knocked her younger sister around on several occasions before. But this was worse than anything that had gone before. Hazel seemed weird; like someone possessed. 'Stark raving mad.'

Hazel had, indeed, passed beyond the point of rational thought. The rage was scorching through her, compelling her to hurt someone, anyone, to satisfy her anger, because some bitch of a woman was trying to come between her and her man. She put her hands around her terrified sister's throat and squeezed, immediately increasing the pressure.

A voice from downstairs recalled her to reality.

'Dinner's on the table, girls,' shouted their mother. 'Get down here please – *now*.'

Hazel let go of Sheila.

'You're evil,' her sister choked out, trying to catch her breath and rubbing her throat. 'I'm telling Mum to have you locked up. You're not fit to live among decent people.'

'I was only playing about,' said Hazel, shocked by her own actions; she hadn't meant to take it that far and was unnerved by what she had done. 'Can't you take a joke?'

'You just tried to strangle me,' said Sheila, getting up off the bed and holding her throat. 'It didn't feel much like a joke to me.'

'Don't be so ridiculous,' sneered Hazel. 'If I'd wanted to strangle you I would have done it and you wouldn't be here to whinge on at me, would you? You know perfectly well that I was just mucking about, so don't make a drama of it.'

369

'I don't think you were just mucking about,' Sheila told her, her eyes narrowing with suspicion. 'If Mum hadn't called upstairs I'd have been a goner.'

'You're being dramatic—'

'No I'm not,' Sheila cut in. 'You nearly killed me.'

'Look, I'm sorry if I hurt you, kid,' said Hazel, changing tack swiftly because she was eager to smooth things over. She didn't want Sheila telling their mother; she didn't want anyone to know about what had happened just now. 'I was just playing about, honest. I obviously don't know my own strength.'

'No you bloomin' well don't,' responded Sheila miserably, rubbing her neck and making a face. 'If that was playing about, I dread to think what you'd be like if you were serious.'

'I tell you what,' began Hazel, becoming chummy, 'how about I make it up to by letting you borrow my red dress?'

Sheila frowned. 'You won't get round me that easily, you know,' she said. 'You half killed me just now. I'm not going to let you get away with it.'

Hazel could feel her temper rising again, but the need to placate her sister was urgent enough to restrain another outburst. 'I'm really sorry, kid,' she apologised again. 'To show you how sorry I am, you can borrow anything of mine you want, as long as I don't want to wear it myself, every night for a month, and I'll do the washing-up for a week, if you promise not to tell Mum. You know how narked she gets when we quarrel; she'll blow her top and we'll both be in trouble.'

Sheila was sorely tempted by Hazel's offer. She had some snazzy stuff in the wardrobe. It was all a bit on the tarty side but glamorous none the less. And it would be nice to have the red frock at her disposal for a whole month. But Hazel wasn't going to get off that lightly, not after what she'd done.

'A month for the washing-up as well,' she bartered.

This annoyed Hazel. Her sister was taking liberties now. But she needed her silence. 'Three weeks,' she said.

'It's a deal,' agreed Sheila.

Their mother's voice came shrieking up the stairs again.

'Have you two got cloth ears or something?' she demanded. 'I told you to come down for your dinner and I didn't do it for the benefit of my health. Your food is getting cold and I want you down here now, this minute.'

'We'd better go down before she bursts a blood vessel,' said Hazel.

Sheila gave a wry grin and the two sisters left the room and went downstairs, united now against parental authority.

Hazel's anger was spent, but her problem wasn't solved. That wretched Rose was still a blight on her life. What was she going to do about her?

'So, have you got your green ration book yet, Joyce?' Rose enquired one day in November when she called to see her cousin on her way home from work.

'Not yet,' replied Joyce, who was sitting in an armchair

371

with a blanket over her legs. Her mother had gone next door to see her sister, and her father was out at work. 'I've got the doctor's certificate that I need, though. I feel a bit embarrassed about applying, seeing as I don't have a husband. I expect I'll get some funny looks.'

'You're entitled to a green ration book the same as every other expectant mother,' asserted Rose. 'Your baby is just as important as a married woman's. You and your baby need the extra nourishment you're entitled to. So you'll just have to ignore any black looks or snide remarks.'

'I know, and I will do it,' said Joyce, who was no longer confined to bed but still had to take things very easy. 'I haven't had much of a chance, being laid up in bed, not knowing if I was going to stay pregnant or not.'

'Now that that scare is over and your pregnancy is progressing normally, you might as well get the extra coupons,' opined Rose. 'Perhaps I can get the ration book for you, if you don't fancy going down the Food Office, or if you don't feel up to it.'

'No, I'll go myself,' Joyce told her. 'A gentle stroll will do me good, and I'll have to get used to being the subject of gossip. There's no time like the present. I'll do it tomorrow.'

A green ration book was issued to every pregnant woman in addition to her ordinary book on production of a medical certificate. Among the additional rations this entitled her to were extra meat, milk and eggs, concentrated orange juice and other edibles considered vital to building a healthy baby.

'Take it steady then,' advised Rose. 'No rushing and tearing about.'

'No chance of that with all the extra weight I'm carrying at the moment,' Joyce said, knitting needles clacking. 'Anyway, I won't do anything to put this pregnancy in jeopardy. One scare is quite enough for me.'

'Are you feeling a bit more confident now, though?' asked Rose. 'Have you stopped worrying about losing the baby?'

'It's still at the back of my mind, naturally. I suppose it will be until the baby is here safe and sound, but yes, I am feeling better about it as time passes and nothing untoward happens,' she explained. 'The doctor says that as long as I take it easy, all should be well. As much as I'd like to come back to work, I daren't risk it.'

'I should think not,' said Rose. 'You'd be thinking of giving up about now anyway. You haven't got all that long to go now, have you?'

'Just a few weeks.'

'Exactly, and you haven't been idle since you've been up and about again, have you?' said Rose, glancing towards the sweater Joyce was knitting for the troops. 'You must have done a fair number of those.'

'I've lost count but I like to keep busy. You've got to do something to pass the time when you're not out at work, and there isn't much you can do when you're supposed to be taking it easy,' she said. 'Anyway, knitted things are so urgently needed by our boys, I'd feel guilty if I was sitting here all day doing nothing.'

'Make the most of it, kid. It's a damned sight warmer

sitting here knitting than going out on the post in the early morning now that the winter is drawing in,' said Rose. 'I thought my fingers were going to drop off this morning.'

'I know the feeling,' responded Joyce. 'Though it isn't warm in here now that coal is getting short and we can't keep a fire in during the day.'

'Which explains the blanket.'

She nodded. 'I've got a hot-water bottle under there too,' she grinned. 'It's freezing in our house most of the time. And when you're sitting about you get cold.' Joyce put her knitting on her lap and looked at Rose. 'But that's enough about me. How are things with you?'

'Fine.'

'How is Alfie, and that divine father of his?' she asked.

'Alfie's fine. I don't know about Johnny. I haven't seen him lately. He doesn't seem to get home week-ends so often recently. Alfie came to us for the weekend last week so I didn't go over to the pub. His grandad put him on the bus and I collected him at this end.'

'It's a good idea for Alfie to come to yours now and again at a weekend, isn't it?' Joyce remarked. 'At least it gives you a break from going there.'

Rose nodded, lowering her eyes.

'Though you might not want a break from it,' her cousin said quizzically.

Rose looked up. 'Meaning . . . ?'

'That you like to go there just in case there's a chance of seeing Johnny.'

'What on earth gives you that idea?'

'Could be the way you go all gooey-eyed every time you mention his name.'

Rose heaved a sigh of resignation. 'Is it that obvious?' she asked.

'Only to me,' said Joyce. 'I doubt if anyone else has noticed anything.'

'His girlfriend has, even though I've been denying it, even to myself,' said Rose. 'She hates my guts.'

'So where do you go from here with Johnny?' asked Joyce.

'Absolutely nowhere,' she replied. 'He's engaged to Hazel, and I'm still a grieving widow.'

'It's nearly a year and a half since you lost Ray,' Joyce reminded her. 'You're not expected to grieve for ever.'

'I know that.' She shrugged. 'But Johnny is committed to someone else, and he has a very strong sense of duty.'

'That doesn't sound very satisfactory.'

'I'd sooner be his friend than not in his life at all,' she said.

'But you'd like more?'

'Leave it, Joyce,' Rose urged her. 'The timing is all wrong. Maybe if things had been different . . . but they're not, so let's change the subject, shall we?'

'All right. There's no need to jump down my throat.'

'Sorry.'

'You're forgiven,' she said. 'Now how about you give me an update on what's been happening at work. I want to hear all the gossip.'

'Right, now let me think . . .' but Rose's mind wasn't really on it. The mention of Johnny had put him at the forefront of her thoughts again: his deep husky voice, his warm smile and the way he made her feel so special when they were together. She missed seeing him and wanted to write to him while he was away – just as friends – but suspected it might be too unsettling for them both. The sensible thing was not to contact him at all. 'We've got lots of people off sick, so we all have to do extra rounds. I've got to go back to work later on.'

'Ah poor you,' Joyce sympathised. 'But that's all run-of-the-mill stuff. Isn't there any nice juicy gossip?'

'No, nothing to get excited about.'

'That'll soon change when they find out about my . . . er . . . little predicament,' she said with a grin. 'It'll be the mother and father of all scandals.'

'That's one piece of sorting office gossip that I won't be taking part in,' Rose said lightly. 'They won't dare make any remarks in front of me.'

'That's the spirit,' said Joyce.

Johnny was lying on his bed in the barrack room, staring at the ceiling and smoking a cigarette. It was the evening and work had finished for the day. Some of the lads were writing letters, others were playing cards; some had already gone to the NAAFI. They had been out on tough manoeuvres all day and everybody was exhausted.

His thoughts turned to home, and Alfie and Ted, wondering how they were and wishing, with a kind of ache, that he was there at the pub with them, especially now that he didn't manage to get home of a weekend very often. A new officer of the tyrant variety had taken over and was very much meaner with weekend passes than the man he'd replaced.

Inhaling on his cigarette, Johnny pondered on the fact that he was missing so much of Alfie's growing years. Firstly because of an error of judgement on Peggy's part, and now because of some Nazi maniac who wanted to rule the world.

Rose came into his mind, as she so often did; too often for an easy conscience, if he was honest. He loved the look of her, the sound of her voice, the way she tackled life head on. Alfie positively lit up when he saw her, and Johnny felt the same way just thinking about her.

He'd been tempted on more than one occasion to write to her. He so much wanted to keep in touch, to know how she was and what she was doing.

'Coming over the NAAFI for a pint, Johnny?' asked his pal who slept in the next bed, interrupting his reverie.

'Yes, mate,' he replied, 'but not just yet. I'll see you over there a bit later on. I've a letter to write first.'

'I'll get one lined up for you then,' said the soldier, and made his way over to the barrack-room door.

Johnny got his writing materials out of his locker and went over to the big table in the centre of the room, excited now that he had made the decision to write to Rose. But as he put pen to paper, he thought of Hazel, and was consumed with guilt. Firstly because he realised that he hadn't given her a thought until now; secondly because he was about to write to another woman.

Was that right? Was that playing the game? If you were committed to one woman, you didn't mess around with another, not according to his rules anyway. It wouldn't be just one letter; the second stage would be longing for a reply, then he'd get his pen and paper out again, feelings would be mentioned, and there would be no going back.

With gloom descending upon him like a change in the weather on a sunny day, he accepted the fact that it wouldn't be fair to Hazel, especially as she was making such an effort with Alfie these days. It was her he should be writing to, not Rose. But he just wasn't in the mood right now, so he took his writing things back to the locker and got ready to go to the NAAFI for a comforting pint with his army pals.

'It's your go, Hazel,' said Alfie.

She didn't reply, so he rattled the dice in the eggcup they were using.

'What was that?' she said, jolted out of her thoughts.

'It's your turn to throw the dice.'

'Oh, right.'

She shook the dice and let it go.

'Three,' announced Alfie. 'Shall I move your counter for you?'

'If you like,' she said, trying unsuccessfully to inject some interest into her voice.

Ludo with a flaming child on a Sunday afternoon, she thought. How much duller could a girl's life get? Talk about plumbing the depths. The lengths a woman had to go to to get her man; it was appalling. If there wasn't so much at stake, she would go out and find someone who didn't have a child in tow. But marrying Johnny offered so much more than just sharing a bed. It would give her access to money, position and protection from war work.

But trying to be Alfie's friend was hard going; especially now that Johnny didn't get home so much. She didn't even have the physical pleasures of the engagement to look forward to; life was just working behind the bar and trying to get along with this dratted kid.

'Six, I got a six so I can have another go,' he was telling her, as though it mattered.

'Go on then, have another go,' she said, yawning.

'A three. Your go.'

How much longer was this awful game going to go on for? she wondered, her patience threadbare. She never had been able to see the point of games, and couldn't take much more of this one. In fact she wanted to throw the whole ruddy thing on the fire, and the boy along with it.

Some people were good with children, and God knows her life would be a lot easier if she was one of them. But no matter how hard she tried, Alfie continued to be just a source of annoyance and resentment to her.

'Fancy a cup o' tea, Hazel?' enquired Ted, who'd been snoozing in the armchair.

Hazel always tried to make sure Ted was around when she did her stuff with Alfie. There was no point in making all this effort if it went unnoticed by the people who mattered. Ted could be relied upon to mention it to Johnny when he came home. She'd always sensed that Ted didn't think much of her, and only tolerated her because of his son. But there was a notice-able change in his attitude towards her when she took some notice of Alfie.

'Yes please, Ted,' she said, the interruption giving her a chance to strengthen her control. 'But I'll make it if you'll take my turn here.'

'No, you stay where you are,' he replied pleasantly. 'You're doing a good job there, keeping young Alfie amused. It's boring for him indoors when it's too cold for him to play out. I'll make the tea.'

'Thanks, Ted.'

'It's your go, Hazel,' Alfie reminded her.

Looking at him as he waited for her to throw the stupid dice, his blue eyes resting on her expectantly and reminding her of how much he looked like his father, she wanted to hit him; to shake him and tell him to go away and get out of their lives for ever. Nothing had been the same with Johnny since this little pest had come on to the scene.

Her rage towards him was so strong, she had to look away and take a deep breath. If she wanted Johnny, which she most definitely did, she had to take the kid as well, as least until she had Johnny safely hooked and could find a way of removing his offspring. So it was vital that she controlled her temper. It seemed that the way to Johnny's heart these days was through his son.

'You don't have to play if you don't want to,' came Alfie's small voice, making her feel guilty and even more furious with him for doing so.

'Course I want to play,' she said, as though surprised at the suggestion. 'What makes you think I don't?'

He shrugged. 'I thought you seemed a bit fed up and bored with the game.'

'I'm not bored and fed up,' she lied. 'I love spending time with you, whatever we do.'

'You're a lucky boy,' remarked Ted, appearing with the tea at exactly the right moment from Hazel's point of view. 'It's very nice of Hazel to play with you.'

Recognition at last, thought Hazel with a boost to her spirits. At least the afternoon wasn't entirely wasted.

'Not at all, Ted,' she said sweetly. 'It's the least I can do. Alfie and I get on like a house on fire, don't we, kid? It's just as well as we're going to be related.'

Alfie didn't reply. Just said, 'It's your turn again, Hazel.'

'Right, here we go then,' she said, making a supreme effort to seem enthusiastic for the benefit of Ted. 'Ooh, look, a six. Does that mean I get another go?'

Alfie nodded and handed her the dice. He was so miserable he wanted to weep. He loathed being with Hazel and knew she felt the same about him. He didn't want to play Ludo or any other game with her but it wasn't good manners to say so. Anyway, she'd find a way of punishing him when no one else was around if he didn't do what she wanted. Even more worrying, she would make something bad happen to Rose. Witches like her had special powers. That was why he couldn't tell his grandfather how horrid she was to him sometimes when the two of them were on their own.

Why couldn't she just go away and leave them alone? He felt sick with dread at the thought of when she and his father got married, because she would come to live here then. If only Rose was here more often. Why couldn't his dad marry her instead of Hazel? His father liked Rose, you could tell when he was with her, and Alfie would love to have her as his stepmother.

'Your go, Alfie,' Hazel was saying.

'All right.' He was struggling to force back the tears as he threw the dice.

On her way home from work one day, around noon, May noticed a stream of women hurrying towards the shops with their shopping bags.

'Cooking apples at the greengrocer's,' explained a neighbour. 'They're coming in at one o'clock.'

'Thanks, luv,' she said, tearing down the street and knocking on Sybil's door to pass on the news before dashing indoors to get some money and her shopping bag.

The queue was already long when the sisters got there because word soon got around when there was news of any non-rationed item being available.

'Still more than half an hour to go until they come in,' said Sybil as they took their places. 'We might just be lucky.'

'I wonder how many they'll let us have,' said May.

'Not many, I shouldn't think, but enough to make a pie, I hope,' she said.

'A pie is the only way to make the apples go round,' remarked May. 'Even if the amount of apple is so small you can hardly see it. As long as there's a bit of a taste inside the pastry it makes everyone happy.'

'How's the job going, May?' asked Sybil.

'Not too bad,' she replied. 'In fact, I quite enjoy it. The other women are all about my age, so we have a bit of a laugh. It's hard work, mind, working in the kitchens, but not as hard as being on the factory floor, and it's only mornings, so I can fit it around my household commitments. Why? Do you fancy joining me?'

'I wouldn't mind but I've promised Joyce I'll look after the baby while she goes back to work. If I start a job I might find it difficult to get out of it when Joyce needs me. I don't want to let her down.'

'It's still not compulsory for women of our age to go out to work.'

'It will be before long, I reckon,' Sybil said. 'Anyway, I feel really guilty not doing a job with all this pressure from the government for women to volunteer for war work.'

'Don't forget all the unpaid voluntary work you do for the Townswomen's Guild,' May reminded her, 'as well as running a national savings group and collecting salvage. If you were to add up all the hours a week you spend doing that, I think you'd find that you do more than your bit.'

'Yeah, I suppose so.'

'Anyway,' began May, changing the subject, 'has Joyce got everything ready for the baby yet?'

'No. She's a bit superstitious about it,' said Sybil. 'Afraid to buy anything in case something goes wrong. But I told her she'll need to get some basics in soon. Mind you, May, she won't be able to get much. It's scandalous what the government give expectant mothers in the way of extra coupons. I mean, how far are fifty coupons going to go when a single nappy is one coupon and most people need thirty-six of them. It doesn't leave much for baby clothes.'

'We'll all help out,' said May. 'This baby won't want for anything with us lot around.'

'That's nice to know.'

Sybil suddenly became aware of a couple of women who lived in their street looking in her direction somewhat furtively and whispering.

'Save my place, May love,' she said. 'There's something I have to get sorted.'

'All right,' said May, watching her sister march towards the women with an air of determination.

'If you've got something to say about me,' Sybil began, confronting them unabashed, her eyes blazing, 'you might at least have the guts to say it to my face.'

'Dunno what you're talking about,' responded one of the women, who was wearing a brown turban with curlers poking out of the front.

'Not much you don't,' said Sybil furiously. 'Come on, let's hear it.'

'You'll be getting all the benefits of a green ration book now,' said the other woman, who was wearing a headscarf. 'We've seen the extra milk you're having left.'

'All that milk must be why young Joyce has put on so much extra weight,' chortled the first woman, her courage boosted by her friend's temerity in speaking out.

'You gossip-mongering pair of cows,' Sybil blasted at them. 'Have you nothing better to do with your time than spread rumours about one of your neighbours?'

'The size of your Joyce tells us it's more than just a rumour,' said the woman in the headscarf.

'So . . . what business is it of yours if my Joyce is expecting?' Sybil demanded.

'It sets a bad example and lowers the tone of the street,' said the woman. 'We've got growing daughters. We don't want them getting any ideas because of her.'

'You'd better keep 'em locked up indoors then,' retaliated Sybil. 'Because that's the only way you can guarantee they won't find themselves in my Joyce's condition.' She paused to draw breath. 'Now if I see you so much as look at my Joyce the wrong way, you'll be hearing about it.'

They both shrugged and turned away. Sybil went back to join May.

'Ignorant beggars,' she said.

'I couldn't come and give you back-up or we'd have lost our place in the queue,' explained May.

'Don't worry about that,' said Sybil. 'I'm more than a match for people like that.'

'You certainly are,' agreed May with admiration. 'When you're on form, no one can touch you.'

It was seven o'clock on a freezing, dark December morning. Out on her round Rose was cold, tired, hungry and fed up. It was most unlike her but she was feeling low; sick of never being warm and always feeling in urgent need of food. She was exhausted by the war and its deprivations. Still, at least the air raids were still eerily absent so there was a lot to be grateful for, but at this moment she was finding it difficult to be thankful about anything. Her husband was dead, the man she was beginning to fall in love with wasn't available, she'd just walked into a wall in the blackout and bashed her head so hard so it was throbbing, and her chilblains were playing up something awful.

The darkness always seemed more isolating in the morning than at night, because there weren't so many people about. The job took longer in the winter too, because she had to feel her way around. She stopped now to open another bundle of letters by the light of the torch, her hands so cold she could barely make them function.

Finally managing to untie the string, she carried on with her deliveries, coming to the part of her round that took in a section of the main road. This was her favourite bit because there were shops here so she didn't have to negotiate front paths in the dark, tripping over privet hedges.

She could hear voices nearby; they sounded like male

voices. Peering into the distance, she could just make out the dim lighting of a stationary trolley bus. Her stomach lurched as the voices rose and it became obvious that there was trouble of some sort. People were shouting; there was a scream. She guessed there must have been some sort of an incident. But there had been no bombs, so that couldn't be the cause.

Hurrying towards the noise to offer assistance, she could see that the AFS were there, their taxis parked near the motionless bus.

'I just didn't see him,' said a man in a bus driver's uniform. With horror she realised it was her Uncle Flip. 'The first I knew was when I felt a bump and realised someone or something must be under my wheels. How are we drivers supposed to see anything in the blackout? People should stay on the pavement and not wander into the road.'

'They're getting him out,' said a fire officer.

Rose saw a fireman crawl out from underneath the bus, the front of which was jacked up. Together with another fireman he drew someone else out. It was a man, and he was moaning in agony.

'You're doing fine,' said the fireman she recognised to be her brother Joe. He was trying to keep the man warm with blankets. 'The ambulance is on its way.'

'My legs,' the man gasped. 'Oh bloody hell, help me, please. It's agony.' He yelled out in pain, his moans becoming fainter before they stopped altogether.

Rose thought he must have died, but her brother was saying, 'You'll be all right, mate; just hold on to me and stay awake until the ambulance gets here. They'll give you something to help with the pain. You'll be fine. Just stay awake. Come on now, please don't go to sleep.'

Rose stayed silent in the shadows. Joe was busy with important work. The last thing he needed was his sister hindering him at this crucial time.

'Can you hurry that ambulance up, boss?' Joe said in a low voice. 'He's bleeding heavily, and unconscious. I can't keep him awake.'

Her uncle bowed his head, and Rose could see that his shoulders were quivering. Her heart ached for him.

'It wasn't your fault, mate,' said the fire officer. 'No one will blame you. The bloody blackout is killing off nearly as many people as the German bombs.'

Rose went over to her distraught uncle, who was shaking violently now. 'Try not to upset yourself too much, Uncle Flip,' she said gently, putting her arms around him. 'You couldn't help it. You can't see in the dark.'

But poor Flip was inconsolable.

'A man's badly hurt because of me,' he said, his voice trembling. 'He might die.'

'You need to go home,' suggested Rose kindly. 'I'll go with you.'

'He'll have to wait for the police to come, luv,' suggested the fireman. 'They'll want details from him.'

'I need to get back on the bus; there are passengers waiting to finish their journey,' said Uncle Flip thickly.

'Wotcha, Rose,' said Joe. 'I didn't realise you were here. You can look after Uncle.'

'I don't need looking after,' their uncle insisted. 'There are people on my bus who need to get somewhere; people going to work on early shifts and others coming off late ones. Anyway, I can't leave the bus there. It's my responsibility.'

'See what the copper has to say,' suggested the fire officer as a police constable appeared on foot.

Although Rose knew she should get on with her round, she didn't feel able to leave her uncle so waited on the periphery of the gruesome proceedings as the ambulance came and took the injured man away. Her uncle was questioned by the policeman, who finally allowed him to get on the bus and continue the journey, asking him to call at the police station later on to make a formal statement.

Rose was humbled by the courage of both her uncle and her brother; Uncle Flip for pulling himself together and continuing to do his duty whilst severely traumatised, and her brother for the calm and kind way he had handled the whole thing. Joe had been on duty all night and still had his day job to do. He wasn't quite eighteen but had the maturity of a much older man. That was what his work with the AFS had done for him.

As Rose continued with her deliveries, she was reminded that not all the heroes were overseas fighting for their country. There were plenty of ordinary people showing their mettle here on the home front. The feeling of melancholy she'd had earlier because of her personal woes had completely disappeared. She was far too full of pride for her brother and uncle to give another thought to her own troubles.

Uncle Flip was officially cleared of all blame for the accident, but the man – a forty-year-old lorry driver on his way to work at the time of the accident – lost one of his legs. Uncle Flip was full of self-castigation.

'He's lost a lot more than his leg, and all because of me,' he said. 'He's lost his livelihood as well. You can't drive a lorry with one leg.'

No amount of reminders that the man shouldn't have been in the road lessened his compunction. Rose thought her uncle would probably live with the guilt for the rest of his life. For all the actual facts and technicalities, it was a deeply personal and emotional matter.

Although he tried hard to hide it, you could see that Flip was haunted by the accident, even when he was playing the fool. He told Sybil and she told the rest of them that he'd known he had to get back on that bus right away or he'd never have found the courage to drive a vehicle again.

The whole thing made Rose see her uncle in a new light. She'd already realised that there was more to him than met the eye when her aunt was in her depression. He'd shown then that he was more than just a jovial joker. Now she knew that he had hidden depths, and his comical persona was no indication of the true character of the man.

★　★　★

The run-up to Christmas was dominated by news from abroad, in particular the Japanese attack on the United States at Pearl Harbor. People were shocked and angry and awaited news of retaliation. When nothing happened except more attacks by the Japanese, there was a general air of gloom until news came through that the United States and Britain had declared war on Japan. America also joined the Allies in the war against Germany and Italy.

'Thank God for that,' said Bill Barton, reflecting the opinion of many British people. 'The Yanks have taken their time coming into the war, but now that they've done it, perhaps we can get the job finished.'

It boosted the nation's confidence, even though every intelligent person guessed there would be a whole lot more bloodshed before this war was finally won. Rose sensed a lifting of spirits as the adult population struggled to find Christmas fare and gifts for their friends and loved ones. The shortages didn't keep the shoppers at home, though, Rose noticed, as she and her mother tried their luck in Oxford Street. The shops and pavements were heaving.

Toys were scarce and expensive but Rose managed to get a clockwork army tank for Alfie which she took over to the Green Cat on the afternoon of Christmas Eve, the gift lovingly wrapped in newspaper she'd painted red because traditional wrapping paper wasn't available. She managed to deliver it into Ted's safe keeping out of range of Alfie's sharp little eyes.

'Hello, Rose,' greeted Johnny when she went into

their living room. 'You must be the only woman in the country who isn't doing some last-minute shopping. Hazel is out there somewhere.'

'It's men who leave the little bit they have to do until the last minute,' she said, thrilled to see him, and glad for his sake that he'd managed to get home to be with Alfie at Christmas. 'But I think most of the population of Shepherd's Bush are out shopping this afternoon. It's like a battleground out there, especially around by the market. I had to fight my way through the crowds when I got off the bus.'

Alfie came bounding into the room.

'Hello, kiddo,' she said. 'Are you all ready for Santa?'

He was at pains to point out to her that he wasn't a little kid, and had known the truth about what happened at Christmas for ages. But yes, he was excited just the same.

'He thinks he's going to get some presents, you see, Rose, that's why he's excited,' teased Ted. 'But that depends on how he behaves between now and tomorrow morning.'

'I'm sure he'll be good, won't you, Alfie?'

'I always am,' he grinned, reminding her so much of his father.

'Cheeky,' she smiled.

'Do you have time to have a Christmas drink with us, Rose?' invited Johnny.

'That would be lovely, thank you.'

She spent a very pleasant interlude with them, chatting and sipping a glass or two of their precious sherry.

By the time she got up to leave, she was feeling extremely festive.

'I think I'm a little bit tipsy,' she giggled. 'I hope they'll let me on the bus.'

'I'll walk with you to the bus stop, just to make sure you get on the right one,' teased Johnny. 'We don't want you finding yourself at Marble Arch.'

'I'm not that far gone,' she chuckled.

She was just leaving when Alfie ran from the room, returning with a package which he handed to her. 'You mustn't open it until tomorrow.'

'Thank you, luv,' she said, hugging him.

The Christmas spirit was palpable around the green as Rose and Johnny walked to the bus stop. The feverish excitement of the season lived on, despite the sadness, horror and deprivation of war. People were weighed down with their purchases, none of which were wrapped up or in bags because of the paper shortage.

'I'm so glad you managed to get home for Christmas, Johnny,' said Rose.

'Yeah, me too,' he said. 'I'm luckier than a lot of blokes. I have to go back on Boxing Day but you won't hear me complaining about that.'

They reached the bus stop and Rose joined the queue.

'Ooh, that's lucky, there's a bus coming already. It isn't often that happens,' she said brightly, turning to him. 'Have a happy Christmas, Johnny.'

'You too, Rose.'

'Cheerio,' she said.

On impulse he moved forward and gave her a farewell hug. 'Ta-ta, Rose. Happy Christmas,' he said tenderly.

He waited while she got on the bus, then blew her a kiss through the window.

Unfortunately this touching scene was witnessed by Hazel, who had just emerged from the market and completely misjudged the situation. In the heat of the moment she rushed up to Johnny and grabbed him by the arm.

'Hello, Hazel,' he said, unaware of the rising storm.

'I saw you,' she hissed, her face distorted with fury. 'I saw you so don't bother to deny it.'

'What are you on about?' he asked. 'I haven't got a clue what you mean.'

'I saw you kiss that Rose,' she said, her voice shrill with rage. 'I saw you do it with my own eyes. How could you, Johnny? How could you?'

He looked at her coldly. 'I did not kiss her,' he denied in an even tone.

'Don't lie to me,' she shouted, causing heads to turn. 'I saw you, just now.'

Angry with her for making a scene in public, Johnny drew her away from the crowds into a side street.

'I did not kiss Rose,' he told her. 'I gave her a goodbye hug, that's all.'

'It looked pretty damned cosy to me,' she said.

'I don't care what it looked like to your suspicious eyes; that is all it was,' he said gruffly.

'I'm not so sure.'

'Oh, I'm not standing here brawling with you in the street,' he said angrily, turning to go. 'You can think what you damn well like.'

'No, Johnny, don't go, please,' she begged him, furious with herself for flying off the handle. 'It was just a misunderstanding, that's all. I'm sorry.'

'And so you damn well should be,' he told her. 'You've made a laughing stock of yourself, and me, and I take a dim view of that, especially when it's uncalled for.'

'I'm really am sorry, please forgive me,' she urged. 'It won't happen again.'

He gave the matter consideration. 'Don't you ever humiliate me in public again,' he said.

'I won't, I promise.'

'You'd better mean it, Hazel,' he said, irritation growing, 'because I won't stand for that sort of thing. I'm a responsible adult. I don't need to be checked up on. I don't want you chasing after me as though I was five years old, accusing me of things I haven't done.'

'It wasn't like that, I just happened to see—'

'You saw what you wanted to see.' His fury was exacerbated by the fact that he had very much wanted to do what Hazel was accusing him of but had managed to resist temptation because of his commitment to her. 'You should know me well enough by now. I do not cheat on people, and that includes you. I really resent the accusation.'

Hazel chewed her lip, afraid that she had burned her boats. 'You've every right to be angry,' she said humbly. 'It was wrong of me to accuse you of anything like that. I know I can trust you. I don't know what came over me.'

'Let's just forget it, shall we?' he suggested coolly. 'I don't want Christmas ruined for Alfie because of a bad atmosphere between you and me.'

'It won't be ruined for him, I promise,' she said, managing to hide the fact that she was extremely miffed that he seemed to care more about Alfie's Christmas than hers. She wasn't in any position at the moment to criticise him about that. She'd already put the relationship in jeopardy through lack of control.

'I'm glad about that. It's important to me that he enjoys himself, after all he's been through,' Johnny said.

'Yeah, I want him to have a nice time too,' she lied.

He turned as though to leave. 'Anyway, I'm going back to the pub now. Are you coming?'

'No, not just yet. I've a few more last-minute bits of shopping to get.'

'I'll see you later then.'

'Yeah. See you.'

Watching him stride off, Hazel admonished herself severely for getting too heavy with him. All she'd succeeded in doing was antagonising him. It was that damned Rose's fault. One of these days I really am going to swing for that woman, she thought venomously, as she made her way through the crowds to Woolworth's.

Chapter Fifteen

Rose fancied that some of the usual festive verve was missing this year in the Barton household. It just wasn't the same without Alan's noisy ebullience, and they all missed Alfie, who had added a sparkle to the festivities last year.

Joyce seemed a lot quieter than usual too. Rose guessed that she was remembering last year, when Stan had been here at the piano, so cheerful and full of life. Even Uncle Flip's attempts at humour fell flat somehow, probably because the accident with his bus was still niggling at his conscience. Mary also seemed subdued when she called in to wish them the compliments of the season, and Rose suspected that she had something on her mind.

But at least the air raids stayed away, and they managed to create something of a party atmosphere, even though their Christmas dinner was rabbit pie, followed by Christmas pudding that barely resembled the pre-war kind and contained chopped prunes to replace the missing dried fruit.

However, appetites sharpened by so little food for most of the time, they all found it delicious and savoured every mouthful. Dad and Uncle Flip had managed to get a few bottles of booze and they all pooled their sweet rations for the big day, which added a touch of indulgence. With working hours being so long these days, they all luxuriated in the precious time off, especially Joe, whose voluntary work for the AFS meant he was hardly ever at home.

Although the atmosphere wasn't as lively as usual, the time passed pleasantly in conversation, card games, listening to the wireless and singing all the wartime favourites. The highlight of the day for Rose came when she opened the package from Alfie, which contained bath cubes from him, and a surprise present from his father: a box of chocolates that must have used the whole of his sweet ration. The latter came with a card that read: 'Just a little something to thank you for all the joy you bring to my son's life. There isn't a gift in existence that could repay you for what you've done for him, but I hope you enjoy these chocs anyway. Johnny.'

The chocolates were shared with the others; the card was put carefully in her dressing-table drawer. Maybe she was being overly sentimental, but she just couldn't bear to throw it away.

The new year of 1942 began on a sombre note because people were still saddened by the fall on Christmas Day of Hong Kong to the Japanese. It stirred British opinion deeply, causing a lot of anti-Japanese feeling. Rose thought it was probably just as well that in their house they hadn't got to hear about the setback until after the Christmas Day celebrations were over.

For Rose and her family personally, the big event on their horizon was the birth of Joyce's baby. Sybil flapped and twittered around her daughter like the proverbial mother hen. The women of the family were knitting furiously for the new arrival, and there was all the usual anticipation as to what sex it would be. Joyce was hoping for a boy who would be a permanent reminder of his father.

One evening in January, Rose was recruited to stay with her cousin while Sybil and Flip went out. They were going to the local pub with May and Bill because there was going to be some entertainment on.

'Thank God they've gone and we've got an evening by ourselves, Rose,' sighed Joyce as soon as the door closed behind her parents. 'Boy, do I need it.'

'Your mum's caring eye is weighing a bit heavy, is it?' Rose guessed.

'Phew, not half,' Joyce confirmed. 'She's driving me right round the bend with her fussing and pampering. Every time I so much as move a muscle she thinks I've started and immediately flies into a panic.'

'It's only natural, I suppose,' said Rose. 'It is her first grandchild.'

'She overdoes it, though. I keep telling her that I've still got two weeks to go, but she says it could come at any time and I shouldn't be on my own in the house.

Even her shopping is done at breakneck speed, which means that I don't get much of a rest from her even then. I keep reminding her that I'm pregnant, not recovering from a major operation, but it falls on deaf ears.' She paused thoughtfully. 'She even does her voluntary work when Dad's here so that I won't be on my own for even two seconds, and God help him if he goes out before she comes back.'

'She means well,' said Rose.

'Oh yes, and I love her to bits,' Joyce was quick to point out. 'But I'm feeling a bit smothered by an excess of motherly attention at the moment.'

'I suppose she's only gone out tonight because I'm going to be here?' Rose wondered.

'She wouldn't have gone if you hadn't been able to stay with me,' Joyce said. 'It was my idea that they went. I pleaded with Dad to suggest a night out to give me some space.'

Rose chuckled. 'I bet that caused a few strong words between them.'

She nodded. 'I'll say. You know what they're like,' she added. 'But it was music to my ears after that awful business of Mum going all quiet and peculiar. And of course, Dad hasn't been quite the same since he ran that man over. So it was good to hear them having a proper barney.'

'Shall I make us a cup of tea?' suggested Rose.

'I haven't been able to touch tea since I fell pregnant, but I'll make you one.' As Rose went to get up, she added, 'No, you sit there. I'll do it, and if you tell me that I should be resting and making the most of it while I can, I swear I'll land you one. I've had enough of that from my mother to last me a lifetime, bless her. I tell you, it's like being five years old all over again.'

'Sounds nice to me,' said Rose. 'But I suppose it would to someone who's out delivering the mail at the crack of dawn every morning.'

'Now you're making me feel ungrateful.'

'Sorry, kid. I didn't mean to. I was just thinking that you'll wish you could have a lie-in and a spot of pampering when you come back to work . . . if you're coming back.'

'I shall have to, to keep myself and the nipper, and being on the post will fit in nicely with the baby because of the early finish. They still urgently need women so I shouldn't have any trouble getting back in. Anyway, that's all got to be sorted out later on. Now I'll go and put the kettle on.'

A few minutes later a shriek came from the kitchen. Rose, hurrying out there, found her ashen-faced cousin holding on to the wooden draining board, looking at her feet.

'My waters have broken,' Joyce said shakily. 'Ooh blimey, Rose, it's starting.'

Rose surprised herself with her own sang-froid in dealing with the situation, and suspected that she managed to keep her head because her cousin completely lost hers. Despite having thoroughly prepared herself by reading up on every aspect of childbirth and discussing the subject at length with the midwife, Joyce was terrified, especially as the pains quickly became so strong.

Fortunately Rose knew that Joe was at home this evening, so she tore next door and asked him to go for the midwife, then went back to Joyce, who was now upstairs in her bedroom, walking around, doubled up in agony.

'Don't tell me to lie down because I can't,' she groaned. 'It's nothing short of torture and I can't keep still. Oh Rose, I don't think I can get through this.'

'Of course you can,' she said reassuringly. 'Everybody else does, and so will you.'

'It's all right for you; you're not the one with the pains.'

'I won't have a baby at the end of it either,' Rose reminded her. 'Just think, Joyce, your own son or daughter. Stan's child. It's worth all the pain to have that.'

'I know; it's just that I feel so rotten.'

'Joe's gone for the midwife, so she should be here soon and that might make you feel better,' Rose told her. 'Now tell me what I can do to help you. Hold your hand, get you a drink of water, anything.'

'There's only one thing that I really want, and that's for my mum to be here. Could you go and get her right away, please, Rose,' Joyce begged with a sob in her voice. 'I know I'm being pathetic, but I really need her.'

'I'll have to leave you on your own while I go to the pub,' Rose pointed out.

'I'll be all right. I've probably got hours to go yet,' Joyce said. 'Just tell Mum to come home, please.'

'Course I will.'

Grabbing her coat, Rose ran down the street to the pub on the corner. So much for Joyce wanting some distance between herself and her mother now, she thought, remembering the conversation they had had earlier. When it came down to it, in certain circumstances there was no one else in the world quite like your mum.

Auntie Sybil was in her element throughout the whole thing; ordering Uncle Flip to keep calm and stay out of the way, then complaining that he wasn't on hand when he was needed to make tea or to carry out some other chore. She was the only one allowed into the hallowed portals of the confinement room, and she came out every so often crying and muttering about how cruel nature was to make women suffer so.

Joyce's son finally made his entrance just before midnight, a surprisingly short labour for a first baby, according to the midwife, who let Rose and her mother go in to see the new arrival, though the room was prohibited to male persons at this stage.

'Well done, kid,' praised Rose, her eyes moist with tears as she gazed at her cousin with the baby in her arms. Joyce's hair was matted with sweat, her face pale and blotchy, but Rose had never seen her look lovelier. 'Congratulations.'

'Thanks. I did it, Rose,' she said, smiling. 'I did it.'

'You did too, you clever thing,' said Rose, kissing her brow and peering at the new arrival. 'He's beautiful.'

'He is, isn't he,' Joyce said, looking down at him adoringly. 'I shall call him Stanley, after his dad.'

Then she burst into tears.

Rose had been right in her suspicions about Mary being worried when she'd visited them at Christmas. She called again one Sunday morning towards the end of January.

'I didn't want to say anything when I called on Christmas Day because I didn't want to put a damper on the day for you, but I haven't heard from Alan and I was wondering if you have,' she confessed.

'Not for a while,' said May, forcing herself to conceal her sinking heart and to look on the bright side. 'Still, he's never been much of a letter-writer. You probably hear from him more often than we do.' She gave a wry grin. 'Young love and all that.'

'I'm sorry if I've worried you, Mrs Barton,' said the sensitive young girl. 'I was getting a bit desperate.'

'I'm sorry we can't put your mind at rest, but I don't think there's any call for panic just yet, dear,' May said kindly.

'Soldiers aren't often in a position to write letters when they're in action,' Bill pointed out.

'And the mail takes ages to get through, with everything being so disrupted,' added Rose.

'I'm sure you'll hear soon,' said Joe, unable to hide his admiration for Mary.

'We'll let you know if we hear anything,' said May. 'Meanwhile, will you join us for a cuppa?'

'Thank you, Mrs Barton,' said Mary in her quiet, polite way. 'That will be lovely.'

'Here, have this chair,' offered Joe, leaping up to give her his seat.

Poor Joe, thought Rose, watching her brother simply melt in the rays of Mary's smile. She was never going to look at him in the same way as he was looking at her. Still, it would make no difference if she did, because Mary was his brother's girl and Joe was a gentleman.

Although everybody was at pains to ease Mary's fears by maintaining a positive attitude, it was obvious to Rose that the whole family would feel easier in their minds when they heard from Alan. They'd been too long without news.

Joe was sitting at a desk opposite an army officer in a drill hall in Acton. There were several of these desks placed around the room, each with a military officer behind it and a young civilian man in front.

The officer looked up at Joe from some paperwork he'd been studying on the desk in front of him.

'Joseph Barton?' he said.

'Yes, sir.'

'I've been looking at your details, in particular the medical officer's report following your examination.'

'Yes?' said Joe, smiling expectantly.

'It seems that you are not physically fit for military service,' the officer informed him briskly. 'So you will be directed into some other form of employment related to the war effort. You'll be notified through the post.'

'Not fit!' exclaimed Joe, astounded. 'That can't be right.'

'Are you saying that the MO doesn't know his job?'

'I'm saying that there must be some mistake. There's nothing wrong with me. I'm as fit as a fiddle.'

'That's a novelty anyway,' said the officer. 'It's usually the other way around: healthy men trying to convince us that they're not fit to go in the army.'

'What's supposed to be wrong with me anyway?' Joe was outraged.

The man looked at the notes again. 'You had a leg injury as a child, apparently.'

'Oh, that. I told the doctor it was nothing. I was playing in a disused building and I fell from an upstairs window and broke my leg in a couple of places. It was years ago. I'd forgotten all about it until the doctor noticed that I have a very slight limp and asked me what had caused it.'

'The accident left you with one leg slightly shorter than the other,' the officer said.

'Only very slightly.'

'You have a limp, Barton,' declared the military man, becoming impatient.

'Not that anyone would notice. In fact I don't think anyone ever has. I certainly never give it a thought.'

'Well, our medical man has picked it up, and you would notice it yourself if you were in combat,' said the officer. 'It would impair your ability to run as fast as the other men. You could put your fellow soldiers at risk.'

'My leg doesn't give me any trouble,' insisted Joe. 'I've been in the Auxiliary Fire Service for a year and it hasn't stopped me doing my duty. Far from it. I went out on some really big fires during the Blitz. I couldn't have done that if I wasn't nimble on my feet, could I?'

'Maybe not, but the army has very strict regulations about this sort of thing, even though we are desperately in need of men.' He paused and looked at Joe with an expression of complete disinterest. 'I'm afraid you don't meet our criteria, so we don't have any other choice than to turn you down. You'll be hearing what work you've been directed into in due course. They might even suggest that you continue with your current employment at the aircraft factory.'

'But—'

'The matter is out of my hands now,' the officer said with an air of sharp finality. 'Now, I have a lot of other men to see.'

Outside in the street Joe was leaden with disappointment and a crippling sense of failure. What sort of a man was he when he wasn't even considered fit to fight for his country? Maybe some men might welcome the chance to get out of it, but he wasn't one of them. People would think he'd pulled a fast one.

So it would probably be the drawing office and part-time work in the AFS for him for the rest of the war, he thought gloomily, as he walked to the bus stop.

It was while he was on the bus that it suddenly came

to him. He realised that there was an alternative; something worthwhile that appealed to him very much indeed.

'A proper fireman?' said his mother that evening over their meal. 'You're going to be a real fireman?'

'He's a real fireman now,' his father felt bound to point out. 'They're not fake fires he goes out to, you know.'

'You know very well what I mean,' she tutted.

'Keep your hair on,' he grinned. 'I'm only teasing.'

'Anyway, I've applied to the London Fire Brigade to become a full-time fireman,' Joe explained. 'I went to the local fire station on my way home. The army turned me down, but I reckon I stand a good chance of getting in the LFB because of my firefighting experience.'

'Good boy,' his father approved. 'You need some bottle to do that job.'

'I'm very proud of you, son,' said his mother. 'And I'm glad you won't have to go away.'

'I'll second that,' added Rose. 'But I'm pleased for you, Joe, for your own sake. I know you've enjoyed your work in the auxiliaries. This seems the next logical step.'

'I'd have preferred to go in the army, but as they won't have me, I might as well try and make a useful contribution to the war via the fire brigade.'

'It's a very worthy occupation,' said Rose.

'I'll get to slide down a shiny pole and be a red rider,' Joe said, keeping it light, thought it did mean a very great deal to him. If they turned him down too, he'd be devastated. Now that he'd had the idea, he wanted to be a regular fireman very much indeed.

'Red rider?' queried his mother.

'Go out to a fire on a real red fire engine instead of in a taxi with old-fashioned equipment on the back,' he explained. 'We'll just have to hope that I'm accepted.'

'They wouldn't be daft enough to turn you down with all the experience you've gained in the AFS,' May pointed out. 'You've proved you're up to the job.'

'Mum's right, Joe,' said Rose, adding lightly because she could see that her brother was anxious about it, 'They'd better take you, because I want to see you in that smart uniform. You'll knock the girls dead in that.'

'I'd better not let you down then, had I, sis?' he said, giving her a nervous smile.

One day a week or so later when Rose got home from work, there was a message for her that had come via the neighbour with the telephone.

'You've to get on the blower to the Green Cat,' her mother informed her. 'They didn't say what it's about.'

Rose's feet barely touched the ground as she hared to the telephone box, her hands trembling as she put the pennies in the slot. Something serious must have happened to Alfie for them to contact her in this way. She'd left the neighbour's number with them only to be used in the case of an emergency.

'Johnny.' She was surprised to hear his voice; she'd

been expecting Ted to answer the phone. 'What are you doing at home in the middle of the week?'

'Compassionate leave,' he explained.

'What?' Her legs felt like water. 'What's happened for you to be given that? It's Alfie, isn't it? Something's happened to him.'

'Yeah, it's Alfie.' She could hear the emotion, despite his even tone. 'Now I don't want you to panic . . .'

'What's happened to him? Tell me, for goodness' sake,' she burst out. 'Has he had an accident, has he hurt himself?'

'No, nothing like that . . . but he isn't very well.'

'Oh my God! It must be serious or you wouldn't have called me.'

'We are worried about him,' Johnny admitted.

'I'll come straight over.'

'Would you, Rose?' he said, sounding relieved. 'I'd be so grateful.'

'I'm on my way.'

Rose had to wait ages for a bus, and when one finally arrived it seemed to travel at snail's pace. Because there had been such a long wait, there was a big queue at every stop and it took forever for people to get on and off.

Her heart was thudding and her jaws were actually clenched with tension as she willed the bus to move faster. She'd have jumped on her bike if she'd known it was going to be this slow. But she'd only gone home from the phone box for long enough to give her mother an update, not even stopping to change out of her uniform.

At last they were progressing: Ealing Common, Acton High Street, the Vale. Then they slowed down and the bus came to a halt altogether. There was some sort of a hold-up ahead. The clippie got off the bus to investigate.

'It's an unexploded bomb, apparently,' she explained to the passengers on her return. 'The road will be closed until the bomb-disposal people have made it safe. No one knows how long it will take them. It's a tricky business.'

The passengers started talking among themselves.

'We could be here for hours,' said a woman in a turban. 'I've got to get to work for the afternoon shift.'

'I'm in a hurry an' all,' said another.

'I'm sure the bomb-disposal boys will get it sorted as soon as they possibly can, folks,' said the clippie cheerfully. 'They do a good job, so we can do our bit by being very patient while we're waiting.'

'It ain't their fault,' said a woman in a blue headscarf. 'It's that bleedin' Hitler.'

There was a roar of agreement.

'Even when he's not bombing us he's still causing a nuisance, leaving his rotten bombs on our streets.'

The clippie got off the bus again, lit a cigarette and engaged in conversation with the driver, who was also taking the opportunity for a smoke. Rose decided it was time to take her journey into her own hands.

'The police won't let you through, luv,' said the

clippie as Rose got off the bus and prepared to walk the rest of the way.

'They wouldn't be doing their job if they did,' added the driver. 'It's far too dangerous. You don't wanna risk getting blown up, do yer?'

'I'll go through the back doubles,' she told them. 'I can't wait until the bomb people have finished. Someone dear to me is very ill.'

They both looked at her sympathetically.

'Well, you mind how you go then,' said the driver, looking towards the crowds who were watching the proceedings behind the rope that was cordoning off the danger area. 'Make sure you keep well away from the main road around here just in case the bomb goes off.'

'I'll be all right,' she said, and hurried on her way.

Not being familiar with the back streets of the area and therefore reliant on her sense of direction, Rose lost her way several times, and was also hindered by a bad attack of the stitch during her mad dash to get to the pub, which was quite a long stretch on foot.

By the time she arrived, her legs were aching and she was out of breath. But when she saw the pale, worried face of Johnny, who answered the side door to her because it was outside of pub opening hours, she was very glad she'd come.

So was he, apparently. 'Am I glad to see you, Rose,' he said thickly.

'What's actually the matter with him?' she asked. 'I was in such a hurry to get here I didn't ask.'

'Some sort of an infection, apparently. The doctor

thinks it's a rare form of meningitis, but he can't be absolutely sure. It's a very unusual case, apparently. The germ has gone to his brain. His temperature is sky high and he's been delirious for days. He hasn't eaten anything since he fell ill, so he's very weak.'

'Oh, the poor little thing,' she said. 'Why didn't you let me know before?'

'We hoped that he would get better and we wouldn't have to worry you with it,' he explained. 'But he isn't showing any improvement so I thought it was time you knew.' He cleared his throat. 'It's touch and go, Rose. We could lose him.'

'If he's so ill,' she said with desperation in her voice, 'why on earth don't they get him into hospital?'

'The doctor said it wouldn't be wise to move him the way he is at the moment. He's better at home. But he'll have to go in if there's no improvement. I think the doctor is thinking in terms of tomorrow, depending on what happens tonight. He's been very good; he's been in several times a day to see how Alfie is. He's hoping that the fever will burn itself out and he'll pull through without any permanent damage to the brain.' Johnny spread his hands helplessly. 'But it could go either way.'

'Brain damage?'

'There is that possibility, yes,' he said gravely. 'At the moment I can't think beyond praying for him to stay alive.'

Rose clutched her head in despair. 'Can I see him?'

'Of course you can, but you'll have to be brave,

because it isn't the Alfie we know in that bed. As I said, he's delirious, and the doctor's told us to go along with him in the hallucinations so as not to distress him even more. So if he says his teacher from school is in the bed with him we pretend we can see her. If he thinks that there are mice crawling up the walls, we just pretend to chase them away.'

'I understand.'

'We've put his bed in the living room,' he informed her. 'We can't leave him on his own. Someone has to be with him all the time because he keeps getting out of bed and wandering off. He doesn't know what he's doing, the poor lad. Dad is with him at the moment.'

Despite Johnny's warning, it still shocked Rose to see Alfie so ill. His face was grey, his lips chapped, two bright red fever spots staining his cheeks. He was also very distressed; he was staring at something the rest of them couldn't see, and looking very frightened.

'He thinks he's in trouble at school,' Ted explained in a low voice to Rose. He was sitting by Alfie's bed, holding his hand. 'He thinks the teacher has come and is giving him a trouncing.'

'Hello, Alfie,' said Rose, sitting on the edge of his bed, biting back the tears.

'I didn't get my sums right,' Alfie said, looking at her without a flicker of recognition. 'Now I'm gonna get the cane. Miss has come to give me the cane.'

Taking Johnny's advice, Rose said, 'No she hasn't, luv; she's just come to see how you are.' She cast her eyes in the same direction as Alfie's. 'She's going now. There you are, your dad is seeing her out.'

This seemed to satisfy the boy, and he lay back in the bed with his eyes closed, thrashing around, his hair glistening with sweat. There was a bowl of cool water and a flannel by the bed. Rose wrung the flannel out and held it to his brow, which seemed to soothe him for a while.

Then he sat bolt upright and started rambling about the Germans. 'They're in the kitchen,' he said, his eyes wide with terror. 'They've got guns and they're gonna shoot us.' He cowered back. 'Get down, get down.'

When he got out of bed to escape from the enemy, Rose went with him and pretended to drive the imaginary intruders away, then led him gently back to bed. Over the next few hours she sat with Johnny at Alfie's bedside. She mopped the sick boy's brow, held his hot little body in her arms when he thought there were Red Indians in the house, and held a cup to his mouth to moisten it with water. Her mind was closed to everything except this sick child and his poor distressed father who was sitting at the other side of the bed, taking his turn with the flannel and trying to soothe his son through his imaginary hell. Ted had opened the pub and was downstairs looking after the bar.

At some point during the evening, Rose was vaguely aware of Hazel coming in. Apparently she'd been called up for war work in a factory and was no longer working at the pub. She didn't stay for long; said she'd just dropped in to see how Alfie was, and left after a while.

Rose was far too preoccupied with Alfie to pay any attention to her.

Rose may not have taken much notice of Hazel, but Hazel took plenty of notice of her. With a mixture of fear and fury, she saw more than just Rose and Johnny sitting beside the bed, tending a sick child like an old married couple. She saw something she knew she would never have with Johnny: the mutual love for another human being besides themselves.

She could fight for Johnny with all of her wits and femininity, but she knew she could never share his love for Alfie. It wasn't in her to have that depth of feeling for anyone. It just wasn't there, and never had been.

As well as not being good with children, she wasn't able to cope with illness either. It frightened and repulsed her; the look and smell of it made her feel faint. She could hardly bear to go near the sick child, let alone hold him in her arms as Rose and Johnny did. It should be Hazel there with Johnny caring for Alfie, but she just couldn't do it.

Seeing them there together, completely absorbed in the child, Hazel felt like an outsider; an intruder almost. Johnny had been distant towards her. Not cold exactly, just preoccupied, which she supposed was understandable. He knew she didn't like illness so didn't expect her to stay and offer assistance.

In some far corner of her heart, the sight of all that caring touched Hazel and almost brought tears to her eyes. But on the heels of this came the bitter taste of inadequacy and envy: that she herself didn't have whatever it was that made people like Rose the way they were.

What was it that made Rose able to do things that Hazel never could? She'd rescued Alfie from a bombed building; she could care for him now that he was sick; she could talk to him in a way that he felt comfortable with. She could get up at four o'clock in the morning and go out delivering the mail, and not seem to mind. And as if all of that wasn't enough, she could also look good without a scrap of make-up.

Walking home with her shoulders down and hands plunged deep into her pockets, Hazel tried to shake herself out of this negative frame of mind. After all, it didn't matter how gutsy and good at everything Rose was, Hazel was the one wearing Johnny's ring, and she would fight with everything she had to keep him and have him as her husband. The sooner the better now that her life had taken such a turn for the worse.

Her cushy job in the pub had been replaced by the harshness of an assembly line in a munitions factory. All day long she pulled the lever of a machine that pressed out the caps for shells; hour upon hour of boredom and physical effort that she wasn't built for. Her shoulders and arms ached unbearably all day. It was dreadful and she made no secret of her discontent. The other women didn't like her; they were always telling her to stop whining and get on with the job.

When she'd been working at the pub, she'd never had any competition; never had to socialise or fit in with other female workmates, as she was the only barmaid. Now she spent the whole day on the receiving end of hostility from her own sex.

They sang along with *Music While You Work*, told lewd jokes, and went out together after work to dances and the cinema. At first they'd tried to include Hazel, but she'd soon put a stop to that. She wouldn't be seen dead outside of the factory with that common crowd.

'Stuck up cow' was a typical insult hurled in her direction. 'I don't know who you think you are. You were only a bleeedin' barmaid before you came here, not a chartered accountant. God only knows how you kept the job with your miserable mug. My cat could do better than you behind a bar if I put a frock on her.'

'I was good at the job,' Hazel had said. 'Anyway, I was more than just a barmaid. I'm engaged to the owner of the pub, so I'll be helping to run it soon.'

'Oh yeah, and that makes you the Queen of England, does it?' one of them had sniped.

'It makes me a cut above you lot, that's for sure,' she'd retorted.

This had caused an outburst of raucous laughter. They mocked her openly; it was terrible.

'There's a name for what you've got, luv,' one of them had said. 'It's called delusions of grandeur. Anyone can pull a pint, after a bit of practice.'

'Not everyone can get the boss's ring on their finger, though, can they?'

'The ring probably makes you more obliging; that's

why he's given you that,' said one of them crudely, causing more laughter. 'You still haven't got the plain gold one.'

'I will have.'

'We'll believe that when we see it,' the woman had said. 'What you need to get into that big head of yours is that none of us particularly likes working here but we came because we were sent here by the government, and some of us are glad of the chance of earn some dosh from an honest day's work. We've got women working here who really are a cut above, and they knuckled down after a while, and tried to fit in with the rest of us.'

'It's bloody hard work,' said someone else. 'But we do it because there's a war to be won and we all have to do what we can to help. So stop being such a lazy, moaning cow and get on with the job.'

Now Hazel experienced a grinding ache of misery at the thought of another shift at that awful factory. She didn't think she could get through another whole day in that dirty, noisy, unfriendly environment. But she'd be sent to prison if she didn't go, unless she had a medical certificate. She'd already been to the Labour Exchange and told them she wasn't physically up to the job. They'd told her that her case wouldn't be considered without medical proof. As there was nothing actually wrong with her, there was no hope of the doctor's co-operation.

Marriage to Johnny was her only escape, and his attention was all being taken up by Alfie at the moment, so she couldn't even broach the subject. It was all so very unfair.

Rose came to, realising that she had dozed off in the chair by Alfie's bed. He was sleeping, and Johnny seemed to have nodded off in his chair too. She glanced at the polished wooden clock on the sideboard to see that it had just turned midnight.

Ted had gone up to bed a while ago. Johnny had insisted that his father try to get some sleep. Earlier in the evening Johnny had told Rose that she needn't feel obliged to stay, respecting the fact that she had other commitments. She'd told him she had no intention of leaving; at least not until she had to go to work in the morning.

It was very quiet and still in the room; just the ticking of the clock could be heard, and the soft sound of Alfie's even breathing. *Even breathing.* It suddenly hit her. Alfie was sleeping peacefully; he wasn't thrashing and struggling against some inner terror. The fever spots had gone from his cheeks too. She gently put her hand to his forehead. It was cool. This was definitely significant, and hope rose in her heart. But she was afraid to be overly confident in case it was only temporary.

She wanted to wake Johnny, to share her hopes with him, but decided against it. The poor man was exhausted, having hardly slept since Alfie was first taken poorly. Let him sleep. Her own lids began to droop and she could feel herself drifting off when she was startled by a voice.

'Hello, Rose.'

She looked up. 'Hello, Alfie,' she said.

He looked around, puzzled. 'Why is my bed downstairs?' he enquired.

'You've not been well, luv,' she said, taking his small damp hand in hers.

'Could I have a drink of water, please?'

'Course you can,' she replied, standing up. 'I'll go and get one for you right away.'

'I'm a bit hungry, Rose,' he said.

'What do you fancy?' she asked.

'Could I have some bread and dripping, please?'

'Course you can.'

'Why are you crying, Rose?' he wondered.

'She's crying because she's happy, son,' said Johnny, awake now and also close to tears. This was the first time in days Alfie had uttered a sensible word, let alone wanted food.

'I'll go and get you that drink now,' Rose said, and hurried to the kitchen, where she collapsed into tears.

'I never thought the sound of him asking for bread and dripping could give me such pleasure,' Johnny choked out, appearing beside her, moist-eyed. 'He's better, Rose, he's come through it; the crisis is over.'

Instinctively they fell into each other's arms, sobbing with joyous relief.

'You go and stay with him, I'll fix him up with some food and drink,' Rose said, drawing back and mopping her tears.

'Thanks, Rose.'

'Thanks aren't necessary,' she said thickly. 'I was glad to be here.'

'I mean for everything,' he said. 'For being here. For . . . being you.'

It was the sweetest thing he could have said to her, and almost brought on a flood of fresh tears. But she bit them back and said, 'Thank you for letting me know he was ill so that I could be here. I should have hated not to be.'

The feeling between them was so strong, it was like a physical presence in the room, and Rose could hardly bear it.

'You'd better tell me where things are around here before you go back to the patient,' she managed to utter in a jokey manner to ease a desperately emotional moment. 'We'll be in dead trouble with him if he doesn't get his bread and dripping.'

Chapter Sixteen

Having witnessed what seemed to her to be the miracle of Alfie's recovery, Rose was imbued with a feeling of gratitude and optimism about life in general. This was reinforced in March when a delighted Joe received news that he had been accepted by the London Fire Brigade, who wanted him to start his training right away.

Things were going well next door too. Little Stanley was thriving and doted on by the whole family, especially his grandmother, who looked after him while Joyce was out at work in her old job at the Royal Mail. The baby had given Auntie Sybil a completely new lease of life, and Uncle Flip had embraced his grandfather status with gusto. There was plenty of local gossip, of course, but the family felt so blessed by the baby's existence as to be almost immune to dark looks and snide remarks.

So although the war news from abroad wasn't good, with Singapore and Java falling to the Japanese, and Malta being battered by Luftwaffe bombs, and shortages at home worsening, with even soap being put on ration, at least the air raids hadn't returned, and Rose felt that there was plenty of reason to be in good spirits.

Then came news of Alan.

The hospital was a large country mansion in Buckinghamshire which had been commandeered by the military for the treatment of wounded soldiers. It took Rose and her parents several hours to get there by train, bus and a large measure of Shanks's pony. Joe was on duty at the fire station and hadn't been able to get away.

'Lovely place, isn't it?' remarked May as they finally reached their destination and trudged along a lengthy, meandering drive to the ivy-covered house. It was set in beautiful grounds with sweeping lawns and a multitude of ancient oaks and other mature trees all burgeoning with new leaf on this sunny but blustery March Sunday. Here and there a wounded soldier could be seen, walking or hobbling on crutches, though the wind was so sharp the garden benches were nearly all empty.

'He's in nice surroundings anyway,' commented Rose. 'That's something to be grateful for.'

'Let's hope he's well enough to enjoy them,' remarked her father.

The official letter from the War Office notifying them of Alan's whereabouts hadn't given them any details as to what his injuries actually were, so they were all extremely apprehensive as they made their way up the wide stone steps to the entrance.

* * *

'Your son is having some difficulty in coming to terms with his condition,' explained the matron, a short, stout woman with warm brown eyes and a weary, overworked look about her.

'Really?' said May worriedly.

'Most people who find themselves in his position take a while to adjust,' she continued. 'It's perfectly understandable, and he will need a bit of time, though some adapt quicker than others, of course.'

'Mmm,' nodded Bill, also looking anxious.

'You'll be surprised how much they can achieve despite the limitations. But Alan has been through a lot, so . . .' she hesitated, as though choosing her words carefully, 'please don't expect too much of him at the moment. It's still too soon.'

Noticing that her parents were now looking whey-faced and petrified, Rose stepped in.

'When you say "his condition",' she began through dry lips, 'what exactly do you mean? Has he lost a leg; is it head injuries or what?'

The matron looked startled. 'Oh dear, I didn't realise you hadn't been told.' She tutted. 'It really is too bad of the authorities to have patients' relatives come here unprepared for what awaits them, and leave us to tell them. Still, that's wartime for you, isn't it? So little time and so much to do. There are such a lot of wounded men, I suppose the administration staff don't have time to go into detail.'

'For Gawd's sake tell us what's the matter with him,' Bill blurted out.

'Yes, of course, Mr Barton,' she said in a controlled manner, as though struggling to stay patient under the burden of too much work. 'Your son was in combat when a bomb exploded close to him and he was caught in the blast. He received several superficial head injures which are almost healed but there was some internal damage.' She hesitated before continuing, her face muscles tightening. 'I'm afraid he has lost his sight.'

There was a stunned silence.

'Blind!' said Bill at last.

The matron nodded.

'You mean totally?' queried Rose. 'Can't he see anything at all?'

'I'm afraid not,' the matron replied.

'He will . . . he will get his sight back, won't he?' said May shakily. 'I mean, there must be something that can be done for him.'

'The doctors have done everything they can, and who knows what might be possible in the future with the progress of medical science?' The matron wasn't without compassion, but she worked with injury and death on a daily basis, and dealt with the most horrific and heartrending cases. 'But as things stand at the moment, Mrs Barton, I'm afraid the damage behind his eyes is irreversible.'

'Oh no,' gasped May, her voice breaking. 'There must be some sort of treatment available. He's a young man with his life ahead of him.'

'Exactly,' said the matron with a barely discernible edge to her voice. 'He has his life ahead of him, which

426

is more than can be said for many of our young fighting men.'

'Yes, I realise that, of course,' said May, feeling well and truly put in her place. 'But not being able to see . . . how will he manage?'

'He'll go to a rehabilitation centre for the blind when he leaves here,' the matron explained. 'They'll teach him how to cope with the basics of everyday life without sight before he comes home, and inform him as to what will be available to him as regards activities, employment and so on.'

'That's something, then,' said May gloomily.

'He can gain a very great deal from it,' said the matron. 'How much is entirely up to him. It's a question of accepting that his life will be completely different as a blind person. Once he fully understands that, he can move forward and do very well, with the right attitude.'

'I think we should move forward now too,' said Rose, more eager than ever to see her brother in the light of the circumstances. 'Can we go and see him now, please?'

'Of course,' agreed the matron. 'If you'd like to follow me, I'll take you to him.'

There were some very badly injured men in the ward: men who had lost limbs, others who were so badly burned their faces were grotesque and difficult to look at. Alan was in the bed at the end of the large room.

'Hello, son,' said May, kissing him on the cheek and trying not to upset him by letting her anguish show in her voice.

'Wotcha, Mum.' Propped up against the pillows, Alan replied without moving his head, which was bandaged at the top, his lifeless eyes staring straight ahead.

'Oh, it's so good to see you, son,' said May, putting her arms around him, carefully because of his injuries. 'We were so worried when we didn't hear from you.'

'Sorry about that,' he said dully. 'There was chaos everywhere out there. We just didn't get the chance to write home.'

'It doesn't matter, son, as long as you're here now.'

'Thanks for coming, Mum. It's a long way for you to travel.'

'It would take more than a bit of travelling to keep us away,' said Rose.

'So . . . how are you feeling then?' asked his mother.

Wonderful, he thought with bitter irony. Why wouldn't I be feeling great when I've so much to look forward to, without any bloody eyesight and my confidence stripped away to nothing like the flesh off my bones? But he said, 'Not so bad, Mum. How about you? How are things at home?'

'We're all fine,' she said, her voice stilted because the situation was so new to her and she still felt awkward. 'Your dad's here with us.'

Alan went through the motions of conversation, sounding outwardly normal. But he was actually locked inside a prison of fear and despair; terrified of this new dark world he found himself in. There was a claustrophobic blackness everywhere and no escape. He wanted to punch his way through it to find the light, but there was none; no escape from the darkness and the over-whelming feeling of vulnerability.

'Why don't you two go and see if you can get us all a cup of tea?' Rose suggested after a while, seeing how distressed her parents were and how bravely they were trying to conceal it. 'I'll stay and talk to Alan.'

As soon as they had left the room, she took her brother's hand and held it in both of hers, feeling his fingers tremble slightly.

'You can drop the act now and tell me how you really feel,' she said.

'Like I'm in the depths of hell,' he told her, his sight-less eyes glistening with tears. 'I can't cope with this one, Rose. I really can't.'

'It must be awful for you,' she sympathised. 'I think I'd be the same if it happened to me.'

'No you wouldn't,' he disagreed. 'You'd take it all on the chin and learn to live with it, which is what I should be doing.'

'You will, given time.'

'That's what everybody here keeps telling me. But I don't have the bottle.'

'That's rubbish! You don't lack for courage. You've just come back from the front, for goodness' sake.'

'This is a different sort of enemy,' he told her. 'One that I'm helpless against.'

'I know it's terrible, but—'

'I know, there are men far worse off than me here in this hospital,' he pre-empted her. 'I've been told that some poor buggers have lost limbs; others have had their faces blown off. One poor devil has lost his mind and screams with terror when he isn't sedated. A lot of men have died and I am very, very lucky.' He paused, looking bleak. 'But as hard as I try, I just can't make myself feel in the least bit lucky. I'd rather have been killed than left with no sight.' Huge tears meandered down his cheeks. 'I just can't do this, Rose. I want to die.'

'Oh, Alan,' she said, caressing his hand, her eyes filling with tears. 'Please don't say that.'

'It's the way I feel,' he choked out.

'I'm so sorry you're having such a bad time,' she sympathised.

'So will everyone else be sorry for me when I get out of here,' he said. 'I'll be an object of pity; a feeble git feeling my way around with a white stick, and having to have people cut up my food for me and suchlike.'

'I'm sure that sort of thing will only be temporary and you'll be able to manage yourself quite soon. They'll teach you how to do things by touch.'

'People will still think I'm feeble.'

'People will be sad for you, it's only natural. They'd be heartless if they weren't. But you can make sure you don't give them any reason to pity you,' she said gently. 'Anyway, you wouldn't know how to be feeble if you tried. You've far too much spirit.'

'How can I be anything else but feeble when I don't have sight to keep me strong?'

'I don't know, Alan, I really don't,' she sighed, with a slow shake of her head. 'But I do know that people cope with blindness and manage to have a useful and happy life despite it. You're bound to feel like this when it's all so new, but you'll get through it. I know you, so I can say that with confidence.'

'That's the whole point; I don't want to get through it,' he said irritably. 'I don't want to fight and be brave any more. I've had enough of all that.'

She caught sight of their parents coming down the ward with a tray of tea.

'Mum and Dad are coming back,' she said, keeping her voice low. 'Don't let them hear you talking like that.'

'I'm not completely heartless, you know,' he said, wiping his eyes and composing himself, and thus disproving his judgement of his own character.

Joe was cycling home from work along the Uxbridge Road one Saturday afternoon in April, thinking about his brother. Blind! The poor bloke. Joe had been devastated when his parents had come home from the hospital and told him. Suddenly he spotted Mary looking in the window of a dress shop. He swung off his bike, stood it up against the kerb with the pedal and went over to her.

'Are you looking for something special?' he asked after they'd exchanged greetings.

'Just window-shopping,' she told him. 'I haven't got enough coupons to buy anything. I'm saving them up for a frock for the summer.'

He was about to commiserate with her when she burst into tears.

Embarrassed and not sure what to do because he

431

was inexperienced with girls, especially weeping ones, Joe said, 'You'll look lovely whatever you wear. You don't need a new frock to make you look nice.'

'Thank you, Joe, but it isn't that,' she said, dabbing at her eyes furtively because there were crowds of people about. 'I'm not crying because I can't have a new frock.'

'What is the matter then?'

'Alan has chucked me,' she told him, her huge eyes filling with fresh tears. 'He doesn't want to see me any more. It's over between us.'

'Oh, I see.' He stood there feeling awkward. 'Look, why don't I buy you a bun and a cup of tea in Lyons and you can tell me all about it.'

'Thanks, Joe, that would be nice,' she sniffed.

'He doesn't mean it,' opined Joe. Mary had told him that she'd had a letter from Alan, obviously dictated to one of the other patients at the hospital, saying that it was over between them and he didn't want to see her again. 'I reckon it's because he's lost his sight. He's probably worried that he'll be a burden to you.'

'How can he be a burden to me when I love him so much?' she pointed out. 'I want to be with him for the rest of my life, Joe. His being blind makes no difference to the way I feel about him. He's still Alan.'

To Joe's surprise, the confirmation of her feelings for his brother didn't hurt any more. He realised that he was no longer interested in Mary in that way. His brother's happiness was what mattered to him now. 'Does he know that?' he asked.

'Of course he does,' she said, sipping her tea. 'I told him when I went to see him at the rehabilitation centre that I'm nuts about him; he's known that for ages anyway. I told him that I would love him through anything. I laid myself on the line for him and he didn't even have the decency to tell me to my face while I was there. He waited until I'd gone home then got someone to write the letter for him.'

'Perhaps he hadn't made the decision while you were with him but thought it over after you'd gone and decided that a letter might be easier for you both,' he suggested.

'He says in the letter that his feelings towards me have changed; that he'll always be fond of me but he doesn't love me in that special way any more,' she told him. 'I've got it in writing. What more proof do you want?'

'He's only saying that so that you'll accept that it's over, and he only wants to end it because of what's happened to him,' Joe told her. 'It's a massive adjustment to make; to suddenly lose your sight like that.'

'But I want to help him,' Mary said. 'I told him that I would always be there for him, that I would be his eyes.'

'Which is probably why he's ended it,' suggested Joe. 'He's a proud man and wouldn't like the idea of having to rely on you. It must be terrible for him. I mean, put yourself in his position for a minute. Shut your eyes and imagine that you can never open them again. That'll give you an idea of what he must be going through. It's a difficult thing for anyone to take.'

'I suppose so.'

'As well as not wanting to be a burden to you, he might feel as though he isn't able to cope with a close relationship at the moment,' Joe suggested. 'I should think it might be difficult for him to consider someone else besides himself until he learns how to come to grips with things as they are now for him. Apart from anything else, he needs to get his confidence back. At the moment he probably doesn't feel able to look after himself, let alone anyone else.'

'You do have a point,' she said thoughtfully. 'I hadn't looked at it from that angle.' She paused, staring into her teacup. 'Should I write and tell him that I understand, and I'll be there if he wants to give it another go later on?'

'I'm the least qualified person to advise you, but I should leave things as they are for the moment,' Joe said. 'I'm fairly sure he'll seek you out when his head's cleared and he's got himself together. If he doesn't get in touch after a reasonable period, then you could approach him.'

'The waiting will be hard; wondering if he'll get in touch.'

'I think you'll find it'll be worth it.'

Mary looked at him with a smile in her eyes. 'Thanks, Joe, you're a really good friend,' she said. 'You've made me feel so much better.'

'Good. I'm pleased about that.'

'Sorry to hear about your brother, Rose,' said Johnny one Saturday afternoon in May when she called to see

434

Alfie. 'Dad was telling me about him. It must be really tough for him.'

She nodded. 'It certainly takes some getting used to,' she replied.

'That's the one thing I dread most,' he confessed. 'I'd sooner anything than to lose my sight.'

'I think that's how he feels about it.'

'Is he back home yet?'

'He came home a few weeks ago.'

'How's he managing?'

'Quite well, thanks,' she fibbed out of loyalty to her brother. She could hardly tell someone outside of the family that Alan was so full of anger and resentment, the whole family was living on a knife edge. If you offered him assistance he was thoroughly disagreeable; if he tripped over something or bumped into it because you hadn't helped him he flew into a rage. There was no living with him at the moment.

'I'm glad to hear that. But how are you?' he asked. They hadn't seen each other since Alfie's illness, as Johnny hadn't been home on leave.

'Fine, thanks. Yourself?'

'I'm all right, apart from wishing that I could get home more often,' he said casually. 'Still, I mustn't grumble.'

'I vowed never to complain about anything ever again after Alfie got better.'

'Yeah, I felt that way too.' He looked at her in such a way that she could feel that special closeness drawing them together. 'It was as though my prayers had been answered.'

'And mine.'

'Talking of Alfie, I was wondering if I could ask you a favour.'

'Of course.'

'Do you think he could come over to your place next Saturday and stay the night?' he asked. 'Only there's a wedding party here on Saturday night and Dad will be kept very busy in the bar. I definitely won't be around to help out because there's no way I'll be able to get home next weekend. I would be much easier in my mind if I knew Dad didn't have to worry about Alfie, and that the lad was happy and being looked after.'

Rose hesitated in her reply, bearing in mind Alan's current mental state. Would the noisy exuberance of a small boy try his temper even more? Would he fly off the handle at Alfie, and scare him? On the other hand, it wouldn't hurt Alan to move out of the limelight for a change. The household revolved around him at present.

'Don't worry if it isn't convenient,' said Johnny, misunderstanding her silence.

'No, no, we'd love to have Alfie; it will cheer us all up,' she told him warmly. 'I'll come and collect him after work on Saturday, shall I?'

'That's so good of you,' he smiled. 'I don't know what we'd do without you.'

'You'd manage,' she assured him. 'But let me go and say hello to that boy of yours.'

As she went up the stairs, she was imbued with a warm and breathless buzz of excitement. Johnny couldn't possibly know the effect he had on her. Her feelings for him were growing with every passing day, and every time she saw him she realised just how much.

Following Rose up the stairs, Johnny was having similar thoughts about her, which put him in something of a dilemma. Hazel was pushing hard for marriage the next time he had some proper leave, as he'd promised. But every time he thought of Rose, he was thrown into emotional turmoil.

But he couldn't let Hazel down. It would be against his principles. She had her faults but she was faithful to him, he was certain of that. So he had to somehow put all thoughts of a future with Rose out of his mind. He knew it wouldn't be easy.

One of the things the Bartons had to be meticulous about now that Alan was home was keeping everything in the same place at all times. He had memorised the layout of the house and the furniture, and even the smallest alteration could cause him problems.

Such was the frailty of human nature, however, that sometimes one of them forgot. That evening, Bill put a chair in the middle of the living room to stand on to put a new bulb in the light socket, and didn't immediately put the chair back. Alan came in and tripped over it and went flying headlong on to the floor, uttering the vilest expletives.

Naturally they all rushed to his assistance.

'Here, let us help you up,' offered Rose, bending down. 'I'll take one arm and Joe will take the other.'

'I can manage myself, thanks very much,' Alan growled. 'My eyes aren't working but everything else is in very good order.' He shrugged them away roughly. 'Just get off me.'

'Have you hurt yourself, luv?' asked his mother, looking worried.

'Of course I've bloody well hurt myself,' he snapped, rubbing his knees as he struggled to get up. 'So would you if you'd just been tripped up because some bloody idiot moved the furniture around.'

'There's no call to speak to your mother like that,' admonished Bill. 'It wasn't her fault. It was mine. It was me who forgot to put the chair back straight away.'

'Don't go on at him, Bill,' said May with a mother's natural protective instinct. 'You can't blame him for being upset, falling over like that and hurting himself.'

'I know, May, and I know you're having a hard time, son,' said Bill, in a more sympathetic tone. 'But try to watch your language, will you, please? All this swearing in the house is upsetting for the rest of us.'

'Oh, I'm going to bed,' Alan grunted. 'It's the only place I can get any peace around here; the only place I'm safe from people leaving stuff about for me to trip over.'

'It's only eight o'clock,' Joe pointed out.

'So what?' said Alan.

'I was thinking you might like to go out for a pint with me as I'm not on duty,' said Joe. 'It is Saturday night, after all.'

'Not for me, thanks.' Alan was on his feet now. 'After taking a tumble I've lost my bearings, so perhaps one of you could point me in the right direction and then leave me to it. Don't any of you try to help me up the stairs; I'm quite capable of doing it myself.'

After he'd gone, feeling his way to his bedroom, a tense silence gripped the family.

'I thought it might have done him good to go out for a pint and a chat,' Joe remarked. 'I would have enjoyed it too.'

'He'll go out with you for a pint some time in the future,' said Rose, deciding that a sisterly chat with Alan might be a good idea. 'The poor man is too troubled to want to do anything at the moment.'

'You're being a bit hard on us all, you know, Alan.' Rose had given him a chance to simmer down, then gone up to the boys' bedroom, where he was sitting on the edge of his bed. 'I know you're having a tough time, but surely you don't have to be quite so bad tempered.'

'Well . . . honestly, fancy leaving a chair out for me to fall over,' he complained.

'Dad's only human; he makes mistakes the same as everyone else,' she pointed out. 'We all have to get used to your not being able to see.'

'My heart bleeds for you,' he said sarcastically. 'You want to try getting used to it from where I am.'

'I know,' she sighed. 'It must be very hard.'

'Hard?' he said scornfully. 'That's like saying the Thames is just a puddle.'

'I know, Alan, and I'm sorry.' Rose mulled the situation over, trying to think of some practical way of helping him. 'Why don't you go down to the pub for a drink with Joe?' she suggested. 'He'd like that. I think he really misses having you as a mate.'

'He doesn't need me now,' Alan said grumpily. 'He's standing on his own two feet in a big way these days, now that he's an upstanding member of the fire service and a bit of a hero. He doesn't need big brother to fight his battles any more, which is just as well, as big brother isn't any use to anyone nowadays.'

'You're right, he doesn't need you in that way any more, and that's a good thing,' she said, ignoring the uncharacteristic self-pity. 'But he still wants your friend-ship and company. He wasn't old enough to have a pint in the pub before you went away.'

'I'm not fit company for anyone,' insisted Alan. 'Having to fumble and feel my way down the street? No thanks.'

'Wait until it gets dark, then everyone else will be in the same boat as you because of the blackout,' she suggested lightly.

'There's no need to be sarky, Rose.'

'I wasn't. I'm just trying to bring your sense of humour back to life.'

'I don't know why you bother when you know I just want to be left alone.'

'I bother because you're my brother and I care a lot about you,' she told him. 'Anyway, you've done Joe plenty of good turns in the past; taking on bullies on his behalf and getting him out of trouble. Why not give him a chance to do something for you in return, like making sure you get to the pub safely?'

'I don't want to go to the pub, so just leave it, will you?' he said his voice rising irritably. 'Now if you don't mind, I want to get undressed for bed.'

'Oh Alan, please don't hide away up here,' she begged him. 'If you don't want to go out with Joe, at least come downstairs and listen to the wireless with the rest of us. It isn't good for you to be alone so much.'

'How many more times must I tell you? I want to be by myself.' He was almost shouting now. 'It's nothing personal, Rose; it's just the way I feel now.'

She left the room because she knew she must respect his right to privacy. But she was worried about him, and didn't seem able to give him so much as a crumb of comfort. She was also concerned about Alfie's visit next weekend because Alan's moodiness was causing such a dreadful atmosphere in the house. This was no place for a little boy.

But she'd promised Johnny she would have him, and she wasn't prepared to go back on her word. She would just have to keep a very close eye on Alfie and make sure he kept well away from Alan.

Rose explained Alan's situation to Alfie on the bus on the way over so that he wouldn't expect her brother to be the same as he used to be: playing about with him, teasing him and always ready for a kickabout. As Alfie seemed to fully understand what she was getting at, she was a little easier in her mind about having him in the house.

But she hadn't taken into account Alfie's unrestrained

enthusiasm for people he liked, and the fact that his skills of diplomacy had yet to be developed.

Alan was upstairs in his bedroom when Alfie arrived, and Rose heaved a sigh of relief. The boy was immediately at home, rolling about on the floor with the dog, greeting everyone with a hug and talking nonstop.

'I see you've brought your ball,' remarked Bill.

'Rose says she'll take me to the park to play with it,' he said.

'You never go anywhere without that bloomin' ball, do you, luv?' said May affectionately.

'Not really. I have to keep practising if I wanna be good at it,' he said. 'I can do kick-ups from my toes for ages without stopping now. Shall I show you?'

'Later on, and not in here,' she said quickly. 'You know the rules. No footie indoors.'

'I'll put the ball in the garden, Mrs Barton,' he said co-operatively.

'Good boy,' said May. 'When you've done that, come back in and have some dinner.'

When Alan responded to his mother's call that dinner was on the table and appeared in the room, Alfie tore up to him and threw his arms around him.

'Wotcha, Alan,' he said, standing back and looking up at him. 'It's me, Alfie.'

'Wotcha, kiddo,' responded Alan.

'Do you fancy coming over the park with me and Rose this afternoon for a kickabout?'

There was a sharp intake of breath from the family.

'Alan doesn't play football now, son,' said May nervously.

'Oh.' Alfie looked thoughtfully at Alan. 'Is that because you can't see?'

The family froze, waiting for the eruption.

'That's right,' grunted Alan.

Alfie thought about this for a moment. 'But I could tell you where the ball is and we could do shots at goal, if I told you which direction to kick. You could do it then, couldn't you?' he suggested, continuing enthusiastically without waiting for an answer. 'We could see who gets the most in out of ten. Rose can be the ref.' He paused, looking towards the window, then chatted on, completely oblivious of the anxiety he was causing. 'As long as it doesn't rain, though, because Grandad said I'm not to play out in the rain in case I catch a cold and get sick again. I think he's fussing about nothing but I'd better do as he says. There's plenty of blue sky at the moment, but—'

'Alfie, will you help me with something in the kitchen, please, luv?' requested May, desperate to prevent the storm from breaking.

But much to everyone's astonishment Alan said, 'All right, kid; just as long as you haven't got any silly ideas about beating me.'

It was strange, Rose thought, sitting on a park bench watching her brother and Alfie playing with the ball, how Alan could accept help from a child with no problem at all, but found it so hard to stomach it from anyone else. Maybe it was because there was no pretence; no fudging the issue. Alfie just said the first thing that came into his head.

But at the same time there was a kindness and sensitivity about him that was surprising for someone so young. On the way to the park, he'd held Alan's hand, chattering away about school and his collection of cigarette cards, and giving Alan a running commentary.

'There's a bunch of kids over the road playing hopscotch on the pavement. Uh-oh, some woman's just come out of one of the houses. I bet she tells 'em to clear off. Yeah, she has; they're going now.' When they reached the main road, he'd said, 'There are crowds of people about so you'd better mind what you're doing with your stick, Alan. You could trip someone over.'

Rose knew that Alan wouldn't have taken that from anyone else, but he just teased Alfie about having verbal diarrhoea and didn't seem to mind at all. Now Alfie was placing the ball in front of Alan's foot for him to kick between the coat and jumper they were using as goalposts. Alan even called Rose over to hold his arm to help with his balance while he kicked the ball, which missed the target.

'Better luck next time,' she said.

'How do I know that you two aren't fibbing so that Alfie will beat me?' he asked jokingly. 'For all I know, I could be getting it in every time.'

'You'll just have to trust us,' she told him, 'and stop being so cynical.'

'You've got more in than me anyway,' laughed Alfie. 'You know I wouldn't lie about that.'

'Oh yeah, there is that, you competitive little monster,' Alan said with a grin. 'So come on then, Alfie. Stop mucking about and show us what you can really do.'

The boy's shot was successful and he leapt in the air, raising his arms in triumph, Rose and Alan cheering him on. Rose was proud of them both: Alan for showing some mettle for the first time since he'd lost his sight, and Alfie for his lovely warm nature.

It was such a sunny afternoon they stayed a while and sat on the bench chatting.

'How are you getting on at the pub these days?' Alan enquired of Alfie.

'All right,' he replied.

'You've changed your tune,' Alan said. 'I heard you hated it there.'

'I did at first, and it isn't nearly as good as living at your house,' he said. 'But I've got used to it now and I don't mind it so much.'

'Do you still think about your mum a lot?' he asked.

'Yeah, course I do,' Alfie said wistfully, but without bitterness or tears. 'She was the best mum in the world, and I'll never forget her.'

'I'm glad to hear it.' Alan thought how far the boy had come since Rose had first brought him home, rebellious and fighting against the world every step of the way. He'd been through so much in his short life, but here he was now, as bright as a button and nice to have around; an inspiration to anyone who was feeling sorry for themselves.

'I think it's time we headed home,' Alan suggested after a while. 'Lead the way, Alfie.'

'Come on then,' agreed the boy, reaching for his hand. 'On your feet.'

Alan spent more time downstairs with the family while Alfie was there than he had in the whole time he'd been home, and everyone was delighted.

When it was time for Rose to take him home, Alfie had a request to make.

'Why don't you come over to our pub with Rose some time, Alan?' he invited. 'You could have a drink with my grandad, and Dad if he's home, and you and I could muck about with the ball on the green. It would be good.'

Alan was about to say that he couldn't do something like that because he was blind when he heard himself say instead, 'Yeah, I'd like that, kid.'

'Really?' beamed Alfie.

'Yeah, really,' Alan confirmed cheerfully. 'I'm not sure exactly when it'll be, but if Rose doesn't mind my tagging along with her, I'll come.'

'Smashing,' said Alfie.

For the first time since Alan's tragic fate had spread its dark, depressing presence through the household, Rose glimpsed a ray of hope.

Chapter Seventeen

By the time the average citizen went to work, Royal Mail delivery staff had already been on duty for several hours, so a break between rounds – as long as they weren't running late – was extremely welcome to the postmen and women. It was necessarily brief but there was usually time to exchange a few words with whoever else happened to be in the canteen.

'How's that baby of yours, Joyce?' asked Elsie, a mother of two sons who were both away in the forces. She was one of the many women who had embraced the employment opportunity bestowed upon her by the war, and reflected it in her cheery manner.

'You might regret asking her that,' teased Rose, grinning over the rim of her mug. 'Once she starts talking about little Stanley you won't get a word in edgeways, and she can keep going for days.'

'Cheek,' objected Joyce with mock umbrage.

'Take no notice of her, Joyce,' said Elsie, smiling at the two of them. 'It's only natural you'd want to talk about your little boy, and I enjoy listening. You wait until Rose gets one of her own; there'll be no stopping her either.'

'Don't worry. It'll take more than my cousin's warped sense of humour to stop me telling you about my lovely boy,' joshed Joyce, and went on to extol the virtues of six-month-old Stanley, who could almost sit up on his own, and who didn't wake her in the night even though he was teething. She then launched into a series of anecdotes about the baby.

Rose was touched by Elsie's interest and wondered if perhaps the general disruption and live-for-today climate of war had lessened the traditionally harsh attitude towards unmarried mothers a little. Naturally there had been a lot of talk at the sorting office initially when word had got round about Joyce's pregnancy. But on her first day back at work, she'd scotched speculation as to the identity of the father by proudly making it known that it was Stan. That had taken the wind out of the gossip-mongers' sails, especially as Stan had been so popular.

It was old news now, of course, but there were still a few disapproving whispers about, Rose suspected. For most people, however, there were far more serious matters to be discussed, such as when the military was going to launch the much-promised second front and get the war won. There was also the ever-topical subject of shortages to be talked over, and this now superseded the antics of Joyce's baby.

'Sweets are going on ration then,' said someone.

'Good job too,' pronounced Elsie. 'At least there

might be something on the shelves in the sweet shops again now. It'll be much fairer for us all.'

'We won't get fat on the ration allowance, will we?' mentioned somebody. 'Half a pound to last a month will only leave us screaming for more.'

'It's better than nothing,' said one positive soul.

The topic got a thorough airing until Elsie changed the subject. 'How's your brother, Rose?' she asked.

'He's doing all right now, thanks,' she replied.

'Oh good, I am pleased,' the other woman responded with genuine warmth. 'Losing your sight is a heck of a thing to have to come to terms with. I don't know how I'd deal with it if it ever happened to me.'

'Me neither,' said Rose. 'I think he still finds it difficult, but he's gradually getting used to it.'

Indeed Alan was a whole lot more positive lately. There hadn't been a miraculous overnight recovery after the breakthrough during Alfie's visit more than two months ago; but that had definitely proved to be a turning point.

It was a gradual process, but little by little Alan had begun to regain his confidence. As he achieved small successes, like walking to the end of the road on his own, or eating his meals without help, he felt less vulnerable and his temper improved. Recently he had made a giant step forward when he'd joined the local branch of an organisation for blind ex-servicemen which offered not only companionship but also advice on everything from coping with such daily trials as having to wash and shave without sight, to learning new skills and discussing employment opportunities. He still had bad days, but there were better ones now too. Joe was wonderful with him. Rose was pleased to notice that Joe's past resentment towards his brother had gone. He was confident in himself now. He didn't need to be jealous of Alan.

Now the conversation ended abruptly as Mr Partridge sailed on to the scene.

'Come on, ladies, be fair now; you're entitled to a break but don't make a flamin' tea party of it,' he said with just enough authority to make them take notice but not enough to alienate them. 'It's time to get your rounds sorted for your second deliveries. We mustn't keep the public waiting longer than we have to, must we?'

Everybody went back to work without argument because they liked and respected him; they also knew that he was right.

That evening a young soldier called Eddie Peck was standing at the bar of a pub in Hackney, drinking a pint of weak wartime beer and staring morosely into space. He was home on compassionate leave, having just buried his mother, who'd died of tuberculosis, and was in the blackest of moods.

Dark-eyed and swarthy, Eddie wasn't normally an emotional man. He preferred to use all his mental energy more profitably by finding ways to make some easy money. But he had loved his mum to bits and her death had caused him such pain. He'd even cried when they'd lowered her coffin into the ground; actually shed tears. He, Eddie Peck, well-known East End hard man, had blubbed like some woman.

He'd always got on well enough with his father, who'd been killed in an air raid during the Blitz, and had learned some neat tricks from the artful old dodger, but the bond with him had never been as strong as the one that had existed between himself and his mother.

But now they were both gone and Eddie was alone in the world. It was Mum he was going to miss, though, despite his being away in the army. Just the thought that she wouldn't be there at home was enough to start the waterworks off again. He couldn't bear to face the fact that he would never hear her voice again, or talk to her or tease her in the way that made her laugh. Mum had been very partial to a bit of fun, bless her.

What a life! He'd lost the only person in the world he had ever really cared about, and his enjoyable and lucrative living had been snatched from him by the government and replaced by the misery of army life and the meagre pay that went with it. Before the war, Eddie had prided himself on never having worked for an employer. He'd survived very nicely by living on his wits and had never even considered any other way of life.

Now, when there was a fortune to be made on the black market, he couldn't be a part of it because he was stuck in army barracks miles away in the country, working in the cookhouse of all places. It was hard work and a terrible comedown for a sharp businessman like himself!

He still had one or two useful contacts in London and was sometimes able to take some dodgy fags back to camp to sell among the lads, but he was home so rarely it was hardly worth the bother; he only did it to keep his hand in, ready for when things returned to normal after the war.

Drinking his beer slowly to make it last, his thoughts turned to another matter: a favour his mother had asked him to do for her after she'd passed on. He mustn't forget to deal with it before he went back to camp. It was a bit of a nuisance, and he couldn't see any point to it himself, but he'd promised her faithfully and he wouldn't let her down. He had a creepy feeling that even death wouldn't stop his mum from knowing what he was up to.

The next morning Johnny got off the train at Paddington station and made his way through the crowds to the buffet, where he joined the queue for a cup of tea. The station was heaving with people, many of them servicemen of all nationalities. There were quite a few Yanks about, he noticed. The noise was deafening: engine steam hissing, doors slamming and the huge volume of human voices all talking at once.

He'd been away for special training at a camp in the country and was on his way home for two weeks' leave so he had every reason to be happy. But it wasn't just ordinary leave; it was embarkation leave. He was going overseas as soon as he went back on duty. The men hadn't been officially notified as to their destination, but wherever it was they would be in the thick of it, that much they could be sure of. Without being unduly pessimistic, Johnny had to face the possibility that he might not come back. This meant he had to put his affairs in order and make certain provisions.

Being a man of a naturally cheerful disposition, it was unusual for Johnny to be depressed. But he was feeling very low now. It wasn't the prospect of the fighting so much as the thought of being away and maybe not making it back. Previously when he'd been in action he hadn't had Alfie in his life. He had been young, free and single then. Now life was in earnest because he was a man with responsibilities.

There had been difficult decisions to make; one in particular had been agonising, and he'd finally forced himself to make it on the train. That was when the gloom had descended. But duty mustn't be shirked, however painful the sacrifice.

On a sudden impulse, he changed his mind about the tea. He left the queue, picked up his kit bag and threw it over his shoulders, then headed towards the underground station.

Delivering the post was so much easier in the summer, Rose thought, as she headed back to the sorting office in the sunshine after her second delivery that day. Doing the round was a joy when she wasn't fighting against the elements. She enjoyed the exercise and the feel of the sun on her face.

The down side of the sunshine was the fact that it

highlighted the shabbiness of everything. The air raids had remained remarkably absent but the landscape showed that this was still very much a country at war. The rubble from the bombed buildings had mostly been cleared now, leaving gaps in the terraces, the bomb sites now overgrown with purple patches of rosebay willow herb and stinging nettles.

There was the usual bustle around the station area, she observed, as she walked past it towards the sorting office, noticing a soldier standing outside. There was something familiar about him, she thought, drawing closer . . .

'Johnny!' she cried, hurrying towards him. 'What are you doing around here?'

'Waiting for you,' he replied. 'I thought you'd probably be finishing about this time.'

On the heels of joy came a bolt of fear. 'Is it Alfie?' she asked. 'Is he ill again?'

'Alfie's fine,' he assured her.

'Oh, thank God.' She gave him a questioning look. 'So if he's all right, to what do I owe the honour?'

'I need to talk to you,' he said, his expression becoming serious. 'Perhaps we could go somewhere quieter.'

'I'll just take my bag in, and finish off my shift officially,' she said. 'I won't be long.'

At Rose's suggestion, they went to Walpole Park and sat on a bench under the trees opposite the lake. A large part of the park had been dug to trenches to be used as shelter during air raids, but sitting here in this shady corner, the war seemed almost not to exist. The school summer holidays were in full swing and there were some children sailing their boats on the water, their high youthful voices floating through the summer air.

'So what's all this about, Johnny?' she asked, turning and looking at him in a questioning manner. 'What do you want to talk to me about?'

'I'm going overseas, Rose,' he replied. 'I'm home on embarkation leave.'

'Oh, oh, I see.' She turned away, feeling crushed. The war seemed very much a reality again.

'When I say home, I haven't actually been there yet, which is why I'm dragging my kit bag about.'

'You've come to tell me you're going away . . . before going home to tell your family?'

He nodded. 'I wanted to speak to you first because I have things to tell you.'

She waited for him to continue.

'I've decided to take your advice and tell Alfie that I didn't desert his mother,' he explained. 'As I'm going away I don't want to leave it unsaid, just in case anything—'

'I think you're wise,' she cut in, to prevent him proceeding along those negative lines. 'Even if you weren't going away, I think it's the right thing for you both.'

'I knew you'd approve, and I'm glad.'

'I'm flattered that my opinion is so important to you,' she told him.

He looked at her, seeing her dark hair shining around her lovely face, her Royal Mail hat having been removed and put on the bench beside her.

'Everything about you is important to me, Rose,' he blurted out.

Her heart swelled with hope as it began to seem certain to her what this was leading up to.

'Which is why I need to tell you about another decision I have made.'

She looked at him, her eyes bright with happy anticipation, her breath short with excitement. This was the moment she'd hoped for and thought would never happen. He was going to tell her that he was in love with her.

'I'm going to marry Hazel by special licence before I go back off leave,' he informed her.

A large rock thrown in her face couldn't have had more impact.

'Oh, oh, I see,' she uttered at last, reeling with humiliation for having harboured such fanciful hopes when she had known all along that he was already spoken for.

'I've been engaged to her for long enough,' he went on. 'It's time I made an honest woman of her.'

'Yeah, I suppose it is,' she said, struggling not to show her devastation.

His brow creased into a frown. 'It won't affect things between you and Alfie,' he assured her. 'I shall make sure she knows that. And Dad will still be around to supervise.'

Rose gave a dry laugh. 'Somehow I don't think Hazel will take kindly to being supervised.'

'I don't mean that literally, of course,' he explained. 'I just want you to know that you'll always be welcome to see Alfie whenever you like.'

'I don't want to stop seeing him until such time as he no longer needs me,' she told him through dry lips, 'but Hazel will be his stepmother, so she'll make the rules while you're away.'

'It won't be a problem,' he assured her. 'I shall make sure of that before I go. Anyway, she's gone out of her way to make an effort with Alfie lately. You know how much my son means to me, Rose. I wouldn't put Hazel in a position of trust if I wasn't sure she would look after his well-being. And his well-being includes seeing you on a regular basis.'

Rose was very angry suddenly, mostly with herself for allowing herself to get into such a state about the man. But she was cross with him too. What was a girl supposed to think when someone wanted to see her before even going home, and told her that she was important to him? Was he so stupid and insensitive as to not realise that she might misunderstand, especially as she knew she had not imagined their mutual attraction for each other.

'Why did you come to see me before going home, Johnny?' she asked, unable to hide the edge to her voice.

He didn't reply immediately; just looked at her, his expression impossible to read. 'I wanted you to know what I'd decided to do about telling Alfie the truth before I broke the news to him,' he explained at last.

'You needed my approval?'

'No. I'd already made the decision.'

'So if that's the case, why did you need to tell me about it so urgently?' she asked. 'Alfie would have told me himself anyway.'

'Because you're important to me, Rose, as I've already told you.' He became agitated. 'I wanted you to know first so that you'd be in the picture, since you're so close to Alfie. Is it such a terrible thing that I've done?' He looked at her questioningly. 'I've obviously made you very angry.'

What could she say? The truth certainly wasn't an option, given his wedding plans. 'No, no, I'm all right,' she fibbed. 'But why the sudden decision to get married?'

'Because I'm going away,' he said quickly. 'I have to make sure my affairs are in order just in case the worst happens and I don't make it back. In other words, I'm behaving responsibly.'

Hazel would be making absolutely certain he did that, Rose thought. She'd been brainwashing him into believing he should marry her for as long as Rose had known him. She took a deep breath to calm herself. After all, the man had a right to live his life in the way he wanted, without explaining himself to her.

'Yes, I can understand that,' she said, forcing a smile. 'If it's what you really want, I wish you all the best.'

'Thanks, Rose,' he said.

'I'll probably see you before you go when I come to see Alfie,' she said quickly, sounding awkward because tears were threatening and she was biting them back. 'But now it's time I went. My mother will have food ready for me.'

'I was going to suggest we grab a bite somewhere. Lyons and the ABC are open.'

'Thanks, Johnny, but no,' she said, standing up. 'Mum will have gone to trouble.'

'Yes, I expect she will, and we can't have food going to waste, can we?'

'Exactly.' She looked at him. 'Are you walking back to the station now?'

'No, I'll stay here for a while to enjoy the fresh air,' he said.

'Ta-ta then,' she said. 'Good luck with Alfie.'

'Thanks.'

Watching her swing off towards the park gates, his misery sank to a new level. He hadn't expected it to be quite this hard. The urge to go after her was over-whelming, but he couldn't trust himself to walk with her even as far as the park gates for fear that his resolve would let him down and he would blurt out the truth: that he was in love with her, and was marrying Hazel only because he didn't feel able to renege on a promise. It wasn't what he wanted, but a man couldn't just ignore his commit-ments because he had fallen in love with someone else.

He hadn't come to Ealing just to tell Rose what he planned to do about Alfie. As she'd pointed out, she would have got to know about that anyway. He'd come because he'd had a sudden and overwhelming longing to see her and just couldn't help himself.

Well, his fate was sealed now. The final decision had been made, so it was time he went home and started to put his plans into action.

Rose was feeling so wretched after her meeting with Johnny that later that afternoon she went next door to Joyce and bared her soul to her cousin while Auntie Sybil was in the Barton house having a chat with her sister.

'It all seems very peculiar to me,' said Joyce, giving little Stanley a crust of bread to suck in his high chair. 'I mean, why would he come all the way over to Ealing after a long journey instead of going home, just to tell you stuff that you'd get to know anyway, unless he was desperate to see you?'

'He values me as a friend, I suppose. Who knows what goes on in his mind?'

'He made a point of telling you that you're important to him, too. There's more to it than friendship,' opined Joyce. 'I reckon he came to see you because he couldn't keep away. He wouldn't feel that way for a friend.'

'That's exactly what I thought until he dropped his bombshell. All the signs were there, or so I thought,' confessed Rose. 'Imagine how I felt. I was expecting him to say that he was in love with me, and he turns round and tells me he's going to marry Hazel by special licence. What a slap in the face that was!'

'I can imagine. It could be that he's cruel or too thick to realise how it must have seemed to you,' suggested Joyce. 'But from what you've told me about him, neither of those things apply, so he met you from work because he just had to see you, and he's marrying Hazel because he doesn't know how to get out of it.'

'He's been engaged to her ever since I've known him, but I didn't think he would ever actually marry her.'

'She's probably put the pressure on.'

'They've never seemed in love, but they could be like a couple of love birds when they're on their own together,' said Rose. 'All I know is that every time I saw him I became more and more convinced that he had feelings for me. It seems I've completely misread the signals.'

'Not necessarily. I've told you, he's marrying this Hazel woman because he's put a ring on her finger and he doesn't know how to get out of it.'

'Maybe.'

'There's only one way to find out, kid,' advised Joyce. 'Confront him with it. Get yourself over to Shepherd's Bush and ask him how he really feels about you.'

'I can't interfere in his personal business just because of my gut instinct,' she stated categorically. 'I might have got it all wrong.'

'If you want him, go and fight for him, girl,' Joyce advised.

'But he's made his decision to marry Hazel,' she reminded her cousin. 'It wouldn't be right to break that up. I don't like Hazel but she is his fiancée, and I wouldn't want to sabotage anyone's relationship.'

461

'Don't be so soft, Rose,' admonished Joyce. 'I was engaged to Bob but I still fell in love with Stan, despite being determined not to. And I don't regret it for a moment. If I'd kept to the rules, Stan would have gone to his grave never knowing how much I loved him, and I wouldn't have had his nibs here. The last thing I wanted to do was hurt Bob, and I'm still dreading having to do so when he comes home. But there are times when you have to follow your instincts; there are also times when you have to take your courage in both hands and seize the initiative.' She watched part of a soggy crust land on the kitchen floor while the baby gurgled and laughed. 'Oh Stanley, you mucky little pup.' She turned back to Rose. 'The bloke is getting married and going away to war. He might not come back. If you want him, do something about it. The worst that can happen is humiliation if you're wrong, and that will soon pass. But don't end up regretting what might have been for the rest of your life because you didn't even try. Go and get him, girl, and don't take too long about it.'

Rose was still uncertain. 'It doesn't seem a very fair thing to do,' she said.

'All's fair in love and war, as they say. But anyway, this is something you'll have to make up your own mind about, no matter what I say,' she said, bending over to kiss her baby son, who deposited a chubby handful of chewed bread into her hair.

'I'll think about it,' said Rose.

★　★　★

One evening a few days later a stranger knocked at the Bartons' front door.

'Does Bill Barton live here?' asked Eddie Peck when May answered the door to him.

'Yeah, that's right,' she said, friendly towards him because he was a soldier.

'Can I have a few words with him, please?'

'He's having his meal at the moment,' she said. 'Can I help you? I'm his wife.'

'Oh. Are you now?' There was a brief hiatus while Eddie pondered on this. 'I'd rather see him myself, if you don't mind,' he said. 'I won't keep him from his grub for long, I promise.'

Assuming him to be someone Bill knew from the pub, May said, 'You'd better come in then.'

She ushered him inside and into the living room, where the family were sitting around the table chattering over their meal.

'You've got a visitor, Bill,' she told him.

'Oh yeah,' said Bill, turning to look at the stranger. 'What can I do for you, mate?'

'Sorry to interrupt you while you're eating,' said Eddie.

'That's all right,' said Bill. 'But as we are in the middle of a meal, perhaps you could make it snappy.'

'This is all very cosy,' approved Eddie. 'Are you always such a happy family?'

'We have our moments, of course, like anybody, but yeah, we rub along together quite well.'

'I can see that.' The instant May had introduced herself as Bill's wife Eddie had spotted a golden opportunity to make some extra dough. It would put an end to their little game of happy families at the same time, too, the smug lot. He was pleased now that he had kept to his word to his dear departed mother and come here. He almost hadn't bothered.

'Anyway, what do you want with me?' asked Bill, rising from the table and looking at the young man. 'I would like to finish my food before it gets cold.'

'I'm Eddie Peck.' He paused for a moment, looking at Bill with a half-smile before adding, 'Lottie's son.'

Rose watched her father turn scarlet, then ashen; her mother had gone a funny colour too.

'My mother was Lottie Barton,' Eddie went on with a slow smile, his eyes never leaving Bill's face, 'otherwise known as Mrs Bill Barton – your wife.'

A hush fell upon the room.

'What's he talking about?' asked Alan.

'Yeah, what does he mean, Dad?' added Joe.

'Is he saying that you were married to someone else before Mum?' Rose enquired.

'He was married to my mother until the day she died a week ago,' pronounced Eddie, 'which, I believe, makes your father a bigamist.' With a great deal of satisfaction he watched the look of absolute horror on every face around the table. 'I'm sure the police will be very interested in what I have to tell them.' He paused again, smiling triumphantly. 'Unless, of course, Mr Barton, you and I can come to some . . . mutually beneficial arrangement in the form of a cash payment.'

★   ★   ★

Johnny chose his words with care when he told Alfie about the past.

'So I wasn't around for you and your mum because I didn't know where you were, not because I didn't want to be with you,' he told him after he'd explained the basics, leaving out anything unsuitable for such young ears. 'Your mother was a wonderful woman. But even someone as good and lovely as she was can get things wrong. Grown-ups do what they think is best, but they don't always get it right.'

They were in the living room at the pub, sitting together on the sofa. Johnny had asked his father to make himself scarce while he had this serious talk with Alfie.

'Couldn't you have looked for us?' the boy enquired.

'I did,' he assured him. 'I searched high and low for your mother before you were born. I followed up every lead and walked the streets looking for her. But if someone doesn't want to be found, it just isn't possible to find them.'

'Didn't she like you?' Alfie asked. 'Is that why she didn't want you to find us?'

'She liked me very much, son,' he said. 'In fact she loved me a lot, as I loved her.'

The boy looked baffled. 'Why did she hide from you then?' he asked.

'One day you'll be old enough to understand about grown-up things. But all you need to know for now is that I didn't desert you, and I never will. I have to go away soon because it's my duty to my country. I am not going because I want to.'

'Will you be coming back?'

'I hope so, son,' he said.

'Will you be away for long?' the boy asked.

'It might be quite a while,' he replied. 'But that won't be up to me. It depends what happens with the war. I have to do as I'm told. We'll just have to hope and pray that I won't be away for too long.'

Alfie looked straight ahead, as though he had already distanced himself from the subject. Then he said in a subdued tone, 'Can I go now, please?'

Johnny had intended to tell him about his wedding plans, but thought it wiser to do that another time as the boy seemed anxious to leave. Enough had been said for now. Anyway, Alfie appeared to get along well enough with Hazel, so the marriage shouldn't be a problem for him. Just because Hazel didn't have Rose's warm and lovely nature, that didn't make her a bad person. He really must stop making the comparison.

'Yeah, of course you can go,' said Johnny disappointedly. He'd hoped that telling Alfie the truth might bring them closer together. But Alfie didn't seem to care one way or the other about what his father had told him.

Alfie sat on his bed with a strange feeling in his stomach that he didn't quite understand. It was kind of soft and happy but made him want to cry too. It had something to do with the fact that his father had wanted him and his mother after all, and hadn't just left them. It was all a bit muddled.

One thing he wasn't confused about was his feelings about his father going away to war. He didn't want him to go, and that was definite. A lot of the soldiers got killed; he knew kids at school whose dads were never coming back.

He wanted his dad to be at home, here at the pub. He liked it when he was around, and it made him sad that he wouldn't be for much longer. He wanted to tell him all these things; he'd wanted to tell him how he felt before. But he couldn't. For some reason he wasn't able to put it into words.

Suddenly he had an overpowering longing to see Rose. She would understand; she would tell him what to do and make everything all right.

'You'll get nothing out of me,' said Bill Barton while the family looked on. 'Not a brass farthing.'

'That's right, Bill, you tell him,' encouraged May, who had moved to stand by his side.

'In that case, I must do my public duty and tell them at the nick what you've been up to.'

'You can tell them what you like,' said Bill, sounding confident. 'It won't do you a ha'p'orth o' good.'

'Bigamy is a criminal offence,' Eddie reminded him. 'You can go to prison for it.'

Rose saw her parents exchange a look. Her mother nodded at Dad. What on earth was going on? This whole thing was getting more bizarre by the second.

'I'm fully aware of that, and had I committed bigamy, that's probably what would happen to me.'

'Are you thick or something?' asked Eddie, looking towards May. 'This lady is your wife, and that's one wife too many according to the laws of this country.'

Bill looked at his three children before continuing.

'I have never been married to any other woman except your mother,' he informed Eddie.

There was a communal gasp from the offspring.

'So you and Mum aren't—' began Rose.

'We don't have a marriage certificate,' her father replied, interrupting her.

'Blimey,' exclaimed Alan.

'Oh God,' said Rose.

'Cor,' added Joe.

'But we have been married in mind, heart and deed since before you were all born.'

'So us three are all . . .' began Joe.

'Bastards,' Eddie finished for him with a raucous laugh. 'So much for your happy little family now, eh?'

Joe was on his feet in an instant, grabbing Eddie by the arm, and drawing his fist back ready to aim a blow.

'Sit down, Joe,' ordered his father with an authority Rose had never heard in his voice before. 'Don't waste your energy on him. He isn't worth it.'

'All right, so you're not actually breaking the law,' began Eddie, 'but I bet your neighbours don't know that you've been living over the brush all these years. Perhaps I should visit your local pub and spread the word about, unless you make it worth my while not to.'

'I've told you, I won't give you a penny, and that still stands,' declared Bill. 'You can tell who you like.

We're strong enough to take it. Nothing you can do will hurt May and me, and I'm sure our children are well established and mature enough to be able to cope with it.' He looked at them, willing them to back him up in front of the intruder at least. 'I hope so anyway.'

All three of them answered in the affirmative.

'Get out,' added Alan, rising to his feet. 'Go on, sling your hook. Go back to whichever hole in the ground you crawled out of.'

'I'm going, mate, don't worry,' said Eddie. 'I don't wanna hang around with a bunch of fakes like you.'

Bill got hold of him and marched him from the house, slamming the door after him. When he came back into the room, he addressed his children.

'Thanks for backing me up in front of him,' he said. 'But I suppose you're all shocked.'

'Well, yeah,' admitted Rose.

'It takes a bit of getting used to,' said Joe.

'It is a turn-up for the books all right,' added Alan.

'We should have told you the truth when you got old enough to understand these things, but somehow we never got around to it,' Bill explained.

'We've always been married in every way that matters, you see,' added their mother. 'We worked hard to build a happy and stable home, and our family meant everything to us. As the years went by, that piece of paper seemed to matter less and less. I suppose the past faded into the background because we were so busy bringing you all up. It has always been our dream to be properly married, though.'

'Are we allowed to know what happened?' asked Rose.

'Yeah, you deserve to know the truth.' Bill cleared his throat and began. 'When I was a lad of seventeen I met a girl called Lottie. She was a very good-looking, confident girl who knew her way around, and I was dazzled by her.'

'She was flighty,' put in May.

'Thank you, May, but let me tell the story,' he admonished. 'Anyway, the next thing I knew she was pregnant. I did the decent thing and married her, but she had a miscarriage so there was no baby. The marriage was a disaster from the start because we were never right for each other. After a few months we hated the sight of each other and went our own ways, though we still lived together for the sake of appearances. Then I met May and we fell in love; Lottie met a man called Tommy Peck and got pregnant by him. There was no way I was going to stay around after that, so I left, and Tommy moved in with her.'

'Lottie didn't mind the gossip then?' said Rose.

'Not Lottie,' he replied. 'It was me who worried about that sort of thing, which is how I got trapped into marriage in the first place. She liked a good time, did Lottie, and had had a good few boyfriends before me. I didn't realise that until after I'd married her.'

'She was a right baggage,' said May.

'All right, May,' said her husband in a tone of mild admonition. 'There's no need to speak ill of the dead.'

'Sorry.'

470

'Anyway, divorce for people like us was even more unheard of then than it is nowadays,' Bill continued. 'Even apart from the fact that it cost money that we didn't have, it was far too shameful. So there was no way we could get married unless Lottie died, and we were all far too young in those days to even think about anything as far away as that.'

May nodded in agreement.

'We had to be together, but we needed to get away from the East End because we knew so many people there,' Bill went on. 'They can say some wicked things when you're involved in a scandal like that. It didn't worry me, but it upset your mother; people calling her a home-wrecker and so on.'

'So we came to west London, and made a new start as man and wife,' said May, taking up the story. 'Our families had disowned us because of the carryings-on, all except for my dear sister Sybil. She and Flip only moved here to be near us, bless them.'

'No one around here knew us so they had no reason to doubt that we were married,' Bill continued. 'We wanted to have a family and bring them up in a stable home environment. We knew we wouldn't stand a chance of that if people knew about our background. You kids would have had a hard time with the other children if the truth had come out, given how cruel children can be. We had to protect you from that.'

May continued with the story.

'It was vital to us that you saw us as a good example when you were growing up. We taught you decency

471

and morality and showed you how to live your lives. If you'd known the truth, you'd have had no one to look up to in your formative years. You're all old enough to make up your own minds now about the way you live, so it isn't quite so important. We've done our part. You're adults now, people in your own right with your own standards and opinions.'

There was a silence while Rose and her brothers digested what they'd heard.

'It's quite a story,' said Rose.

'Not half,' added Alan.

'So what do you think of your respectable parents now?' asked May nervously. 'Are you ashamed of us?'

'Don't be daft,' said Rose.

'There are times in life when you have to follow your heart even if it means breaking the rules,' explained May. 'Your dad and I knew we had to be together; we knew it was the right thing . . . and here we are, more than twenty-five years down the road and still going strong.'

'And here *we* all are, happy, well-adjusted adults,' said Rose. 'You gave us life and a good solid upbringing and are still giving us support. The rest doesn't matter. Does it, boys?'

'Not to me,' said Joe.

'It isn't up to us to question your judgement about something that happened before we were even born,' said Alan.

'Thank God for that,' said May. 'I thought you might be angry with us.'

'After all you've done for us?' said Alan. 'Not bloomin' likely.'

Rose and Joe murmured their agreement.

'There's one thing I am going to ask you to do, though,' said Alan.

'What's that?' asked his mother.

'That you achieve your dream and get married,' he grinned. 'You've no excuse now, have you? You're a free man, Dad. You can make an honest woman of her whenever you like.'

'Indeed I can, son, and the sooner the better as far as I'm concerned,' said Bill, grinning and slipping his arm around May's shoulders.

Chapter Eighteen

Having been thrashing around in the sheets for most of the night, Rose was feeling gritty-eyed and achy when she got up for work at four o'clock the next morning.

It wasn't so much the bombshell her parents had dropped last night that had kept her awake, as the issues it raised in her mind. Mum and Dad were so staunchly conventional, she could never have imagined them ever putting so much as a toe over the line. But they had done, quite dramatically, and as a result of it the Barton family had been created. Had they stuck to their principles . . . well, that just didn't bear thinking about.

And here she was, about to let the man she loved marry another woman without even putting up a fight. She was prepared to let him go away to war to face possible death without telling him how she felt about him. Come on, Rose, show a bit of mettle, girl. You've stood back for long enough.

As she cycled through the streets to the sorting office, she vowed to take action as soon as she possibly could after work. One way or the other, the matter would be resolved before this day was over.

Hazel awoke that same morning with a glorious sense of well-being. She had every reason to be happy because she had finally landed her man. In a matter of days she would be Mrs Johnny Beech. It was all arranged. He'd booked them in at the register office, and they were having a small reception afterwards at the Green Cat, where she – as the bride – would be the centre of attraction. Yippee!

There was only one minor snag: she'd used all her clothing coupons so wasn't able to buy a new outfit to get married in. She would have been more economical with them had she known Johnny was going to name the day. But it had come right out of the blue. She hadn't even had to nag him into remembering his promise to her. Miraculously, he'd raised the subject without any prompting. Never mind that it had come about because he was going overseas. That wasn't a problem.

Neither was the lack of new clothes, not really, because she could make herself look good whatever she wore. She had perfected the art of making the best of herself over the years. The important thing was that at last they were going to get married. Finally she could escape from this house, she thought blissfully, listening to her sister snoring in the other bed. No more family irritations and house rules about taking your turn with the washing-up and not staying out too late at night. She would do exactly as she pleased once she was married, because she would be the mistress of the house.

To add to her joy of the moment, she didn't have to go in to work at that dreadful factory today. She had a day off in lieu because she'd worked a shift on Sunday. Her days on the assembly line were numbered anyway, thank God. Once she was in possession of that vital document, the marriage certificate, she would tell the know-alls at the Labour Exchange that she was a married woman now and needed at home to look after a child so would be leaving the factory, and there wouldn't be a damned thing they could do about it.

For the moment, however, she was going to enjoy a nice lie-in. When her sister had gone to work she would get up and wash her hair with some of Sheila's shampoo. As long as she remembered to top the bottle up with water to the original level, Sheila would never know the difference, seeing as she was thicker than a pile of planks.

Later on, when the lunchtime session at the Green Cat was over so that there would be no fear of her having to lend a hand, she would make herself look glamorous, then go over to the pub to see her intended.

There were heavy footsteps on the stairs and the bedroom door was flung open.

'Time to get up, girls,' said her mother in a loud, shrill voice. 'Wakey, wakey, rise and shine.'

'I've got the day off,' Hazel reminded her, wincing at the volume of sound.

'Oh yeah, course you have. I remember you telling me now,' said her mother, who was in her dressing gown and curlers. 'So it's just that sister of yours I've got to get out of her coma. Come on, Sheila, time to get up.' She went over to Sheila's bed and gave her a vigorous shake on the shoulders. 'Come on, out of bed or you'll be late for work.'

While her sister moaned and muttered, Hazel lay back and luxuriated in the relaxation, the fact that her sister had to get up for work and she herself didn't adding to her pleasure.

She could hardly believe that her life had taken such a turn for the better at last. Everything comes to those who wait, she thought. It had taken her a long time to bag Johnny Beech, but she'd done it in the end.

'Would you mind looking after Alfie while Dad and I pop out for a short time, Hazel?' asked Johnny that afternoon. 'Only we want to go to see a pal of ours down the market, to offer him our condolences. We've heard that the poor man has had a telegram telling him that his son's been killed in action.'

'Oh, what a shame. Of course I'll look after Alfie. Don't you worry about it,' said Hazel, who didn't relish the idea of having to play nursemaid but was making a supreme effort to hide her true feelings.

Johnny shouted upstairs for Alfie to come down from his room.

'Grandad and I have to go and see Syd, the green-grocer in the market,' Johnny explained to his son. 'He's had a bit of bad news and we're going to pay our respects. So Hazel is going to look after you.'

'Alfie will be all right with me, won't you?' said Hazel matily, because it was imperative that she didn't do anything in front of Johnny to put the wedding plans in jeopardy at this late stage. 'I'm practically family now.'

He nodded. 'Can I go out to play while you're gone?' he asked his father.

'As long as you don't go far,' replied Johnny. 'I don't want Hazel wondering where you are and having to go out searching the streets for you.'

'He'll behave himself,' said his grandfather, winking at Alfie affectionately. 'He's never any trouble. Come on then, Johnny, let's be on our way. Poor old Syd needs all the support he can get at the moment.'

'Coming, Dad,' said Johnny, and hurried from the room and down the stairs.

Alfie was sick with dread at the idea of having Hazel as his stepmother, even though his father had told him that she had no intention of trying to take his mother's place. His father seemed to think it would be good for a boy of his age to have a woman about the place.

Maybe it would be if it was a woman like Rose. But not horrid cold-eyed Hazel, who made his stomach churn just by being there. Even when she was being nice to him, he knew it wouldn't last and she would soon be looking at him as though she hated him, and reminding him of the time she'd bent his fingers back and told him what would happen if he didn't do exactly what she told him. He daren't tell anyone or talk back to her, for fear of what she'd do to Rose.

Now she was speaking to him. 'So what are you going to do now?' she asked. 'Are you going out to play?'

At the moment he didn't want to go anywhere because he was afraid he might cry. He was so miserable and afraid at the idea of this horrid woman living here at the pub, he just wanted to be on his own. If only Rose was here; she would know what to do.

'Dunno,' he said.

'I think you should go out,' she suggested, eager to get rid of him. 'It's a nice day. A young boy like you needs to be out in the fresh air, not hanging around indoors with a face like a wet lettuce.'

'I'll just go up to my room to get my marbles to take out with me, and then I'll go,' he said.

'All right,' she shrugged. She didn't care where he was as long as he wasn't around her. Now that the wedding was all booked she didn't need to pretend to be nice to him when they were on their own together. It was only when Johnny was around that she had to put on an act.

She was planning on having a nice leisurely time with her feet up, reading her copy of *Woman's Own*, and she didn't want some kid spoiling it.

Johnny had a great deal of admiration for the traders of Shepherd's Bush market. The area had suffered extensive damage during the Blitz, and the market had been threatened with closure. But the stall-holders had helped to clear the area of rubble themselves and the market was up and running again within a matter of days.

'We came over as soon as we heard, Syd,' said Johnny now to his greengrocer friend.

'So sorry, mate,' added Ted. 'You must be gutted.'

'Devastated,' he confirmed.

'There's nothing anyone can say to help you really,' said Johnny.

'No, but I appreciate your coming over, boys.' A short, stockily built man of about fifty, with a veined, weather-beaten face, Syd was standing by his almost empty greengrocery stall, smoking a cigarette. 'You're never really prepared for it, are yer? He was away at war so I knew he might not come back, but I never faced up to it. I blanked that part out and looked forward to his coming home. They won't get my boy; he'll outsmart them every time, I thought. Then I get a telegram and that's that. He's gone, and there ain't a thing I can do about it. Makes you think, dunnit? Makes you remember all the things you wished you'd said while there was still time.'

While Ted made sympathetic utterances, Johnny was shocked into silence as the significance of Syd's words hit home. He himself was going away to war, and he'd taken care of his obligations in case the worst happened by telling Alfie the truth and agreeing to marry Hazel.

But the most important thing of all had been left undone. With a sinking heart he realised that he hadn't taken care of the one thing that really mattered to him: his feelings for Rose. What if he didn't make it back and she never got to know how he felt about her? What was he doing marrying Hazel when he didn't love her and never would? Why was he forcing himself to meet a commitment that wasn't right? It was Rose he wanted to share his life with.

'I couldn't stay at home even though I don't have much to sell,' said Syd, his bloodshot eyes filling with tears. 'I just had to get out of the house for a while. Being indoors was making me morbid. My daughter is with the missus so she'll be all right while I'm out earning a crust, even though it's more like just a crumb or two these days.'

'You're best out among people,' sympathised Ted.

'I can't help the wife when I'm at home anyway. The poor love has taken it hard,' he said sadly. 'I can't make her grief go away, can I? I reckon the women take it harder than us men, you know.'

'The maternal bond is a special thing,' said Ted. 'A child hurts itself and the mother feels the pain, so they reckon. But that doesn't mean we aren't deeply affected by these things too, even though it isn't the done thing for us men to show our feelings.'

Syd nodded, drawing on his cigarette and looking disconsolately into the distance.

'Johnny's going overseas when he goes back off leave,' mentioned Ted.

'Ooh, blimey, the best of British luck to you, son,' said Syd. 'I'll be thinking of you.'

'I'll be all right,' Johnny said, forcing a hearty tone. 'They tried to finish me off at Dunkirk and didn't succeed, so I shall do my best to make sure that they fail again this time.'

All Johnny wanted to do was to get on the bus to Ealing. He needed to see Rose urgently. But it would be unkind to leave while Syd still wanted to talk. The poor man had suffered a cruel blow. The least his mates could do was to give him a little of their time and attention.

Hazel was lying on the sofa engrossed in her magazine when she heard the rat-a-tat of the door knocker downstairs. Sod it! Who was that come to disturb her peace? It couldn't be anyone connected to the pub because it was out of hours and that was the family's private front door. She decided not to answer it. Whoever it was would come back later if it was important enough. The knocking started again, only louder and more determined. Honestly, the nerve of some people. She remained where she was. If she ignored it, they'd give up and go away eventually.

Alfie, who had stayed in his bedroom rather than go out, heard the knocking at the front door. But he couldn't go down and answer it in case Hazel flew into a rage because he hadn't gone out to play as she'd told him to. He couldn't see who the caller was through the window because his room looked out over the back yard.

A feeling of terror gripped him suddenly, making his heart thump and his mouth go dry. It was so quiet inside the flat, he daren't move in case Hazel realised that he was here instead of outside as she thought. He hated being alone with Hazel, and wished that his dad and grandad would come back.

*　*　*

'Oh for God's sake,' Hazel muttered to herself when the caller continued to knock at the door. She decided that she'd better go down and find out who it was and what they wanted. 'Whoever you are, you're gonna get a piece of my mind, disturbing decent people when they're trying to relax.'

Hurrying down the stairs, muttering under her breath, she opened the door.

'Hello, Hazel,' said the caller.

'You?' scowled Hazel. 'What the hell are you doing here?'

'I've come to see Johnny,' explained Rose.

'He's not in.'

'I'll wait then,' Rose told her. 'Is Alfie about?'

'No, none of them are in, so sling your hook.'

'I'm not going anywhere,' declared Rose, 'not until I've seen Johnny.'

'Bugger off.'

'If you'd rather I didn't come inside,' Rose said as Hazel went to shut the door, 'I'll wait out here until he comes home and catch him then. The weather's fine so I'll sit on the green in the sun.'

Hazel daren't risk letting the evil bitch be alone with him. God knows what she'd get up to. 'What do you want to see him about?' she asked.

'It's a personal matter.'

Hazel thought about this. 'You'd better come in and wait, then,' she said, opening the door wider.

As soon as Rose had stepped over the threshold, Hazel closed the door after her and said, 'Right, let's

484

have it. Tell me what you want to see my fiancé about.'

'I've told you, it's personal, and none of your business.' Rose had come here determined to stand her ground and wasn't going to be put off.

'Are you thick or something?' Hazel burst out, almost beside herself with rage. 'In a few days' time I'll be Johnny's wife, so his business is my business.'

'Not necessarily . . .'

'You've no right to come here demanding to see him,' Hazel blasted at her. 'I don't want you anywhere near the place. You definitely won't be seeing Alfie once Johnny has gone away, whatever he's told you to the contrary, because I shall be in charge then and I won't allow you to see him.'

'I should have thought you'd be only too pleased to have him off your hands,' said Rose. 'You don't strike me as the maternal type.'

'I'm not, and I have no intention of changing my ways. I'm not looking after someone else's brat,' Hazel made clear. 'I shall leave all that to his grandfather. But I'll be making the rules. Oh yes, I shall decide what goes on around here.'

'We'll have to see what Johnny has to say about that when he gets back, won't we?' said Rose.

'You can tell him what you like and I'll deny it,' Hazel informed her without so much as a qualm. 'As he's engaged to me, and you're of no significance, it's obvious who he'll believe. Anyway, once he's gone abroad he won't know what's happening back here, will he? Even if he did find out somehow, there would be nothing he could do about it as he'll be across the ocean somewhere.'

Rose studied Hazel's attractive face, observing the harsh mouth, the cold eyes in which Rose had never seen any evidence of genuine warmth. 'You don't love Johnny at all, do you?' she stated as a fact rather than a suggestion.

'What a thing to say. You've got a cheek—'

'If you did love him,' Rose cut in, 'you'd want to make sure everything is kept as he wants it to be while he's away. You're just using him for your own ends.'

'Is that right?' she mocked. 'Some sort of an expert on human behaviour, are you?'

'No. But I do have enough common sense to recognise a fraud when I see one.'

'There's nothing wrong with a girl looking after herself,' Hazel said. 'If you want a decent life you have to get it in whatever way you can.'

'You're unfeeling,' said Rose, appalled. 'You're just a self-seeking cow.'

'I don't have to listen to this,' said Hazel, making for the street door and opening it. 'Get out, go on. Clear off.'

'Certainly,' said Rose, taking a step forward. 'I'll enjoy sitting in the sun while I'm waiting for Johnny; the further away from you the better.'

Hazel's eyes narrowed, expediency giving her a change of heart. She closed the door swiftly, before Rose could leave. 'I want to know why you want to see Johnny,' she demanded. 'I have a right to know, so come on, let's have it.'

Rose considered the matter and decided that there was no real point in hiding it from her.

'You won't like it,' she warned.

'Just get on and spit it out.'

'All right, you asked for it. I want to see Johnny because I am going to tell him that I'm in love with him.'

'You wouldn't dare.' Hazel's eyes were bright with fury.

'That's where you're wrong, Hazel,' Rose told her. 'I intend to do it, and you won't stop me.'

'You've got a nerve.'

'It is a bit pushy, I admit, but I have to do it. There's no other way.'

'He'll laugh in your face.'

'I don't think so,' Rose disagreed. 'I'm almost positive he feels the same about me. I'm going to ask him to marry me instead of you.'

Hazel gave a dry laugh. 'I always knew you weren't the brightest button in the box, but I didn't realise that you were stark raving bonkers. I don't know which world you're living in, but in this one the man does the proposing.'

Rose shrugged. 'So I'm going to make an exception to the rule. I can't afford to be feeble about it with him going away to war.'

'You talk about me being unfeeling,' rasped Hazel, her face scarlet with fury. 'What about you, deliberately setting out to break up someone's engagement?'

'The difference between us is that I really love him,'

Rose said. 'I admit it isn't a nice thing to do, but there are times when you have to do what you know is right, even if it isn't actually very kind. Anyway, it isn't as if it will break your heart to lose him. It'll upset your plans, that's all.'

'You're round the flamin' twist, woman.'

'We'll see about that,' said Rose. 'Now if you don't mind, I'll go and wait on the green. I don't much care for the company in here.'

Rose was completely unprepared for what happened next. Hazel hurled herself at the front door and stood against it, facing inwards with her arms spread, barring Rose's way, her eyes burning with malice.

'You're going nowhere, lady,' she stated, her voice oddly distorted. 'Anything you have to say to my fiancé you'll say while I'm present. I'm not stupid enough to let someone as devious as you be alone with him.'

Before Rose had a chance to say anything, Hazel grabbed hold of her firmly by the arms and tried to drag her towards the door to the bar. Caught off guard, Rose was at a disadvantage.

'Get your hands off me,' she said at last, managing to pull herself free. 'What on earth do you think you're doing?'

In reply Hazel lunged at her and pushed her through the door behind the bar area with such force Rose fell against the counter, hurting her arm. While she was still shaken from this, Hazel opened the flap and gave her an almighty shove into the saloon bar, empty and silent at this time of day.

The violence of Hazel's temper added to her strength, and Rose hit her head on the corner of one of the tables before falling to the floor. As she tried to get up, Hazel pushed her down and kicked her in the ribs.

'That's where you belong, on the floor of the bar,' said Hazel, who had lost control completely. 'You'll stay there until I say otherwise. The flat upstairs is for family members only, which you never will be no matter how much you scheme to worm your way in.'

Looking at Hazel and seeing malevolence exuding from every pore, Rose realised that she wasn't just a spiteful, jealous woman; she was also a very dangerous one.

Unbeknown to either of them, Alfie had heard the whole thing from the top of the stairs. He'd crept out of his room after he'd heard Hazel go down to answer the door, and sat on the stairs almost paralysed with fear and horror at the things Hazel was saying.

Now hearing her get rough with Rose, he was galvanised into action. He tore down the stairs and rushed into the bar, where Rose was on the floor with Hazel standing over her. As he watched, Hazel kicked her.

'Leave her alone,' he said, throwing himself against Hazel and pummelling her stomach with his fists, which were no threat whatsoever to Hazel's superior physical strength. 'Leave Rose alone.'

'Keep out of it, Alfie,' Rose begged him, concerned for his safety at the hands of this woman. 'Go upstairs and stay there until your dad gets back.'

'I'm not leaving you on your own with her,' he said, his voice trembling with fear and emotion. 'She's wicked.'

Hazel gave him a withering look. 'Have you been earwigging?' she asked.

'I heard everything,' he replied, too upset to pretend. 'But you won't be able to do bad things to Rose, like you've always said you would, because I'm going to tell my dad and he'll do something to make sure you can't, even though he's got to go away.'

'Like hell you're gonna tell him,' she said, clutching him hard by the arm and pushing him out of the way so roughly he fell against a chair and hit his head, causing him to cry out. 'Now get out of here, and if you breathe a word about what you've heard, you'll regret it. Remember, your father will be going away; he has to go whatever happens here, so he won't be able to help you. One word about this and I'll make you pay.'

Rose struggled to her feet and went to Alfie's assistance.

'Are you all right, luv?' she asked, seeing the bump on his head which was already beginning to swell. 'Let's get out of here and get that looked at. I'll see your dad later.'

But Hazel had other plans. 'Oh no you don't,' she said. 'You're staying here. You're not talking to Johnny unless I'm there too.'

'Don't be so stupid, Hazel,' Rose warned. 'The boy is hurt. He needs medical attention. I'll take him down to the hospital straight away.'

Hazel was at a loss to know how to handle this. These two people had been the bane of her life for too long. Just when she'd got things going along nicely with Johnny, one or other of them wrecked everything for her. Rage burned to the roots of her hair. Why couldn't this woman leave her alone? Hazel had come so far in her quest to get Johnny to the altar, and was on the verge of a better life. Now Rose was going to spoil it for her if she wasn't stopped.

Hazel picked up a heavy glass ashtray from one of the tables and brought it down on Rose's head, watching as she crumpled to the floor; crying out then lying still. There was just a fleeting moment of satisfaction for Hazel before panic set in as she realised what she'd done. She stood there cemented to the spot, shaking and wanting to be sick. Alfie was on his knees beside Rose, sobbing and begging her to wake up.

Realising the enormity of her actions, Hazel dropped the ashtray as though it was scalding her, and took flight. She ran from the pub and across the green with no idea of where she was heading. She was shaking so much she could hardly breathe or make her legs work. She'd killed someone, which meant she would be hanged. Oh God, what was she going to do?

Inside the pub, Alfie was desperately trying to get a response from Rose.

'Please, Rose,' he sobbed, holding her hand. 'Please wake up. Please don't be dead.'

She didn't move; just lay there with her eyes closed.

She was very white and there was blood on the floor by her head. Although Alfie was almost too terrified to think straight, something barely remembered came into his mind, and he went to the telephone on the table in the hallway at the bottom of the stairs and dialled 999.

'Ambulance, please,' he said. 'Someone's tried to murder my friend. Please send someone quick. She's down on the floor. I think she might be dead.' He listened carefully, then replied, 'I'm at the Green Cat pub in Shepherd's Bush.'

Having been told that an ambulance would be there as soon as possible, Alfie had an overwhelming longing for his father and grandfather. But mostly he wanted his dad.

He went to the side door of the pub and ran out on to the street, rushing up to the first person he saw, who just happened to be Mr Brown from the paper shop on his way to post a letter.

'Can you help me, please,' Alfie blurted out. 'Could you get my dad; he's down the market with Grandad. They've gone to see Syd the greengrocer. Could you tell him to come home quick? I can't go because I've got to stay here.'

'What's the matter, Alfie?' the man asked, noticing a reddish bump on the boy's head. 'Have you had a fall?'

'No, I'm all right. Please get Dad, please, Mr Brown, I'm begging you.'

'All right, son, calm down, I'll get your father as

quick as I can,' he said, and hurried towards the market while Alfie went back inside to stay with Rose.

'Thanks again for coming to see me, boys,' said Syd when Johnny and his father were about to leave. 'It's nice to know that people care.'

'Anything at all we can do, mate, you know where we are,' said Ted.

'It's times like this you know who your friends are.' Syd looked at Johnny. 'Good luck, mate. I'll be asking after you when I call in at your place for a pint.'

Johnny thanked him and they turned to go.

'I'm not going straight home, Dad,' Johnny told Ted. 'Something's come up and I've got to go over to Ealing. I'm going to get the bus.'

'That's a bit sudden, isn't it?' remarked his father. 'You didn't say anything about it when we came out.'

'I've only just realised that I have to go there.'

'But Hazel is waiting for you back at the pub,' Ted reminded him. 'She'll do her nut when I arrive back without you. Surely there's nothing so urgent you have to go without letting her know first?'

'It is urgent, Dad, believe me,' Johnny said. 'Tell her I'll explain later.'

'All right, but don't blame me if she's got the hump with you when you get back.'

'I won't.'

'I think I'll call in to see how old Bert Hutchins is on my way home, as I'll be practically passing his place,' Ted said, referring to one of their regular customers,

493

an octogenarian who hadn't been well lately. 'I'll only stay long enough for him to know we haven't forgotten him.'

'Give him my best, and I'll see you at home later,' said Johnny and hurried off towards the bus stop.

Shortages didn't keep people away from the market, Reg Brown noticed as he elbowed his way through the crowds, his eyes peeled for Ted Beech and his son. There was something very wrong at the Green Cat. The lad had looked frightened out of his wits. There must have been someone there with him because they wouldn't go out and leave the boy on his own. He knew the family well enough to be sure of that. Maybe he should have stopped to find out what was going on, but it had seemed more urgent to do what the lad had asked. The poor kid had been in a hell of a state.

Punters were packed around the second-hand clothes stall and he had a struggle to get through as he headed for Syd's stall. It was a warm day and the air was heavy with the smell of sweat, cigarette smoke, dust and drains.

'Ted and Johnny have gone,' said Syd when Reg finally reached his stall.

'I must have missed them in the crowds. Still, as they're on their way home anyway, it's all right. I told the boy I'd get his dad to come back pronto. Some sort of trouble there, I think.'

'They're not going straight home, though,' said Syd. 'I heard Johnny say he was going to get the bus to Ealing, and Ted's going to call in on old Bert Hutchins.

'How long ago?'

'Ooh, a good few minutes.'

'Oh no. I promised the boy I'd get his dad sharpish,' said Reg, putting his hand to his brow worriedly.

London Transport is one thing I won't miss when I'm abroad, Johnny thought as he stood in the queue waiting for the bus, eager to be on his way because he was desperate to see Rose. He didn't feel good about letting Hazel down, but she would soon find someone else. Mulling it over, he doubted if she had ever loved him, or anyone, in an all-consuming way; she was far too self-centred. He shouldn't have let things get this far. He'd never been eager to marry her, even before he'd met Rose. She wasn't the love of his life and never would be. Peggy had been his first love. Rose would be his last.

Finally there was a bus.

'About time too,' muttered someone in the queue.

It seemed to take forever for the queue to move. If the bus was full up by the time his turn came and he had to wait for the next one, he thought he would go mad. But they were still moving. Good, he had his foot safely on the platform.

'Move along there, please,' urged the conductress. 'Come on, folks, don't hang about.'

Above the clamour of the passengers and the strident tones of the clippie, he could hear someone calling his name. Peering back to the bus stop, he saw Reg Brown from the newsagent's frantically waving his arms and shouting. He couldn't hear what he was saying because of the noise in the bus, but whatever he wanted it must be urgent because Reg wasn't given to doing anything of an extrovert nature.

'Make your mind up, mate,' said someone as Johnny tried to get past the passengers boarding the vehicle. 'There are people trying to get on, and you're holding us up.'

'Let the man through,' said the clippie, who'd seen Reg's dramatics on the pavement. 'He's got to get off the bus urgently.'

The passengers made way, and he finally leapt off the platform on to the street.

Johnny knew that he would never forget the scene that greeted him when he went into the bar. Rose was lying on the floor with Alfie sitting beside her, holding her hand in both of his and talking to her in a low voice.

'When you're better I'll come over to Ealing and we'll go for a game of footie in the park with Alan. We'll take the dog with us. It will be fun, Rose.'

When he saw Johnny, he got up and rushed over to him.

'Oh, Dad,' he said, sobbing and wrapping his arms around his father.

'What happened, son?' asked Johnny.

'Hazel attacked Rose. She pushed and kicked her then hit her on the head with an ashtray and I think she might have killed her. Please don't let her die, Dad, please.'

496

'Calm down, son,' Johnny said, holding Alfie close. 'I'm here now. I'll take care of everything.'

On his knees, he observed Rose's ashen face and her ominously still body. Trembling, he felt for a pulse and found one. It was weak but she was alive.

'Thank God,' he said, leaning over and gently kissing her brow, his voice thick with emotion. 'Hang on in there, Rose. Don't leave me. I love you.'

Her eyes flickered open. 'Alfie,' she began weakly. 'You must protect him from Hazel. She's dangerous.'

'Alfie's here with me, safe,' he assured her gently, pulling his son down beside him so that she could see him. 'We'll both be here when you're feeling better.'

She looked at them with a half-smile then closed her eyes, striking fear into Johnny's heart.

Everything seemed to happen at once after that. The ambulance arrived, and at the same time Johnny's father rushed in to the bar.

'What's going on?' He saw Rose. 'Oh my Gawd, what's happened to her?'

'Rose has been hurt.'

'I can see that. I mean how did it happen?' said Ted as the ambulancemen came in with a stretcher.

'Alfie will tell you the basics, and you and I will have a chat about it later on,' Johnny told him. 'I'm going in the ambulance with Rose. Take care of Alfie for me, will you, Dad? He's been a proper little hero. But the poor kid's upset.'

From inside the ambulance, before they closed the

doors, Johnny caught a glimpse of Alfie and his grand-father standing in the street, pale and solemn, watching them go. Something had happened just now that had moved him immensely, despite being consumed with fear for Rose. Alfie had called him Dad for the first time, and had hugged him like he never wanted to let him go.

It had taken adversity to bring them together, but he knew somehow that it was a permanent thing. Wherever he was in the world, and whatever fate befell him, there was finally a bond between himself and his son; and all because of dear Rose. Even when she was at death's door, she still touched all their lives. 'Please God, let her pull through,' he said aloud.

For the first time since he'd known her, Johnny saw real fear in Hazel's eyes when he confronted her at her front door the following evening.

'How's Rose?' she asked nervously.

'She has a nasty head wound, masses of bruises and is recovering from concussion,' he informed her coolly. 'But she's alive. No thanks to you.'

Her relief was palpable.

'Yes, I thought you'd be pleased to know that you won't have to face the death penalty.'

At least she had the grace not to insult him with a denial.

'Things got out of hand,' she explained, wringing her hands. 'I don't know what happened.'

'You hit her over the head with an ashtray and left her for dead, that's what happened.'

'I meant, I don't know what possessed me to do it,' she tried to explain. 'One minute I was arguing with her, the next she was on the floor and I was running away.'

'How could you do that, Hazel, just leave her to die?' he asked.

'I panicked; I wasn't thinking straight.'

'So you ran off and left a small boy to deal with a seriously injured woman.' He shook his head in disgust. 'That's an unforgivable thing to do.'

'I told you, I was in a panic.' She looked at him. 'I was scared stiff, Johnny; absolutely terrified of what I'd done.'

'Serves you damn well right.'

Knowing that she hadn't committed murder made Hazel feel less vulnerable and more like her old self.

'Anyway, the woman provoked me,' she said spikily. 'Turning up at the door like that, saying such awful things.'

'I've heard all about it from Rose and from Alfie,' Johnny told her. 'I don't need another version, thank you. Honestly, Hazel, I've always known you were no angel, but I didn't think you'd stoop to attempted murder.'

'Attempted murder.' The official term shook her. 'You mean she's going to report it to the police?'

'If it was up to me, she would have done so already and you'd be behind bars,' he told her. 'But Rose doesn't want to take it any further provided you stay away from her. She just wants to put the whole thing behind her, and have you out of our lives for ever.'

'*Our* lives?'

'That's right, Hazel; mine and Rose's, and Alfie's too, of course.'

She shrugged. 'Very nice,' she said in a barbed tone.

'I didn't set out to hurt you,' he explained. 'When I finally faced up to my feelings for Rose, I felt bad about having to let you down, even though you were trying to push me into a marriage I think you knew I didn't want. Then I came home to find what you'd done to Rose and I've since heard what you've been up to behind my back for a long time: threatening Alfie and scaring him half to death; scheming to get both him and Rose out of my life.' He gave her a shrewd look. 'You soon discovered how useful Alfie could be to you when they started calling women of your age up for war work, didn't you? If you could get me to make you his stepmother before I went away, you would be able to come off war work. Oh yes, Hazel, I'm not as daft as you think. I guessed you had your own agenda and that was the reason for all the rush, but I went along with it because I thought I owed it to you to marry you, having been weak enough to allow you to persuade me into setting a date for the wedding. But now that I know what's been going on, I don't feel in the least bit guilty for being in love with Rose; just very relieved to have had a lucky escape, for myself and Alfie.'

She didn't say a word; just stood there looking downcast.

'You're to stay away from him and Rose when I'm

not there, do you understand?' he said. 'Rose won't be so lenient if you go anywhere near either of them again, I promise you. At the first sight of you, she'll call the police.'

Hazel knew she was beaten. She'd known in her heart that she'd lost him the day that Rose had come into their lives. There had been something tangible between them from the start, which was why Hazel had felt so threatened by her.

But compared to thinking she'd murdered someone and was likely to face the hangman's noose, losing Johnny was not such a big thing. She'd been living in a state of terror ever since she'd left the pub yesterday, expecting the police to come to the door to arrest her for murder at any moment. Knowing that she was free was sweet news indeed. Even the dreadful factory didn't seem quite so bad compared with the prospect of prison and the death cell.

It was time to move on and look for someone else; someone easier to manipulate.

'I shall stay well away; you can rest assured of that.' She never wanted to see any of them again; all they'd done was cause her grief. 'That's a promise.'

'Good.'

She stepped back and took hold of the door. 'Goodbye, Johnny. Good luck when you're away.'

'Goodbye, Hazel.'

She closed the door and Johnny walked away, relieved to have put the whole affair behind him.

★ ★ ★

Rose married Johnny on the penultimate day of his leave. As she came out of the register office into the sunshine on his arm, she felt strong enough to face his departure and whatever the future held, despite still having stitches in her head and bruises on her body from Hazel's kicking.

His love raised her up and made her feel as though she could cope with anything. Besides, she had to stay positive for Alfie and his grandfather. It was ironic how Alfie had learned to love his father almost on the eve of his departure. It would make the parting more painful for the boy, but she was glad it had happened because it meant so much to them both.

'Congratulations,' said her mother, hugging her then moving on to Johnny to do the same.

'That goes for me too, luv,' said her father. 'I hope you'll be as happy as me and your mum are.'

'Your turn next to do this,' smiled Rose.

'We would have made this a double wedding, but we wanted it to be your day,' said her mother.

Joyce appeared carrying little Stan. 'No going back now, kid,' she grinned at Rose. 'And by the look on your face that's just the way you want it. You look lovely.'

'Thanks, Joyce.'

Shortage of time, exacerbated by Rose being laid up, and lack of clothes coupons meant the bride hadn't been able to get anything new to wear, but she looked very pretty in her best frock, a pale blue crêpe de Chine which hugged her waist then fell in a gentle flare. She was carrying a spray of summer flowers, and had a few in her hair. Johnny stood proud and handsome beside her in uniform. A beaming Alfie was standing close by, holding his grandfather's hand, thrilled about having a new family.

As they all clustered around the bride and groom to wish them well, and Uncle Flip appeared with his old camera and some film he'd had since before the war, Rose thought how blessed she was to have them to help her and Alfie through the days ahead without Johnny.

Joyce had heard that Bob was coming home on leave soon. She was going to tell him about Stan, and hoped that somehow she and Bob could be friends. Alan and Mary were back together again, and she was here with him today. Once he'd regained enough confidence to feel whole again, and with encouragement from Joe, he'd wanted Mary back as she'd hoped. He'd made them all so proud, the way he was coping with his blindness. To pass the time he'd renewed his interest in the piano, after discarding his talent in favour of other, more exciting things when he was a boy, and had got on so well he had agreed to be accompanist to Rose and Joyce when they resumed their charity singing some time soon. He had also found more gainful employment that would need the full use of his other senses; he was due to start training as a switchboard operator at a munitions factory next week.

Dear Joe was still enjoying his job in the fire brigade, and keen to work his way up in the service which had been the making of him. His personal life was better too now that he had a girlfriend – a local girl called Jill. Rose would miss living at home, but her place was at the Green Cat from now on, looking after Alfie and helping Ted to run the business. She was going to stay on with the Royal Mail as well, working from the Shepherd's Bush sorting office, and would be making regular trips on the trolley bus to see the family.

But now there was a disturbance in the making.

'Give the camera to me, for goodness' sake, man,' Sybil was saying to Uncle Flip. 'Let me do it.'

'No. I'm going to take the picture.'

'You're not, you know,' insisted Sybil. 'I'm not going to let that precious bit of pre-war film get ruined because you don't know how to use the camera.'

'What are you talking about, woman?' he objected. 'Of course I know how to use it.'

'How come you're putting your finger over the lens then?' she demanded.

'I wasn't ready to take the photo. I'd have taken my finger away if I was,' he told her. 'Honestly, I don't know what you take me for.'

'You're probably better off not knowing,' she quipped. 'But if you're going to take the picture, get on and do it before we all turn grey waiting.'

Rose laughed out loud at this quarrelsome but comical couple, and the others joined in. The war had turned the whole world upside down, and her own life was about to change dramatically again. But some things stayed the same . . . fortunately.

The Sparrows of Sycamore Road

Pamela Evans

Through good times and bad, the Sparrow family has always stuck together. But as the Blitz ravages London in 1940, each of the Sparrows has their own battle to fight. Nancy finds herself volunteering as a porter at busy Paddington station – a world away from the smart West End dress shop where she used to work. Young Mickey is sent to the front line, while little Leslie suffers as an evacuee. Nancy must summon all her strength to support her loved ones, but they are unaware the woman they rely on hides a painful secret . . .

An unforgettable saga about an indomitable family, who refuse to let the war dampen their spirits or dim their hopes for a brighter tomorrow.

Praise for Pamela Evans' well-loved sagas:

'A good traditional romance, and its author has a feeling for the atmosphere of postwar London' *Sunday Express*

'There's a special kind of warmth that shines through the characters in Evans' novels . . . An uplifting love story with all the right ingredients' *Lancashire Evening Post*

'This book touched me very, very much. It's lovely' *North Wales Chronicle*

'A superb and heartwarming read' *Irish Independent*

0 7553 2147 2

headline

Now you can buy any of these other bestselling books by Pamela Evans from your bookshop or *direct from her publisher*

FREE P&P AND UK DELIVERY
(Overseas and Ireland £3.50 per book)

Part of the Family	£5.99
Town Belles	£5.99
Yesterday's Friends	£5.99
Near and Dear	£5.99
A Song in your Heart	£5.99
The Carousel Keeps Turning	£5.99
A Smile for all Seasons	£6.99
Where We Belong	£5.99
Close to Home	£5.99
Always There	£5.99
The Pride of Park Street	£5.99
Second Chance of Sunshine	£5.99
The Sparrows of Sycamore Road	£5.99

TO ORDER SIMPLY CALL THIS NUMBER
01235 400 414

or visit our website: www.madaboutbooks.com

Prices and availability subject to change without notice.